Pretty Woman

Also by Fern Michaels
in Large Print:

About Face
Beyond Tomorrow
Crown Jewel
The Future Scrolls
Kentucky Sunrise
Listen to Your Heart
No Place Like Home
The Real Deal
Weekend Warriors

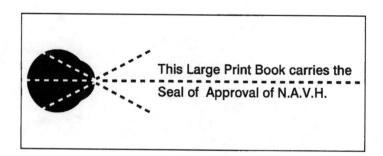

This Large Print Book carries the
Seal of Approval of N.A.V.H.

Pretty Woman

FERN MICHAELS

Waterville, Maine

Published in 2006 by arrangement with Pocket Books,
an imprint of Simon & Schuster, Inc.

The text of this Large Print edition is unabridged.
Other aspects of the book may vary from the original edition.

Set in 16 pt. Plantin.

Printed in the United States on permanent paper.

Library of Congress Control Number: 2005922633
ISBN 1-58724-931-6 (lg. print : hc : alk. paper)
ISBN 1-59413-132-5 (lg. print : sc : alk. paper

Pretty Woman

As the Founder/CEO of NAVH, the only national health agency solely devoted to those who, although not totally blind, have an eye disease which could lead to serious visual impairment, I am pleased to recognize Thorndike Press⋆ as one of the leading publishers in the large print field.

Founded in 1954 in San Francisco to prepare large print textbooks for partially seeing children, NAVH became the pioneer and standard setting agency in the preparation of large type.

Today, those publishers who meet our standards carry the prestigious "Seal of Approval" indicating high quality large print. We are delighted that Thorndike Press is one of the publishers whose titles meet these standards. We are also pleased to recognize the significant contribution Thorndike Press is making in this important and growing field.

Lorraine H. Marchi, L.H.D.
Founder/CEO
NAVH

⋆ Thorndike Press encompasses the following imprints: Thorndike, Wheeler, Walker and Large Print Press.

Prologue

Vickie Winters looked down at the picture she was holding in her hands. It was the last thing to go into her travel bag. Her eyes flooded with tears as her index finger traced her best friend's likeness, the tears she was desperately trying to hold in check, finally rolling down her cheeks. Best friends since sandbox days. Keeper of each other's secrets. Inseparable. Better than sisters. Their other friends used to envy them their special relationship. Close as thieves, they'd said. They'd even gone into business together and made a success of that business. But, like all things that were near to perfect, it had ended. Her grief at what she was feeling was so total, she almost blacked out before she managed to get her feelings under control.

Her hands shaking, Vickie wrapped the picture in a pair of sweatpants to make sure it didn't get broken during the long overseas trip. The sound of the zipper closing on the bag was so loud in the quiet room, she flinched.

All Vickie had to do now was carry the

bags downstairs, where a chauffeur waited to take her bags to Adeline Simmons's house for the early-morning ride to the airport. She was to spend the night at the Simmons mansion with her new employer, but she would go over there later in the evening.

When things had gone sour between her and her best friend Rosie, she'd answered an advertisement for a traveling companion to wealthy heiress Adeline Simmons. The salary was mind-boggling. The lure of foreign travel had attracted her, too. Eating in five-star restaurants was an added plus. In addition, Adeline Simmons was a hoot. In more ways than one, she was actually looking forward to her new job. She was going to miss Rosie, though.

How could a relationship that was so deep, so wonderful, so near perfect, go awry?

She wasn't going to cry again. She'd shed all the tears she was going to shed for Rosie Gardener. If Rosie wanted to ruin her life, so be it.

Adeline said she needed to say good-bye to Rosie. On the eve of Rosie's wedding, she was going to her house to say good-bye. How weird was *that*?

Ten minutes later, Vickie watched as Adeline Simmons's chauffeur stowed her trunk and suitcases in the back of the custom Rolls Royce. She waved airily as he drove off. Now all she had to do was drive to Rosie's house, ring the bell, and if Rosie didn't kick her butt out the door, say good-bye, and leave. Never to darken her doorstep again. Ha!

Her stomach in knots, Vickie lowered the canvas roof of her Mustang convertible. Maybe the warm June breezes as she drove around the corner would help her calm down. Maybe she should have walked. Too late now, she was already in the car. When she stopped for the traffic light at the corner she looked at the dashboard clock. It was ten minutes past nine. Maybe the reason her stomach was in knots was because she hadn't eaten anything since she'd wolfed down a stale donut at noon. The idea of a piping-hot pizza and a cold beer suddenly appealed to her. It would also fortify her for the meeting with Rosie.

Her eyes on the late-evening traffic, Vickie slowed for a stop sign, made a left on West Jones and another left onto Tattnall Street where the Crystal Beer Palace was located.

Vickie pulled into a parking space and had one foot out of the car when she heard voices coming from the Porsche that was parked to her right. One of the voices sounded familiar. When the voice turned low and intimate, she looked up and recognized Kent Bliss, the man Rosie was marrying at ten o'clock the next morning. The only problem was, it wasn't Rosie hanging on to Kent and kissing him full on the mouth. She dropped back onto the seat. She inched the door closed before wiggling over to the passenger side of the car for a better look at what was going on.

No, it definitely was not Rosie mashing her body against Kent's with her tongue down his throat.

Vickie cracked the passenger-side door and almost fell out in the process. She was just in time to hear Rosie's intended say, "What say we have a little quickie before we have our drink."

"Oooh, Kent, you are so wicked. Naughty and wicked. Okay," the young voice chirped.

Now what am I supposed to do? Wait till the quickie is over? Go inside and take my beer and pizza with me? What if I'm standing in the lobby when Kent and the young girl enter? Vickie debated all of ten seconds before she fit the key into the ignition and backed out of the parking space, sans lights. She didn't turn the lights on until she was once again on West Jones Street.

Her thoughts jumbled, Vickie drove by rote until she reached Rosie's house. She parked, got out, and walked around to the back, where she could see lights. Rosie must be in the kitchen. Maybe she was having a case of the jitters or having a late-evening snack.

Damn, what am I doing here anyway? The last time she'd gone there the visit had ended in an ugly scene. She'd stormed out, leaving Rosie crying hysterically. Both of them had said hateful, ugly things to one another, something they'd never, ever done before.

Before she could change her mind, Vickie jabbed at the kitchen doorbell. From somewhere in the house, possibly the dining room, where Rosie would have her wedding presents set up, she could hear heavy footsteps. "Who is it? Kent, is that you? You know you aren't supposed to see the bride until right before the wedding."

Vickie clenched her teeth just as the outside light went on. "It's Vickie, Rosie."

"Vic! Oh, God, you came! I am so happy to see you! Come in, come in! Oh, God, Vickie, I wanted to call you a hundred times. Tell me you reconsidered and are going to be in the wedding party. Please tell me that's why you came."

Vickie felt her eyes start to puddle. She stared at her lifelong friend, whose freckles made a bridge across her plump face. Her dark chestnut hair was set in giant rollers, and her ample, size fourteen frame was decked out in a scarlet sweat suit. She was in her bare feet. Vickie shook her head slightly. She thought her heart was going to break when Rosie stepped backward, her back stiffening.

"I . . . I came to say good-bye, Rosie."

"I'll be back, Vickie. A honeymoon doesn't last forever. Seven days is nothing." Rosie's voice sounded so desperate, Vickie closed her eyes, dreading what she was about to do.

"Not you, Rosie, me. I'm going away. I got a job, as a companion to Adeline Simmons. We're leaving for Europe in the morning. It's a cushy job, and it pays very well. All my expenses are paid. I'm closing up my house this evening and leaving my car in the Simmons's garage till we get back."

Rosie's jaw dropped. "But . . . but what about my wedding? What about the business? Tell me this is all a big joke. Why would you do . . . such a thing?"

Vickie shrugged. "Have your lawyer talk

12

to my lawyer. I think that's how it's done. I told you the last time I was here, Rosie, that I wouldn't be at the wedding. My feelings haven't changed. You are making a serious mistake marrying Kent. I don't want to go through that whole ugly scene again, okay? I just came to say good-bye and to wish you well. Did you buy him that new Porsche?"

Rosie bit down on her lower lip. "I wish you hadn't come here, Vickie. And, yes, the Porsche was my wedding present to Kent. Why can't you be happy for me? Why are you so jealous of me? Did you really think that because I weigh twenty-five pounds more than you, that no one would look at me? So what if I'm a size fourteen and you're a size six. My weight and size don't bother Kent. He says it's just more of me to love."

"And you believe that! Rosie, open your damn eyes! He's a loser. He owes everyone in town. He chases anything in a skirt. I just saw him having a quickie in his brand-new Porsche just ten minutes ago. Don't ask me how he's doing it in that racy car, but he's doing it. I saw him, Rosie. With my own eyes. I can even tell you who he was with, Sara Armstrong. She just turned eighteen two weeks ago. I saw the announcement in the paper because her parents threw her a wingding birthday party. She and Kent were at the Crystal Beer Palace. Read my lips, Rosie. You're marrying him tomorrow morning, and he's out there screwing an eighteen-year-old the night before! What's wrong with this picture?"

Rosie Gardener sat down on one of the kitchen chairs. Her expression was sad when she said, "I had no idea you hated me so much. I can't comprehend your jealousy, Vickie. Why did you come here? Can't you stand to see me happy? I would be delirious if it was you getting married. I think you should leave now, Vickie."

She had to try one more time. "Rosie, listen to me. I don't hate you. I love you. We were best friends. And because of that relationship, I take it personally when I see someone bent on hurting you. What kind of friend would I be if I didn't try to warn you? I do want you to be happy. You're so desperate to get married, you're settling for that loser. He's going to milk you dry if he hasn't already. That's all I have to say. Bye, Rosie, have a good life!"

"You have the nerve to say that to me after what you just told me! Get out of my house! I never want to see you again. Never, do you hear me, Vickie?"

Vickie turned at the door. "If you ever really need me, Rosie, my lawyer will know where I am and how to reach me."

"You don't have to worry about that, Vickie Winters. It will be a cold day in hell before I call on the likes of you," Rosie vowed through her tears.

Vickie quietly closed the door behind her. She carried the sounds of her friend's sobs with her out to her car. She felt lower than a snake's belly as she drove away. She wasn't wrong about Kent. Knowing that might make it a tad easier to live with what she'd done.

As she drove around the corner to her own little house, Vickie tussled with the memory of her and Rosie walking hand in hand on the first day of school. They were both excited and yet scared at the same time. Right before they walked up the steps to the school, they'd stopped, hugged each other, giggled as they swore to each other that they would be best friends for life. Then they'd galloped up the steps for the first big adventure of their lives.

It was all so long ago, but the memory was just as vibrant and fresh as that day so many years ago. Maybe she didn't have any right to expect a childhood promise to last forever.

1

Three Years Later

Rosie Bliss feigned sleep in the early-morning light. There had been a time when she'd loved lying in bed watching her husband get dressed for the day. Two years and fifty-one weeks ago. Now, she dreaded opening her eyes in the morning to watch him fuss and fiddle and primp like some movie star.

Oh, Kent had the looks of a movie star, that was for sure. He could have doubled for George Clooney with his dark unruly hair and bedroom brown eyes. It was the rest of him that didn't go with the image. She'd found that out, too, two years and fifty-one weeks ago.

She sneezed. The jig was up. Rolling over, Rosie turned on the bedside lamp and sat up. She hugged her knees close to her chest. No mean feat with the extra pounds she'd put on over those two years and fifty-one weeks. She waited now for the verbal onslaught she knew was coming.

When she finally got tired of waiting, she said, "Well, let's get on with it so we can both start our day."

Today he wouldn't look at her. She wondered what *that* meant. Once she had cared about every little thing he did. She'd done everything but turn herself inside out to please the man she'd married. It had taken her exactly seven days, the length of their honeymoon, to figure out it was never going to happen.

The realization that her friend Vickie had been right made the knowledge all the more bitter. So she'd doubled her efforts to win her husband's love. She'd bought him outrageous gifts, mountains of pricey clothes, a Rolex, a Mont Blanc pen, a speedboat, a flatscreen television set, any number of electronic toys, the memberships at the country club and the Olympus Gym in the hopes of a smile and maybe a lovemaking session. It never worked.

Rosie wondered if Kent even remembered that it was their wedding anniversary. She bit down on her tongue to make sure she didn't blurt it out. Instead, she let her gaze go to a small television set perched on the corner of the dresser. Kent liked to hear the local news while he got ready for his day. Her ears perked up when she heard him make a sound. Maybe it was a grunt. He rarely spoke so early in the morning. He did point to the screen. She grimaced as the morning news anchor rattled on about the Wonderball lottery drawing that was going to be held that night. Someone, the news anchor said, was really going to win 302 million dollars, the largest Wonderball drawing ever. He went on to say people were coming to Savannah from other states, mostly South Carolina and North Carolina, to buy tickets. The wait in line, according to the newsperson, was up to four hours.

Rosie blinked when she heard her husband say, "I bought a hundred dollars' worth of tickets yesterday. Man, I could spend that money in a heartbeat."

Rosie swung her legs over the side of the bed. "It's always about money with you, isn't it, Kent?" she observed quietly. "Between the two of us we make almost half a million dollars a year." There was no need to remind him that four hundred and fifty thousand of the half million dollars was money she earned. Kent just played at selling real estate and looking nice for the customers he drove around all day long in his Porsche.

Rosie stood up, moved closer to her husband. He deliberately inched away. He still wasn't looking at her. Today of all days. She bit down on her bottom lip again to prevent herself from mentioning their anniversary. She sniffed his aftershave. She loved the way he smelled so early in the morning. Rather like a woody glen on a clear summer day.

She was a fool.

She hated the anxiousness in her voice when she said, "Will you be home for dinner, Kent?"

"Probably not. I have appointments right through seven o'clock."

She was angry now. She couldn't remember the last time they'd had dinner together. She couldn't remember the last time they'd done *anything* together. Sex was something other people had. She felt her insides start to shrivel at the coldness in his voice.

"I think, Kent, it would be a good idea for you to come home to dinner this evening. This is *June*." Maybe mentioning the month would trigger his memory. "You haven't sold a house or a piece of property in three months. You haven't contributed a cent to this household since we got married. Since I am the breadwinner, I want you home for dinner." She was surprised at the ring of steel in her voice.

Kent jerked at his tie before he turned around. He stared at her, a look of revulsion on his face. Stunned, Rosie backed up two steps. "And if I don't come home for dinner, what are you going to do, Rosalie? Are you going to cut off my allowance?"

Damn, when am I going to learn? When did I turn into such a gutless wonder? Her spine stiffened imperceptibly. She summoned up the steely tone again. "Worse. I'll sell your car. The one I'm still paying for. The one you trade in every year. On your salary, you should be able to lease a Volkswagen. After I do that, I'll drive over to the country club and cancel our membership, and your membership to that prestigious gym where you pretend to work out. Effective immediately. Depending on my mood at that point, I might or might not sink that damn speedboat. Dinner will be at seven. My advice would be to show up on time."

Rosie slammed, then locked the bathroom door. She sat down on the edge of the Jacuzzi and cried.

She was a fool.

A stupid fool who still had feelings for her handsome husband. A husband who made no pretense of even *liking* her, much less loving her. A husband who'd never said a kind word to her. However, he had said bushels of unkind words. He hated her weight, hated her freckles, hated her pug nose, hated her curly brown hair, hated her clothes. Loved her money. Loved her prestigious address. And, of course, he loved himself. And yet she stayed with him. *I'm not just a fool, but a stupid, ignorant fool.*

She should have had the guts to kick him out of the house two years and fifty-one weeks ago. But, because she was a fool in love, she'd thought their marriage would get better. Just like every other dumb woman who fell for a bad apple. Even when she knew it was getting worse, she'd hung in there, hating to admit she'd made a mistake, so she turned pretense into an art form. Her housekeeper, Luna Mae, said she was in denial.

Luna Mae was right.

Well, it's time to do something about it. Tonight I'm going to lay down a whole new set of rules, and if Kent doesn't like those rules, then Kent can leave.

Bitter bile rose in her throat. If he left her, everyone in town would talk and gossip. Luna Mae Luna would look at her with pity. Thank God Vickie wasn't around to say, I told you so. She'd have to

21

turn into more of a recluse than she was already. If she did that, she'd go from a size sixteen to a size eighteen. Fat women's clothes. She'd been a size fourteen when she married Kent. Now she was a size sixteen as long as the garment came with elastic. Her favorite word these days, *elastic*.

Not only was she a stupid, ignorant fool; she was a mess, too. Physically as well as mentally.

A bold knock sounded on the bathroom door. Kent apologizing? Not in this lifetime. "What?" she barked tearfully.

"Open the door, Rosie."

Luna Mae.

Rosie hitched up the bottom of her pajamas and opened the door. She fell into her housekeeper's arms, hoping for kind words and solace. It wasn't to be.

Luna Mae Luna, aka Charlotte Bertha Hennessy, fixed her steely gaze on her employer before offering up a solid whack on Rosie's behind. "I heard everything, and yes, I was eavesdropping outside the door. Are you ever going to learn? When are you going to stop taking his crap? That weasel has made you a laughingstock in this town. I hear *everything* when I go to the market. I even overhear things I'm not supposed to hear. Things your husband says about you at the club. You're a standing joke, Rosie. We've had this discussion a hundred times, and you don't do anything."

Luna Mae Luna had been a homeless person when Rosie, who'd been eighteen then, had found her and brought her home to Rosie's mother, who had cleaned her up, then hired her on the spot. Luna Mae was a female Mr. Clean, opinionated, a hell of a cook, and read the Bible every day. She'd gone to seed, as she put it, after her boyfriend, a man named Skipper who had sixty-seven tattoos and a cat, crashed and burned on a racetrack. She'd cremated him, what was left of him, with her last cent, taken his mangy cat, and lived on the streets begging for handouts. Skipper, his ashes in an urn, sat on the mantel in her bedroom. She talked to him every day. She'd cremated Buster the cat, too, when he'd used up all his nine lives. Sometimes she talked to Buster when she got really lonely.

If there was anything or anyone Luna Mae truly loved, it was Rosie because Rosie had been her savior.

"You need to grow some balls, honey, and kick that man's ass all the way to the Mason-Dixon line. He doesn't love you.

He loves your money, child. When are you going to see that? When it's too late, that's when. You're letting the business slide. I'm one person. I can't keep doing it all. I'm thinking it's time for you to do some major sucking up and call Vickie. You need her, Rosie. You really do."

"No, Luna Mae, I can't do that. I was so ugly to her the last time we talked. I don't even know where she is. I thought she would keep in touch, but she didn't. Let's be honest here. If the situation were reversed, I wouldn't call her either. Besides, how can I admit how wrong I was and how right she was?"

"You just say it, honey. Friends understand things like that. She can't be that hard to find. I can ask around. I'm sure someone in town has her address. Like the post office," she added slyly. "Look, you two girls loved each other. She only wanted what was best for you, just the way I did. Vickie didn't say anything to you that I didn't say. You took it from me but not from Vickie."

Rosie rubbed at her temples. "I thought she was jealous. Pride is a terrible thing, Luna Mae. Okay, enough of this. In case you forgot, today is my wedding anniversary. I want you to make a big dinner, standing rib roast, Kent's favorite. I want scented candles, lots of fragrant flowers. Use Mom's linen tablecloth, the good silver and crystal. Dinner is at seven. Then I want you to go to the movies. A double feature. Can you do that, Luna Mae?"

Luna Mae nodded. "It isn't going to work, Rosie. I hate saying this, I hate being so blunt, but the man doesn't love you. A fine dinner with real silver and crystal is not going to make a difference. He doesn't even remember it's your anniversary. Why do you want to torture yourself like this?"

"Because I have to."

"Baby, you can't still love that man. He's not worth your little finger. Okay, okay, that's enough talk about *him*. What would you like for breakfast? How about some waffles with blueberries?"

Rosie looked at her housekeeper. She was tall and skinny, with double braids that were now gray hanging down her back. Granny glasses perched on the end of her nose. Rosie knew Luna Mae forgot to look through them and was forever squinting. Two round circles of bright rouge dotted her bony cheeks. She wore no other makeup. A five-carat diamond graced her middle finger. Luna Mae called it her personal headlight. She was never without it, even in soapy water. Skipper had given it to her after he won a big race. It was supposed to be their nest egg in their retirement years.

"Waffles and blueberries sound just fine, Luna Mae."

At the doorway, Luna Mae turned to call over her shoulder. "Wear something festive today. It will lift your spirits."

Rosie snorted her opinion of that statement. "They don't make festive in size sixteen, Luna Mae."

"Then do something about it," Luna Mae snapped. "You're carrying around enough blubber on your person to sink a ship."

Rosie burst into tears when she slammed the bathroom door shut for the second time. She hiccuped, blew her nose, squeezed her eyes shut, then stripped down to the buff. The mirror was something she avoided like a plague, especially when she was naked. Today she stared at her unflattering figure with wide-open eyes. She looked like a washboard, with all her rolls of fat. She couldn't see her belly button. Every ounce of fat on her body was dimpled.

Rosie stared at her naked body for a long time.

She wasn't pudgy; nor was she chubby or plump. She was fat, fat, fat, from her neck down to her toes.

Whirling around, Rosie stared over her shoulders at her buttocks. This time when she bit down on her lower lip, she tasted her own blood.

Rosie thought she could hear the floor rumble when she stomped her way to the shower, her face a grim mixture of misery and determination.

Thirty minutes later, Rosie presented herself in the kitchen attired in a cranberry sleeveless shift with matching sandals. Festive it wasn't. Luna Mae rolled her eyes as she poured coffee before sliding two delectable-looking waffles onto Rosie's plate.

"I changed my mind, Luna Mae. I'll just have the blueberries and a piece of toast. No butter or jam. No sugar on the berries either, and no cream in my coffee."

"Yes, ma'am," Luna Mae said, saluting smartly. "Now you're getting it, girl."

"Instead of that rich dinner I suggested earlier, let's have poached red snapper. I have to go to the post office, so I'll stop at the fish store. Baked potatoes, green salad, maybe some snap peas and baby carrots. Sorbet for dessert. No rolls, no butter. Just seasonings. For the record, I have nine, that's n-i-n-e rolls of fat from my neck down to my thighs. Later, I'm going to measure my thighs. While I'm out, I want you to call that sporting goods store out by the River Walk, and have them deliver a treadmill, a StairMaster, and an Exercycle. When they deliver it, have them put it all in the sunroom. No one ever goes in there. Take one of the television sets from another room and hook it up in there."

"You know *he's* going to have something to say about all this, don't you?"

"Yes, I guess he will, Luna Mae. As you well know, this is my house. My parents left it to me. That means I can do whatever I want here. Kent's name is not on the deed. Now, ask me if I care if he says anything about the equipment."

Luna Mae pushed her granny glasses up to the bridge of her nose. She actually peered through them. "Do you care, baby?"

"No. This toast is delicious. These blueberries are scrumptious, and the coffee stinks without cream and sugar. How long do you think it will take me to lose fifty-five pounds, Luna Mae?"

"A year if you do it right. More coffee?"

Rosie held her cup out for a refill. She looked around at what she considered her mother's kitchen. It was warm and cozy. Comfortable, too. The word *homey* came to mind. It was a yellow kitchen, the color of sunshine on a warm summer day. The dishes were yellow, too, with a bouquet of green mint in the middle to match the handles on the everyday flatware. She particularly loved the yellow teakettle sitting on the stove. It was probably her favorite thing in the whole kitchen. Then again, maybe her favorite things were on the shelves — her mother's teapot collection. Teapots she'd collected from all over the world. Luna Mae washed them twice a year.

Admiring the pretty, comfortable kitchen, Rosie asked, "Why do you suppose Kent never liked this kitchen or liked eating in it? I don't feel comfortable eating in the dining room because it's so formal."

Luna Mae jammed her hands on her skinny, bony hips and glared at her boss. "Because kitchens represent family and unity. In a time of crisis or a time of happiness, people tend to gather in the kitchen. It's homey, comfortable, safe. It's where the stove is for coffee or tea. Liquor is kept in the cabinet. If you want a single word, then I'd have to say a kitchen is a commitment. That man you married doesn't know the meaning of the word. He's a wannabe. You know it, and I know it.

"Now, what's on your agenda for today other than going to the fish market and the post office?"

"Nature's Decorations," Rosie said, referring to the business she ran out of her three-car garage, "is crying for my commitment. I have orders to pack up for UPS, orders to process, and I need to meet with the photographer to go over my Christmas catalog. I think, if I stay focused, I can double the business I did last Christmas."

Luna Mae twirled one of her long braids between her fingers. "Do you think any of your customers suspect you sell them weeds?"

Rosie grimaced. "They're only weeds when I start out. The finished product is a work of art. The best part is, weeds are free. It's just the lacquer, the paint, and the sparkles that cost money. It's a win win for me. Vickie was the only one who believed in me when I started this. Remember how she and I used to go out in the country and fill our cars with weeds on the weekends? Then we'd dry them out, decorate them, and fill our bank accounts. She hasn't touched any of her share of the money from the business, do you know that? I wonder why."

"Vickie is a woman of principle. Like I said before, you owe her an apology, Rosie." Luna Mae shook her head. "Well, you better get a move on because UPS will be here at three o'clock. If you need me, call me on the intercom, and I'll help you pack up the orders. Since dinner is going to be so simple, I won't need much time to prepare it.

"Would you look at that!" Luna Mae said, pointing to the television set where excited people standing in line to buy lottery tickets were jabbering to a reporter interviewing customers. "It's an obscene amount of money. I'm going to buy a ticket today. What do you think my chances of winning are?"

"Probably one in a billion. You might as well save that dollar because you aren't going to win. I'll see you later."

"Spoilsport. I'm buying it anyway." Luna Mae grinned as she set about clearing the table.

Her errands completed an hour later, Rosie stopped at the local gas station. "Don't bother with the windshield or oil, Bobby, they're okay. Just fill it up, and can you bring me a copy of the paper when you come back?"

"Sure, Miz Bliss. You sure about the oil? You want to buy a lottery ticket? Tonight is the big night."

"The oil is fine, and there's no way I'm going to get in that line," Rosie said, motioning to the triple line that ran around the building.

"No problem. I'll get you a ticket. I work here, and rank has its privileges. How many do you want, Miz Bliss?"

"It's like throwing money away, Bobby, but I'm game. I'll take five dollars' worth. Let the machine pick four tickets, and the numbers for me are 1-3-6-7-9 and the Wonderball number is 2." Rosie handed over two twenty-dollar bills. While she waited for her tank to fill and Bobby to return, she thought about her husband buying a hundred dollars' worth of tickets. With her money, of course. She wondered where her husband was at the moment and what he was doing. Did she still care for him, or was it that she was so humiliated she felt she had to care? She thought about how she used to melt when he touched her arm, or smiled at her. She *had* loved him. What a fool she'd been. Vickie had been so right about everything. She'd wanted to be married so desperately, to validate herself somehow. Being Mrs. Somebody had been the most important thing in the world to her.

She wished now that she had insisted on a prenuptial agreement. Vickie had suggested it, but she'd been outraged with the suggestion. She needed to talk to a lawyer to find out if Kent had any claim to her business, a business she'd incorporated with Vickie long before she'd married Kent. She crossed her fingers that the corporate veil would protect her.

Stupid, stupid, stupid.

Yet, deep in her gut she knew that if Kent showed up for dinner with a bouquet of flowers, she'd smile, hug him, and all her wicked thoughts would disappear until the next time he berated her. She was a stupid, gutless wonder. If he remembered that it was their anniversary, then she felt confident he would show up for dinner if for no other reason than to get his hands on the gift he would expect her to give him. Wasn't he going to be surprised? She hadn't bought him a thing. But in her heart of hearts she knew full well that he was not coming home for dinner.

Bobby returned with the lottery tickets, the newspaper, and her change. "Those numbers you picked are all single digit. For some reason the Wonderball number is

33

always a high one. You picked a low one. I don't think you're going to win with those numbers, Miz Bliss, they're just way too low. Usually the high numbers win. For some reason the machine printed out five separate tickets instead of one. Sorry about that."

Rosie shrugged as she shoved the tickets and her change into her purse and waited for the young man to remove the gas hose and close the tank. "It doesn't matter, one or five. If I win, Bobby, you'll never have to pump gas again, and I'll put you through medical school."

"I'll hold you to it, Miz Bliss." The lanky teenager laughed as she drove off.

Back home, Rosie parked the car, put the fish in the refrigerator, and walked back to the garage. She really needed to move to a warehouse or bigger quarters. The business was getting too big for her to operate out of her garage. She also needed to think about hiring more full-time as well as part-time help.

She was on her own today. Originally, she hadn't planned on working at all because it was her anniversary. She'd given her help the day off. She'd planned on going to the hairdresser, getting a mani-cure, pedicure, and a full-body massage.

Now, for some strange reason, none of that seemed to matter. What mattered was her flourishing business.

She and Vickie had started the business with $1,790 between them. The biggest expenditure had been the ads in newspapers and magazines. The cost of the sprays, the paints, the shipping cartons, and other incidentals had been charged to their respective credit cards. Inside of six months, they were rolling along and looking forward to a busy holiday season. That first year they earned out, after expenses, a cool thirty thousand dollars that they put right back into the business. The second year they tripled their profits and actually took salaries. The seven-page glossy catalog they'd created for Nature's Decorations had put them over the top in the third year.

They'd hired two full-time workers the fourth year so they could spend more time traveling in their truck to other states to pick weeds. The fifth year they paid off the truck and bought a van. They also added two additional pages to the catalog. By the end of the eighth year, they netted four hundred thousand dollars. In year nine, they took a bad hit with the drought in the South, and their net profits plummeted to the hundred and fifty thousand mark. Year ten found them flush again. Year ten was when Kent Bliss entered her life.

Rosie shivered when she realized she was now in her thirteenth year of business. Thirteen was such an unlucky number.

The pile of orders filled the in basket. There had to be at least three hundred. She hadn't checked her Web site to see how many orders were logged on there. She estimated it would be around seven hundred. Bottom line, she was backlogged. How in the world was she going to get all these orders out and still go to North Carolina with Luna Mae this weekend to pick cattails? Maybe if she didn't sleep, she could pull it off.

Luna Mae had offered to go to the Senior Citizen's complex to post a notice for any seniors wanting part-time work. Over the years she'd found that the college kids she hired for the summer months liked to call in sick at the last minute and take off for the beach. They were not dependable. Her two full-time moms had demanding personal lives, and often had to take off if they couldn't find a sitter or if their kids were sick. She was at the mercy of her employees. More often than not, she worked through the night, catching a nap here and there.

Rosie could feel the stress building between her shoulder blades. It wasn't just the business either. Her life, her future, were on the line. She shook her head to clear her thoughts. She needed to take an inventory of what she was going to do today. Along with all her other problems, she was running late.

Normally, she was here in her workroom by seven-thirty, getting the weeds ready for spraying or painting. Her gaze swept the entire first section of the garage. She was running low on thistle, one of her best sellers. The cat's ears, another of her best sellers, were down to a dozen or so. The creeping buttercup and Virginia creeper weren't as plentiful as she'd thought. She made red check marks on her inventory list.

As she moved down the wall, she noted that she had more than enough mustard leaves, nettle, plantain, milkweed, lady's thumb, and horsetail. She looked over to the left to sift through a huge box of dandelion and crabgrass that had been thoroughly dried and was ready to be worked on.

Rosie pulled on a canvas apron, the kind barbecue chefs wear, donned her goggles, and headed to the far end of the working garage, where she would spray a light polyurethane onto the weeds. Yesterday's weeds were ready for the spray painting and glitter. She looked over at her worktable to see the Christmas centerpiece she'd made three days ago. It was going to be photographed for the cover of the catalog later that afternoon.

Rosie touched one of the gilt leaves. She smiled. Perfect.

Startled, Rosie turned around when she heard Luna Mae tromping through the garage. "You forgot to open the doors, Rosie. Do you want to pass out from the fumes? I brought you some coffee, and the paper. You left it on the front seat of the car. You might want to take a look at the front page. You go ahead and read the paper, and I'll pack up the boxes for UPS."

Rosie removed the goggles, hitched her foot on a stool to drag it closer to the worktable before she flipped open the paper. She frowned. Why did Luna Mae want her to see a picture of a funeral cortege? She read the caption under the picture. Adeline Simmons's funeral. There was a picture of Vickie dressed in black from head to toe with a wad of tissues in one hand and a white rose in the other hand.

Vickie Winters was back in Savannah. Rosie felt light-headed at the knowledge.

Was Adeline Simmons's death an omen of some kind? She shook her head again to clear her thoughts.

"Say something," Luna Mae shouted from the far end of the garage.

"Mrs. Simmons, patron of the arts, died peacefully in her sleep. I'm sorry that she had no immediate family to grieve for her. It's sad when someone dies," Rosie shouted to be heard.

"Read the article, Rosie. It says Mrs. Simmons left that big old house in the historic district to Victoria Winters, her loyal companion. I'm thinking Vickie could probably use a good friend right about now."

"If that's what you're thinking, perhaps you should stop by and offer your condolences. I really don't want to talk about this, Luna Mae."

The skinny housekeeper tugged at her braids, twirling the ends this way and that. "See, that's part of your problem. You never want to deal with a situation. You walk around it, you look at it, you sniff at it like a dog, then you turn away because you don't want to deal with it. Your husband is a case in point. Vickie was a case in point.

You better shape up, Missy, or I'm moving on. I need to live in harmony."

Rosie hated it when Luna Mae turned belligerent. She'd never even come close to winning any kind of verbal fight with the housekeeper. She didn't even try anymore. It was simpler to let Luna Mae talk until she was talked out.

"You aren't going to start that *feng shui* stuff again, are you?" Rosie asked.

"There are people who would benefit from the Chinese art of harmonic placement. You are not one of them. First you have to be cosmically enlightened like I am." Luna Mae sniffed and tossed her head to make her point.

Rosie adjusted her goggles with her left hand. Her right hand was busy shaking an aerosol can of lacquer. "You don't have a very high opinion of me, do you, Luna Mae?" The words came out strangled, like she was choking back a sob. Luna Mae finished packing up the cardboard box she was working with before she ran to her employer.

"Baby, I have a *very* high regard for you. I don't like some of the things you do, but that's okay. You don't like some of the things I do. However," the housekeeper said as she wagged a finger under Rosie's nose, "I never delude myself, nor do I lie to myself. I like who I am. I didn't like being Henrietta Bertha Hennessy so I became Luna Mae Luna. You and your mother helped me get my act together, and for that I will be eternally grateful. I'm trying to do the same thing for you so you don't waste any more of your life. Life is too precious to spend it being miserable. Pride, Rosie, is a terrible sin." Luna Mae shook her head.

"You know what I'm going to do? I'm going to go to that mansion and welcome Vickie back to Savannah. It will give me great pleasure to tell her we were both right and how miserable you are."

Rosie stopped spraying the Virginia creeper that was laid out on a rough board in front of her. She pulled off her goggles. "Don't you dare! I forbid you to do that! If you do, I'll fire you!"

Luna Mae worked her facial muscles into something that passed for a smile. "Like I said, pride is the deadliest sin of all. You just made my point for me." She turned and marched back to her end of the garage. She called over her shoulder, "If you fire me, then I'll go to work for Vickie. I bet she'd love to have me help her in that big old house she just inherited."

Rosie clamped her hands over her ears.

41

She could feel her world starting to crumble around her. She wanted to stomp her feet and cry the way she had when she was a child. She knew she wouldn't do either of those things because she was no longer a child, and her world, such as it was, was of her own making. What she had to do was make sense out of her life, deal with it, then get on with that life. If she faltered or screwed up, she'd just have to deal with the consequences.

What a fool she'd been!

2

Mrs. Kent Bliss — that's how she thought of herself — looked in the long pier glass. She took the hit full on and didn't flinch, wince, or cringe in any way. A fat lady glared back at her. It didn't matter that the fat lady was dressed in designer wear, that her hair was swirled into a fashionable do, or that her makeup was flawless. She was a fat lady, pure and simple. No denials here. Those days were long gone.

Everything was wrong. It had gone downhill from the minute she opened her eyes that morning. What exactly had triggered the hatred she was feeling for herself and those around her? Her anniversary, which her husband didn't acknowledge? The look of revulsion she'd seen on his face? Vickie's coming back to town? Was it the pity she saw in Luna Mae's eyes? Or was it her naked reflection she'd seen in the vanity mirror this morning?

All of the above.

Rosie turned away from the pier glass. She was wearing high heels that made her trundle as she moved forward. Like a lumbering walrus. She kicked them off. Now she could just *plop* her way along, her weight coming down solidly on her feet. She slipped into a pair of straw sandals. In the great scheme of things, it really didn't matter if they matched her burnt orange linen dress. Her grandmother's pearls adorned her neck. She wore no other jewelry except her wedding ring.

The wedding ring drew her eyes like a magnet. It was an embarrassing piece of jewelry. It had been so hard to pretend to Kent that she liked it. It was platinum, or so he said, no bigger or thicker than the hoop that came with a cheap key chain. Kent said it was elegant and spoke volumes. She'd wanted a thick, gold band. Something that could be easily seen, something that said she was Mrs. Kent Bliss. All the ring on her finger said to her was that she was just another circle on a cheap key chain.

Rosie was almost to the door when she walked back to her dressing table for her watch, a Swatch with big numbers. Kent made fun of it. She liked it because the numbers were big, and she could see the time at a glance without having to squint. She strapped it on her right wrist. Kent had something to say about that, too. He said she just wore her watch on her right wrist to annoy him and as an attention getter. When someone looks like you do, he'd gone on to say, the last thing you wanted to do is call attention to yourself. She hadn't worn a watch after that. She liked wearing her watch on her right wrist because she was left-handed. Strapping the watch on her right wrist now was an act of defiance.

Too much, too little, too late.

Her head high, Rosie left the room and walked down the long hallway to the grand circular staircase. She moved slowly, glancing at her watch when she reached the bottom. It was a quarter to seven, and there was no sign of her husband.

Luna Mae was standing at the bottom of the steps, her arms folded over her skinny chest. In honor of the occasion, she was attired in a zebra-striped jumpsuit, one of a hundred or so that hung in her closet and her favorite mode of dress.

Luna Mae only got dressed up for weddings and funerals.

"There were no calls while you were getting dressed, Rosie. Dinner is ready whenever you want me to serve it. Just leave everything, and I'll clear it away when I get back."

Rosie looked around the massive foyer. It was big enough to house a whole suite of furniture. A round table with a huge bouquet of vibrant crepe myrtles from the gardens sat in the middle. The crepe myrtles always bloomed in June. She'd had many of them, the deep pinks, the vibrant purples, and, of course, the snow-white ones, at the church the day she got married. The color of the flowers brought out the deep pinks and greens in the paintings that hung on the foyer walls. Her mother always said a house was judged by the foyer because that was what people first saw when they entered.

Her mother had liked clutter; Rosie didn't. When she'd taken over the house, she'd stored most of the furnishings in the attic. All were priceless antiques. But as far as she was concerned, the table in the center, the colorful paintings, and the burnished floor, along with the circular staircase, made their own statement.

Rosie missed her parents, who had died within months of one another. Luna Mae had consoled her at the time by saying her parents were a unit, a set. One couldn't function without the other. Back then, she hadn't believed the housekeeper, but the more she thought about it these days, the more she was inclined to agree with Luna Mae. It was hard to conjure up a memory of her mother that didn't also include her father. It was true, they were joined at the hip. Her mother would start a sentence, and her father would finish it. Her father would mention something, and her mother would fill in the details. Side by side, holding hands, always touching, always smiling at one another, her parents never argued, never said cross words to each other. At least she had never heard any.

As a child, she remembered being envious of the affection and love they felt for one another. Not that they ever neglected or ignored her. Still, there were times when she'd felt like an outsider. She remembered telling Vicki once that when she got married she didn't want a marriage like her parents' because there was no room for anything else in the marriage except the two of them.

How foolish she'd been to think that. Her parents' marriage was vastly superior to her own! She shrugged away her regrets. She needed to get on with her plans for the evening.

"I'll let you know, Luna Mae. I have a feeling you won't be going anywhere tonight. Kent should be home by now. You can serve me my dinner promptly at seven."

"Baby, he might be running late. Give him a few minutes' grace. You aren't going to cry, are you?"

"I don't have any tears left, Luna Mae. If he isn't here by ten minutes past seven, I want you to serve me my dinner, then I want you to go upstairs and pack up his belongings in trash bags. Tomorrow morning, call a locksmith and have the locks changed. Put all his stuff at the top of the steps or kick them to the bottom. It really doesn't matter to me. Just don't pick them up."

"Isn't that kind of drastic, Rosie?"

Rosie's temper flared. "You've been haranguing me for four years about getting rid of Kent. Now that I'm doing it, you're questioning my decision? Make up your damn mind, Luna Mae. Whatever I do is for me, not for you, or Vickie, or Kent. You kept after me the whole year of our engagement, then you never let up for these last three years."

Luna Mae turned away. "I just want you to be sure you know what you're doing before you do something you might possibly regret. Think this all through and don't act in haste is all that I'm saying."

Rosie made her way to the dining room and sat down at the head of the table. Kent's seat. What did it matter where she sat? In her gut she knew he wouldn't be joining her for dinner. Despite the thought, she got up, pushed the chair back into place, then sat down on a chair to the right. She sat primly, her hands folded. She had a clear view of her watch and the moving hands.

When the minute hand on the Swatch crawled past the twelve, Rosie knew with deep certainty that her husband hadn't taken her invitation seriously. He did what he wanted when he wanted, and answered to no one. It was all about Kent. Never about her. Never.

Somewhere deep inside her, the last thread of hope that somehow, some way, she could salvage her marriage disappeared. Her marriage, which had begun three years ago to the day, was now over.

Rosie was about to call out to Luna Mae when she appeared at her side, dinner plate in hand. She set the food in front of Rosie, poured wine into the wineglass, then stepped back.

"Thanks, Luna Mae. This looks good. You can . . . pack Kent's things now."

"Rosie, are you sure you want me to do that?"

Rosie eyed the fish on her plate. She'd never felt less like eating in her life. She dug the fork into the meaty side of the filet. "I'm sure, Luna Mae."

Somehow, Rosie managed to eat everything on her plate, even the skin on the baked potato. She was on her second glass of wine when Luna Mae appeared with coffee and the sorbet. It was eight o'clock.

"How's the packing going?"

"I'm almost done. Are you okay, Rosie? Do you want me to sit here with you?"

"No. I need to sit here so I can punish myself for being so stupid. I need to feel my humiliation and what I allowed that man to do to me. I need to wallow. Just let me do what I have to do. Finish the packing and don't worry about me."

Rosie dutifully took a bite of the sorbet. She thought it too tart, so she pushed it away. She reached for the black coffee, sipping at it. She longed for a cigarette. A habit she'd given up for Kent because he didn't like the smell. She reached behind her to pull at the door of the buffet. A full carton of cigarettes was inside. In case she ever had a nicotine fit. Well, she was having a nicotine fit that very minute.

The hands on the Swatch moved slowly, around and around, until the numbers told her it was twenty-five minutes past ten. The dining room was full of smoke, the candles burned to the ends, the flowers wilted.

A bottle of Budweiser in her hand, Luna Mae sat down in Kent's chair. "How long you gonna sit here, kiddo?"

"Until he comes home. Like I said, I need to get my face rubbed in it one more time. Think of me as a masochist. When he does come home, Luna Mae, I want you to go outside and take the distributor cap off his Porsche. I know you know how to do that. Put the boat keys someplace safe. I called the bank this afternoon and had them transfer all my money to a new account. I left twenty-five dollars in it for Kent's use. I canceled all our joint credit cards before I got dressed this evening. He's going out of here this evening, or whenever he gets here, the same way he arrived, with nothing. Don't look at me like that. I knew he was going to be a no-show. Consider it a preemptive strike."

"Baby, you are on a roll. If you're serious about all of this, I was thinking earlier, maybe you should hire yourself a personal trainer. That way you won't make excuses when you don't feel like exercising or if you think you're too tired. What do you think?"

Rosie eyed the puddle of candle wax that was still burning and hissing, bits of wax spurting onto the linen tablecloth. "I think that's a great idea."

"You fixed okay for money, kiddo?"

"I'm fine. I never touched my parents' insurance money. The house is paid for. I've been living off the business. Some months it's touch-and-go, but I make it. I'd have a lot more if I hadn't been so generous with Kent. We'll sell the Porsche and the boat. That will give me a bit of a cushion. Oh, I also canceled his club membership as well as the gym. I think he has a few weeks on the gym, though. It doesn't really matter at this point."

"Rosie, I don't know where your backbone came from all of a sudden, but I certainly approve. All I can say is, it's about time."

Rosie looked down at her lap. Her hands were folded the way she'd folded her hands at the table when she was a child. She spoke hesitantly, her face warm with what she was going to share with her trusted housekeeper. "Kent and I haven't . . . we didn't . . . it all stopped right after we got back from our honeymoon. He was the one who wanted the twin beds. Because of his back, he said. I only approached him once. It was a humiliating experience. I've smelled perfume on him so many times I've lost count. He said grateful clients would hug him, and that's why he smelled like a French whorehouse. He had an answer for everything. Look at me, Luna Mae. I bought my husband. I paid for him. That's all he wanted. My money. And I wanted to be Mrs. Bliss. End of story."

Luna Mae looked puzzled. "What happened today to make you kick up your heels? Today was just like any other day around here. What did I miss?"

"I saw, I really saw, the way he looked at me this morning. I repulsed him. Yeah, Luna Mae, I saw that. He didn't try to hide it either. And the fact that I knew he wasn't going to remember that today is our anniversary. I must have had some kind of premonition or something because I didn't knock myself out buying him a gift the way I did last year and the year before. Now you know it all."

"Rosie, I'm so sorry. I wish it had worked out differently. You have so much love in you to give. It's his loss. He's never going to find anyone better than you," Luna Mae said vehemently.

Rosie reached out to pat the housekeeper's hand. "I appreciate your loyalty, Luna Mae, I really do. I don't know what I would have done without you these past three years."

"Do you want me to clear the table, Rosie?"

"No, not yet. Is that a car I hear?" Rosie looked down at her watch — 10:35.

"Yes, I think so. I'll be in the kitchen. If you need me, yell."

"Why? Your ear will be pressed against the door," Rosie responded, a sickly smile on her face.

A minute later, Rosie looked up to see her handsome husband towering over her. She reached out and deliberately fired up a cigarette she didn't want. "You're late," she said through a plume of smoke.

"I told you this morning I couldn't make dinner, Rosalie."

"Yes, you did. I guess you didn't hear me when I said it was imperative you be here. You smell like . . . soap. Your hair is wet. I guess you must have just taken a shower at some woman's house. The club is closed. I don't really care. I'm just making conversation." Rosie blew another puff of smoke in his direction, her eyes daring him to say something. Kent remained quiet, a puzzled expression on his face.

Rosie looked down at her watch. "Ooops, it's time for you to leave. Your stuff is all packed at the top of the stairs. You better call a cab."

"What the hell are you talking about, Rosalie?"

Rosie crushed out the cigarette she was holding. "What part of 'your stuff is all packed at the top of the stairs' and 'you better call a cab' don't you understand? The bottom line is, I'm kicking you out of my house. The way I see it is this, you have two options. You can go peacefully, or I can call the police and have you ejected." She looked down at the Swatch watch on her right hand. "I'll give you ten minutes. If you kick the bags down the stairs, you'll save time."

"I'm not going anywhere, Rosalie. What the hell's gotten into you?"

Rosie felt pleased at the note of panic in her husband's voice. "Yes, Kent, you are going somewhere. Where, I don't care, but you are leaving my house. In ten minutes. Have your lawyer call my lawyer. Luna Mae!" she shouted.

Luna Mae poked her head in the dining room doorway. "I want you to call the police in eight minutes."

"Okay."

Kent reached up and straightened his tie. He looked wrinkled, unlike his usual pristine self. The Rolex winked on his wrist. Rosie wished she could snatch it off his arm. He sat down and leaned forward. Rosie reared back against the chair she was sitting on. "Obviously we need to talk," he said, his voice sounding jittery.

Rosie's chair scraped backward. "You see, you aren't getting it. I'm tossing you out of my house. I don't want to be married to you any longer. I'm sick and tired of your affairs. I'm sick and tired of being humiliated in town. I don't like people talking about me behind my back. I'm sick and tired of you mooching off me. Work like everyone else does. By the way, the car stays here. That's why you have to call a cab. I'm selling it. The boat, too. I canceled the credit cards, and there's no money in the bank. I also canceled the club membership and the gym, but there are a few weeks to go on the gym membership."

"You can't do that!" Kent sputtered, a look of panic on his face.

"You aren't listening to me, Kent. I *already* did it. I did it because I knew you wouldn't be home for dinner. You don't want to risk staying here. I might do something to you while you're sleeping. Your time is running out." Rosie looked down at the Swatch to make her point.

"Luna Mae, call Mr. Bliss a cab. If he doesn't want his stuff, we'll have a bonfire!"

"Okay."

"You fat bitch! You aren't going to get

away with this," Kent snarled, his face turning ugly.

A lump formed in Rosie's throat. She managed to talk around it. "Today was our anniversary."

Kent looked at her, bug-eyed. "Is that what this is all about? For Christ's sake, you're like a little kid when it comes to that romantic stuff." He looked uneasily at the burned-down candles and the wilted flowers.

Rosie looked at the Swatch again. "Four minutes and counting."

"Will you stop that! I'm not going anywhere. Where the hell am I supposed to go at this hour of the night?"

Rosie shrugged. "I don't care where you go. You aren't staying here. Go to the woman you just left. Or does she have a husband who wouldn't approve? Three minutes."

Kent's arm snaked across the table to reach for Rosie's dress to yank her forward. In the blink of an eye, Luna Mae was in the room and had the melted candle wax that was still dripping in her hand. She tossed it at him, getting him on the right cheek. "Take your hands off her!"

"You pitiful hippie reject. You'll pay for this," Kent yowled in pain.

"Don't go there, Kent."

"Luna Mae, call the cab *and* the police."

"Okay, okay, I'm going," Kent snarled. "You know what, you're a disgusting blimp. You turn my stomach. Just sleeping in the same room with you made my skin crawl. I'm glad to be rid of you. At least I can stop pretending where you're concerned."

Rosie didn't flinch at the verbal onslaught even though she felt like she was dying. She hated that Luna Mae was hearing her husband's low opinion of her.

"Why did you marry me, Kent?" She made the words sound like she was asking about the current weather conditions.

"For a meal ticket. What other reason would I marry a walrus like you? I want half of everything," he bellowed.

A car horn shattered the night.

"Cab's here," Luna Mae chirped. "I bounced the trash bags down the stairs."

Her heart in shreds, Rosie looked straight at her husband. "Your meal ticket's just been canceled. Now get the hell out of my house and don't ever come near it again. Like I said, have your lawyer call my lawyer."

"You're nothing but a fat pig with big feet. I was ashamed to be seen with you.

Why do you think I never wanted to go anywhere with you?" Kent bellowed as he grabbed the bags and made his way to the front door Luna Mae was holding open.

When the front door finally closed behind her husband, and Luna Mae shot the dead bolt, Rosie collapsed against her, sobbing.

"Cry, baby, get it all out now. Tomorrow is a whole new day and a whole new life. Tonight belongs to the past. It's over and done with. The man isn't worth your little finger."

"Did you know he thought all those things about me, Luna Mae?"

Always brutally honest, the housekeeper mumbled, "Yes."

"He didn't even *like* me. How am I going to live with that?"

"By not thinking about it. I'm going to make you a cup of hot chocolate. Go up to bed, Rosie. Sleep in the guest room tonight. Tomorrow, I'll take out those twin beds and get Drew the gardener to help me move the big bed back into your room. Go on, scoot. Oh, by the way, while I was in the kitchen I saw on TV, they picked the lottery number, and I didn't win. I'm glad I only bought one ticket. Here," she said, holding out the slip of paper to Rosie.

Rosie reached for it and smiled. "I told you, you wouldn't win. Kent bought a hundred dollars' worth. I wonder if he won." She handed the ticket back to Luna Mae, who refused to take it. Rosie shoved it in the pocket of her dress.

"I hope tomorrow is a better day than today. I feel like someone sucker punched me. Thanks for everything, Luna Mae. I don't know what I would have done without you."

"You would have managed. Go on now, I'll be up with the hot chocolate in a minute. No more crying. I want your promise."

Her eyes wet and shiny, Rosie held up her hand and muttered, "I promise."

Wide-eyed, Rosie watched the hands on the clock move toward the six. She reached out and pressed the button before the alarm went off. She hadn't closed her eyes once during the long night. Instead, she'd tortured herself reliving each day of her marriage. How was it possible, she wondered, for one person to be so incredibly stupid? While she'd never wanted a claustrophobic, all-encompassing marriage like her parents had had, she had hoped for at least a little closeness, a little sharing, a certain camaraderie with secret knowing smiles once in a while. A pat to the shoulder, intimate things whispered in her ear from time to time wasn't too much to expect. She'd bombed out from the git-go.

Did she love Kent Bliss? Or did she love the idea of love?

She'd been thirty-three when she married Kent. Men weren't looking at oversize women who were thirty-three. They wanted skinny twenty-three-year-olds. She'd been too shy and introverted at twenty-three to seek out men. Besides, men wanted willowy blondes with tiny waists. She didn't qualify in either department. Four years ago, when Kent Bliss winked at her in the post office, she'd actually looked around, unable to believe that he was winking at her. She'd blushed and smiled. Then they'd struck up a conversation while they waited in line. Since he was ahead of her, she watched as he bought money orders. That should have been her first clue. A man without a checking account just wasn't normal.

She remembered how her heart had fluttered when she found him waiting for her outside. She'd been so flustered she could barely talk. He'd asked her to go for coffee. She'd gone with misgivings. Misgivings because she couldn't imagine why someone like Kent would be interested in someone like her, who was so overweight with no social skills when it came to men. If she had ever known how to flirt, she'd forgotten the rules. The best she could hope for was that she didn't embarrass herself. Kent spent the whole time talking about himself, which was okay with her because she was tongue-tied. He'd scoped her out that day, asking where she lived, what she did for a living.

God, how she'd loved the look of him. Loved the way other people looked at the two of them. She felt proud, honored, to be in his company. She'd been one sick puppy back then. She had to have been blind at the time not to see what Luna Mae and Vickie called the handwriting on the wall.

After that first meeting, Kent stopped by for breakfast, then he stopped by for dinner. He never stayed, always saying he had a meeting or a late showing. She'd bought into it to her friend's dismay. Their first date had been a total disaster. Dinner at a fast-food restaurant, the service so fast, she hadn't finished her meal when Kent whisked her to the movies. He hadn't held her hand or even leaned close to her. His cell phone rang six times during the movie. Six times he excused himself and went out to the lobby. She watched the movie by herself.

There were more dates like that one, with a peck on the cheek at the end of the night. They were dates, though, and that's what she wanted. At the time.

No one had been more surprised than she when Kent offered her a ring, the diamond so small she had to squint to see it. A chip actually. She told herself a diamond was a diamond, and if he couldn't afford better, it was all right with her. Luna Mae had just clucked her tongue when she saw it. Vickie had laughed outright. She'd told them to back off and leave her alone.

Rosie's face burned now when she remembered the night she'd invited him to her bed. He'd looked at her, a stunned expression on his face. He stammered something that sounded like he had a low sex drive and hoped that wouldn't make a difference. She'd bought into that, too, making excuses to herself.

She spent a lot of time wondering how someone so lean and hard, so good-looking, so polished, so suave, could have a low sex drive. She finally decided she wasn't enough of a turn-on for her fiancé. She bought sexy magazines, bought sexy clothes, boned up on sexual techniques. He'd laughed at her. She'd been so wounded, so hurt, she'd hunkered down and hidden out for weeks, refusing to face him. Then he'd shown up with a wilted daisy one night and asked her to forgive him. He'd even brought her a box of Crackerjacks and let her find the silly prize. Of the entire four years of her relationship with Kent, that was her only positive memory.

The door opened. Rosie sat up. She looked at Luna Mae before she swung her legs over the side of the bed. "Before you ask, no, I did not sleep. I stared at the ceiling all night long trying to figure out if I overreacted. I didn't. What's for breakfast?"

Luna Mae was dressed in a blue-and-white seersucker jumpsuit whose huge pockets had gold zipper closures. She wore her braids pinned to the top of her head like a coronet. "It depends if you're waffling where the diet is concerned. I, myself, am having pancakes."

"I'm dieting. How about a yogurt, some fruit, and toast?"

"I can do that. I'll have it ready by the time you shower and dress. At what point are you going to start trying out that exercise equipment?"

"Before lunch. I need to work this

morning, Luna Mae. Remember now, call the locksmith this morning. I already changed the code on the alarm. While you're on the phone, call the Porsche dealer and have them tow the car to the dealership. Tell him we'll take whatever we can get for it provided it's a decent offer. Do the same with the boat in the marina. Also look into getting me a personal trainer."

Luna Mae's closed fist shot in the air. "Yessss."

Thirty minutes later, Rosie was peeling an orange when Luna Mae said, "Shhh, listen to this. The winning ticket for that big $302 million Wonderball was sold right here in Savannah. They don't know yet who the winner is, though."

"With my luck, it was probably Kent who won. He bought a hundred dollars' worth of tickets." Rosie didn't even look at the screen when the numbers flashed.

Luna Mae switched channels. "If you had that much money, what would you do with it, Rosie?"

"I don't have a clue. Don't dump what-ifs on me this morning. It's all I can do to handle the what-ises. Kent's going to be coming by here today at some point. I know it as sure as I'm sitting here. Don't let him in the house and keep the doors locked. I'll use the fans in the garage and open the window but not the doors. Call the police if he shows up."

"Yes, ma'am. Are you okay, baby?"

Rosie's eyes filled. She shook her head. "One day at a time, Luna Mae. If I can get through today, tomorrow will be better. The day after that even better. I don't want to talk about it anymore, Luna Mae."

"Then we won't talk about it anymore. Are you going to need me to help with packing the orders?"

"I don't think so. If Alice and Danny show up, I have it covered. I need to print out the orders from the Internet and process them. The first printing of the Christmas catalog is going out in July. The cattails are going to be a big seller. I'll even go so far as to predict they'll be 85 percent of our Christmas business. I can't make up my mind which one I like best, the gold or the silver cattails. I'll see you later."

Luna Mae looked down at the half-eaten yogurt, the toast that was barely nibbled on, and three-quarters of the orange. If Rosie kept eating like this, she'd shed those fifty-five pounds in two weeks. And that wasn't good.

3

Jason Maloy stared through the slats of the blind that covered the window of his office. Was that his employee, Kent Bliss, getting out of a cab? He watched, frowning, as the man counted out change from his pocket. He continued to frown as he watched Kent stretch his neck, adjust his tie, and shrug his shoulders inside his sport jacket.

Jason Maloy didn't like Kent Bliss, never had, but the man added a touch of class to his company. He looked good sitting up at the front desk. And he was a charmer. The Porsche he drove didn't hurt either. Everyone knew he wore a Rolex watch because he made a point of looking at it a hundred times a day.

Women flocked to Kent, the buyers and the lookie-looks. Unfortunately, he wasn't much of a salesman when it came to properties, but he was a hell of a salesman when it came to promoting himself. He'd probably bedded every single female in town and half the married ones. He worked just enough to keep up his million-dollar status on the boards, which sounded pretty grand but, at a 3 percent commission, yielded him a less-than-grand paycheck. The rest of the time he golfed, played tennis, or hung out at the ritzy country club where his wife had a membership. Why work when he had a stay-at-home wife who footed his bills?

Jason was behind his desk when Kent rapped on the plate-glass window of his office. "Can I talk to you, Jason?"

"Sure, come on in. You look . . . awful. Is something wrong, Kent?"

"Yes, and no. I'm sure I can straighten it all out, but in the meantime, I'm in a real bind. Rosalie and I had a terrible argument, and she kicked me out. She took my car, cut off my credit cards, the club, the whole ball of wax. I had to stay at a Comfort Inn last night. I need an advance on my last sale, Jason. I hate to ask but I have exactly thirty-three dollars in my pocket."

I'm loving this, Jason thought to himself. "Sounds to me like your wife wears the pants in your family. I thought she was a pretty easygoing young woman. You a kept man, Kent?" Yes, sir, he was loving every minute of this.

"No, I'm not a kept man, Jason. I resent you implying that I am. I forgot our wedding anniversary. Every man forgets something once in a while. Rosalie just needs to calm down a little. Can I use the company car?"

Jason pretended to think about the matter as he massaged his freshly shaved chin. The decision would have been easy and simple if the man standing in front of him had a humble bone in his body. But Kent was arrogant and cocky, traits Jason hated with a passion.

"Well?" Kent said impatiently.

"I never forget my anniversary, Kent, and I don't know any man who has. It's one of those sacred days that's burned into your brain, like Mother's Day. I don't like it when my employees carry their personal problems here to my business. I'll float you this one time. I suggest you give up the fun and games and sell some properties. You can use the company car until you can make other arrangements. That means one week. You're going to have to use some of your thirty-three dollars to buy gas, because the tank is empty. Give this to Camilla," he said, scrawling his name across a pink slip of paper. "She'll write out a check for your commission. You have three appointments today. I want to see at least one sale within the next week, or your ass is grass. Do we understand each other?"

"Yes, Jason, we understand each other. I never thought you were the type to kick a dog when he was down." Without another word, Kent turned on his heel and left, the keys to the company car in his hand.

"Miserable excuse for a human being," Maloy muttered under his breath. He watched through the window as Kent stormed his way to the battered company car that had 126,986 miles on it. He grinned as he watched Kent chug out of the parking lot. *Oh, how the mighty have fallen.*

Maloy swiveled his chair back around so he was facing the door. He liked Rosalie Gardener. His wife liked her, too. To him, she'd never been Rosalie Bliss. He and his wife Harriet had talked about Rosalie once because neither one of them could figure out how and why she had married Kent Bliss. Harriet said it was because she'd needed someone after her parents died. She didn't want to be alone. He'd always thought Kent had bamboozled her and just wanted a free ride. He laughed then, thinking about the bumpy ride his salesman was experiencing at that very moment.

As his wife was fond of saying, all good things eventually come to an end.

"Bravo, Rosalie!"

Kent rattled into the gas station on fumes. He turned off the engine and waited, embarrassed to be seen driving the clunker he was sitting in.

"Hi, Mr. Bliss! Where's the Porsche today? Is it true you guys won the lottery?" The kid was so excited he could barely get the words out of his mouth.

"What the hell are you talking about?" Kent snarled as he peeled a five-dollar bill off his slim wad of money. No point in buying more than five bucks' worth of gas because the damn car would probably conk out, and he'd be stranded. "Five dollars' worth, Bill."

"Bobby. My name's Bobby. I get it, you guys are playing it cool, huh?"

"Bill, Bobby, same thing. Put five dollars in. Make it snappy, okay? Since I don't know what you're talking about, just cool it, okay."

"Yeah, cool. I can't serve you. You're in the self-serve lane. You have to pump it yourself. I only pump when you're in full-serve. Those are the rules. Sorry."

When there was no further response,

Bobby hopped first on one foot then the other. His wild exuberance seemed to melt away at the ugly look on Kent Bliss's face.

"So, did you or didn't you and Miz Bliss win the lottery? The lottery commission issued a statement saying the ticket was sold out of this station. Miz Bliss bought five dollars' worth of tickets. I got them for her myself. She had all low numbers. Single digit if I remember correctly. My boss said other people bought low-number tickets, too, so maybe it wasn't your wife who won. Do you want the gas or not, Mr. Bliss?"

What the hell is this kid talking about? Kent climbed out of the clunker and walked around to the gas tank. It took him a full five minutes to get the rusty cap off. *Damn, now I'm going to smell like gasoline.* He looked over at the kid, who was staring at him. He felt embarrassed all over again to be seen with this junker.

While he waited for the gasoline to gurgle into the dry tank, Kent started to think about what the kid had said. He felt a wild adrenaline rush at the mere thought that his wife, soon to be ex-wife, might have won the lottery. Was it possible?

As far as he knew, Rosalie never bought lottery tickets. She thought it was a waste of money, whereas he couldn't wait to buy them in the hopes of finding the pot of gold at the end of the rainbow.

If she had won, it would certainly explain her actions of the previous night. Well, hot damn. He was so excited, he yanked the hose out of the tank, spilling gasoline everywhere, even over his tasseled loafers. He cursed loudly and ripely as he clicked it off and jammed it into place.

"Six dollars and eighty-five cents, Mr. Bliss."

"I only wanted five dollars' worth."

"Maybe that's what you wanted, but you pumped six dollars and eighty-five cents."

Kent dug in his pocket for two singles and handed them over along with the five-dollar bill. "Keep the change, Bill."

Kent prayed the clunker's engine would turn over, and it did. He chugged out of the station, not knowing if he was furiously angry or elated.

Three hundred and two million dollars! He'd seen a rerun of the drawing on the early-morning news. That's what the Wonderball jackpot had turned out to be.

Rosie looked up when Alice, her number one full-time employee, entered the garage. She started to babble the minute she tied on her canvas apron. Alice knew the business almost as well as Rosie did. She was full of nervous energy she transferred to her work. She could pack a carton at the speed of light, spray a line of weeds, and not miss a spot while she talked nonstop. Alice was one of those people who actually worked her eight hours and was proud of her productivity at the end of the day.

"What do you need me to do today, Rosie?"

Rosie raised her paint goggles to stare at her helper. Alice was a butterball with frizzy hair and eyes that were bluer than a summer sky. Her foot was tapping to some unheard music. Within minutes she'd clip on her Sony and earphones, then she'd really rock through her work hours.

"I'm going to have Danny pack up orders today. Luna Mae will help later this afternoon. I want you to process the Internet orders, then you can help me with the painting and spraying. There are 867 Internet orders, and we have very little finished stock. Luna Mae and Danny are going to make the trip to North Carolina this weekend, and I'll be here working. If you can use the overtime, I can use the help this weekend."

"You got it!" Alice said, dancing away. She returned a minute later, removed her earphones, and pointed to the small over-head television set Rosie kept on just for company.

"I don't believe it. What kind of idiot would pick numbers like 1, 3, 6, 7, 9, and 2."

"Obviously someone very smart since they won," Rosie said, adjusting her paint goggles again. A heartbeat later she removed them. *"What did you say?"*

Alice didn't hear what Rosie said. Her earphones were back in place and she was already dancing down to the far end of the garage. Rosie looked up at the television again, the numbers searing her eyeballs.

It couldn't be. Impossible. She squeezed her eyes shut, opened them again, but the numbers were gone from the screen. The announcer had moved on to other things.

Her numbers.

She had to move, too. *Oh God, oh God, oh God!*

Rosie tossed her goggles onto the table, and shouted, "I'll be right back." Alice ignored her as she snapped open a card-board carton.

Rosie ran as fast as she could up the walkway to the back verandah and into the kitchen, where Luna Mae was cleaning out the refrigerator. She whizzed by her to the back stairway, where she galloped up the steps, shouting for Luna Mae to follow her.

When she reached the guest room Rosie doubled over as she gasped for breath. "In a million years, Luna Mae, you are never, ever, going to believe this. Look!"

Luna Mae gasped in shock when Rosie pulled her five lottery tickets out of her purse as she fumbled for the winning ticket. "Look, Luna Mae! Look!"

For once in her life, Luna Mae was speechless. She flopped down on the unmade bed and stared at the ticket her wild-eyed employer had handed her. She raised her eyes to stare at Rosie. "You won! You're the mystery winner!"

Rosie backed up and literally fell into the rocking chair, the dress she'd been wearing the night before at her feet, exactly where she'd dropped it before she got into bed.

"I know. Oh, God, Luna Mae, what am I going to do? Kent will want half. Are you listening to me? He'll want half! It won't matter that I kicked him out last night before I heard about this. Half! Tell me what to do, Luna Mae. I can't think."

"Well, baby, you better think fast," Luna Mae said, giving the ticket back to Rosie, "because I think that's your husband who just pulled into the driveway. He can get in the house because the locksmith hasn't been here yet. He can't know. How could he know? You just found out yourself. Stay here, baby. I'll go down and boot him out. That's what you want, isn't it?"

"Yes. No. Luna Mae, I can't think. The only way he could possibly know is if he went to the gas station and Bobby remembered the numbers and told him. Go. I don't want to talk to him. I need to think. If he gives you trouble, call the police."

The minute the door closed behind the housekeeper, Rosie struggled to take a deep breath. Her mind was racing as fast as her heart. She bent down to pick up the dress she'd worn the night before. She was about to fold it up for the cleaners when she remembered Luna Mae's lottery ticket, which she'd shoved into the pocket of her dress. She fumbled and finally pulled it out. Her hands were so feverish she kept dropping the tickets from her purse onto the floor.

The winning ticket went under the cushion on the rocking chair. Luna Mae's ticket went with the remaining four. She put them all together, crunched them into a ball, then tossed them in the wastepaper basket. Five tickets. Five nonwinning tickets.

Proof that she hadn't won the lottery. At least for Kent's benefit.

She felt like a criminal.

Rosie almost jumped out of her skin when the knock sounded on the guest room door. Before she opened it, she ran into the bathroom, flushed the toilet, waited a few minutes, and opened the door. She pretended to be surprised at the sight of her husband.

"What are you doing here, Kent? I thought I made myself perfectly clear last night that this house is off-limits to you. Luna Mae, call the police."

"Yeah, you do that, Luna Mae." Kent sneered. "Call the newspapers while you're at it. We'll all look real good on the news. Me saying you kicked me out because you won the lottery and didn't want to share with me. I know all about it, Rosalie." He sneered again for her benefit. "That's why you were so quick to hustle me out of here last night. You knew you won before I got home. It isn't going to work. I'm going to get the best lawyer in the state and claim my rightful half of that $302 million."

Rosie held on to the back of the rocking chair. She prayed she wasn't going to black out. "What in the world *are* you talking about, Kent?"

"Don't play innocent with me, Rosalie. The kid at the gas station congratulated me when I stopped for gas. He said he sold you the winning ticket."

"Bobby said that! I don't believe it," Rosalie said, feigning surprise. "He must have me mixed up with someone else."

"Yeah, right. He sounded pretty sure to me." Kent was turning sneering into an art form.

"First of all, Kent, I kicked you out of here before the lottery went off. You left here at ten minutes of eleven. We didn't even have the television on if you recall. I heard this morning that the winning ticket was sold here in Savannah. That's all I know. Take a look in the wastebasket. Those are my tickets. All five of them. They're yours if you want them. Now, get out of my house before *I* call the police."

Rosie reached out to grasp Luna Mae's hand. Both of them were trembling as they watched Kent almost kill himself as he raced to the wastepaper basket. He took the tickets over to the window to look at them. He cursed then, long and loud, his face turning ugly and threatening.

Waving the crumpled tickets like a weapon, he advanced on the two women. "The kid said you won. He said you had all low numbers. I think you're trying to pull a fast one on me. Give me the keys to my goddamn car."

Rosie drew herself up to her full height and stared her husband down. "The car has my name on the title because you have bad credit. That means it belongs to me. Get out of my house, *NOW!*"

"I'm going, but not because you're scaring me. I'm going back to that gas station and talk to everyone who works there. The kid said you won. That's good enough for me."

"Well, it isn't good enough for me." Before Kent knew what was happening, Rosie snatched the tickets out of her husband's hand. In the blink of an eye, she stuffed them down her bra. "My proof that I did *not* win," she said. "You have now crossed the line, and you're harassing me. I want you out of here."

Kent shot his wife another ugly look before he stomped his way out of the room. Both women ran to the window to watch him climb into an old car and back out of the driveway. They huddled together, shivering. Rosie started to cry.

"I married that man. I thought he was the answer to all my prayers. Do you believe he had the nerve . . . Oh, God, now what's going to happen?"

"Rosie . . . where's the ticket?"

"Under the cushion on the rocker. I remembered sticking *your* ticket in my pocket when you showed it to me last night. I don't think I'm going to get away with this, Luna Mae. The machine will show that the five tickets, including the winning one, were rung up at the same time. Maybe they have a time stamp or something. Bobby, the boy who pumps gas and got me the tickets, said something was wrong with the machine and it printed out individual tickets instead of all five sets of numbers being on one ticket. He said I was never going to win because my numbers were so low. He remembers. On top of that, I promised him if I won, he'd never have to pump gas again, and I would put him through medical school. Oh, God, Luna Mae, what did I just do?"

"You panicked just the way I panicked. We both need to calm down and think about this. For the moment, you pulled it off. Your husband was like a scalded cat when he left here. He'd already spent half of his share in his head. He saw the tickets, and he has to take your word that you weren't the winner. It could have been anyone. Thousands of people bought tickets the day of the drawing. The boy could have made a mistake. As to your promise to him, you can always do that anonymously through an attorney at some point in time. You bought five tickets. You produced five tickets. Yes, if they check, they're out of sequence. I'm sure we can come up with a likely story of some kind. You can say you gave me the ticket. The one I gave you could have been given to you at an earlier time. I bought mine before you bought yours."

Rosie rubbed at her temples. A headache was starting at the base of her skull. "You know what they say, Luna Mae. You tell one lie, then you have to keep telling more lies to cover up the first one. I'm not being greedy, I'm really not. I just don't want to give that man one more cent. Maybe I could put his half in a trust and be the conservator and dole it out to him in small amounts. I'd do that." Her voice was so desperate-sounding she couldn't believe it was her own. She felt light-headed all over again.

"Stop it, Rosie. Let's go downstairs and have some coffee. Or, let's not go downstairs and have coffee. Sitting here talking it to death isn't going to get us anywhere. I say we get on with the business at hand

and discuss it tonight. There is nothing anyone can do until you decide to go public. You have a whole year to do that. Another thing, when that gas station owner gets wind of all this, the story is going to change. The boy was not allowed to buy tickets. You have to be eighteen. I know he got them for you, but he had the money in his hand and he paid for them, then took those tickets and handed them to you. I will bet you my new gold shoes that his story is going to change by the time the six o'clock news comes on this evening."

"See, see! This is what happens when you lie. I didn't know you had to be eighteen. He offered to get them for me. I had no intention of buying a ticket when I stopped for gas. Now I involved an innocent kid! Bobby's going to college in the fall, so maybe he is eighteen."

From down below a horn sounded. Luna Mae looked out the window. "It's the locksmith. We'll talk more at lunch. Hide that ticket somewhere safe, Rosie."

Rosie threw her hands high in the air. "Where is it safe?" Luna Mae was already out of earshot and didn't hear the pleading question. In the end, Rosie left the ticket where it was, under the flowered cushion on the rocking chair.

★ ★ ★

Kent Bliss steered the company car into the parking lot of a 7-Eleven, where he bought a large coffee to go. He rolled down the window, allowing the warm, muggy air to creep inside. At first he gulped at the coffee, hardly noticing that he'd burned his tongue. Then he started to sip it as he fired up a cigarette. He only smoked once in a while, mostly when he felt overwhelmed. Like now. He hated the smell of cigarette smoke, and it made his contact lenses foggy.

His own crafty nature told him his wife had lied to him. Probably because if the situation were reversed, he would do exactly the same thing. The big question was, how could he prove it. Rosalie wasn't a liar, and yet, she'd lied to him. He was sure of it. Three hundred and two million dollars were three hundred and two million reasons to lie.

What, he wondered, was his best course of action? Should he return to the old house and beg his wife to take him back, swear on the Almighty that he would mend his errant ways? Rosalie would never fall for that line. The cold, determined look on his wife's face last night was all the proof he needed to know he'd shot his load and was now reaping the consequences.

Kent thought about the thirty-three-hundred-dollar check in his wallet. He had to cash it and find some kind of cheap efficiency apartment to rent. He also had to rent a decent car, then he was going to have to work his ass off so he didn't end up in a Motel 6 or the Comfort Inn indefinitely. He would be reduced to eating in Bojangles or Burger King and getting his coffee at fast-food places. The flip side of that was he could learn to cook. The idea was so horrible, he didn't give it another thought.

"Bitch!" he seethed.

He thought about the last three years of his life. They'd been about as perfect as you could get. He hung out at the country club, played golf and tennis, dined there almost every night with a woman of his choosing. He drove a candy apple red Porsche, told time by his Rolex, and worked an hour or so a day. It was obvious to him now that he should have paid a *little* more attention to the wife he despised.

He thought about his dry-cleaning bill and laundry bill. That was going to eat into his advance big-time. With no credit cards to use, he would have to pay cash for everything. He wouldn't be sending flowers to anyone for a long time or buying trinkets for his many lady friends.

"Bitch!" he seethed again.

On top of everything else, he had to hire an attorney. Lawyers wanted money up front. He wondered what his chances were of getting alimony from his wife. He started to wonder how long she'd been planning his demise. Her cold-hearted actions the previous night didn't sound to him like a spur-of-the-moment decision.

Kent turned the key in the ignition, praying the car would start. It did, but with an unholy backfire. Furious at his circumstances, he floored the gas pedal, but the old car wouldn't go faster than thirty-five miles an hour.

Two hours later, Kent had cashed the check from his boss, paid a deposit at the Days Inn Suites on Bay Street. It made him feel a little better that he was still in the historic district near the City Market, only a block off River Street. He had modular furnishings, and most amenities, along with an adjacent parking area. He could live with the rent. He had no other choice.

He brought the trash bags that held his belongings into the suite and hung his suits on wooden hangers. Later he would put away the rest of his things.

At the Avis car rental agency he was mortified when he was told he needed a credit card to rent one of their cars. He had to call his boss to vouch for him, which Jason did grudgingly. He drove off with a Ford Mustang convertible, the top down. He'd sweet-talk one of the secretaries into driving the clunker back to the agency later.

Kent skipped lunch, something he rarely did, and concentrated on the four appointments Jason Maloy had assigned him. He oozed charm and charisma as he showed customers three houses and one lot. By four-thirty, he had contracts on two of the houses and one on the lot. The deal on the third house, he was sure, would be consummated the following day.

He was on his way to his new home by four-thirty but, at the last minute, decided to stop at the gas station to fill up the Mustang. He hoped the kid would still be on duty. He wanted to get to the bottom of what he considered his wife's betrayal before he went to see an attorney.

Kent pulled out his charm and charisma again as he pulled into the full-serve lane. Bobby hustled over, a wide grin on his face. "New wheels, Mr. Bliss?"

"Yes. By the way, I want to apologize for

this morning. I was a little sharp with you, but the day started off wrong."

"No problem. So, did you guys win or not?" the boy asked as he removed the tank cap.

"Nah. My wife showed me her tickets. She bought five of them, right?"

"Yeah. The machine wouldn't print them all on the same ticket, so she had five separate ones. Guess she had a high number in there. My boss said Wonderball never had a single digit winning ticket. You know, numbers one through nine."

"What made you think she won, Bobby?" Kent asked casually.

The boy shrugged, his eye on the clicking numbers of the gas pump. "Miz Bliss picked the numbers herself. They were all low. That's all I remember. Everyone has been asking me the same thing all day long. We sold over fourteen thousand tickets over a two-day period, right up till the cutoff time. Most of the buyers were from out of state. Maybe they didn't check their tickets yet. Lots of people had low numbers according to my boss. I could have sworn it was her, though. That'll be eleven dollars even, Mr. Bliss."

Kent pulled off a ten-dollar bill and a single and handed them to the boy. "See ya," he said, turning the key and driving off. "You know what, kid, I think you're right," he muttered to himself as he pulled out onto Whitaker Street. He drove fast, his brain reeling until he came to West Bay, where he made a left. He parked his car, put the canvas top up, and headed for his new living quarters.

Vickie Winters stepped down off the steps of the decaying Simmons mansion. Dusk was her favorite time of the day. The heat and humidity weren't as bad, and the city moved a little slower.

She loved Savannah, always had. Just the name alone conjured up misty images of days gone by, frosty mint juleps, Spanish moss dripping from the magnificent live oaks, beautiful, stately old mansions like the one she'd just stepped out of. Even if you were a Yankee saying "Savannah" for the first time, you couldn't help saying it with a Southern drawl.

Vickie was glad to be home. She'd missed the slow Southern pace while traveling with Adeline Simmons. Now she was back, and she was lonely. All her old friends were either married with families or had moved on.

It was time for her to move back to her

own house around the corner from her old friend Rosie Gardener Bliss. The thought made her heart thump inside her chest. A day hadn't gone by in the three years she'd been gone that she didn't think about Rosie and their friendship.

With no family of her own, Adeline had left her decayed mansion and a sizable monetary bequest to Vickie. She never had to work again if she didn't want to. By early next week, she would have all the details taken care of and it would be okay for her to move back into her own little house. She was toying with the idea of donating the old mansion to the town's historical society. Providing they agreed to refurbish it. If not, she'd hold on to it and pray she could keep up with the taxes and maintenance.

Her honey blond hair in a ponytail, wearing shorts, a lemon yellow tank top, and running shoes, Vickie half jogged, half ran up and down the streets until she was a block from her old house. Just around the corner from Rosie's house, which was just as old as Adeline Simmons's mansion. But Rosie's house was in mint condition.

Vickie slowed to a snail's pace as she approached her own little house. Actually, it was more a cottage than a house. An aunt on her father's side of the family had left her the cottage complete with antiques in every room. She'd modernized the kitchen, added a new bathroom, and restored the bathroom on the second floor. It was a comfortable house, and she had been happy in it. It cried out for a child or a dog. Not necessarily a husband, something that was in short supply in Savannah. Not that she was looking for a husband.

The word *husband* brought Rosie to her mind again. Rosie had been so desperate to get married so she could say she had a husband. She wondered if she was happy.

Vickie looked up at her house, opened the small gate, and walked up to the tiny porch where she used to sit late at night in the summer when she couldn't sleep. She sniffed, smelling the confederate jasmine and the tea olive trees that were in bloom. How she loved the sweet scent. The jasmine needed to be trimmed and cut back a little. It was now climbing around the white columns that held up the roof. She loved the look. The stone steps were full of emerald green moss. She stepped on them gingerly as she walked up and opened the door.

The little cottage smelled musty, and the furniture was covered with sheets. The plantation shutters were closed to ward off the brutal summer sun. Tomorrow when she came to the cottage, she would remove and wash the dust covers, air out the house, have her old car serviced, do some grocery shopping, look at the want ads in the paper, and start to get on with her life. She wondered if the utilities would be turned on by morning. There would be no way she could move in until the air conditioners were functional. She could get by with her cell phone, but she did need electricity. She plugged in the refrigerator so if they did turn on the power at eight o'clock tomorrow as promised, the refrigerator would immediately start to cool down. She could clean it out later.

Getting her little house ready would be a joy. The last year with Adeline in failing health had been incredibly stressful. She was almost finished fulfilling all the promises she'd made to the elderly lady. It was time to move on with the rest of her life.

Vickie sat for a few more moments before she got up to leave. She locked the door and left. She walked around the corner, her heart beating extra fast as she approached Rosie's house. Dusk had given way to full darkness, so she didn't worry about craning her neck to see if there were lights glowing in her old friend's home.

The front was dark, but there were lights in the rear of the house, the kitchen, dining room, laundry room, and the back verandah. The garage area was well lit, with four cars parked side by side. Alice's, Danny's, Rosie's, and Luna Mae's cars. Where was Kent's flashy Porsche? She moved closer to the old-fashioned lamp at the corner of the street and looked down at her watch. Kent should be home by now. She shrugged as she walked on, then broke into a jog.

It was after midnight when Rosie walked through the garage, doing one last check before she closed and locked up for the night. She always smiled with satisfaction when she saw the cardboard cartons packed, labeled, and waiting for UPS. They were stacked six deep from floor to ceiling. Despite the personal turmoil, she'd been experiencing, with Danny's and Alice's help she'd accomplished more than she could have hoped for. They had made a serious dent in the Internet orders.

Working had been good for her. While her brain went in a thousand different directions, her hands obeyed her and did what they were supposed to do.

Hands on her hips, Rosie looked around

the garage. Not bad for a little Southern girl who knew nothing about business. Oh, she'd made her mistakes, many of them, but each one had been a learning experience. Together, she and Vickie had perfected their system, and what she was looking at was the end result.

"Where are you, Vic? God, how I miss you," she whispered as she closed and snapped the padlocks on the main garage door.

Inside the house, she walked through the kitchen, the hall, and down past the sunroom. Luna Mae had left the lights on, the exercise equipment glaring at her. "Damn." She'd forgotten her intention to start exercising. She'd also forgotten to come up to the house for a heart-to-heart talk with Luna Mae the way she'd promised earlier.

Tomorrow was another day.

4

Rosie climbed out of the van with her snake boots in hand. She perched, half-on, and half-off the running board she'd insisted on when she bought the Chevy Tahoe for Nature's Decorations. She kicked off her sneakers and pulled on the snake boots that came up to her knees. More so than in the past, snakes and water moccasins were plentiful this year for some reason. Probably it had something to do with the monsoonlike rains they'd been getting since spring.

She loved coming down to the river to pick her weeds. The tangy marsh smell mixed with the wild confederate jasmine reminded her of her youth. It also reminded her of Vickie and the thousands of times they'd come to this very spot to pick the feathery plants that were almost too pretty to be called weeds. They'd given the various kinds of wild growth names that they'd laughed over, but the names had stuck. Vickie hated wearing the snake boots, but Rosie insisted.

Rosie wished she had the guts to walk

over to the old Simmons mansion and ring the doorbell and throw herself into Vickie's arms. She didn't have the guts, it was that simple. And yet, she'd had the guts to kick her husband out of the house. She gave herself a mental shake as she moved away from the van, a burlap bag in her hands.

A light mist was falling, the ground wet, making it easier to pull the weeds out by the root. She'd listened to the weather report in the car. It was supposed to rain all day. Damp weeds were the best because if they were too dry, the delicate leaves and thistlelike balls tended to blow away when touched. When she picked them damp or even soaking wet, all she had to do was hang them upside down and let them dry naturally. It was easier then to spray the first coat of lacquer or hair spray, depending on which weed she was working on.

Rosie eyed a round clump of pampas grass with its flowering shoot. She clipped and snipped for an hour, carrying the huge flowers back to the van. She moved on then, to the tall grass, where she started to yank what she and Vickie had christened, Princess Silk. Princess Silk was a half-inch-wide, foot-long, satiny stalk that she used to fill in her different arrangements. The only problem with the Princess Silk was the sharp edges that required gloves for harvesting and thick latex gloves when she was working on them in the garage.

Suddenly, an uneasy feeling settled between her shoulder blades. She looked around, realizing just how vulnerable she was all alone down by the river. Her arms tingling, she made her way back to the van to place the wet Princess Silk in the backseat. She should have told Luna Mae where she was going, but she hadn't been awake. Luna Mae might think she was still sleeping and not want to wake her. She snorted at the thought of sleeping. If she'd had an hour of sleep last night, it was a lot.

Then she saw her in the distance. She looked better to Rosie than the finest-wrapped Christmas present.

Neutral ground.

"Vickie!" she shouted, joy ringing in her voice.

"Rosie!" Vickie responded, the same joy ringing in her voice.

They moved at the same time, their arms outstretched as they started to babble, neither one knowing what the other one was saying. They hugged one another, tears dripping down their cheeks.

"I can't believe it's you, Vic! God, you look good. I think I thought about you every day since you left. Are you back for good?"

"You look just as good, Rosie. You *porked* up a little," Vickie chided. "I thought about you, too. And, yes, I'm back for good."

Excitement ringing in her voice, Rosie said, "What are you doing *here?*"

Vickie laughed. "Hey, it's Thursday. We always came to the river on Thursdays. I see the Princess Silk is as lush as ever. Need some help?"

"Are you kidding! I can use all the help I can get. Do you want back into the business? Actually, you still own part of it. I never had my lawyer call yours to sever our partnership. Hope springs eternal, that kind of thing. Jeez, it's really starting to rain. Let's go to Dolly's Cafe for coffee and do-nuts like we used to do. That was always the best part of our Thursday morning river expeditions. I'll meet you there. So, do you want back in?" Rosie didn't realize she was holding her breath until Vickie responded.

Vickie's eyes were wary, yet hopeful somehow. "You said you didn't want to see me or talk to me ever again. I wasn't jealous, Rosie. I swear to God, I wasn't. I thought you were making a mistake. If you still want me, the answer is yes, a thousand times yes."

Rosie threw her hands in the air. "I want

you! I want you! You were right about Kent, too. I knew it in the first week. I kicked him out Tuesday night. We'll talk at Dolly's." Rosie shouted to be heard over the sudden crackling thunder and downpour.

Vickie nodded excitedly. "Okay. I'll see you at Dolly's. My treat!"

Kent Bliss watched his wife and her best friend from behind a row of pampas grass. He adjusted the soaking-wet hood on his sweatshirt as he looked down at his pristine white tennis shoes, then cursed under his breath. He'd never be able to clean the thick, gray mud off them. He wouldn't be able to throw them away either since he was now living on a budget with no credit cards at his disposal.

He'd been all set to scare the hell out of his wife until Vickie Winters showed up. Now he was going to have to wait for a more opportune time to put the fear of God into the woman who had just ruined his life.

He tried once more to clean the mud from his sneakers on a mound of green moss. It didn't work. Now he had green grass smears all over the sides, even on his shoelaces. His tennis socks were full of sharp burrs. He would have to throw those away, too. That was okay, he had plenty of socks, but he didn't have a second pair of two-hundred-dollar sneakers.

Kent's expression turned mean and ugly as he turned the key in the ignition and flicked on the windshield wipers. Now that Vickie Winters was back in his wife's life, he was going to have to rethink his plans. He would have plenty of time to think and plan today because no one wanted to look at houses or property in the rain. Maloy would expect him to man the phones, but he knew how to get around that. He was an expert at pretending to look busy.

Kent fretted all the way back to his depressing orange-and-brown efficiency at the Days Inn to change into his work clothes.

"You aren't going to get away with this, you mountain of blubber," he snarled.

Dolly's Cafe was a small establishment filled with huge baskets of live greenery, cozy nooks, tantalizing aromas, and a bustling staff, all of whom wore infectious smiles even so early in the day.

Rosie arrived first and was shedding her snake boots when Vickie pulled up alongside her. She grinned. It was like old times, the two of them meeting at Dolly's. It was like the past three years had just flown away on the wind.

Vickie climbed out of the car and immediately linked her arm with Rosie's. "So, how's it going, *partner?*" She chuckled.

Rosie beamed. She felt like singing as she held the door for her friend. "Oh, look, our booth is empty. Hurry up, Vic, before someone snatches it."

Almost immediately, a carafe of coffee was placed in the center of a table that already held silverware, napkins, and cups. Vickie reached for the pot and poured. She added cream and sugar. Rosie shook her head. "Besides kicking Kent out, I've gone on a diet. I bought a bunch of exercise equipment and am going to hire a personal trainer."

"Good for you, Rosie. Want to talk about it? If you'd rather not . . ."

"No, no, no. I want to talk about it. I *need* to talk about it, Vic. I just don't know where to start. This probably won't mean anything to you, but I did try to find out where you were after the first week. I didn't try hard enough, I guess. I kept hoping you'd send me a card or something. Not that I deserved it. I did hope, though."

Vickie brushed at her honey blond hair before she leaned across the table. "Start at the beginning. It's okay, Rosie, this is me you're talking to. I'm not going to judge you. I'm your friend, remember."

Rosie leaned back in the booth. She bit down on her lower lip before she sipped at her coffee. "I feel like such a fool. You were right about everything. So was Luna Mae. It was me. I wanted to be married. I wanted to be Mrs. Somebody. Let's face it, Kent is a very good-looking man. Unfortunately, it's all a facade. I don't think I loved him. I *know* he didn't love me. He loved my money. The truth is, I bought myself a husband. The only time he was ever nice to me or smiled at me was when I gave him an expensive present. It had to be expensive, Vic, or he'd make a comment about its being a white trash present. I learned real quick what I had to do if I wanted that smile. I went through just about all of my money. I didn't touch my parents' insurance money, though. I didn't sink that low.

"I knew he was having affairs. I saw the way people looked at me. If he worked an hour a day, it was a lot. Luna Mae kept jamming it in my face, and you know what, Vic, I ignored her. I pretended she never said a word. Luna Mae went after him once with a butcher knife when he said I stank like a smelly farm animal. I didn't say a word. He rarely came home for dinner, preferring to eat at the club. I got the bill. They were always dinners for two, lunches for two. The credit card bills were astronomical. I just paid them even when the jewelry he charged wasn't for me.

"I was so miserable, I started to eat. As you can see, I packed on fifty-five pounds. Food became my best friend, and it doesn't talk back to you. Kent said he was ashamed to be seen with me. I ate more. He said I didn't look good in the Porsche I bought him. He hated me, and I knew it, but I didn't do anything about it. How sick is *that?*"

Rosie was like a runaway train, the words tumbling out of her mouth at almost the speed of light. "When I woke up on Tuesday morning, our third anniversary, I knew he wasn't going to remember. I said I wanted him home for dinner, and when he looked at me I could see the revulsion on his face. I guess I snapped because I cut off everything. I even had Luna Mae take the distributor cap off his Porsche. I had the dealer pick it up yesterday. I'm selling it. I cut him off at the club, the charge cards, the whole ball of wax. He didn't come home for dinner that night. I sat at the table the whole time, waiting. He came home at ten-thirty, and I kicked his ass out. I had Luna Mae pack his stuff in trash bags. He didn't know what hit him. I haven't gone to a lawyer yet, but I will. We changed all the locks on the doors, too.

"The business is doing great, Vic. I need more help. I can't keep up with the orders. There's more I have to tell you, but I want to hear about what you were doing and what's been going on in your life. Don't leave anything out. God, I'm so glad you're back. You have no idea how happy you just made me."

The waitress appeared.

"I'll have pancakes with a side order of sausage," Vickie said.

"Just melon and toast for me," Rosie said. She smiled when Vickie nodded approvingly. "Okay, shoot. Tell me *everything.*"

Vickie leaned back as she tugged at her loose-fitting jersey that was the same color as her summer blue eyes. She smiled. "Believe it or not, there isn't all that much to tell. I fell into the job with Adeline. She was a dear, sweet lady who was living on borrowed time, and she knew it. She wanted to travel through Europe the way she had with her husband when they were young. They had a yearlong honeymoon. I guess you can do that when you're rich. So, that's what we did. She was my tour guide. I pushed her wheelchair, and we went everywhere. She had the time of her life. The last year we didn't do much traveling because her health had started to fail. We had a nurse with us all the time.

"We spent the last six months in Paris. I met a man while we were there. He's an American lawyer at the American embassy. Oh, Rosie, this guy is *hot!* I'm in love with him. I don't want to live in Paris, though. He has to stay through the end of the year. He said he's coming back here for New Year's, then he's really going to sweep me off my feet. We'll see. He calls every day. We e-mail several times a day. He's really a nice guy. You'll like him. I want you to be my maid of honor if . . . if we make it down the aisle."

"Oh, I'd love to be your maid of honor, but give me a chance to take off this weight. I don't want to embarrass you. I'm happy for you, Vickie."

"First of all, Rosie, you could never embarrass me. His name is Calvin Rhodes. He's tall, dark, and . . . ordinary. He wears glasses, and his hair is starting to thin on the top. It doesn't bother him. He's one of those guys comfortable in his own skin. He's got a wicked sense of humor. Adeline loved him. He could make her laugh, and that was important. He flew over for her funeral. He didn't have to do that, but he did. He's caring, compassionate, and a gentleman. It wasn't hard to fall in love with him. Six months is a long time to wait, though."

"It'll go by in a heartbeat now that you're coming back to work. The Christmas catalog goes to press next month. We're going to be inundated. I have to find a bigger workplace. The garage, even though it's huge, simply doesn't have enough room. We need more help, and supplies are sparse. You'd think weeds would be plentiful. What I picked this morning won't get me through one day's orders."

"Wow! The business really did take off while I was away. Rosie, I never touched the money. Not once. You should take it back."

"Absolutely not. Nature's Decorations is as much yours as it is mine. The reason it took off is because I was working twenty-four/seven. You do things like that when you're miserable. I worked around the clock, getting by with catnaps. Working kept my mind occupied, so I didn't dwell on my disastrous marriage. Why didn't I listen to you? I'd give anything if I could erase those four years of my life."

Ever practical, Vickie said, "You can't erase those years, Rosie. They happened, and, hopefully, you'll be a better person for the experience. Like Adeline said, everything in life is a learning experience.

"Rosie, think about this. Adeline left me that big old house. I've been thinking of donating it to the historical society even if it isn't in the historic district. But maybe we should use it for the business. It has twenty-two rooms and a six-car garage. I've been staying there since I returned, but I'm moving back into my own little house today. What do you think?"

Rosie reared up in her seat. "What do I think? I think that's the answer to our prayers. A room for each weed! We can do the packing in the garages. It will make it easy for UPS when they come for pickups."

"The wraparound sunroom will be perfect for the painting and spraying. It's air-conditioned, so even if it's humid the way it is here in the summer, we won't fall behind.

"As soon as I get settled and clean up my house, we can start moving stuff into the mansion. The best part is we can both walk to work." Vickie clapped her hands in glee.

Rosie burst out laughing. It was so good

having Vickie back and on her team. They'd hardly missed a beat and had picked up where they left off three years ago. There was nothing better than a true friend. Nothing.

Vickie filled their coffee cups again. "You hinted that there was more to tell me. C'mon, Rosie, did you meet someone? What's the secret?"

Rosie leaned across the table, Vickie did the same thing. Rosie looked around furtively, so did Vickie. "I won the lottery Tuesday night," she whispered.

Vickie was stunned. "You did!"

"Uh-huh. I didn't realize it till yesterday morning, though. It's a long story. We can talk about it later. Kent suspects I won because he talked to the boy at the gas station who actually bought the tickets for me. I think I have it covered for now. I have a whole year to claim it, so I'm not in a hurry."

"Oh my God, Rosie! The odds of that drawing had to be like one in a billion! You actually won! I heard there was only one winner. I don't know what to say."

"I don't know what to say either. I'm still in shock. Kent is not going to give up on this. We'll talk about it later, okay? I start to twitch and shake every time I think about it."

"I can understand why. Okay, we've diddled around long enough. I have to go to my house and start to clean."

Rosie suddenly turned shy. "Want some help?"

"Damn right I want some help. I was wondering if you were going to offer." Vickie pulled some crumpled bills out of her pocket and placed them under the saltshaker. "Let's go, partner."

The receiver pressed to his ear, Kent Bliss waited for someone on the other end of the line to pick up the phone. Like he cared one way or the other. He was just sitting there, going through the motions for the benefit of his boss. He hadn't done cold calling in years, not since he'd married Rosalie Gardener. Now, though, it was a whole new ball game.

He hated the position he was in. And he damn well hated his wife. With a passion. He broke the connection when there was no response after seven rings and stared out the window. On rainy summer days he liked to do lunch at the club with some willowy blonde, then head for a classy motel or hotel to while away the dreary afternoon.

His life until a few days ago had been wonderful. While his fingers punched out another number he tried to remember if he knew a sharp lawyer who would take his case on a contingency basis. Everyone wanted money up front. That limited his options.

He wasn't used to dealing in pennies and small change. He liked bills, the bigger the better, and he loved the solid gold money clip Rosalie had given him one year for his birthday. The clip had five one-hundred-dollar bills in it.

Whom did he know at home on a rainy Thursday afternoon? Husbands had a bad habit of showing up at home for lunch or even leaving the office early if it was raining. He should know since he'd slid out way too many back doors over the years.

What lie could he come up with to explain why he was staying at the Days Inn? The house was being fumigated, his wife was away, the roof leaked? He could probably bluster his way through any explanation he needed to come up with. But how was he going to explain that he no longer had a cell phone? Everyone who was anyone had a cell phone. You needed to have good credit to get a cell phone. Rosalie was the one with the good credit rating. His own wouldn't allow him to buy a package of gum on time.

How would he explain driving a Ford Mustang? The red Porsche had been his trademark. That and his Rolex. The kind of women he liked to associate with, were impressed by those two particular power items. They liked that he tipped big and bought them memorable little gifts. He also let it be known that he, too, liked gifts. *Expensive* gifts. If the woman was foolish enough to give him a silly gift, he scratched her right off his list. He loved it when they called and asked him what they had done wrong and why hadn't he called. Sometimes, when he was in a hellish mood, he'd blurt out, "You can't afford me."

Sometimes he even told the woman on the other end of the line that she bored him.

Another turnoff was cotton underwear because it reminded him of his wife. He insisted on lacy, sexy undergarments. Thongs gave him an instant erection, like the one he was experiencing right now just thinking about them.

He turned when he heard footsteps behind him and looked up to see Jason Maloy.

"Bad day, eh, Kent."

"It's raining," Kent snapped. "When it rains everyone goes to the club or to the mall. This is just a waste of time. I'm going to lunch."

111

"Lunch! I thought you'd be brown bagging it, Bliss. Like in the old days, when I first hired you."

"You're busting me, Jason, and I don't like it. I'm entitled to a lunch hour. If you look around, you'll see I'm the only one here today. The reason I'm the only one here is because no one wants to do business or talk with a real-estate salesman when it's raining. It's pouring outside in case you haven't noticed. I sold your three properties and the lot. My million-dollar status is still intact. That's more than anyone else sold around here in the last month. I'd appreciate you cutting me a little slack if you don't mind."

"Well, sure, Kent. Take all the time you need. Don't come back to the office if you don't want to. I'm betting you aren't going to make it, Mr. Bliss, without some woman in the background picking up your bills. Oh, one other thing. You better get yourself a tax man so you can make some estimated tax payments on the commissions I've paid you this quarter. Uncle Sam doesn't like it when you don't give him his fair share, and neither does the governor of the fine state of Georgia. I don't think your wife is going to have her tax man continue to take care of your business. Nor will she want to file a joint return with you if she booted you out. Just wanted to give you a heads up, Kent."

Son of a bitch. He hadn't thought about that. Kent stood up and reached for his jacket. Now he had something else to worry about. He didn't bother to say goodbye as he ran from the office and through the parking lot to his car. He was drenched within seconds. He cursed long and hard when he started up the Mustang.

This was all Rosalie's fault. He wondered what would happen if he showed up at the house and asked her for a loan to tide him over. He almost choked on his own anger. He knew it wasn't an option. Even if he had the nerve to show up at the house, he'd want to put his fist through her fat face. No, it wasn't an option.

He needed to find a lawyer.

Kent drove up one street and down the next, anything to avoid going back to the Days Inn to watch television.

Before he knew it, he was cruising past the house he'd lived in for the past three years. He'd liked the house, liked the freedom he'd had to come and go with absolutely no responsibilities. Rosalie had taken care of everything. She'd been like a puppet whose strings he'd jerked whenever he wanted something.

Four cars were parked by the garages. That had to mean the weed business was doing well. Rosie hadn't returned with the van. He wondered what that meant. He did a second cruise by, but nothing had changed. He rolled around the corner and noticed the van in the driveway of Vickie Winters's old house. So the two of them were buddy-buddy again. That couldn't be good for his cause, that was for sure. He did a second drive-by, hoping to see something. He didn't know if he dared risk a third time around the block. Some nosy neighbor might call it in to the police, and they'd roust him.

Fuming at his circumstances, he drove away, stopping at a Taco Bell for food and coffee. At least he wouldn't have to leave a tip.

"I should kill you for what you've done to me, you bitch," he muttered under his breath. He grabbed his food and peeled out of the drive-through line.

"You are going to pay for this, Rosalie. One way or another."

5

Rosie rolled over on the big marital bed that had never been a marital bed, aware that she was alone. But then, that was nothing new. She'd slept alone since she'd returned from her honeymoon, exactly three years and seven days ago. She sat up and swung her legs over the side of the bed. It was 3:10 in the morning. She'd dozed off, sleeping perhaps two hours. This had been her pattern since the night of her anniversary. Some nights she didn't sleep at all. When one made a mess of one's life the way she had, sleep was a luxury. Obviously one she didn't deserve.

She got up the way she always did and walked over to her rocking chair. She dragged it over to the big bay window that overlooked the gardens and the side of the garage. Earlier, before climbing into bed, she'd pulled the drapes wide and opened the window all the way. The sheer curtains billowed in the warm night breeze. She drank it in greedily before she sat down in the rocker. The scent of tea olive and jasmine tickled her nostrils.

Rosie did her best to shift her thoughts into neutral but knew it wouldn't work. Maybe it was the feeling of being so alone, the darkness of the night, the uncertainty of tomorrow. Whatever it was, she hated the feeling.

The lottery ticket under the cushion she was sitting on felt hot to her backside. She'd looked at it a thousand times in the past two weeks. Each time she picked it up, her hands started to shake. Three hundred and two million dollars was an obscene amount of money. Even now, one week later, she still couldn't comprehend the sum. She wiggled on the chair, uncomfortable with her thoughts. Damn, was she ever going to be able to sleep again? Maybe when she was finally divorced. Or maybe she wouldn't sleep again until she resolved the lottery ticket business.

The only good thing that happened in the past two weeks was her reconciliation with Vickie. Just thinking about Vickie brought a smile to her lips.

Movement down in the yard brought her to her feet at the same moment her bedroom door opened. She turned to see Luna Mae, resplendent in a long, flowing, scarlet gown shot through with gold threads, advance into the room.

"Shhh, don't make a sound, Rosie, and back away from the window. You bypassed the alarm system when you opened the window. I told you not to do that, baby. A window screen does not afford the same protection as a closed, locked window. Did you ever hear the word *ladder?* Someone's in the yard. I heard a noise but couldn't identify it. I got up, looked out the window, and saw this shadowy figure down below. It might be a good idea to start thinking about getting a dog. I don't trust that husband of yours. I think we should call the police."

"I don't trust him either, Luna Mae. Let's go downstairs. Don't turn any lights on. If we call the police, it will be in the papers tomorrow, and Kent will see it. It will give him satisfaction, and I don't want that. Besides, I'm sure it's Kent out there prowling around. We are not going to play into his hands. The only thing I am really certain of is, he is not going to give up. He's convinced I won the lottery, and he wants his piece of it. Just so you know, Luna Mae, I'll never claim it if I have to give him half."

"That's my girl." Luna Mae reached for the cordless phone. "Just in case we have to dial nine-one-one."

Together they walked down the hall, careful to stay away from the outside windows, with the moonlight filtering through the vertical blinds. There were no creaky steps on the staircase as they made their way to the bottom and out to the dining room and kitchen.

"Whoever it was I saw was over by the corner of the garage next to the gardens," Luna Mae said from her position by the kitchen window.

"That's where I saw him, too. It might have been a her, it was really too dark to see," Rosie said.

"It doesn't matter who it is. No one should be in the yard prowling around at three o'clock in the morning. Whoever it is, is up to no good. That's a given." To Rosie's horror, Luna Mae said, "They could murder us in our own beds. Criminals know how to disarm alarm systems. That's why we should get a dog."

"All right, all right, Luna Mae, you made your point. We'll get a dog, and I will not open the windows anymore. Don't even think about going outside."

"Me? Go outside? I don't think so."

"Good. Maybe whoever is out there is intent on stealing the stuff in the garage. His or her loss since just about everything

118

has been moved to the Simmons mansion. Do you think I should start calling it the Winters mansion now that Vickie owns it?"

"I think you should call it whatever you want to call it. What should we do now, Rosie?"

"Give me the phone, and you go back to bed. I'm going to go on the treadmill. Tomorrow, today actually, is my first day with the trainer. I at least want to *pretend* I know what I'm doing. Like learning how to set the timers and to turn the damn things on and off."

"Rosie, you will be an open target with those wraparound windows in the sunroom. The moonlight is a little too bright. I see by that determined look on your face you're going to do it regardless of what I say. Just don't turn on any lights."

"Go! I'll be fine."

"I'm not going to sleep. I'm going to make some coffee."

The words were no sooner out of her mouth than the front doorbell rang. The two women stood in the dining room, huddled together, their startled gazes locked.

"Maybe it's the police saying they found the prowler," Luna Mae whispered.

"We didn't call the police, Luna Mae," Rosie whispered in return.

"Maybe the police were patrolling the area and spotted him. They do patrol, you know. My God, you aren't going to open the door, are you?"

"No, I am not going to open the door, Luna Mae. I'm also not going to live in fear in my own house. However, I am going to the front window and peek out."

"I'm going with you. When we get that dog, we should also get a gun. Don't you move one step till I get the butcher knife." Rosie nodded as the housekeeper scampered into the kitchen to return with a wicked-looking knife that she held out in front of her.

The doorbell pealed again.

The two women's sweaty bare feet made a sucking sound as they ran across the wood floors to the front window.

"It's Kent!" Rosie gasped, horror registering on her face.

The doorbell rang a third time.

"Go back to the kitchen. Here's the phone. I want to see what he wants."

"Oh, baby, no. This is not a good thing. I don't think you should open the door."

"Go, Luna Mae."

Any other time, Rosie would have been mortified to have her husband see her in clinging jersey pajamas that cleaved to her ample body. She squared her shoulders, reached up to press the button to turn on the outside light. She unlocked the door and opened it. She blocked the doorway, her arms crossed over her chest.

"It's three-thirty in the morning, Kent. You're lucky I didn't call the police. What do you want?"

He looked terrible, with dark circles under his eyes, his clothes wrinkled and messy. He badly needed a shave, and his hair was standing on end. He looked like he'd lost weight. His appearance pleased Rosie.

"Can I come in, Rosalie? I know it's late, but I couldn't sleep. We need to talk."

Suddenly, Rosie felt more powerful than she'd ever felt in her life. "I think you have me confused with someone who might care about what you think or feel." She reached out to close the door.

"Please, Rosalie."

Rosie tilted her head to the side. "Are you groveling, Kent?"

Kent's head reared back. "No! Yes, if that's what you want. Listen, Rosalie, I'm sorry about . . . everything. I didn't realize how much I . . . I want to make it up to you. I know now I was a lousy husband. I was never married before," he whined.

Rosie's eyes almost bugged out of her head. She could just imagine Luna Mae in the kitchen covering her mouth so she wouldn't laugh out loud.

"Are you . . . are you saying you want to come back to me? That you still want to be married to me? Is that what you're trying to say, Kent?"

"Well, yes," Kent said, looking everywhere but at Rosie.

Rosie smiled. "In that case, maybe you should come inside. I don't think my neighbors need to hear this. By the way, you don't look like your usual dapper self this morning, Kent. You poor thing, you have had a rough time of it these past two weeks, haven't you."

Kent sighed with happiness. He had it in the bag. He was sure of it. Rosalie's smile was all he needed to see. She still loved him, still needed him.

"You have no idea, Rosalie. No idea at all."

"Well, sure I do, Kent. I've been alone, too. Now let's make sure I understand all this. You want to come back here. Move back in, is that right?"

"Nothing would make me happier."

"You want things to be just the way they were, is that right?"

"You bet."

"No, no, no. If you want to come back, we need some new rules. Let's be real careful here. Tell me if this is how you see your return. You're going to continue working for Mr. Maloy. You will work hard, coming home for lunch every day, work through the afternoon, be home for dinner at six-thirty, spend your evenings with me. Every evening. There will be no more evening appointments. You and I will cozy up in front of the TV set and eat snacks. Just another old married couple.

"We'll sleep together and have sex *every* night, after which we will cuddle. We'll shower together in the morning, then have a lovely breakfast. We don't need that cliquey, snobby country club. We'll be spending too much time together to go there, and it's such a waste of money. We will just be so busy trying to get pregnant. I can see it now! I see us having four, maybe five children. Three girls, two boys. You get to name the boys, I get to name the girls. Lordy, I will put on soooo much weight. It will be worth it, though. Yes, five kids. And we'll trade in the Porsche for a VW Beetle. They're so fashionable. And cute. Just perfect for you to scoot around in. Oh, and you will turn over your check to me every week to help with all the household bills and such. You can take an allowance. We need to build up our bank account. The one we'll open when you come back. No credit cards either. If we can't pay cash, we don't buy it. Is that how you see your return, Kent?"

Kent stared at his wife, a look of horrified disbelief on his face. It looked to Rosie like he was having a hard time breathing.

"In the past, Kent, it was all about you. Now, sweetie, it's all about me."

"You're out of your mind, Rosalie. No man in his right mind would agree to conditions like that. C'mon now, stop fooling around. Let's be realistic."

"What part didn't you like?" Her voice was so neutral one would have thought she was discussing a particular cut of meat from the local butcher.

"The whole damn thing. I said I was willing to come back if we picked up where we left off. No, no, no, I don't and won't accept those terms."

"Hey, honey, I didn't ask you to come back, now did I? You were crawling around in my backyard at three o'clock in the morning, not the other way around. I guess you didn't understand when I said it's all about me now. Take it or leave it."

Rosalie quickly opened the door and

waited, knowing exactly what her husband would do. He didn't disappoint her. She smiled. He shook his fist in her face, the same look of hatred and revulsion on his face that she'd seen two weeks ago.

"Bitch!" he seethed.

"Bastard," she shot back.

He wasn't moving. What he was doing was doubling up his fist. Rosie backed up, alarm on her face.

"Eyow!" Luna Mae bellowed at the top of her lungs like a Ninja as she rushed to the foyer, the butcher knife straight out in front of her, her nighttime pigtail swinging wildly. Kent barreled through the door. Rosie slammed it shut and locked it.

Rosie's eyebrows shot upward, almost to her hairline. "What do you call that move you just performed?"

Luna Mae sliced the air with the butcher knife. "Luna Mae with a butcher knife! It worked, didn't it. I bet he lost half the tread off those Brooks Brothers loafers of his."

For some reason Luna Mae's comments made Rosie laugh. She collapsed on the steps and howled. "I wish you could have seen yourself. Hell, you even scared me. Do you believe the gall of that man? He really thought he could waltz right in here, and I was going to fall all over him.

"We are going to get that dog, and we're also going to upgrade our alarm system. The only thing I'm having trouble with is that I was such a fool. Getting my nose rubbed in it again and again makes it that much easier to follow through with the divorce. And dealing with the lottery ticket," Rosie said sotto voce.

"Okay, I think I'm going to go into the sunroom and read the directions on my new exercise equipment so I can at least appear to have a brain when the trainer gets here. What's for breakfast?"

"Puffed rice, skim milk, blueberries, black coffee, and one slice of toast."

"Oh."

"Do you want to know about lunch?"

"I don't think so. I did lose seven pounds in two weeks, though. One of these days, I'm going to start jogging."

Luna Mae waved the butcher knife as she rearmed the alarm system. "Good night, baby."

" 'Night, Luna Mae."

Rosie didn't cry until she closed the French doors that led to the sunroom. She didn't just cry, she bawled and howled her misery that she'd been stupid and naive enough to marry a man who loved her money but hated her.

Well, it was a whole new game now, and she was the one who would set the rules.

Just because she'd been stupid once didn't mean she had to be stupid forever.

Rosie yanked at the instruction manual hanging off the bar on the treadmill. The instruction booklets for the StairMaster and Exercycle were on the floor. She sat down on the window seat to study them. By seven-thirty she knew how to adjust all the different gizmos. The only thing she didn't do was try them out.

Rosie headed for the second floor to shower. Her trainer was due at nine o'clock, which meant she had to eat her skimpy breakfast by eight o'clock.

A new day.

The doorbell rang as Rosie was walking toward the sunroom to wait for her personal trainer. She looked down at her watch. Two minutes to nine. He was early. She liked that. Rosie hitched up her sweatpants, which felt a tad loose with the seven pounds she'd lost. She drew in a deep breath, wondering what kind of trainer she was getting for a hundred bucks an hour. Luna Mae said that Savannah's Olympus Gym, one of many in a chain across the country, told her Jack, no last name, was the best of the best.

Rosie opened the door and hoped the disappointment she felt at the sight of the trainer didn't show on her face. She'd expected a tall, bronze Adonis with pecs and abs and a white, toothy smile. What she was seeing was a man about her own age — in his late thirties — perhaps five-ten, with a receding hairline, muscles, and a disarming grin showing a crooked eye-tooth. His eyes were brown, the color of freshly cooked chocolate pudding. Nice, warm eyes. His nose, she thought, looked like it had been broken more than once.

"Hi. You must be Jack," Rosie said, holding out her hand. "I'm Rosie . . . Bliss, soon to be Rosie Gardener. No, I'm Rosie Gardener. I want you to think of me as Rosie Gardener. You okay with that, Jack? I don't want to confuse you."

Jack grinned. "I'm okay with it if you're okay with it. Are you ready to get started?"

"No. Well, I am and I'm not. I plan to do my best. You aren't going to work me till I drop, are you?"

"Yep."

"Oh."

Rosie led the way to the sunroom. It was almost bare of furniture. Luna Mae had

had most of the wicker furniture carted out to the back verandah. Other than the exercise equipment, the weights, the books on healthy exercising, the only piece of furniture was a wicker chair with a bright green-and-white-striped seat cushion. For her to collapse in after her workout, Luna Mae said.

"First things first, Rosie," Jack said. "I want you to fill out this questionnaire. Don't skimp on the answers. I always call the doctor to find out if there's anything about you I need to know. So, before you do that, call your doctor and tell him that he can give me the information I request, so we can get that out of the way. Here's my cell phone."

After speaking to the doctor and giving the phone back to Jack, Rosie began on the questionnaire. Ten minutes later, Rosie handed the clipboard back to the trainer. She watched as he carefully read every single entry. Then he wrote something on the back of the first page, probably the doctor's assessment of her condition.

"Okay, we're good to go. We're going to do some warm-up stretches, followed by a few sit-ups, some jumping jacks, then we'll tackle the machines. I brought a book for you on weight training. I want you to read it. We won't be doing that for a while, but I do want you to read it soon. And the book on nutrition. I mapped out a week's worth of meal plans. I want you to stick to it religiously. Any questions?"

"How long is it going to take me to get rid of forty-eight more pounds?"

Jack looked at his client. "As long as it takes," he said coolly.

Rosie nodded. "That was the right answer, Jack. If you'd given me a time, I would have booted you right out of here. Just so you know, I'm serious here, okay?"

"Okay, Rosie, let's do it . . ."

An hour later, Rosie walked the trainer to the door. Actually, she limped her way to the door. "Eat a protein bar after you shower. I put a few in your kit until you can buy your own. Take a *hot* shower. You did good for the first day. Stick to the schedule I made up for you to follow on my off days. I'll see you the day after tomorrow."

"Just so you know, I hate your guts," Rosie said before she slammed the front door. She heard the trainer laugh. She stopped in midstride to listen. It was a wonderful sound. She couldn't remember the last time she'd heard a man laugh.

Luna Mae appeared out of nowhere. "How'd it go, baby?"

"I'm dead. I just don't have the good sense to keel over. I hurt. You need to buy me some protein bars. And my menus are in the kit. I guess you'll have to go to the store. If I can still walk after I take a shower, I'll be over at Vickie's. Not her real house, the Simmons house. We're about ready to commence business. We can use your help today, Luna Mae. Damn, it's raining. That weatherman is all fouled up. He predicted sun and fluffy white clouds. Do you think it's an omen of some kind, Luna Mae?" To her ear her voice sounded overly anxious.

"No, I don't think it's an omen. That guy never gets it right. Remember last winter he said cool and sunny, and we got two inches of snow?"

Rosie shrugged as she limped her way to the stairs. "Among other things, I'm getting shin splints," she grumbled.

"Stop whining, Rosie. No pain, no gain."

"Shut up, Luna Mae."

The housekeeper pulled out Rosie's weekly menus from her exercise kit and laughed as she checked her purse for the car keys. She was about to set the alarm and lock the back door when a technician from the alarm company appeared. She looked at him questioningly. "We keep getting a signal at central that says there's an electrical short somewhere. I have to check it out. It's going to take a couple of hours."

Resigned, Luna Mae checked the man's ID card before she let him into the house. Then she ran upstairs to Rosie's room. She stuck her head in the bathroom and explained what had happened. "You have to go to the store, baby. I'll leave the grocery list and your menus on the counter. I'm going to stay right behind that guy every step of the way."

"Okay, Luna Mae."

On his way to work at Maloy Realty, Kent Bliss passed Rosalie on the road. He pretended not to see her. He felt as awful as he looked. Jason Maloy and the others in the office would undoubtedly think he'd been out catting around all night now that he was a free agent. How they'd laugh if they knew.

He parked the Mustang, making sure the canvas hood was secure before he stomped his way into the office. With the rain coming down as it was, he knew it would be another day of cold calling, with few if any results. He also knew he had to erase his scowl and his fears and as Maloy said, put a smile on his face.

The receptionist of the day, whose name was Sylvia, winked at him. "Another hard night, Kent?"

"Ha-ha," Kent grunted as he walked into his office. A small gold gift-wrapped package sat in the middle of his desk. He undid the gold ribbon and opened the box. He smiled. He loved receiving presents. He carefully removed the tissue to see a solid gold key chain with a gold Porsche charm. The card read, I miss you. It was signed, Allison.

The box indicated the key chain came from Tiffany's. His slick brain raced. He could hit Swanson's pawnshop on his lunch hour. If he was lucky, he could get around seventy bucks for the chain. Enough to pick up his dry cleaning, fill his gas tank, buy some cigarettes for emergencies, and a few fast-food lunches or dinners. If he met up with Allison What's-her-name, he'd simply say he'd lost the key chain.

This was what he had been reduced to.

Kent removed his jacket and hung it on a hanger before he rolled up the sleeves of his white shirt. He sat back down and pulled the phone list he'd worked on previously closer to the phone. He needed reading glasses, but there was no way in hell he was going to perch that banner of middle age on his nose. Squinting worked just fine. He had a magnifying glass in his drawer that helped him read small print.

Before he picked up the phone, he found himself wondering who or what he hated more, cold calling or his wife.

His wife.

Jason Maloy entered the office, shaking the excess rain from his oversize umbrella. "You're actually early today, Kent. That's what I like to see. Nose to the grindstone and all that." Kent wanted to tell him to shut up, to leave him alone, but he kept quiet. He needed this pissy-assed job until he could make other arrangements. He nodded, picked up the phone, his signal that Maloy should move on and let him do his job.

He'd been so sure he could convince Rosalie to take him back. Where did she suddenly get that backbone she'd showed in the early hours of the morning? From winning the Wonderball lottery, that's where. If it weren't for that, she would have taken him back in the blink of an eye.

All he had to do was prove she'd won and was sitting tight until they got divorced. Well, he could fight that, saying he loved her and didn't want a divorce. He needed a really good lawyer. One of those barracudas who went for the jugular. Hiring a lawyer like that would require a sizable retainer, something he didn't have at the moment. He knew people who had bought divorce kits and represented themselves. But they were mostly people who really didn't have any assets and just wanted out of a marriage the cheapest and quickest way possible.

Sometimes lawyers took on high-profile cases for a contingency fee. A $302-million win should qualify as a high-profile case.

The pencil Kent was holding snapped in two. His devious mind kicked into overdrive. The nonwinning tickets were the key to everything. He was sure of it. He'd had them in his hand, and Rosalie had snatched them away at the last second. Those tickets were the proof that she'd won. Somehow she'd tossed in a ringer. Why else would she have snatched them away from him? And, of course, the kid, Bobby, who remembered selling Rosie the tickets, could help him.

The big question was, how was he going to get hold of those tickets, assuming Rosalie hadn't thrown them away?

Kent racked his brain then. Were any of his possessions left behind? Could he lie and say certain things weren't in the trash bags? Did he have stuff in the attic? Of course, he had all kinds of stuff in the attic. Old tennis rackets, old golf clubs, boxes of books he'd never read, stuff from his youth, old suitcases. Pictures.

Damn. He was feeling better by the moment. Maybe there was light at the end of the tunnel after all.

A smile stretched across his face when he thought about the $302-million jackpot.

6

Rosie zipped through the supermarket at top speed. By the time she reached the checkout counter there wasn't one item in her grocery cart that appealed to her. Still, she was going to have to acquire a taste for unappealing food. *Will I ever be able to eat mashed potatoes and gravy again?* "Not in this lifetime," she muttered to herself. She paid for her groceries, loaded them in the back of the van, and started off. She had one more stop, the fish store, where she was to buy salmon. Though she had always preferred beef or pork to fish, from here on in it was going to be a staple in her life, so she might as well get used to the idea.

When she stepped out of the van ten minutes later, the rain was coming down in hard-driving sheets. The moment she opened her umbrella, a strong gust of wind turned it inside out, and another gust ripped it out of her hands.

Rosie ran to the fish store and was immediately handed a wad of paper towels by one of the clerks. She gratefully mopped at her face and hair as she placed her order. Since she was the only one in the shop, she was back out in the rain in less than eight minutes. Since she was already soaked to the skin, she walked around to the passenger side of the car to toss in the fish bag. She was about to close the door when she sensed movement by her feet. She looked down and saw a dog cowering under the car. She dropped to her knees, unmindful of the rain. She coaxed the scrawny dog out and stroked its face, not caring if he snapped at her or not. "Oh, you poor thing. Come on, I won't hurt you." Reacting to Rosie's tone, the dog bellied out but didn't get up. "Are you hurt?"

Luna Mae had said they needed a dog. This was a dog. A dog that needed her. Unsure if it was hurt, she was careful when she picked him up and lowered him to the passenger seat, brushing the fish bag onto the floor. "It's okay, it's okay," she crooned over and over as she climbed in the car for the drive home.

The moment she hit her long driveway, Rosie leaned on the horn. Luna Mae, her face filled with worry, rushed out into the rain. "What?" she screamed, as Rosie hopped out and ran to the passenger side of the car. She opened the door and pointed.

"He was under my car at the fish store. I don't know if he's hurt or not. I just scooped him up, and he let me, Luna Mae. He wasn't the least bit afraid of me. Do you think he's sick? Should we call a vet? What should we do?"

"Let's get him in the house and decide. He's shivering. He looks half-starved to me. Careful, baby."

Luna Mae was a whirling dervish once they were inside the house. She ran to the laundry room for towels. The dog allowed himself to be wrapped snugly, and only re-laxed when Rosie cradled him in her lap. She continued to croon to him as she gently rubbed the towel he was wrapped in. "Do we have anything for him to eat? I know we don't have any dog food, but can you fix him something till we can get some? How about hamburger?"

"I can do that. Maybe mixed with a little cheese. Poor thing. Oh, look, he's sleeping. He must feel safe. He's *big*, Rosie. Looks like a shepherd-Lab mix to me."

"Who cares what he is. He needs us. Cook already, Luna Mae."

The housekeeper risked a glance at her employer out of the corner of her eye. Rosie's fierce hold on the dog told her that at last she had someone to love, someone who would love her in return. Right now it didn't matter if that someone had four legs.

"Yes, ma'am," Luna Mae said smartly. "I'll microwave some chicken and rice and add some broth. The hamburger meat is frozen. Between the two of us I think we can get this dog on the mend. He's not crying or whimpering, so I think he's just tired, hungry, and scared. Tomorrow, you can take him to a vet. I don't think he needs to be traumatized any more today."

"I think you're right. Do you think you could call Vickie for me? I don't want to move and wake him up. He's big, but he isn't heavy. I think you're right about him being starved, too. He was probably looking for food in the Dumpster. Tell Vickie she has to carry on today without me. This is more important. She'll understand."

"All right, boss. We both need to get out of these wet clothes. The worst kind of cold to catch is a summer cold. Just let me get the dog's food going, then I'll call Vickie for you."

Ten minutes later, the dog's food was finished and cooled. Both women were still in their wet clothes dithering about waking the dog up. In the end, the decision to wake or not wake the dog was taken out of their hands by an earsplitting whistle coming from the keypad on the alarm system. The dog woke and started to shake as he looked around fearfully. Rosie held him close, murmuring words of comfort.

The technician entered the kitchen, a wide grin on his face. "Sorry about that, folks, but I had to test the system. You're good to go now. Just sign my work order, and I'm out of your hair." Luna Mae obliged him. A moment later he was gone.

Rosie squirmed off her chair, no mean feat with the dog still in her lap. She sat down on the floor with the dog while Luna Mae set a bowl of chicken and rice in front of him, along with a bowl of water. The dog looked at the food for a moment before his wobbly legs gave out on him. Rosie reached for him. "Maybe he's too weak to stand up to eat. I'll feed him. You go get dressed, then you can feed him while I dress."

Rosie filled the palm of her hand with the rice-and-chicken mixture. The dog ate it daintily. From time to time, Rosie scooped water into her hand so he could lick at it. "Good boy. You're getting it. Before you know it, you're going to be just fine. We'll get you checked out, give you a bath and some vitamins, and we'll be best buddies." She kept feeding him as she talked softly.

"I know you probably have a name, but in a million years I'll never guess what it is, so I'm going to have to give you one. I'm not even going to look for your owner because whoever they are, they would have found you by now if they were looking. You're mine. You hear me, you're mine." The dog raised his head and looked at his new owner with total adoration. Rosie's eyes filled.

Rosie got up when Luna Mae appeared in the kitchen dressed in an electric blue jumpsuit with silver zippers on the sleeves and legs. "Your turn," she said, sitting down on the floor. The dog immediately started to whimper when Rosie left the kitchen. "She's coming back, boy. You are a boy, aren't you? Like you're really going to answer me." Luna Mae laughed. Using her fingers, she took a pinch of food and held it out to the dog. He or she refused it and looked away.

"Okay. You're a one-woman dog I see. Big mistake, I'm the one who cooks the food. Come on, just a little." The dog obediently opened his mouth. "You understand, don't you. Yes, I think you do. Let me tell you a little secret, big guy, you are in good hands. There is no doubt in my mind that you are going to live like a king and rule this domicile." Luna Mae continued to feed the dog until the bowl was empty.

Rosie ran down the steps in her bare feet in time to see the dog struggling to his feet. He made his way to the back door. The two women looked at one another. "I think he has to *go*. It's pouring rain. Let's put some papers down and see what he does."

Rosie reached for the morning paper that was still on the kitchen table, folded it, and laid it down by the back door. The dog looked at them, at the paper, then lifted his leg. Both women clapped their hands. "Good boy," they chorused.

"He's a boy all right," Luna Mae chortled.

"Now what?" Rosie asked, as the dog brushed up against her leg.

"This is just a guess on my part, Rosie. I never had a dog, but I watch Animal Planet on TV. We'll feed him again in a few hours. He needs to drink, though, or he'll dehydrate. And he's probably been on the loose for some time since he's so skinny. He has to build up his strength. We can call a vet now if you want."

"Let's see how he does over the next few hours. I don't want him to get scared. I think I'll go in the sunroom and read some of those books Jack left for me. He's still wet, so let's keep him wrapped up and warm. Bring a bowl of water for him, okay?"

"Do you want me to serve you lunch in there, too?"

Rosie glared at her housekeeper. "Don't ever again refer to an apple, a cracker, and two stalks of celery as my lunch, Luna Mae. My idea of lunch is a ham-and-cheese sandwich with pickles and chips on the side and a piece of pie for dessert."

Luna Mae laughed until she couldn't laugh anymore. "When you're a size eight you can have that for lunch."

"I'll never be a size eight, Luna Mae, so just shut up and bring the damn food. For your information, I'm not even hungry."

Luna Mae continued to laugh as Rosie walked to the sunroom.

"You'll learn to love her the way I do. Sometimes she's a pain in the butt, but she means well. She'll be taking care of both of us," Rosie said to the dog as she tickled him behind his ears. The grateful dog almost purred when she wrapped him in a thick pink towel until only his snout was sticking out. Rosie curled into the wicker chair with the green-and-white-striped cushions.

A day off to do nothing but sit. With her new best friend. What could be better?

The clock on the reception room wall said it was 2:45. Kent had been cold calling, asking whoever answered the phone if they were thinking about selling their house. He'd been at it for over five hours with two maybes, one definite yes, and all the rest definite no's.

It was still pouring rain outside. Should he stay here in the office or go back to the Days Inn and his orange-and-brown efficiency? He still had a week to go on his gym membership. He could go there, pretend to work out, and shoot the breeze with the guys who lived to flex their muscles. If he remembered correctly, there was a scrawny young lawyer who worked out around this time every day. Maybe he could get some free advice. Yeah, yeah, that's what he would do. Anything was better than sitting here counting his pennies, moaning and groaning about his circumstances, and phoning people who hung up on him the minute he stated the reason for his call.

Kent turned off his computer, shoved his list of prospective house sellers into the middle drawer of his desk, and took off.

He didn't wave good-bye or look back to see if Jason Maloy was watching him through the window. Just then, he didn't give two shits what Jason Maloy thought or did.

The owner of the nationwide Olympus Fitness Centers cast a critical eye over his domain. The Savannah gym was the flagship of the chain. Savannah was where his father and uncle built and ran the operation before Jack took over. The OFs, or Old Fogies as they called themselves, still came in from time to time to check on things. They were due today, and Jack Silver wanted everything just perfect. As far as he could see, everything was A-1. The OFs shouldn't have a complaint as best he could tell.

The locker rooms and showers glistened. The small kitchen in the back not only gleamed, but it smelled clean. The equipment was the latest, the workout rooms tidy and neat. There was nothing he could do about the body smells. At night, when everyone else was sleeping, the gym was cleaned and disinfected from one end to the other.

The payroll numbered twenty-five, all longtime, loyal employees who were interested in a healthy, fit life.

Jack smiled to himself, knowing the OFs were due any second, always timing their arrival for the start of the afternoon aerobics class.

The gym was full today with local businessmen and housewives. It must have something to do with the rain he decided. People didn't feel like working or staying home. The steady beat of falling rain had a tendency to make one sleepy. That was his own assessment, and he didn't know if it was true or not.

Jack walked around the desk and out onto the main floor. He liked this part of the day, when he could walk among the members to check their progress. He knew every member, could recite their vitals, remember the dates they'd enrolled and the progress they'd made. Like Albert Beeker. Big Al, as he thought of him, had come in seventy pounds overweight. He'd looked like a donut without the hole in the middle. That had been eight months ago.

"How's it going, Al?" Jack said, coming up behind the weight bench.

"It's going good, Jack. Hell, man, I can tie my shoelaces without fainting. Best thing I ever did was come here. I went square dancing with my wife on Saturday night. That was a workout in itself."

"I'm proud of you, Al." Sincerity rang in the owner's voice as he moved on until he stopped at the StairMaster and a guy named Mike McIntyre.

"You're lookin' pitiful from where I'm standing, McIntyre. What are you going to do when I put those ten-pound weights around your ankles and make you go full throttle? My grandmother has more speed than you do. C'mon, you can do it. Move, man, move!" McIntyre increased his tempo to the trainer's delight. "I'm watching you, remember that. I want to make sure you get your money's worth."

Overall, Jack decided, everyone was progressing nicely. He could leave on the weekend to check out four of his other gyms. In two days, including the flight time, he could hit North Carolina, South Carolina, Alabama, and Florida. The following week he'd head up the East Coast. With no family other than his father and uncle, he was the Olympus's roving ambassador slash owner.

Jack looked at his watch. His father was running late. Must be the rain. He glanced up to see a member walking out of the locker room. His eyes narrowed as he looked at the man's tailored shorts, the pricey sneakers, the clean, ironed tee shirt. He smirked at the designer sweatbands the man wore on his wrists and around his forehead. Since the man didn't sweat, he'd never been able to figure out why he wore them. He was fit and trim, though. And he was tanned. Like the OFs, the man always managed to show up right before the aerobics class started. He also made a practice of walking around so the women could see him. He usually left after the aerobics class, more often than not with one of the women.

Jack Silver detested Kent Bliss.

He watched as Bliss walked over to one of the treadmills. He set the timer, turned it on, and started walking, his arms swinging at 4.5. "I hope you fall off," Jack muttered under his breath.

Jack thought about Rosie Gardener Bliss. She had to be this turkey's wife. Something was going on there. Normally, he didn't hire out as a personal trainer, but when Luna Mae Luna had appealed to him, he couldn't say no. He told himself it was because her name appealed to him. He'd liked Rosie Gardener. He remembered how he'd laughed when she'd said she hated his guts. He wondered what she really thought of him.

Jack walked over to the treadmill. "How's it going, Mr. Bliss? You okay? You look tired. Maybe you should bring it down to 3.5."

"I'm fine. Let me worry about my speed. If I fall off, I won't sue you."

"That's what they all say, Mr. Bliss. Turn it down. *Now.*"

Kent was about to offer up a sharp retort when he looked into the trainer's eyes. He adjusted the speed on the treadmill and immediately felt better. He looked away.

"We're having a triathlon in November. Are you going to sign up, Mr. Bliss?"

"Probably not. I'm too busy to give up a whole day."

"I'll send you a notice. You might change your mind. By the way, your membership is up at the end of the month. It might be a good idea to renew it before you leave today. We only have two other openings."

"I'll let you know," Kent responded.

Before Jack walked away, he said, "Say hello to Rosie for me." So much for fishing for information.

Kent stepped off the treadmill. "I didn't know you knew Rosalie."

"Yes, I know Rosie. Nice lady. Excuse me, my father's here, and I need to talk to him."

Son of a bitch. If this guy knows Rosie, then he knows I can't afford this place, Kent thought. It would be all over town. The membership was four hundred bucks a year. If he paid it now, he'd seriously deplete his cash. Still, he couldn't let the trainer think he had no money. Besides, he needed this place like he needed the country club. There wasn't much he could do about the club, but if he paid the four hundred bucks for the gym he'd know he'd be able to pick up a woman anytime he felt like it.

Kent moved over to the Exercycle and climbed on. He had a perfect view of the women on the aerobics floor. He sized them up one at a time, finally deciding on a dark-haired, long-legged beauty. He even knew her name, Heather Daniels. Her father owned a Buick dealership. They'd spoken once or twice, nothing important, hello, nice to see you. She was a flirt. He liked that. He'd seen her eyeing his Porsche. Of course she drove a Buick and worked at the dealership. What he didn't know about Heather Daniels was whether she had her own apartment or lived at home.

The buzzer went off on the Exercycle. Kent slid off and walked over to the

StairMaster. The way the machines were positioned, he could see Heather in the mirror even though his back was to her. That had to mean she could see him, too, if she was looking into the mirror in front of her.

Kent climbed away. He never broke a sweat. He hated sweat, his own or anyone else's. He really hated using the machines because he knew people dripped sweat. God alone knew what kind of germs a person could carry out of the place.

Ten minutes before the aerobics class ended, Kent stepped off the machine and headed for the showers. He'd timed his arrival at the desk just as Heather exited the women's locker room. He withdrew his money clip from his pocket and peeled off four one-hundred-dollar bills just as Heather reached the desk. "Hey, Jack, here's the money for my renewal. I'll get the receipt next time I come in."

Nonchalantly, Kent looked around. "Hey, Heather, hold on a minute. I want to ask you something."

"Hello, Kent."

Kent cupped her elbow in his hand, and said, "I wanted to ask you about leasing a Buick until I can get my Porsche repaired. If you have the time, let's go for a drink."

Heather smiled and nodded.

Kent grinned as he strutted out of the gym.

Jack Silver scowled.

The restaurant was small and intimate, with small banquet rooms whose doorways were strung with colorful hanging beads. They tinkled and made a noise when anyone parted them to walk through. They also afforded a certain amount of privacy. Unless one stopped and peered intently through the beads, it was impossible to see who was sitting at the small tables — tables small enough for one to reach across and hold a partner's hand.

La Petite was known for its ambiance, terrible food, and colorful drinks. And it was cheap. It was a meeting place for lovers, a place where late-night assignations were finalized. More often than not, most of the couples were married . . . to someone other than their dinner companion of the moment.

Kent was well-known to the establishment, probably their best customer up to a few weeks ago. *This place,* he thought, *is a little more discreet than the country club. A lot cheaper, too, now that I'm on my own nickel.*

A single yellow rose in a small nest of

ferns sat in the middle of the table.

Kent smiled at his companion across the table, his pricey porcelain caps, compliments of Rosie, gleaming in the dim, intimate light. He risked a quick glance at the Rolex on his wrist. Perfect timing. Too late for lunch, too early for dinner. Hopefully, in two hours, after several glasses of wine, he could convince Heather to go to her place, providing she had a place. Once he was there, he could say he was hungry. Women still believed the way to a man's heart was through his stomach. He could play that up real good and say he *loved* home-cooked dinners. Women loved to oblige.

Heather was sizing him up just the way he was sizing her up. He had to figure out what would appeal to this leggy creature.

They made small talk laced with sexy innuendos. He was almost certain he had it in the bag and wouldn't be spending the night at the Days Inn when Heather leaned across the table, and whispered, "So, Kent, tell me every man's best-kept secret. Are you a boxer or jockey man?"

He hadn't had sex in over three weeks. She was a turn-on. He tried to squelch the erection that threatened to erupt. "That's why they call it a secret. If you *really* want to know, you'll have to check it out yourself."

She giggled. Only the young ones giggled. Another turn-on. "When?"

Kent wiggled his eyebrows. "How about now?"

Heather giggled again. "You mean we should go for it right here in this banquet room! Are you an exhibitionist?"

Kent leered at her. "Sometimes. How about you?"

She wasn't giggling now. She was *purring*. "All the time. I'm game if you are."

Whoa. Kent looked at the beads moving in the breeze the A/C created. As hard as he was, he didn't think he could *do it* here in this little room. He was a creature of comfort.

"How long will it take to get to your place?" he asked huskily.

She was still purring. "Seven minutes."

Kent's mind raced. "Tell you what, sweetheart. I'll settle up here and meet you at your place. I'll give you five extra minutes to *get ready* for me. All I need is your address."

She rattled it off. "All I need is sixty seconds. If that." There was a sexy growl in her voice now. He grew harder. Sixty seconds meant naked. He loved naked.

155

"You're wasting time, sweetheart."

She was up and gone in a heartbeat.

Kent groaned as he shifted in his chair. He pulled out the money clip and peeled off a ten-dollar bill. That covered the wine. He'd always been a big tipper, but that was then, and this was now. He fished in his pocket and pulled out four quarters. Ten percent would have to do.

Fifteen minutes later he was ringing the doorbell of a fashionable condo. His jaw dropped when Heather threw open the door. "Like the doormat says, Welcome! Oooh, you're wearing way too many clothes."

He was, and then he wasn't. He reached for her, but she danced away. All he could see through his lust, which was threatening to strangle him, was a tangle of arms and legs as Heather jiggled to some unheard music, offering up high kicks, her breasts bouncing up and down before she collapsed on the oversize sofa. Kent made a run for it and landed on top of her.

"Show-off," she whispered, before his lips clamped down on hers.

"You ain't seen nothing yet, honey."

7

Rosie sat on the upstairs verandah with her dog. She sniffed, imagining she could smell autumn in the air. She wondered how that was possible since they were in the midst of what people called the dog days of summer.

She was alone, but she was content. Vickie had taken a long weekend and flown to Paris to see her beau. How happy Vickie had been when Rosie'd seen her off at the airport. She couldn't help but wonder if she herself would ever be that happy. She missed her, though, and she missed Luna Mae, who had also taken a long weekend to go to some NASCAR race where she would meet up with old friends. It was just her and Buddy, the name she'd given to the dog she'd rescued.

Buddy had filled out and was a healthy, happy, devoted dog, never far from Rosie's side.

Rosie reached down to scratch behind the big dog's ears. He growled with pleasure. She smiled.

Her life, which she had thought was in

chaos a few months ago, was almost right side up. She'd lost eighteen pounds and two dress sizes. She had a new friend in Jack Silver. She liked talking to him after her workout. Not about her personal life although she sensed he knew about it, but more about owning a business, tax problems, and exercise routines. He liked Vickie, Luna Mae, and Buddy. Yes, Rosie liked him. Maybe more than she should. One night she'd fantasized about him until her entire body flushed crimson. He seemed to like her, too, but as a friend. She suspected Jack Silver did not mix business with pleasure.

It was almost three months since she'd kicked Kent out of the house. So far he had not filed for divorce. That was something she was going to have to do. She'd gone to see an attorney, but when it had been time to enter his office, she'd bolted and run. She had yet to schedule another appointment. Maybe she would do it tomorrow after her exercise workout. Maybe.

Then there was the matter of the lottery ticket that still rested under the cushion of the rocker in the spare bedroom. She had to make a decision where the ticket was concerned even though she had months to go before she was required to turn it in.

She'd read up on everything she could get her hands on in regard to lottery winners and marital assets. There was no easy out for her. She would have to give half of her winnings to her husband, and it wouldn't matter if they were divorced or not, because they'd been married at the time of the drawing.

There might be a solution, however, if she wanted to avail herself of it. Vickie and Luna Mae had both come up with the idea. Just turn the ticket over to them, and they would claim the prize, then transfer all the money back to her when things quieted down. She had to admit, she was thinking more and more about agreeing to that.

The three years of her disastrous marriage weren't all Kent's fault. Yes, he'd married her for a comfortable life. Yes, he hated her; yes, he'd used and verbally abused her. Yes, he'd cheated on her, spent her money on other women. Yes, to almost everything where Kent was concerned. But the sticking point, the bottom line, the part she was having trouble with was, she had allowed it. In her desperation, and *desperation* was the right word, to belong to someone, to be known as Mrs. Somebody, she had allowed everything to go on until she was so miserable she'd made herself sick. She had to share the blame, too.

However, did sharing the blame mean she had to share her lottery win with him? The law would say yes. It wouldn't matter to a judge or a jury that she had kicked him out *before* she knew she'd won the lottery. If she cheated him, wouldn't that make her as bad as he was? Did she care?

Rosie shook her head to clear it. She must be really screwed up. No one in her right mind, under these circumstances, would do anything differently than she was doing.

All she was doing was making excuses for herself.

She hated all this heavy-duty thinking. Hated when she got to the part where she couldn't even give the money away. Oh, she could give *her* half away, but not Kent's. This was when she got a throbbing headache. She squeezed her eyes shut, hoping to ward it off, but it came anyway. She felt like crying.

The dog, sensing his mistress's distress, hopped onto the chaise lounge and snuggled close to her. She stroked his silky back as the tears flowed.

The hot tears that she couldn't hold in check dripped on Buddy's head. He whined softly as he tried to wiggle closer. "What I don't understand, what I could never accept, was why Kent hated me so much. I'm not *that* ugly, I wasn't *that* fat in the beginning. Why was I so stupid, so blind, that I allowed myself to become a laughingstock in this town? It was me, not him, Buddy. I could have booted him out of here anytime I wanted to. I didn't want to. I needed that humiliation, needed to see the revulsion in his eyes. That doesn't say much for me, now does it? I wish you could talk, Buddy.

"You know what else? He's not getting half that money! I'll burn the damn ticket before I share it with him, or else I'll have Luna Mae and Vickie give it all away. After we do that, then I'll tell him what I did. Boy, I can't wait to see the look on his face. One nice word, that's all it would have taken, and I would gladly have shared even though I bounced him out of here. One nice word, sincerely meant, Buddy. I guess Kent was true to himself, he wasn't going to do or say anything kind or nice if he didn't feel it."

Rosie meant to take Buddy outside. She really did. Instead, she headed for the refrigerator. Her mouth started to water when she saw all the good things she was no longer allowed to eat. Oh, God, why did Luna Mae buy all this stuff? Moon Pies. A whole box full. Pineapple coconut ice cream. Three quarts. Brownies. Half a box. Cheese. Wonderful, golden yellow cheese. Pounds of it. What to eat first? If she was going to fall off the wagon, why couldn't she eat a little of everything? No one would know unless Luna Mae kept a mental inventory of the contents. Did she care? She decided she didn't as she ripped off a chunk of yellow cheese. Tears rolled down her cheeks as she chewed and munched.

When Rosie finally closed the refrigerator and freezer doors, she felt sick. Even worse, she was disgusted with herself. "What's wrong with me, Buddy?" she sobbed. The big dog whined and nuzzled her hand as she tried to pet him. She continued to sob. "I just blew all the hard work I did. Oh, God! I thought I turned over a new leaf in my life. This just proves I have no willpower, no backbone. I'm a waste of a human being!" Rosie felt her legs crumble underneath her. She allowed herself to slump to the floor, where she cried even harder. Buddy did his best to lick away her tears.

A long time later, Rosie struggled to her feet. Her eyes murderous, her chin determined, she cleaned all the goodies out of the refrigerator and freezer. When she was done, the only thing left was a loaf of five-grain bread, vegetables, fruit and yogurt. She didn't feel one bit better but she was determined not to repeat this mistake again. Never again!

"C'mon, let's take a walk around the yard, then it's time for bed. Maybe, if I'm lucky, I'll feel better when I wake up. Maybe a lot of things."

The big dog was on his feet in an instant, padding along at her side.

Woman and dog. For now, it was enough.

They were like old friends these days, she and Jack Silver. She liked snapping and snarling at him, marveling at his composure, his low-key approach to her and everything in general. When he was in a bad mood and trying not to show it, she'd be sweet and *noodgey*. Most times she could cajole him out of his dark moods.

She liked Jack, really liked him. He was never anything but positive where she was concerned. His words, "You can do this," had made a believer out of her. She worked hard, following the rules, not wanting to disappoint him or herself.

Rosie stepped off the treadmill, wiping at the perspiration dotting her forehead. "I think I'm ready to go up to 4.0, don't you think?"

"Another week or so. We'll see. I'd like to see you run in the morning. Do you think you can handle that? I can meet you the first few times you go out, then you're on your own. You can take Buddy with you. It will be good for him."

"Sure. Does that mean I'll take the weight off faster? I know, I know, I'm obsessed with the weight. It's not coming off fast enough. I haven't deviated from the diet, I've done everything you said. I weighed myself this morning, and I don't like the numbers on the scale."

Jack stretched his neck as if to loosen up some tight kinks. "I told you to stay off the scale, didn't I, Rosie?"

"Yes, you did. That's the only rule I've broken. I won't do it again. It's not that I want instant gratification. I don't know what it is." Rosie hung her head in shame. "Wait. That's not true. I lied to you just now. I . . . I . . . . yesterday, I was feeling sorry for myself and I . . . I ate everything that was in the refrigerator. Not all of it, but some of everything. I totally blew my diet. I ate so much I made myself sick and even then I kept on eating. Then I had a real good cry." She held up her hand. "You don't have to say anything. I cleaned out the refrigerator. There's nothing left but good stuff." Her tone turned belligerent. "Don't ask me to promise not to do that again. I don't want to make a promise to you I might not be able to keep. I hope I don't falter again, but I might. If I do, I'll deal with it. Now, can we move along here?"

"How long did it take you to put on that weight?" Jack asked curiously. Not bothering to wait for a reply, Jack continued. "I want you to be hard on yourself. That's important. You have to want this, work at it. No one can do it for you but yourself. Now, I suggest you make a chart and post it in the kitchen. The time, the date, what you binged on and *why* you did it. It's the 'why' that's important, Rosie. One more thing — you can't disappoint me, you can only disappoint yourself. You're embarking on a lifestyle change. Food is at the top of the list. Conquer it and you're halfway home."

Jack watched as Rosie's head bobbed up and down as he was talking. He wanted to clap her on the back, praise her for telling him the truth, but he didn't.

Rosie stared at her trainer. "I started putting on weight when I finished college. I put on the last fifty-five pounds during my three-year marriage. Before you can ask, I ate because I was so miserable. I really don't want to talk about this."

"Why? It's the crux of your problem. Why were you so miserable? What happened when you finished college? What size were you when you *started* college?"

"There was nothing in your contract that said I had to answer personal questions, Jack. I might like to ask a few of you. How would you like that?"

"Ask away. I don't have a problem. I'm the same weight I've been my entire adult life. What do you want to know?"

She wanted to know everything there was to know about him, but she didn't ask. "Nothing."

Jack chuckled. "I guess that means you think I'm perfect."

Rosie grimaced. "I wouldn't go that far, Mr. Silver."

"Does that mean you aren't going to answer my questions?"

"Yep, that's what it means."

Jack shrugged. "Listen, Rosie, I want to ask you something. We're sponsoring a triathlon the day after Thanksgiving. It's a hundred dollars to enter. All the money goes to the local SPCA and a few other charities. We do it twice a year. The money from the March marathon goes to a battered women's shelter. We do other indoor competitions at the gym, with money going to the Scouts and local organizations. We usually have a good turnout."

Rosie stepped on the StairMaster, her heart fluttering in her chest. "You expect me to run more than twenty-five miles?"

"No, no. It involves a ten-mile run, a five-mile bike ride, and a three-mile canoe trip on the Savannah River. There's a trophy prize donated by the store owners. You have three months to get ready. You can do it, Rosie."

Those four little words, "You can do it," were all she needed to hear. "Okay, Jack. Sign me up. How many people will there be?"

"Just about everyone from the gym. Usually about two hundred people counting the outsiders. We try to raise $25,000. If we don't make it with the enrollment, then the gym throws in the difference. Why, does it make a difference?"

"No. I was just curious. Men and women, huh?"

Jack laughed. "We don't discriminate."

He hesitated for just a second before he said, "Your husband signed up yesterday."

At the trainer's words, Rosie lost her footing and tumbled off the StairMaster. Jack was on his feet in a flash, his arms out to catch her. Startled, she looked into his eyes, her own filling with tears. Either she was nuts or light-headed, but she thought he was going to kiss her. She reared back.

"I'm sorry," she mumbled, refusing to meet his gaze. "Guess I lost my footing there for a minute. It just goes to show you have to pay attention to what you're doing." She climbed back on the StairMaster but remained silent. Jack said she could do it. She would be competing against her athletic husband. Jack said she could do it. Forget the idea that maybe he was going to kiss her. Just forget it. Don't even think about it. It never happened. It was all wishful thinking.

"Listen, Rosie," Jack said rather abruptly. "I just remembered something I have to attend to. I don't know how I could have forgotten. I won't charge you for this session. You know the routine. I'll bring the forms for the triathlon next week. Let's plan on Monday morning for our first run."

"Yeah, sure," Rosie said flatly. She didn't

let the tears come until she heard the door to the sunroom close. *What the hell is it about me that turns men off? What's wrong with me?* She swiped at her tears with the sleeve of her shirt.

She continued her workout with a vengeance, crying the whole time.

Outside in the driveway, Jack sat in his car staring at the house, his insides feeling shaky. He'd wanted to kiss Rosie. Really wanted to kiss her. That had been a little too close for comfort. He never mixed business with pleasure. For that one split second, he thought *she'd* wanted to kiss him, too.

There was something about Rosie that triggered something in him. Something he hadn't felt since his wife had died of ovarian cancer four years ago. On rare occasions he had dated women, but none of them measured up to his wife Martha. Rosie had what Martha had, an inner goodness, a soft vulnerability. She was as determined as Martha had been. He realized now how she must have taken his personal questions. She'd probably felt that she was under attack. It was a stupid mistake, a *personal,* stupid mistake.

He slipped the car into gear and drove off, mentally calculating how many hours it would be until he saw Rosie again. Next time, though, it would be all business. Client and trainer. Nothing more.

It was midmorning when Rosie dressed in a powder blue pantsuit. She was stunned at how big it was on her frame. The pants actually slid down over her hips. She couldn't go out looking like this. She rummaged in the back of her closet until she found a short-sleeved multicolored shift that was what Luna Mae called a one-size-fits-nobody outfit. Obviously, she needed to buy some new clothes.

She was going to see a lawyer, a man Luna Mae said was a pit bull when it came to divorces. A lawyer who stripped every husband whose wife he represented, leaving the husband with nothing but his name. Luna Mae and Vickie both insisted Kent would try to get everything he could out of her. Well, that wasn't going to happen. He would get nothing from her because he'd brought nothing to the marriage except his person. She wasn't going to think about the lottery ticket.

"It's too hot to take you with me, Buddy, and I can't leave the car open with you in it. I won't be long. Here's a chewy — my old slipper — and your water bowl is full."

The dog looked up at her, his eyes sad. Rosie knew the dog understood everything she said. Sometimes, he could even anticipate her. It boggled her mind.

It was a short drive to Timothy Donovan's office. Rosie turned the radio on so she wouldn't have to think about Jack Silver. Thinking too much about Jack Silver would give her a headache. At the moment she didn't need a headache. To prove her point, she hummed along with Roy Orbison singing "Pretty Woman." She wondered if anyone would ever refer to her as a pretty woman. Thoughts of Jack Silver wormed their way into her thoughts again. She'd been *that* close to the trainer. Why had she reared back when he'd touched her? Kent's ugly comments rang in her ears. Who would want to kiss or hug a sweaty tub of lard? Not someone like Jack Silver, that's for sure. Maybe someday. Yeah, right, and pigs fly.

Rosie squared her shoulders. She could make it happen. All she had to do was follow the rules, work like hell. If she believed in herself, anything was possible. "I-will-be-a-pretty-woman when it is time. I can do it. I *will* do it." The silent affirmation was all she needed to perk up her sagging ego.

Rosie was feeling pretty good when she swerved the van into the attorney's parking lot. It didn't look crowded at this time of day, and she was able to get a parking space close to the door.

Luna Mae had given her the skinny on Tim Donovan. According to her housekeeper, men quaked in their boots when they found out their wives had retained him to represent them in divorce cases. More than one errant husband had thrown in the towel the minute his own lawyer told him who opposing counsel was.

Tim Donovan hated cheating husbands and the lawyers who represented them. It was only hearsay, but the story was his own father had cheated on his mother, then she'd lost everything and had to hold down three jobs to support him and his sister. Luna Mae went on to say Donovan would suck the blood right out of his clients' husbands if he could. It was also said that Donovan's colleagues respected him and warned their clients what they were up against if they were foolish enough to try to hide assets or in any other way stick it to their former wives.

Rosie thought she would be in good hands if Donovan took her on.

A small, tasteful sign perched among the

lush shrubbery indicated that Donovan shared the building with a dentist and an architect. It was called the Donovan Building by most people.

The building was not ostentatious in any way. It was, however, neat and tidy and constructed of old brick that years of sun and the elements had polished to a glossy rose color. The grass was thick and lush, the walkway, made of pink flagstones, was bordered with multicolored flowers. Crepe myrtles, the South's answer to lilacs, bloomed profusely. All in all, the Donovan Building had a cozy, welcoming look to it.

Rosie walked up the flagstone walkway and entered the building. She proceeded down the hall to the last office, which was to the right of an atrium that was so pretty she stopped for a few minutes just to admire it. It also served to quiet her twanging nerves.

When Rosie stepped into the reception area, she was on time, to the minute. She was ushered into Timothy Donovan's office the moment the lawyer's secretary walked around the desk to greet her.

Standing in the doorway, Rosie made her assessment of the lawyer, who was getting up, his hand extended. They eyed one another, neither blinking or looking anywhere but directly into each other's eyes, as they shook hands. Both appeared satisfied. Donovan motioned Rosie to a deep comfortable chair across from him.

The first thing Rosie noticed, other than the man's tidy desk, was the box of tissues sitting on the corner of the desk within easy reach of the client. For tearful wives no doubt. Well, she wouldn't be using them today or any other day.

Rosie simply smiled at the attorney. Donovan responded by leaning back in his chair, a huge grin splitting his homely features. *We're going to get along just fine,* Rosie thought.

He didn't look like a lawyer, more like a schoolteacher, with his shell-rimmed glasses and rosy cheeks. He had a wonderful smile, warm and welcoming. His body language said, *I'm going to take care of this and make it all come out right.*

"Tell me what I can do for you, Rosie. By the way, I want you to call me Tim. First names are more comfortable. Now, start at the beginning and tell me why you're here. Don't leave anything out no matter how inconsequential you think it might be. Can you do that, Rosie? By the way, is it Bliss or Gardener? My secretary wrote down both names."

"My married name is Bliss. My maiden name was Gardener. I want my name back. Do you mean you want me to start at the moment when I first met my husband?"

"If it works for you, it works for me. I can always ask questions when you're finished. I hope you don't object to my taping this meeting. My secretary doesn't do shorthand, and says she can't read my writing. Besides, it makes for good record keeping."

"I don't have a problem with a tape." Rosie leaned back in the comfortable chair. "I met Kent a little more than four years ago . . ."

When she finished her sorry tale forty minutes later, Donovan asked her if she'd like coffee or a soda pop. She declined both. "I guess what I want to know is, does Kent have any claim to anything I have, like the house and my business? Both were mine before the marriage. He contributed absolutely nothing."

"If it was yours before you married Kent, then it is yours now. Does your husband sell real estate?"

"That's his job description. Once in a while he sells something. I never knew from year to year what he made until I saw our income tax statements. Most of this is my fault. I was an enabler. I didn't know that term until my friend used it. I no longer wish to be his enabler. I just want out of the marriage. I suspect he will try to make things difficult for me."

"No, he won't. If he gives you one iota of trouble, you call me any time of the day or night, and I will take care of Mr. Bliss. Now, what is it you would like me to get for you from Mr. Bliss? Or is it just your regulation pound of flesh?" His eyes twinkled with this last statement, proof that he knew how to extract said flesh.

Rosie flushed. "Absolutely nothing. I know he's going to fight me. He is not above asking me to pay him alimony. To keep him in the style to which he grew accustomed."

Donovan shook his head. "That isn't going to happen. Where does he work? I will have him served at his place of employment. Do you know if he has an attorney?"

"I don't know. I am ashamed to admit I know very little about my husband, Tim."

"That's going to change real quick, Rosie. You will know more about him when this is over than you ever wanted to know. I know his type," he said grimly.

Rosie nodded. Luna Mae was right. She liked Donovan a lot.

"I'll get right on this and have him

served with divorce papers by the end of the week. If he gets in touch with you, call me ASAP. Don't delay. It's imperative that you understand and do exactly what I tell you. Now, is there anything else?"

Rosie inched forward on the chair. "Can I ask you something . . . *hypothetically?*"

Here it comes, Donovan thought. *It's always hypothetical.* Still, he wasn't prepared for what he heard.

"The community property laws being what they are in most states, Georgia included, what would be the rule if someone won, say a large sum of money from something like . . . bingo or maybe the lottery when they were in the midst of a divorce?"

"I'm not sure, Rosie. I suppose the person who won would have to prove it was his or her money that allowed him or her to play whatever he or she was playing. There have been cases that went to court for just such a matter. I can't say that I paid much attention because I'm strictly a divorce lawyer. Do you know someone who won a large sum of money?"

Rosie nodded. "It's . . . it's a rather . . . a rather large sum, Tim."

"What's a large sum, Rosie, a hundred thousand?"

Rosie jumped up and walked over to the

window that overlooked a patio of sorts in the back of the building. She looked down at a fishpond to see huge goldfish swimming lazily from one end of the pond to the other. Colorful lawn chairs and small tables with umbrellas sat under an old oak tree. She surmised the employees ate lunch outside on nice days.

Her voice was raspy when she blurted, "Three hundred and two million dollars!"

The attorney gaped at his new client. "That sounds like the sum of money won in the Wonderball lottery a couple of months ago."

Rosie bit down on her lower lip.

"Did . . . did your . . . ah, *hypothetical* friend who is about to get divorced win the lottery, Rosie? I seem to recall hearing that the winning Wonderball ticket was sold here in Savannah. Unfortunately I didn't buy a ticket."

Rosie found her tongue again. "Do you think you could do some research on the matter and let me know? I'll be more than glad to pay . . . for . . . for my friend."

"So then it isn't a hypothetical matter. There actually is a person who won the money."

Rosie stared at the attorney. "Yes, there is such a person. They haven't come forward because . . . because of what we just discussed. The ticket for Wonderball is good for one year from the date of purchase. It says so right on the back of the ticket."

The attorney threw his hands in the air. "There you see, you learn something new every day. I didn't know a lottery ticket was good for a year."

"Most times it's just for 180 days. Wonderball is a full year."

"The person who won the ticket . . . does he or she have it in a safe place?"

Rosie thought the lawyer's voice sounded anxious. She thought about the flowered cushion on the rocker in the guest room. "Semisafe, I'd say."

"Semisafe isn't good enough, Rosie. Whoever has the ticket in hand is the owner. You realize that, don't you? I hope you can explain that to your . . . ah, friend."

Rosie ran her fingers through her hair. "I'll explain it to her. She isn't in a hurry to claim the prize. Tax ramifications and the soon-to-be-divorced husband could be a real problem. On top of that she needs a good tax man, a good accountant, and an excellent attorney. She's not hurting for money, so she can take her time right up until the eleventh hour if it comes to that."

It was the attorney's turn to get up and walk over to the window. He, too, stared down at the fishpond. The fishpond had been his idea. Perhaps because his father had never taken him fishing because he was always out chasing other women. His gut instinct told him Rosie Gardener's hypothetical friend was herself. He turned around.

"Let me do some research on the matter, Rosie, since there's no hurry. I'd like to get your divorce filing done, then take on the lottery issue."

"What would be wrong with my friend's giving the ticket to, let's say, two other friends, and letting them claim the money?"

The lawyer shrugged. "Personally, I don't think I'd do that. I think I'd put the ticket in a safe-deposit box for the time being. Matters like that have gone to court. You would all be under oath, especially if the soon-to-be-ex got wind of what was going on. You cannot lie under oath, but then you already know that."

Rosie sat back down on the comfortable chair. "I would imagine lawyers would stand in line wanting to represent the husband."

"That's the understatement of the year,

Rosie. Like I said, let me have my paralegal do some research on the matter."

Rosie stood up. "Do I pay you or the secretary?"

"Neither. We'll send you a bill. Take my card and remember what I told you. Call me any time of the day or night. You can always reach me either on my cell, at home, or here in the office. You can beep me, too. I'm just a number away.

"From here on in, I don't want you to worry about a thing. I'll do all the worrying for both of us."

Outside in the hall, Rosie stopped at the atrium and looked around again. She took several deep breaths before she could gather up the energy to walk outside to the parking lot. She was just about to open the van door when she heard someone call her name.

"Hey, Rosie!"

Rosie whirled around. "Jack! What are you doing here?"

"I was at the dentist. It was time to get the pearly whites cleaned." He grimaced to show off his teeth. Rosie laughed.

"Since you weren't at the dentist, and the architect is closed for vacation, I guess you were in Donovan's office."

Rosie nodded. "I hired Mr. Donovan to

represent me in my divorce. Everyone says he's quite good."

Jack threw his head back and laughed. Rosie loved the sound. Suddenly, she felt warm all over.

"Half, if not three-quarters of the women in this town owe their well-being to Tim Donovan. He's a hell of a nice guy. Works out once in a while at the gym. Hey, you want to go for some coffee? I could use some caffeine about now."

"Sure. How about I meet you there? Where?" she called over her shoulder.

"How does Ryan's sound to you?"

"Sounds good to me."

"I'll see you there in ten minutes."

Rosie used up the ten minutes telling herself coffee with Jack Silver didn't mean anything other than they had met by chance and were going to have a cup of coffee together. A chance meeting. Nothing more. Jack was just being friendly and nice because that's the kind of guy he was.

Would I like it to be more than a friendly cup of coffee? Damn straight I would.

8

Inside the cafe, Jack pulled out Rosie's chair and took his own seat. "Best table in the house." He grinned. "You can see everyone coming and going. Listen, Rosie, I'm sorry I had to postpone our run this morning, but I had something I had to attend to. We're on for tomorrow, right?"

"I hope your confidence in me proves out. Treadmill walking and running is a little different from running on asphalt. I'm game, but if I wimp out before the end, don't hold it against me."

Jack settled himself more comfortably in his captain's chair, his elbows propped on the arms. The picture of a man who didn't have a worry in the world. "Never happen! How's the business going, Rosie? You haven't talked about it lately."

Rosie looked around the little cafe. She'd only been here once, and it had been re-decorated since. Possibly new owners. "It's going great now that Vickie is back from her three-year European jaunt with Mrs. Simmons. She's out of the country right now, but she's due back sometime this morning. She went to Paris to see her fiancé. We hired a lot of college kids for the summer. They think it's a hoot to walk along the river and pick weeds. We're almost up to speed. We're going to be adding a few more pages to next year's Christmas catalog. You'd be surprised what a few more pages in a catalog can do for your profit margin.

"Also, Luna Mae got this brainstorm a few months ago and acted on it just last week. There are three or four senior citizen living units here in town. I want to say they're like halfway houses with chaperones. Not really assisted-living facilities but close. They're in some of the big old mansions that have gone to seed. Anyway, when the college kids leave at the end of the month, the seniors are going to step in. Luna Mae is going to shuttle them back and forth. She said they're eager to do something besides playing cards and watching television. It's a good way to supplement their social security now that they can earn money and still collect on their pensions. It's not hard work, and we certainly have room since we took over the Simmons mansion. The best part is I don't have to be there twenty-four/seven. The paperwork alone is taking me hours now that we're rolling along."

"That's great. I'm happy for you, Rosie. They should do a spread on you in the Sunday paper. Local girl makes good, that kind of thing. Think of it like this, not only are you making a living for yourself, you're providing jobs for other people and selling a product that's a weed. It's the American Dream."

Rosie blushed. She never knew quite what to do when someone like Jack paid her a compliment. She shrugged. "How are things at the gym?"

It was Jack's turn to shrug. "Things slow down in the summer. That's okay, I can use the break. Once September rolls around, we go full tilt."

Rosie looked up at the waitress. "I'll have the fruit bowl, a bran muffin, and black coffee."

"I'll have the same thing," Jack said.

This was the perfect time to find out who and what Jack Silver was. "How long have you worked at the gym?" She hoped she didn't come across as coy but more like an interested friend.

Jack looked at her over the rim of his coffee cup. It sounded to him like she didn't know he *owned* the Olympus Fitness

Centers. He played along. "It seems like forever. A long time."

Rosie smiled. "I guess that means you like what you do? Are you the top trainer? Luna Mae said you were the best and would only settle for you."

"Your housekeeper drove a hard bargain. I'm glad she did. That's just another way of saying I'm pleased with your progress. At some point, I'd like you to join the aerobics class."

Rosie turned brick red. "Yeah, right! I-don't-think-so."

Jack frowned looking perplexed. "Why not?"

"So people can say I look like a beached whale?" Rosie's voice sounded bitter. "No thank you. All those little size sixes who don't have an extra ounce of fat on them hopping around while I flounder. Don't bring it up again, okay?"

"Jesus, Rosie, I'm sorry. I didn't think . . . you're right about the little sizes, but you're wrong about the beached whale part. Right now you have a little more poundage on you than you should have, but you're working on that. Stop being so hard on yourself. You have my word that I will not bring it up again."

Jack shook his head. "Kent Bliss did a

number on you, didn't he? Don't look back, Rosie. Only forward."

Rosie speared a piece of kiwi fruit onto her fork. It was halfway to her mouth when she said, "Once words are said aloud, you can't take them back. Sometimes I think verbal cruelty is worse than physical cruelty. Yes, Kent did a number on me, but I have to take responsibility for it, too. I should have kicked his lazy ass out the first time he said something that offended me. I didn't. Luna Mae said every dog has his day, so I will just wait patiently for mine."

Open mouth, insert foot, Jack thought. *One of these days I'm going to learn to mind my own business.*

Just as he was wondering what it would feel like to kiss Rosie, the door to the cafe opened. He looked straight into Kent Bliss's eyes. And then he looked at Heather Daniels. He lowered his gaze to Rosie, who was looking for the ripest strawberry in the bowl, unaware that her husband had entered the cafe.

Jack lowered his head, and said softly, "Rosie, don't look up. Your husband just came into the cafe." *One more time, Silver, open mouth, insert foot.* He watched in horror as his breakfast companion's face turned white. *Just like a woman,* he

187

thought, when she ignored his words and looked up, then down at the fruit left in the bowl in front of her.

Rosie dabbed at her lips. "I think I'm finished. How about you, Jack?"

"I'm done." He slapped bills on the table, walked around to pull back her chair. The only way out of the restaurant was past the table where Kent and Heather were sitting.

Jack was so proud of Rosie, he thought the buttons on his Izod shirt were going to pop off when she stopped at her husband's table, looked down, and said, "How are you, Kent?" She waited for a response, and when there was none, she said, "This is Jack Silver, I'm Mrs. Gardener Bliss," she said to Heather Daniels, whose jaw dropped. She openly gaped at the woman towering over her. Then Rosie threw her hands in the air and said, "I seem to have this awesome power over people that renders them speechless. Bye," she trilled.

She felt like a noodle that had been cooked too long when she made it to the van and sagged against it.

"What you just did in there was a work of art. I've never seen anything so slick in my life. You just ruined their day. You do good work, Rosie," Jack said cheerfully. He reached out to open the door of her van for her. In her haste to get inside, Rosie lurched forward, her foot catching on the running board of the van. Jack had no other recourse but to wrap his arms around her to prevent her from falling. Their eyes met. He knew his own were glassy. Hers were wet, like she was going to cry any second. She smelled sweet and powdery, and there was a woman scent about her that was all hers. He watched as she licked at her lips, and just as he was going to lean forward to kiss her, she said, "You can just stop feeling sorry for me, Jack. I don't want your pity!" She jerked free and scrambled into the van, pulling the door shut.

"Son of a bitch!" Jack blurted. "Dammit, I wasn't feeling sorry for you, Rosie. I just wanted to kiss you. What the hell is wrong with kissing?" Of course Rosie couldn't hear his tortured words because she was blasting out of the parking lot at full speed.

Inside the cafe, Heather Daniels glared across the table at Kent. "*That* was your wife!" She might as well have said, "that *creature from the Black Lagoon* is your wife!"

Kent's mind raced. What the hell was Rosalie doing with the owner of Olympus

Gyms? Was she having an affair? Was that why she'd booted him out of the house? Rosalie having an affair! It was almost too ridiculous for words. Still, it would explain Silver's snotty attitude toward him. And to think he'd tried to impress him by plunking down four hundred clams. He tried to put the picture of his wife and Silver out of his mind by concentrating on the problem at hand.

There were two ways to play this. One would be for him to agree with Heather that his wife was a mess. The other would be for him to take the high road and down-play it and stick up for Rosie. He chose the latter, deciding it would only make him look better than good. Rosie and Silver. He wanted to laugh out loud. Then his eyes narrowed as he tried to figure out what they had in common, if anything.

"That's not very kind of you, Heather. Rosalie has had some problems. I think she's working on them. She's a very kind, compassionate person once you get to know her. Just because we're getting di-vorced doesn't mean I have to make her out to be something she isn't."

Heather looked properly chastised. She immediately compared herself at a size eight to Rosie's size fourteen, maybe a twelve. Women couldn't help it if they were homely. Just because she herself was beautiful didn't mean everyone was. She knew how lucky she was. Rosie was probably trying to compensate and not doing a very good job of it. She nodded. "You're right, Kent. I'm sorry. That was so rude of me. I don't know what I expected in regard to your wife. You never mention her. I just didn't know she was so . . . *big.*"

Kent listened with half an ear as he contemplated the breakfast menu. He'd tricked Heather into buying breakfast because he was down to his last two hundred dollars. Earlier when she'd asked to go to breakfast, he'd said no, thinking he would have to pay for it. She'd coaxed and pleaded, saying her fridge was bare, and she needed to eat something. Like he didn't. Finally, he'd acquiesced, and said, "Okay, but you're buying." She had happily agreed.

"There's big, and then there's big," he said gently. "Just because you have a perfect figure and are beautiful, you should never knowingly put down someone else. I thought better of you, Heather." She looked like she was ready to cry. *Good. That means she'll buy some food and actually cook tonight.*

Kent had been putting off asking Jason Maloy for another advance and trying to stretch out his money until the closings on his recent sales came due. He wished he had something more to pawn.

"I'm really sorry, Kent. I'm jealous, that's my problem."

"Jealousy is not a very becoming trait. If you knew Rosie, you would like her."

"No, Kent, I wouldn't like her. I'm in love with you. She's my adversary. I could never like her."

She was in love with him. Ho-hum. Like he didn't already know that. He wished she would show her appreciation a little more with some pricey gifts. Maybe he needed to hint a little more. Or, be more blatant. Sometimes Heather was on the thick side. She was much too frugal. Actually, she was downright *cheap*.

Kent smiled over the top of the menu. "I think I'm going to have a real Southern breakfast. How about you, honey?"

"I'll just have juice, coffee, and a muffin. I don't want to end up looking like . . . like my neighbor."

Kent gave his order to the waitress. "I think I'll have two eggs over easy, grits, biscuits, and gravy, and a side order of bacon and sausage. Oh, and three blueberry pan-

cakes. Decaf coffee and a slice of melon."
Eating a hearty breakfast would take him through lunch, too, and he wouldn't have to worry about his stomach until dinner-time. He needed to start eating more, and on a regular basis like normal people. He couldn't afford to lose any more weight.

Heather tugged at the skimpy dress she was wearing when she noticed a man looking at her thighs, knowing full well Kent would have something to say about it later. Hoping to wipe away the annoyance she was seeing on his face, she said, "How would you like to go to the house on the river this weekend, Kent? There won't be anyone there, just us. And the servants, but they won't bother us."

She was sucking up. That was good. At least he'd get to eat like a king. He shrugged as he sipped at his coffee.

"And, I thought I'd cook tonight if you don't mind staying in. We could watch some movies, then we could . . ."

"Just like an old married couple on Sat-urday night," Kent muttered. "How cozy."

It was exactly what he wanted, and she'd come up with the idea all by herself. Now he had to move in for the kill. His leased Mustang was costing him way too much money.

"So when are you going to get me a vehicle?"

"Anytime, darlin'. I talked to Daddy about it last week. He said we, as in you and I, could consider the silver one you were admiring, as ours. Since I have my own car, you can use it and get rid of that tacky Ford you're driving. Are you *ever* going to get your Porsche back?"

"Only if Rosalie has a change of heart. Right now she's not too happy with me since I'm the one who wanted out of the marriage. Everything will be settled in due time. It doesn't pay to rush things when so much money is at stake." Kent hoped she didn't ask how much money or want details. He felt pleased with himself. Either Heather was incredibly stupid, or he was incredibly smart at snowing her. He preferred to believe it was the latter.

"You seem to be having a problem with this, Heather. We should clear the air now before we get any more involved."

"No. No, I'm just . . . Like I said, I'm jealous. I want you all to myself, and at the same time I want to scratch out your wife's eyes for making you go through this. It's so unfair. You are just the sweetest man, darlin'."

Kent smiled again. "I'll see if Jason can

get along without me this weekend. It would help if I sold a house or two in the next few days. That man is so greedy. He has dollar signs in his eyes."

"Isn't that the truth!" Heather crumbled her muffin but made no attempt to eat it.

Kent watched her out of the corner of his eye. Something was bothering her. He let her stew. Sooner or later it would come out. Heather wanted what she wanted when she wanted it. He'd met and conquered spoiled brats like her before. All he had to do was keep her on a short leash. He looked up, his eyes guileless. "Is something wrong?"

"Yes. No. Oh, I don't know. I feel so guilty, Kent. I know you're having a tough time of it with the divorce and all. When you asked me for a temporary loan, and I said no, it has just been eating at me. Daddy always said neither a borrower nor a lender be. I guess I took that to heart. I'm sorry now."

Kent's eyes narrowed. That little episode had been one hell of a harrowing experience. In his wildest dreams he'd never thought she would say no when he'd asked her for the loan, but she had.

Kent reached for a slice of the crisp bacon. He waved it in the air like a baton.

"Don't you go worrying your pretty little head about it. I'm going to the house after work tonight to talk to Rosalie. Being the fine person she is, I'm sure she'll loan me some money till we settle up. As I said, Rosalie is a kind person. I'm the one who wanted the divorce, not her. Maybe we better not plan on dinner. Rosalie will probably want me to have dinner with her. She's like that. So genteel. I'm still fond of her in my own way."

Heather was sputtering now. "But darlin', what if she tries to . . . to . . . seduce you or something like that? Sweet cakes, that would just undo me. I won't have a moment's rest until you're out of there completely."

So predictable. "Well, Heather, I'm not going to be out of it for some time yet, so you had better get used to the idea. Until we're legally divorced, Rosalie is still my wife."

The muffin on the plate in front of Heather was a mountain of crumbs. "I know that, and I just hate it. I just hate it, Kent! If I loan you the money, you won't have to go to your wife's house tonight, and we could keep our plans intact. I won't even charge you interest or make you sign a note like your wife would."

196

"Heather," Kent said patiently, "Rosalie is not like that. She would simply hand me a wad of cash, and that would be the end of it. Rosalie knows I am a man of my word, just the way she is a woman of her word. Now, let's finish our breakfast so I can get to work."

Heather pouted. Kent ignored her. He knew that within an hour of their leaving the restaurant, Heather would go to her bank and come to the office and hand him an envelope. *So predictable.* Still, he had to let her know how much he needed. How could he do that without seeming calculating?

Kent finished the last slice of bacon. He drained his coffee cup, then patted his lips. "There is not a more generous person on this planet than my wife. If I ask her to loan me five thousand, she'll give me ten thousand and wink. That's Rosalie."

"Really. She is generous," Heather said snidely. Kent squelched her with one look.

Kent waited while Heather paid the bill. He felt no shame or embarrassment whatsoever. Outside, he pecked her lightly on the cheek before he walked right and she walked left.

As he walked to the office, Kent looked down at his watch. If he was any judge of character, Heather would be in his office in less than thirty-five minutes.

Kent was flirting outrageously with a walk-in, a customer who was looking for a house in the historic district. He knew immediately that she was a snowbird and he turned on his Southern charm. The woman was tall, shapely, and as much of a flirt as he was. He had her elbow in the palm of his hand and was ushering her toward his office just as Heather breezed through the door, a thick envelope in hand. She took in the scene before her, calculated the woman's age, her designer clothing, the fine webbing at the corners of her eyes, and smiled. She held up the envelope for him to see before she tossed it in the air. Kent caught it deftly. He offered up a megawatt grin that lit up the dreary room, then blew her a kiss.

Heather stomped from the office, a murderous look on her face that didn't bode well for the unsuspecting snowbird.

Rosie woke to the sound of the alarm. Buddy hopped on the bed, his energy knowing no bounds as he flip-flopped to the top, then to the bottom. Clearly, he wanted to go out. His mistress obliged by dutifully trotting down the hall, down the steps, and opening the back door for him. She was surprised to see Luna Mae in the kitchen with coffee made. She was sitting at the table smoking a cigarette, reading the paper, and drinking her coffee. Rosie grimaced. No one got up at five-thirty in the morning unless they had to. She let Buddy back in, poured herself coffee, and carried it upstairs.

What to wear? Everything she owned seemed to belong to the gray family. Drab. Almost like prison garb. Not that she had much to choose from. She yanked a pair of light cotton sweatpants off the shelf and a tank top that was now loose on her frame. She pulled on thick cotton socks and her heavy-duty sneakers. Then she pulled her hair back into a ponytail.

She wanted to be sitting on the back steps, coffee in hand, when Jack arrived to go running. Buddy was chomping at the bit. The poor thing needed more strenuous exercise than the meandering walking they did every night after dinner.

"I'm nervous, Luna Mae. What if I wimp out and can't do the run?" she fretted as she was filling her cup for the second time.

"If you drink any more of that coffee,

you will wimp out because you'll have to go to the bathroom. How's that going to look?"

"Do you have to be right all of the time, Luna Mae? Can't you be wrong once in a while? Just once," Rosie grumbled.

"No point in being wrong. Did I tell you Skip's old friend asked me to marry him this weekend? I told him I'd think about it."

Rosie's heart stopped, or at least she thought it did, at her housekeeper's words. "You told me you hated men. You said you were never going to get hitched. You said you couldn't be disloyal to Skip's memory."

"That was then. This is now. Racing is in my blood. Skip's dead. I'm alive. End of story."

"Tell me you're making this all up to get a rise out of me. Luna Mae, I'm talking to you."

"I think your trainer is here. You better get a move on. Send Buddy back if you wimp out, and I'll come and get you."

"Like hell. We will pick up this conversation when I get back. I mean it, Luna Mae."

Luna Mae's face took on a dreamy look. "I knew Dale Earnhardt you know. I cried when he died."

Rosie wondered if she was supposed to know who Dale Earnhardt was. She shrugged as she trotted out the kitchen door, Buddy at her side, to join Jack, who was running in place, a huge grin on his face.

"Morning, Rosie! You ready to set the world on fire?"

Rosie grimaced. "I'm the smoldering type," she quipped. *God, did I just say that?* From the look on Jack's face, he looked like he was wondering the same thing.

"I'm ready as soon as I do a few warm-up stretches. Buddy's ready, too."

Ninety minutes later, Rosie limped up the driveway. Buddy raced ahead but kept coming back every few seconds to offer moral support. When she finally came to a dead stop, Buddy raced back and nudged her forward. She groaned as she staggered into the house.

"You're sitting in the same spot you were in when I left you, ninety minutes ago," Rosie gasped. "What's wrong with you, Luna Mae?"

"More to the point, what's wrong with you? I'll go upstairs and turn on the shower. If I were you, I'd go in with my clothes on and worry about it later. Do you want me to rub you down with some liniment?"

"That smelly stuff you rub on your knees? No thank you. Yes, to the shower. Oh, God, I don't know if I can make it up the steps. I did it, though. I ran the whole five miles. What's for breakfast?"

"One egg, one croissant, and a dish of strawberries," Luna Mae responded.

Rosie sighed. "There is a God. I knew it. How about two eggs?"

"One egg. Do not try to bribe me just because I'm in a dreamy good mood."

"Shut up, Luna Mae. Walk behind me in case I fall backward."

Buddy barked shrilly, his signal that they should all move forward.

"I hate Jack's guts. He kept goading me. I wish you could have heard him. He was merciless. When he told me I could stop I wanted to kiss him."

Luna Mae clucked her tongue. "You've been wanting to kiss that man from the minute he walked in here. He's a pretty good catch in my opinion."

"Shut up, Luna Mae."

Luna Mae laughed all the way to the top of the stairs. "He really is a good catch. I think he likes you, too. If you'd stop being so standoffish, he might give you a tumble. You know, Rosie, all men are not like your husband. There are some wonderful, caring men out there who could make you happy if you'd give them half a chance. I wish you'd be a little more friendly. Just a little."

"Shut up, Luna Mae. Didn't anyone ever tell you not to mix business with pleasure? Jack Silver is my trainer. I am his client. End of story."

Luna Mae turned on the water in the shower and shoved Rosie in, clothes, sneakers, and all.

Nothing in all the world felt as good as the hot water pounding her body. Not even Christmas morning. It felt better than eating two wedges of double-chocolate thunder cake.

And to think she had to do this all over again tomorrow morning.

9

Kent walked through the house on the Savannah River trying to figure out if it was even remotely possible for him to own it someday. Heather said it had been in the family for a couple of hundred years. Her father and his father before him had been meticulous about keeping it up. On the open market, it would probably sell for 3 or 4 million dollars. The commission would be staggering. Still, to own it, to live in it, would make him a force to be reckoned with. He could cohabit with Heather. For a while. Cohabit didn't necessarily mean marriage.

As a sexual companion, Heather had no equal. She was up for *anything* — the more experimental, the better she liked it. She was also capable of tiring him out. Something he hadn't thought possible.

On their arrival, she'd banished the servants to their respective cottages, locked the doors, stripped down, and they'd stayed stripped down until an hour ago, when they got dressed to head back to town. Double-digit sex in two days was mind-boggling. In a way, he couldn't wait to get back to town. Pure and simple, he was exhausted by all the bedroom gymnastics. He'd never thought he'd want to return to the Days Inn and just hang out, but it was what he craved.

Kent threw his overnight bag, which he hadn't even opened, into the silver Buick that had materialized just as they were ready to leave for the river house. It was plush, several steps up from the Ford, but it wasn't his Porsche. Damn, now he had to think about Rosalie and Jack Silver. They were up to something, and, whatever it was, it wasn't going to be good for him.

He knew he needed to keep his wits about him. In his gut he knew she was holding the winning lottery ticket. She was just waiting, biding her time, thinking when they were divorced, she'd claim it. Well, it wasn't going to happen. If he had to, he was prepared to contest the divorce.

There had to be a way to find out for certain if there was a ticket or not. He groaned at the thought of trying to break into the house or making unexpected visits to throw Rosalie off her stride. If there was one thing he knew how to do, it was rattling Rosalie. He wondered just how much he could suck up when it came to his overweight wife. As much as he had to, he decided. Just as he was sure he could keep Heather on a short leash.

"Darlin', this was one of the nicest weekends I've had all year," Heather said. "We have to do it again, real soon. I just love it out here by the river. Daddy keeps saying we need to use this place more, or he's going to sell it. He's just so busy with the dealership, and he's going to be opening another one soon. Mama hates it here. She says the moss hanging from the angel oaks is ugly, and it depresses her. She doesn't like the river smell. And, can you believe this, she doesn't like this gorgeous, green moss. It looks just like an emerald carpet to me. Drinking juleps on the verandah is my idea of a perfect end to a wonderful day out here. Do you love it as much as I do, Kent?"

"Definitely. You should tell your daddy to give you the property, then you could move out here."

Heather was wearing a pair of skimpy white shorts and a bright red tank top with no bra. He could see her nipples straining against the flimsy material. Any minute now, if she didn't move, he was going to slam her against the car and take her right here, out in the open. She moved.

"Oh, darlin', didn't I tell you? The house *is* in my name. Daddy deeded it over to me when I turned eighteen. Mama insisted. It can't be sold, though. Daddy wants it to stay in the family. We would all have to agree if one of us wanted to sell it. I don't think Daddy even cares anymore. He hasn't been out here for years."

"Really," was all Kent could think of to say.

"I'm ready if you are, darlin'."

Kent climbed behind the wheel and started the engine. The Buick was a nice car, but it wasn't his Porsche. A Buick was a family car. He belonged behind the wheel of a candy apple red Porsche, not a family car.

At the end of the driveway, Heather ordered him to stop the car. "I always like to look back. To me this is the most beautiful spot on earth. I grew up here. My fondest memories are of this river house."

Kent had no idea Heather was so sentimental. He watched as tears rolled down her cheeks. For one wild moment he actually felt protective of her. He was stunned at what he was feeling.

He tried to see the river house through Heather's eyes. The long and stately row of angel oaks lining the winding driveway created a beautiful, lacy umbrella where the sun made dancing patterns on the cobblestones. At the last bend in the driveway he could see the stately old river mansion with the massive white pillars. Diamond-shaped windows, some of them stained glass, winked in the bright sunlight, casting hundreds of miniature rainbows. He sniffed, savoring the river smell mixed with the heady scent of the confederate jasmine. He nodded. For some unexplained reason, he reached across for Heather's hand. He squeezed it reassuringly. She smiled through her tears.

Heather's voice was a whisper when she turned around in her seat. "Can you picture little children running through the moss and making little hidey-holes in the trees to leave notes for each other? Can you see a swing on the tree in the front lawn hanging between the moss? I used to have one. I would always try to swing high enough to reach for the moss, but I was too little. Then the swing broke and was never replaced."

Kids, Kent thought. Kids meant babies first. That meant he would be a father and at some point in time a grandfather. *Jesus.* A wild look crossed Kent's face. He floored the gas pedal and shot out onto the country road, leaving a trail of dust and gravel behind.

Monday morning turned into one of the nicest days of late summer, in Kent Bliss's opinion. So nice, in fact, he decided to walk to work. His arms swinging, humming under his breath, he walked the short distance, stopping for coffee at a Krispy Kreme. He eyed the sugary confections and at the last second bought two blackberry jelly donuts with frosting on top. He could do with something sweet for a change. He was still trying to figure out how he'd dropped eight pounds while eating mostly fast food. Stress, he decided, living on the edge and not knowing from one day to the next what was going to happen.

Donuts and coffee in hand, he opened the door to the realty office ten minutes later to see the receptionist trying to signal him. For what, he wasn't sure. Maybe the man wearing a vibrant Hawaiian shirt standing in the waiting room. Perhaps a referral. He set his purchases down on a table next to a stack of *People* magazines.

Kent was about to walk over to the man when he saw the receptionist shaking her head, her eyes wide and anxious. He mouthed the word, "what," but he was too late. The Hawaiian shirt advanced, his hand outstretched. "Kent Bliss?"

Kent grasped the man's hand, and said, "Yes, and you are?"

"The guy who's serving you these divorce papers. Have a nice day now." Kent looked down at the sheaf of papers in his hand. He felt like a fool.

There was a squeaky whine in the receptionist's voice when she said, "I tried to warn you."

"Well, you should have tried harder, Eileen," Kent snarled. He marched back to his office and slammed the stapled papers onto his desk. He realized he'd left his coffee and donuts in the reception area, so he had to go back for them. He shot Eileen a hateful look, pleased at the way she cowered in her chair.

Damn, I didn't expect Rosalie to really go through with it. He thought it would take her at least a year to get her ducks in a row, and then *maybe* she'd file. Here she was, a few months later filing for divorce. Rosalie never did anything quickly, she usually had to make a blueprint, study it, revise it, shelve it for a while, then start over because of some minute little detail. This quick filing was suspicious. Either it had something to do with the winning lottery ticket he was convinced she was holding, or it had something to do with Jack Silver.

Kent bit into one of the jelly donuts. *Just what I need, a sugar high.* As he chewed and sipped, he perused the document in front of him. *Who is Rosalie's lawyer?* He blanched when he saw the name Timothy Donovan. He'd screwed around with enough divorcées to know Donovan was every woman's dream attorney. Well, he'd just have to get a better lawyer than Donovan. One who was merciless *and* greedy.

It was midafternoon before Kent found time to make inquiries concerning a divorce attorney. He pulled his Rolodex closer and started by calling just about every female he knew who had gone the divorce route. All, with the exception of a woman named Heidi Anders, extolled the virtues of one Timothy Donovan. Heidi's story was a lot different. She said not only did she lose, she lost big, and her husband's attorney was a sleazebag named Steven Wiley. "He was so slick, I never knew what hit me," she complained. She went on to recite a litany of other men who had used the same sleazebag, and all of them had come out winners. "He's expensive, too," she said. "When am I going to see you again, Kent?" There was no future with Heidi Anders other than the fact that she smelled good. She'd been working at the perfume counter at Dillard's since her divorce. Plus, she worked on commission. No expensive gifts coming from that direction, that was for sure.

"As soon as I get this mess I'm in cleaned up. Keep your chin up, honey. I'll call you." Kent drew a big red X through Heidi's name in the Rolodex. At least he had a starting point. He wondered just what expensive meant. With Heidi it could mean five hundred dollars. Or it could mean five thousand. If he remembered correctly, her husband headed up a twenty-man CPA firm that brought in big bucks. He wondered what she'd done to incur her husband's wrath. She was certainly beautiful and shapely. Like he cared. He snapped the Rolodex shut and yanked out the Savannah phone book.

Kent looked down at his desk calendar. Maloy would have no complaints. He'd kept his nose to the grindstone and now had four new listings, four outright sales, three pending sales, and four more showings to go to tomorrow. His boss would laugh all the way to the bank. Hell, he himself might even get a giggle or two. Then he thought about the feds and the state and realized he wouldn't be doing any giggling. Bastards. They took one-third of everything he worked for. One-third of all his commissions would go to them. He'd still be a pauper. He heaved a sigh of relief that Heather had come through with the ten thousand dollars. It would tide him over until he received the commission checks he was due. He'd worry about paying her back later on. He knew how to play that game. Actually, he was an expert at the game. With no equal. He felt proud of himself as he reached for his jacket. It was time to pop into the sleazebag's office. Why bother with an appointment? People paid more attention when you showed up with an attitude and a cash retainer.

Kent jotted down the attorney's address, knowing it wasn't in the best section of town. *Less overhead,* he told himself. He didn't say good-bye to any of the employees. He did straighten his tie and tug at the cuffs of his dress shirt, however.

Thirty-five minutes later, Kent pulled into the parking lot adjacent to the strip mall in which Steven Wiley practiced law. His offices were almost at the end of the run-down strip, sandwiched in between a

Dollar Store and a mom-and-pop candy store.

Kent stepped out of the car and immediately started to laugh when he stepped on a weed that came halfway up his leg. He looked around. The asphalt was cracked and splintered, the center full of potholes where giant weeds grew like trees. He wondered if he should call Rosalie to tell her what a bonanza this lot could be for her business. He was still laughing to himself when he opened the door to the offices of Wiley and Wiley, Attorneys-at-Law.

Green pull-down shades adorned the plate-glass windows to ward off the brutal Savannah sun. A bell tinkled over the glass door, which also had a green shade on it. Gold lettering on the door said it was the offices of Wiley and Wiley. Kent doubted there were two Wileys. It was probably meant to sound impressive. Two attorneys for the price of one. Senior and Junior. Wisdom and chutzpah. Hopefully.

A young girl with a peaches-and-cream complexion and natural blond hair looked up from the computer she was working on. "Can I help you, sir?"

Kent smiled his winning smile, the smile that he liked to think made women drop at his feet. The girl responded to his smile with one of her own. Jailbait?

"I don't have an appointment. I stopped in on the off chance one of the Wileys could see me. I can make an appointment now or come back later if this isn't a convenient time." He looked around the empty office to make his point. The girl smiled again, revealing a marvelous set of teeth.

"It's really slow in the summer. I think Mr. Steve can see you. Now if this was September, you'd be standing in line outside. I'll just be a minute. Take a seat."

The office was shabby but clean. The magazines were current, the paper, today's edition. The plants looked healthy and vibrant. Kent was surprised at how comfortable the chairs were. He leaned back and closed his eyes as he wondered how old the young girl was. He thought she was young enough to be impressed with the Buick and his age.

He looked up when she said, "Mr. Steve can see you now."

Kent winked as he let his eyes rake over her supple figure. She was wearing a white halter top that showed off her tan. He wondered what her name was. He asked when she winked back. "Candice," she said. "You can call me Candy."

Kent couldn't resist. "You must drive those college boys out of their mind." He winked again.

"I had a conquest or two before I graduated." She laughed.

Hot damn. No jailbait here. If someone had mentioned the name Heather Daniels at that moment, Kent would have said, "Heather who?"

Heidi Anders was right. Steve Wiley even looked like a sleaze in his polyester suit, greasy hair, and ankle-high boots. He was skinny, almost gaunt-looking, but his dark eyes were speculative and wary when he held out a hand that was clammy with sweat even though it was ice-cold in his office.

"Kent Bliss," Kent announced, crushing the man's bony hand. He was pleased to see that the attorney didn't flinch.

"Steve Wiley. Have a seat. Would you like a cold drink or some coffee?"

Kent shook his head as he sat down in one of the chairs facing the lawyer. He pulled out the divorce papers that had been served on him earlier and handed them over.

Wiley pulled out a pair of wire-rimmed glasses. He perched them on the end of his nose to skim through the papers. "Okay, what's your side?" He leaned back in his high-backed red leather desk chair, steepled his bony fingers, and looked at Kent over the rims of his reading glasses.

"Okay, here's my story. I stepped into a good thing, and I screwed it up. I didn't love my wife. She said she loved me, but I think she was in love with the idea of love, and I sure as hell didn't measure up to the white knight she imagined she married. I'm not denying that. She got me accustomed to a very nice lifestyle, the country club, charge cards, Rolex, Porsche, the whole nine yards. Then she yanked it away from me because I forgot our anniversary. She booted my ass out at ten-thirty at night. I have an efficiency at the Days Inn. She cut everything off. I've been living on my wits, existing on fast food and working my ass off to get some cash.

"Look, my wife is no beauty. I'm a guy who likes a good-looking woman with a nice figure on my arm. Rosalie is fat and plain. She's a nice person, but she just isn't my type. We have nothing in common. She simply can't turn me on even if I close my eyes. Do you see where I'm coming from here?"

"Yes. You want to have your cake and eat it, too. Did you contribute to the household bills? Did you have joint accounts?

Who paid the bills?"

"We had a joint checking account. My wife is well-off. She was very generous while we were together. I'm not denying that either. She had her life, and I had mine. And, before you can ask me, yes, I had lots of affairs. I don't know if she did or not. I think she's seeing someone now, but I'm not sure. I want alimony. If she hadn't gotten me used to a rich lifestyle, I wouldn't be in this mess now. By the way, I sell real estate."

"Did you contribute to the household? What happened to your paycheck?"

"I kept it and spent it. Rosalie never asked for a penny from me." Kent squirmed in his chair. "I know how this all sounds. If you want to call me a gigolo, go ahead."

"What about gas for your car. Who paid for that?"

Kent shrugged. "I used a credit card. At the country club, I just signed for everything."

"Did you ever pay even *one* bill? Think."
"No."

"Did you ever give your wife money?"

Kent had the good sense to look embarrassed. "No."

"And you want alimony?"

The disbelief in the lawyer's voice stunned Kent. This guy was supposed to be a scumbag. He was acting like a *real* lawyer. "Look, Mr. Wiley, Rosalie asked me to marry her. Not the other way around. She made it all so tempting it was hard to say no. Of course she's going to deny that, but I can't help it," Kent lied. "No guy worth his salt would turn down the perks she was offering."

"Did you sleep together? Did you have sex?"

"A few times. Each time it was a disaster. She just turned me off. Her thighs rubbed together and she had this . . . this . . . odor. No matter what she did, she always smelled like paint and turpentine." It was all lies, but who cared at this point? This was a man he was talking to, a man who would understand.

Wiley jotted notes on a legal pad. "Did the two of you acquire anything together during the marriage?"

"No. Rosalie had her business already when we were married. It wasn't as lucrative as it is now. The house was left to her by her parents when they died. It's worth a fortune because it's a historic house. The business is incorporated. If I wanted money, I just wrote a check. Sometimes it was a long dry period between commission checks. She was agreeable and never said a word. She never asked for anything. Not a penny. If I'd had money to spare, I would have given it to her had she asked." *Another lie. So what. This guy's eating it up like candy.*

"So you were a kept man."

"So what if I was? She was the one doing the keeping. It was all her idea. Now she probably found someone more to her liking, and she booted me out. Listen, there's more." Kent took a deep breath and told the attorney about the lottery ticket. "I'm telling you, she won it. I know her. I saw it on her face. The kid at the gas station is sure of it. You can talk to him if you don't believe me. She booted me out the night of the lottery drawing. She has a whole year to claim it. If you listen to the news, then you know no one has come forward to claim the money. The ticket was sold the afternoon of the drawing at the gas station where my wife buys gas. The kid who works there, his name is Bobby, will verify everything I just told you. She's got that winning ticket. I want my half."

Wiley bounced forward. "Are you sure about this?"

"Of course I'm sure. Rosalie is sneaky.

You wait, she's going to have the house-keeper or the best friend say they won it. She trusts them. She doesn't want to give me my half. By law, she would have to split it."

Kent swore he saw dollar signs flashing in the attorney's eyes. "How can you be so sure, Mr. Bliss?"

"Call me Kent. I'm sure because of the kid Bobby, who pumps gas. He told me he asked my wife the day of the drawing if she'd bought a ticket, and she said no. He offered to get her one because the line was around the block. She gave him one set of numbers, and said the machine could pick the other four. Five tickets, five dollars. The kid said he told her, 'You're never going to win because you picked all low numbers. Single-digit numbers.' She laughed and said it didn't matter because she wasn't going to win anyway. She also promised him if she did win, he would never have to pump gas again, and she would pay his way through medical school. The kid was really bummed when she didn't come forward.

"Rosalie showed me the tickets, all five of them. But, there wasn't one ticket with all single-digit numbers on it. Not one. I just don't see the kid making a mistake like that. He was certain. Look, talk to him yourself and just remember, no one has claimed the money."

Wiley scribbled furiously. Kent thought he had an itch the way he was wiggling and squirming in his chair. "This is all very interesting," the lawyer muttered.

"If we can prove it, what would be your cut?" Kent asked bluntly.

"We need to talk about that, Mr. Bliss. I won't be billing you by the hour, that's for sure. How does 15 percent sound, Mr. Bliss?"

"Fifteen percent sounds just fine, Mr. Wiley. Now, how can we force Rosalie's hand?"

"I'm not sure. I need some time to think about it. I know someone who works for the lottery commission. I'll make some inquiries. In the meantime, keep this close to your chest. You haven't told anyone have you?"

"Other than Rosalie, no. She knows I suspect she's holding the winning ticket. Hell, I outright accused her. She can be as stubborn as a mule. The kid might be the clincher. She did make a promise to him, a costly promise. She'd be embarrassed and ashamed if he and his family confronted her. If it hit the newspapers, she wouldn't like that."

Wiley played with his Mont Blanc pen, doodling on the yellow pad as he stared across at his new favorite client. "I'm just thinking aloud here. Maybe there's a way to get the printout of the numbers from that particular lottery machine. Of course, I will want to talk to the boy and his family, too. This needs a lot of careful thought. If we act in haste, we might jeopardize your position. Give me some time to think about all this. I'd like to see you back here one week from today. My retainer is five thousand dollars."

"Do you take cash?"

"Of course," Wiley said suavely. "I thought you said you were destitute."

"I am. I borrowed money from a friend. I'll leave my card with you." He scribbled off the number of the Days Inn and his apartment number. "If you don't reach me, leave a message, and I'll return your call. I can see myself out. You just stay here and start thinking."

In the reception area, Kent pulled the envelope out of the inside pocket of his jacket and counted out five thousand in hundred-dollar bills. Candy stared, wide-eyed at the money. "I need a receipt, and I need an appointment for the same time a week from today. I don't need an appointment card. I'll remember."

Candy nodded as she scheduled the appointment. "Of course. I do hope everything went well."

"Just swell, honey. Wanna have a drink?"

"I can't right now. I get off at five. I'd be happy to join you then."

"Why don't we meet at say, five-thirty in the lounge of the Hilton?"

Candy nodded agreeably as she handed over the receipt with a flourish. "Ah, your name is Wiley, too, I see," Kent said, pointing at a name plate on her desk.

"Steve's my uncle. Actually, I'm his paralegal, secretary, gopher, niece, and chauffeur." Kent laughed.

Nothing like keeping it in the family. "See ya." Kent winked at her before he left.

10

Kent Bliss whipped out his brand-new cell phone, courtesy of Heather Daniels. It's a family plan, she'd cooed. Heather was doing everything in her power these days to make him happy. The cell phone made him *really* happy. He felt like he was back among the living again.

Just then his world was right side up. But things could change in five minutes. He was juggling too many things and not getting enough sleep. Prowling around outside Rosalie's house late at night, trying to figure out a way to get inside to look for the Wonderball ticket, then worrying about covering his tracks with Heather, who was becoming much too demanding, made for a short temper.

The lawyer he'd hired was so scummy that Kent was having second thoughts. Still, whatever he'd told him was confidential. According to Steven Wiley, the lottery commission was ticklish about giving out information. Of course, he'd said, if one wanted to pay for such information, it was available to the tune of ten thousand dollars. There was no way he could put his hands on ten thousand dollars, and the lawyer wasn't about to advance it. Maybe he didn't have a good case after all. He needed to think about that a little more.

The upcoming Labor Day weekend was perfect for a little breaking and entering, with Vickie and Luna Mae leaving Rosalie alone. He couldn't believe his luck when, hiding in the bushes last night, he'd overheard his wife and Luna Mae talking on the upstairs verandah. For one heart-stopping moment, the dog had gone wild, almost jumping off the verandah until Rosalie calmed him down and turned on the floodlights. He'd gotten out of there, quicker than a rat the minute the lights illuminated the area. It was okay, he finally had some information he could act on.

Rosalie ran in the mornings for an hour. At night, she walked the dog. Whoever would have thought Rosalie would get a dog. He felt pleased that she felt the need for a dog as protection against him.

Kent yanked the Rolodex closer to him. Some men had little black books; he had an entire Rolodex of his conquests. He flipped through the little cards until he found the H's. Hillary was her name. He dialed the number and, his pencil tapping on the smooth surface of the desk, waited for someone on the other end of the line to pick up.

He thought he recognized Hillary's voice, but his greeting was cautious just the same. "Hillary?"

"Yes."

"Kent Bliss. How are you, Hillary?"

"You scoundrel. It's been three years! Where have you been, sweetie?"

"Trying to stay out of trouble. I didn't want to make problems for you once I heard you called off your divorce proceedings. Did you ever go through with it, or are you and what's-his-name back together?"

"In the end, sweetie, we decided to stay together. I had too much on him, and he didn't want to part with what he knew my lawyer would find. Once he knew that we knew about all the money he had stashed in the Caymans, he saw the light of day. We lead separate lives. Bring me up to date, sweetie."

"Separate lives, eh? The only way to go. My wife and I went through exactly the same thing. Listen, how about meeting me for a drink. I'm free right now, how about you?"

"Best offer I've had all day. Where?"

He was flush at the moment. That meant he could pay for some fancy drinks and keep up appearances. "How about the Hyatt Regency in, say, twenty minutes?"

"I'll see you then."

Kent hung up the phone. He wished he could remember what Hillary looked like. She'd been older, that was all he could remember. Rich and older. The best kind because they were *very* generous. Hillary's husband owned a string of very profitable high-tech surveillance companies. Globally. Hillary said his net worth at one time was in the hundreds of millions of dollars. She'd also told him that half of their ten-thousand-square-foot mansion had one of everything he carried in his firm. All Kent needed was one little gizmo, and he was home free. *Damn, I wish I could remember what Hillary looks like.*

Seventeen minutes later, Kent strode through the Hyatt lobby like a permanent resident. He headed straight for the Mariner's Bar, where it was dim and dark. Perfect for late-afternoon drinks. He settled himself in a burgundy leather-backed booth and immediately ordered a Stinger. He gulped at it. Something told him he was going to need a glow on to handle Hillary. He wondered what her last name was. It rhymed with flower, that was all he could remember. Lowry, that was it.

He was draining his glass when Hillary Lowry approached the booth. He got up immediately and kissed her cheek. He wanted to sigh with relief. She was tall, willowy actually. And she'd had a magnificent face-lift. Breasts looked to be high and firm. More surgery. But the hands were a dead giveaway. They said she was fifty if she was a day. It didn't matter how many rings and bracelets she wore.

He could handle it.

"You're lookin' wonderful, honey," Hillary purred. She oozed into the booth and stretched like a contented feline.

Kent's eyes lit up. Now he remembered everything there was to remember about Hillary. "You're looking pretty good yourself, Hillary." It wasn't a lie. He hoped she could see the admiration in his eyes. The truth was, she looked hungry. For him. They were all hungry for him. He was glad now he'd turned his cell phone off. What he didn't need right now was for Heather to call him.

Kent signaled the waiter and ordered a double scotch on the rocks for Hillary and another Stinger for himself. They made small talk, laced with sexual innuendos. He needed to get into her house. "So, where is *Mr.* Lowry these days?" He let his hand trace the hard length of her thigh. She still worked out. That was good. She'd been a hell of an acrobat three years ago.

"Right now, *Mr.* Lowry is in South America. For all I know they might be heading up some uprising or something. He just hops on planes and goes wherever the action is. It makes him feel important. All those high-tech toys you boys like to play with. My section of the house is . . . *secure.* That was part of our settlement terms. I don't like to brag, but my attorney, who, by the way, is the best in the business, got me exactly what I wanted. Of course I didn't get the divorce, but that's okay, too. A 90-million-dollar nest egg is nothing to object to."

Good-bye Heather. You can have your Buick and your cell phone.

"I can't tell you how impressed I am, Hillary." Then he said the words that made her eyes light up. "And you deserve every penny of it. Your husband should be drawn and quartered for the way he treated you."

Hillary moved closer. "That's what I always liked about you, Kent. You understand women. If you don't have any pressing engagements, let's go to my place. You can follow me in your car. We can have a really nice dinner on the deck. My housekeeper is *my* housekeeper if you know what I mean. As an added plus, she doesn't speak a word of English. It's a good thing I'm fluent in French. My husband has his own valet, who takes care of him. He also travels with him." She looked up expectantly to see Kent's reaction.

"What are we waiting for? We have three years of catching up to do." He tossed some of Heather's money on the table. He wondered if his own eyes looked as hungry as Hillary's. Probably so.

He thought about his game plan on the drive to Hillary's house. They'd drink. A lot. They'd have sex, then when Hillary was asleep, he'd prowl through the rooms to find what he wanted. The gizmo that would give him the ability to disarm Rosalie's alarm system. He knew he wouldn't have any trouble picking the locks. He'd done it before. Of course the ideal scenario would be for Hillary to give him a tour of her husband's wares. If he remembered correctly, she knew each time a patent came out, what it was for, and how it was used. It was called, according to Hillary, staying one jump ahead of her husband.

She was such a bitch. A rich, needy bitch.

"Are you sure that you don't mind going shopping with me, Vickie? I really need new clothes. Nothing fits because I've dropped twenty-six pounds. And it's been so long since I've bought . . . you know . . . pretty stuff. You have such good taste. I invariably buy the wrong thing, and Luna Mae gets after me telling me I look like a *schlump*. I don't even know what a *schlump* is, but I assume it's nothing good. I want some bright colors, some fine material. Nothing *serviceable*. I'm sick and tired of brown, gray and black! I want to lighten up my life. And, if we have time, can we go to that new drop-in spa in the mall? You don't even need an appointment. I saw a television commercial where they pamper you and even serve you wine."

"Great idea! I'm game. Grab your checkbook, your credit cards, and let's go!"

Rosie was like a giddy schoolgirl when she hooked her arm with Vickie's as they strolled into the mall forty minutes later.

"High-end stores or low-end?" Vickie asked, her eyes twinkling.

"Definitely high-end. I've got plenty of plastic. I want some of everything from the skin out."

"Gotcha! Victoria's Secret for the undies! They have some great animal-print underwear. Are we looking for sexy?"

"Absolutely! By the way, I'm buying all

this stuff for *me*. I want things that will make me feel good when I put them on. Me. This is all about me so don't read anything into this shopping spree that isn't there. I know you're going to buy stuff for what's-his-name. I don't have a what's-his-name in my life, just me."

Vickie burst out laughing. "What's-his-name is Calvin and he does have a passion for black lace. I kind of like it myself."

The women were as thorough as scavengers as they ripped through the pink store.

Rosie did a lot of blushing and stammering as she picked out gossamer bras and skimpy bikini underwear. Kent had made fun of her white cotton underwear. She picked out every color there was except white. She'd blinked at the animal-print thongs, wondering how in the world one adjusted to something like that. Maybe when she was down to her desired size eight, she'd try one just for fun.

Seven-hundred and forty dollars later, Rosie left the store with bulging pink and white striped bags. "I never spent so much money on underwear in my life!"

"Didn't it feel good?" Vickie asked.

Rosie laughed. "Oh, yeahhhh," she drawled.

"Next stop, Nordstroms. I have a personal shopper. All we have to do is ask for her, she'll take us to a small sitting room, serve us wine while we wait for her to bring us things we might want to buy. It's a grand experience. It's all about service. Be careful, Rosie, you can get hooked on shopping. By the way, when was the last time you went shopping?"

"A hundred years ago. I've been shopping through catalogs. Because of my size, my choices were limited. Okay, okay, my catalog shopping days are over."

Vickie's personal shopper, whose name was Ann Marie, turned out to be a small, compact woman who reminded Rosie of a human dynamo. As Vickie explained what they wanted, Ann Marie scribbled on a small notepad. Then she ushered them to a small private sitting room with deep, comfortable chairs. She herself brought them wine in fine crystal glasses before she left the room to do Vickie's bidding. Soft music filled the room.

Vickie held out her glass to clink it against Rosie's glass. "To you, my friend," Vickie said. "For having the good sense to make life-altering changes. I am so proud of you, Rosie."

Rosie smiled. "One step at a time. I'll get there, but it's going to take time. This is one step on the road to me getting there. Thanks for being such a good friend, Vickie."

"Hey, you've been a good friend to me, too. My money is on you. I *know* you can succeed in whatever you want to do."

They talked then, two old friends, of many things, Vickie's trip to Paris, Luna Mae's senior moments, and the crucial gossip, which concerned Jack Silver's bachelor eligibility.

Rosie leaned forward. "Sometimes I dream about him. Really good juicy dreams. I like him, Vickie."

"I know you do. You know what else, I think he likes you, too. I see the way he looks at you and the way you look at him. Stop blushing, Rosie."

Rosie was saved from a reply when Ann Marie appeared with a clothing rack stuffed with clothes every color of the rainbow. There were skirts, blouses, dresses, suits, slacks and sweaters, purses, scarves, and shoes.

Rosie gave herself up to the two women as she tried on one outfit after another, listening to what matched with what and what jacket could be worn with slacks or a skirt. She enjoyed every minute of this unique shopping experience. Within minutes her mantra was, "I'll take it!" Three hours later, Rosie plopped down on the chair and sighed. She had no idea how much money she'd just spent and she suddenly realized she didn't care. She loved *everything*.

"Wise choices, Rosie," Ann Marie said. "And the choices were all yours. Everything is stunning. Wear it all in good health."

Rosie jumped up, held out her credit card, and grinned from ear to ear. Turning to Vickie, she said, "And, they deliver once everything is altered. I'm going to put this store's number on my speed dial."

"Okay, girl, this is all about you!" Vickie said. "It's about time. Now I think it's time to hit the Paradise Spa so we can get ourselves pampered a little more. Shopping is so exhausting!"

Rosie pocketed the charge receipt, slid her credit card back into her wallet. "I'm ready whenever you are."

It was six o'clock when the two women exited the Paradise Spa. Both had new hairstyles, new makeup, French manicures, and bright red pedicures.

"I feel like a million bucks," Vickie said.

Rosie wanted to say she felt like $302 million, but she didn't. Instead, she laughed and couldn't stop until Vickie clapped her on the back. Even then she couldn't stop. Finally, she gasped, "For the first time in my life, it really is all about me. I love it, love it, love it!"

"I can't believe this!" Rosie said in stunned surprise to Vickie and Luna Mae. "We're actually caught up and have time on our hands. I'll tell you something else that's hard for me to believe. It's Labor Day weekend. Where has the time gone? First it was June, then July, and then those dog days of August, and now here we are in September. Time is moving entirely too fast." She was grumbling and didn't know why. Yes, she did know why. Vickie was flying off to Paris *again*, and Luna Mae was going somewhere for *another* NASCAR race. She was going to be alone with Buddy. *Again.*

Maybe she should think about getting a hobby. Running and exercising took up just so much time. Shopping! She could go shopping again.

"You sound . . . disgruntled," Vickie said, concerned. "Are you sure you don't mind if I go to Paris? I'll stay if you want me to, Rosie."

Rosie looked across the massive worktable at her best friend. "Don't be silly. I was just wondering what I was going to do with myself for four long days. I think I'll go shopping. I think I need a hot pink blouse to go with that tan suit I bought. It will be a new experience shopping by myself. I'm driving you to the airport, so we should be on our way."

"Don't look at me that way, Missy. I'm not giving up my weekend. Curly is waiting for me. I might give him my answer this weekend. I'm thinking more and more that I want to be married."

Rosie shook her head. "Shut up, Luna Mae. I don't want to hear that married stuff. Those race car guys are just a bunch of mooches. They're after your money. Why can't you see that?"

Luna Mae plopped her bony hands on her skinny hips. Her chest heaved with indignation. "Maybe for the same reason you couldn't see it yourself four years ago. Don't be telling me what to do, Missy."

"Luna Mae, you told me yourself that Curly person hit you up for a loan after you got back from your last road trip. Did he pay you back? No, he didn't. The man doesn't even have a car, for God's sake. He rides a scooter. Drunk driving, that's why. You admitted it to me. I don't want you to make a mistake like I did."

Today, Luna Mae was resplendent in a shimmery, silver jumpsuit with bright red lightning bolts scattered over it along with seven different zippered pockets. Today, the pockets were full.

Luna Mae huffed and puffed as she paced the room. "I'm going to tell you what you told me, mind your own damn business. If I make a mistake, it will be my mistake, and I won't have anyone to blame but myself."

"He lives in a rented trailer, Luna Mae, with six other men. He doesn't even have a bed and sleeps in a sleeping bag. Don't deny it. You told me so yourself. And, he's ten years younger than you are. He doesn't have a pot to spit in. Tell me where's the romance here? You're getting old, Luna Mae, and I don't want some roustabout taking advantage of you."

Vickie moved toward the door. World War III was about to break out. She could see it on both women's faces. Rosie was afraid Luna Mae was going to leave her, and she would be totally alone. Again. Just like when her parents had died, and she'd homed in on Kent. She herself would be getting married soon. Things would change again for her and Rosie. This time, though, she had to agree with Rosie. And she said so.

"That's it! That's it! I'm out of here. I'll see you on Tuesday. Then again, maybe I won't see you on Tuesday," Luna Mae said coldly.

"Luna Mae!" Rosie screeched. But the housekeeper was gone, the door slamming so hard, the pane of glass rattled. Rosie viewed it with alarm. "I'm just trying to help you!" she screeched again.

Vickie leaned against the doorjamb, her arms crossed against her chest. "Did you listen, Rosie? If it's any consolation to you, I don't think she'll go through with any kind of wedding plans. She's feeling good right now that she met up with all her old friends, and they remembered her. Let her enjoy this bit of happiness. Luna Mae has a lot of common sense. When push comes to shove, she'll do the right thing. If she doesn't, then oh well." Vickie shrugged dramatically. "I think we should head for the airport. The lines are really long these days, and I don't want to miss my flight. You're sure it's okay for me to go?"

Rosie worked her facial muscles into a smile. "Of course it's okay. Buddy and I will be just fine. I've got a pile of new books to read, a few television shows to catch up on. After I drop you off, I'm going shopping for that blouse. I probably won't even miss you guys," she lied.

"Okay, as long as you're sure. Let's rock and roll, partner!"

★ ★ ★

It was almost six o'clock when Rosie parked the car outside her garage. She'd found the hot pink blouse she'd wanted but had kept on shopping, focusing this time on sportier clothes. The back of the van was filled with boxes, bags, and garment bags. She didn't want to think about all the money she'd spent on herself . . . again. If she continued to lose weight, she would either have to get all the clothes she'd bought today and on her shopping spree with Vickie altered, or she'd have to go shopping again. Neither thought struck her as unpleasant.

It took her three trips to carry her purchases into the house, Buddy poking and sniffing at the bags to see if there was anything for him. There was, a squeak toy that made a barking sound and a package of bacon-flavored chewies. His tail swishing importantly, the big dog carried his toy and chew over to the carpet by the sink, lay down, and proceeded to bite into the toy.

Rosie laughed. Buddy's idea of playing with a toy was getting the squeak mechanism out, then he lost interest in the toy. She was careful to lock the door and set the alarm before she carried the bags and boxes upstairs. All day long she'd had the feeling someone was watching her, following her as she went from store to store. But each time she stopped to look over her shoulder, there was no one who appeared to be watching or following her. In other words, no sign of Kent. Even so, the itch between her shoulder blades wouldn't go away. In fact, it was still with her. Hence the rush to get home to Buddy, who she knew would protect her with his last breath, and the ultrasophisticated, state-of-the-art alarm system she'd had upgraded when Kent left.

Rosie ripped at the bags and boxes, holding up each new article of clothing, folding it and stacking it in neat piles on her bed. Should she or shouldn't she strip down and try on some of the things she'd bought? She frowned. She still felt uncomfortable looking at her nude body. When she showered, she turned on the water before stripping down so the mirror would be foggy. She knew she was a coward, but she didn't care. She could, however, count the rolls of fat that still remained. She didn't *feel* as much like a washboard as she had the day of her anniversary. Her nine rolls of fat were down to three.

Everything she'd bought today had either come off a table or rack. She was al-

most certain everything would fit and perhaps be a little roomy. She'd concentrated mostly on workout outfits and casual clothes. She did buy one fancy outfit, though. Capri pants with an elastic waist and a matching piqué top whose neckline, armholes, and hem were circled with appliquéd daisies. It was a top that was meant to be worn outside and not tucked in — it was an end-of-the-summer clearance sale item. At best, she might be able to wear it once or twice before the end of September. Now, if she were a true Southerner, she would never wear white after Labor Day.

Maybe she'd wear one of the new outfits tomorrow morning when she ran. She was up to eight miles a day. But Jack was no longer running with her. It was just Buddy who kept her company. Jack didn't know she was up to eight miles. He thought she was still at six. Tomorrow she was going to strive for the full ten. She was on her third pair of running shoes, too. Jack had drilled into her the importance of balance that would come from wearing good, solid running shoes. She'd bought two new pair today. She was saving the old ones but wasn't sure why. Maybe because her blood, sweat, and tears were in those shoes.

Buddy appeared in the doorway, his plastic food bowl clamped between his teeth. He set it down and barked. Rosie dropped to her knees to tussle with the big dog. They rolled over and over, with Rosie giggling and Buddy barking playfully. "Okay, I guess it is dinnertime. There was a time, Buddy, when I couldn't wait one minute past six o'clock for dinner. Can you believe I no longer find food a must? Guess that means my stomach has shrunk, and that's a good thing." The black dog looked like he was listening intently. Rosie laughed again as she picked up the bowl. "Okay, time for dinner."

Rosie continued to talk to Buddy as she made her way downstairs and into the kitchen, where she fixed the dog's food and prepared her own dinner. She ate a can of tuna, a garden salad, three crackers, and, for dessert, a wedge of melon. Her beverage was a glass of Diet Coke with a slice of lemon. She was entitled to a glass of red wine, but she liked to save the wine for later, when she sat out on the upstairs verandah before going to bed. At that time she also smoked one cigarette. Jack said it was okay for now. Later, he didn't want her to smoke any cigarettes at all, which was okay with her. Whatever it took to get her to her goal was okay.

clothes and, after taking a nice hot shower, pulled on a silky nightshirt that felt soft and delicious against her skin.

The glass of wine and a cigarette in hand, Rosie opened the French doors leading to the second-floor verandah. Now she was finally ready to wind down from her day.

Two hours later, Rosie walked through the house again, double-checking all the locks on the windows and doors. She knew she was becoming obsessed with her safety. Exactly who and what she was afraid of, she didn't know. Probably Kent. She walked back upstairs and crawled into bed.

Rosie crossed her fingers that she would get more than a few hours' sleep. She looked over at the small bedside clock with its bright red numerals. She'd been lying here for two hours, her mind racing. Finally, she got up and ran over to the rocking chair. She knew she wouldn't be able to see the lottery ticket in the dark, but she could feel it. Satisfied that it was still there, she crawled back into bed. *Maybe I'll sleep now.*

Maybe.

Rosie wasn't the only person who couldn't sleep. Jack Silver finally threw off the sheet that was covering him. He stalked his way to the bathroom to take a shower. At three o'clock he was in the kitchen making coffee and frying chicken. For a picnic.

The plan that had come to him as he was tossing and turning hours ago was to show up at Rosie's doorstep and take her on a picnic. With a picnic basket in hand, how could she turn him down?

He leaned against the sink sipping his coffee as he tried to figure out how Rosie Gardener — he refused to think of her as Rosie Bliss — had crept into his heart to replace his beloved Martha. When he wasn't looking? What a stupid thought. There was just something about Rosie that tugged at his heart.

He knew she was alone for the holiday weekend, just as he was. His father and uncle had gone to South Carolina for some golf tournament. They didn't golf, but they did like to watch the game.

Maybe he should have gone on the road to stay on top of the fitness centers. Maybe a whole hell of a lot of maybes. The bottom line was he was lonely and didn't know what to do about it. Most of his and Martha's friends had drifted away, busy with their growing families or else relocating because of business.

Being alone, especially on holidays, was the pits.

Jack counted out six eggs and put them on to boil. Maybe he would pickle them. He liked pickled eggs. The big question was, did Rosie like pickled eggs? He poured more coffee before he turned the chicken, all white meat breasts. No skin. He was frying them in canola oil.

What else did one take on a picnic? Vegetables? Fruit? Well, he had plenty, apples, melons, peaches. He grinned. There wasn't anything better in the summer than a sweet, juicy Georgia peach. Martha had been crowned Miss Georgia Peach when she was nineteen. He wished then the way he'd wished a thousand other times that he and Martha had had a dozen little Marthas or Jacks. It wasn't meant to be.

Some days he could barely remember what Martha looked like. Other days, she was front and center, the very core of his being. During those times, his eyes would get wet, and he'd start feeling sorry for himself. That's when he'd set out, regardless of the weather, and do a ten-mile run, sometimes fifteen miles. It never helped.

Rosie.

He didn't even know if Rosie liked him.

Sometimes he thought she did. Other times he was certain she didn't. He discounted the many times she said, "I hate your guts." They were just words because he worked her hard. Most times she would smile or grin to take the sting out of the words. He really liked Rosie. A lot. Maybe too much. He'd always made a point about not getting involved with his female clients. It just wasn't good for business or for his emotions, which oftentimes ran too high. He tried telling himself that Rosie was different. Maybe, he told himself, somewhere along the way, he might want to get involved with her if she was willing. He liked her honesty, her determination, the way she felt comfortable enough to speak her mind and tell him off. She reminded him in some ways of his deceased wife, Martha. It wasn't her looks, it was something else he couldn't quite put his finger on. What he knew in his heart and his gut was that Martha would have liked Rosie Bliss.

His picnic plan was to scoop Rosie and Buddy up, drive to the Silver family home on the Savannah River, the house he'd grown up in. The house that had been his and Martha's. Martha had loved the river house and refused, right up to the end, to go to the hospital, saying she wanted to die by the river and have her ashes scattered on that same river.

He didn't often return to the river house because he couldn't deal with the feelings and the memories. This picnic today was a test of some kind. He knew it as sure as he knew he was standing here frying chicken at three o'clock in the morning. Jack turned the chicken again. It was golden brown, true Southern fried chicken, his own variation on his mother's recipe, which had been handed down from generation to generation. How surprised his mother would be that he knew how to cook as well as he did. And bake, and clean up his messes just the way she and Martha had taught him.

Jack picked up the tongs and set the chicken to drain on a wad of paper towels. He looked at the timer. Two more minutes to go on the eggs. He spent the two minutes washing and drying the fruit. While the eggs cooled in cold water, he skinned stalks of celery and carrots, washed them, and put them back in the crisper until it was time to pack the picnic basket.

He wondered if he was going to be picnicking alone. Maybe he needed a line. What were guys saying these days when they tried to pick up girls? He had to admit he had no clue. He'd simply been out of circulation too long.

Jack felt a groan building in his stomach. When it finally escaped his lips, he sounded like a bullfrog in acute distress.

Two bottles of wine. One red, one white.

He was good to go.

That's when he panicked. *What the hell am I doing?* Jack sat down with a hard thump. He could be letting himself in for the biggest disappointment of his life. Rosie was probably going to say no.

Rejection was a terrible thing.

Rejection was a truly humbling experience.

Jack watched the hands on the kitchen clock. It was only 4:45. Rosie said she got up around five, sometimes five-thirty. She liked to do her run no later than six. She would be home by seven. Maybe if he showed up at ten minutes of six, she'd cancel her run, and they could run together out on the dirt road along the river. Providing she agreed to go on the picnic in the first place. He wondered if he was putting the cart before the horse.

Maybe.

Damn, he hated that word, *maybe*.

By five-thirty, Jack had finished the pot of coffee, gone to the bathroom three times, and packed the picnic basket. He dithered around for another ten minutes trying to decide if he was acting foolish.

"The hell with it!" he said aloud. He grabbed the picnic basket, shut and locked the door behind him. He drove the seven blocks to Rosie's house. He'd never felt so jittery in his whole life. Maybe he was going through a premidlife crisis of some sort.

Jack pulled into the driveway just as the downstairs lights came on. He waited till two minutes to six before he climbed out of his car, picnic basket in hand. He marched up the walk, then up the steps to the front verandah, where he rang the bell, three sharp peals of sound. Inside, Buddy barked.

The door opened. He had an impression of bright yellow. Rosie was wearing yellow, her hair pulled back from her face, and new running shoes.

"Jack!"

"Rosie!" *Well, that was certainly brilliant.*

"Are you going to run with me this morning?"

Jack stepped forward. "Listen, Rosie, I'm a stand-up guy. You might not think so, but I am. I have all my own teeth, and I admit my hair is thinning a little. I shower regularly, I'm in shape. I can cook and take care of myself. I have a good-paying job, and I'm a responsible member of the community.

"I drank a lot of coffee this morning because I got up at three and couldn't go back to sleep." He hopped from one foot to the other because he had to go to the bathroom again. "So, because I couldn't sleep, I decided to fry some chicken, boil some eggs, and I was thinking, 'picnic.' What the hell, I had this basket they gave me when I bought my new truck, and I never used it. Comes with silverware, napkins, and all kinds of junk. You just have to put the food in it. Like I said, I thought about a picnic, and then I thought I don't know many people I'd like to invite to go on a picnic. You were at the top of the list."

Rosie stared at her trainer. "Uh-huh."

Jack took a step backward. "What does that mean, uh-huh?"

"It means . . . it means . . . just that, 'uh-huh.' Let me get this straight. You're standing on my doorstep with a basket of food. You have all your own teeth, your hair is thinning, you can cook plus you're a stand-up guy and have a job. And you have to go to the bathroom because you drank a whole pot of coffee. I want to make sure I didn't miss anything. How am I doing so far? Go to the bathroom already!" she ordered. Buddy chased him all the way down the hall, his tail wagging furiously.

Rosie stood in the doorway trying to comprehend what was going on. *Did Jack Silver just ask me to go on a picnic? Is it a date?* She was glad now that she'd put on one of her new lightweight workout outfits.

Jack joined her in the doorway. She was close enough to smell his aftershave. "I thought we could run together when we got to the house."

"House?"

"The old family homestead down the river. I grew up there. It's real nice. Perfect spot for a picnic. I thought we could spend the weekend there. There's more food there, too. You can have your own bedroom. Buddy can have his own, too. Whatever." He was so flustered he was disgusted with himself. "You look like a canary."

Rosie tried to hide her smile. "A canary! Couldn't you have said a daffodil or something a little more flattering?"

Was he always going to open his mouth and stick his foot in it when he was around Rosie? "I like canaries," he mumbled. "I like the color yellow. I think what I'm trying to say here, and not doing a good job of it, is to tell you you look pretty. You are a pretty woman, Rosie Gardener Bliss and I'll sock anyone in the eye who says you aren't." He took a deep breath, then continued, "So, I guess you don't want to go, is that it?"

Rosie laughed. "Are you kidding! I'd love to go on a picnic! I haven't been on a picnic since I was ten years old. If you're inviting me for the weekend, I have to grab some stuff. Do you mind waiting?"

Jack realized he'd wait forever if she said the word. "Don't take all day," he grumbled. "What I meant was . . ."

"Don't take all day," Rosie said, turning and running up the stairs. She was back down in seven minutes flat. She'd just jammed everything into one of the shopping bags she'd brought home yesterday.

"I'm ready. I just have to turn on the alarm and lock up. Unless you have to go to the bathroom again. Do you?" she teased.

"No," he mumbled again.

In the car as she buckled her seat belt, Rosie looked across at Jack. "Is this a date?"

Jack's jaw dropped. Was a picnic a date? "Yeah," he said. "I rang your doorbell. I invited you. I cooked. Yeah, it's a date."

"Okayyyy." *Maybe I should have bought that thong underwear after all.*

11

His car parked around the corner, Kent Bliss made his way in the dark to the garage where he'd once kept his Porsche. His ass was dragging. There was no other way to put it, delicately or otherwise. Hillary Lowry had sapped every bit of strength from his body. She'd pouted when he said he had to leave at five o'clock, but he needed the cover of darkness to do what he wanted to do.

He still couldn't believe his good luck when Hillary had shown him what she called her husband's trophy room. She'd turned her back to answer the phone, and he'd simply pocketed the gadget guaranteed to disarm any alarm system anywhere in the world. He'd also taken the instruction pamphlet and jammed it into his pocket. All he'd had to do was move each display item on the shelf a little to the right or left, and no one would ever be the wiser. He'd felt magnanimous as he trailed behind Hillary, saying he'd seen enough and it was time for *action*. Hillary had started stripping as they walked down the hall.

So damn easy.

Now he was inside the garage, a pair of $29.95 binoculars he'd picked up at Radio Shack pressed against his eyes. It was finally starting to get light out. As soon as Rosalie left with the dog for her morning run, he would have an hour to get inside the house and out before she returned. He wasn't worried. An hour would be more than enough time. Rosalie was a creature of habit. She would have hidden the lottery ticket someplace where it would be convenient to check on it at a moment's notice. It was another way of saying Rosalie was lazy. Fat and lazy.

"Oh-oh, what have we here?" Kent muttered to himself thirty minutes later when a car pulled into the driveway. A Mercedes. The crown jewel in the Daimler line. He cursed under his breath when he saw Jack Silver get out of the car with what looked like a picnic basket in hand. *Son of a bitch,* he seethed. Now what? Were they going to picnic at home or get in the car and go somewhere? A picnic basket had to mean they weren't going to run this morning.

Kent's tired eyes narrowed. So, Rosalie was having an affair with Jack Silver. He wanted to laugh at the ridiculousness of the situation. Jack Silver and his wife. It was too damn funny for words. He continued to wait and watch, the binoculars pressed tightly against his eyes so he wouldn't miss anything.

Ah, this was looking good. They were getting in the car with the dog. For some strange reason the sight made him angry. He waited a full ten minutes before he left the garage and made his way to the kitchen door. In his pocket, he had what he called a burglar's pick. He'd gotten locked out of too many houses when showing them to prospective buyers. Jason Maloy had given him the pick and showed him how to unlock a door. Of course, they always told the owner and made a joke of it.

It was full light now, and shortly the sun would be riding high, lighting up the first day of the holiday weekend.

The gadget he was holding in his hand must have been designed for a child. He'd had no trouble figuring it out in the thirty minutes he'd spent waiting for Rosalie to make her appearance. He pulled a pair of latex gloves out of his pocket. Even though his fingerprints were all over the house from having lived there, he didn't want to leave any fresh prints.

The lock and the dead bolt opened

easily. He quickly entered the house and immediately went to the keypad, where he held the small high-tech box up to the alarm and keyed the numbers. The beeping he heard made him nervous. The little green lights on the box were skittering all over the place as it figured out the sequence of numbers. He had the code in less than forty-five seconds. He punched the reset button. A loud sigh escaped his lips.

It was safe to prowl around the house to his heart's content.

First things first. He pulled out his cell phone. He had to call Heather. He knew she was going to be spitting mad. After a night like the one he'd just spent, he really didn't care. He was probably going to wake her up. She was such a spoiled brat. He took a minute to compare the sex he'd had with Heather with what he'd done with Hillary last night. Heather was better, but Hillary was richer. No contest.

"Hey, baby, rise and shine . . . Oh, did I wake you? . . . Heather, how many times do I have to tell you not to wait up for me . . . Sweet cakes, I wanted to be alone last night. I do have a life besides the time I spend with you . . . What do you mean did I forget this weekend? Of course not."

What the hell was this weekend? "Oh, yes, of course, we were going to go to your house on the river. The truth, baby, I did forget. Maloy has me so bogged down with paperwork I don't know if I'm coming or going. I have to finish it up. I spent all night *working* . . . I can be at your place by one o'clock. You'll have to drive though. I'm just too tired . . . If you're going to whine and ruin the weekend by acting childish, then maybe I should just stay home and finish the rest of my paperwork and get some sleep . . . Don't worry about me. I can stop by Rosalie's house. She always has a big shindig over the holiday . . . One o'clock is just fine with you? Good, I'll see you then." *So predictable.*

Kent's second call was to Hillary. He just knew he was going to call one or the other by the wrong name one of these days. He really needed to stay alert. Hillary's sleepy voice came over the wire. "Well, hello," she purred. "Are you calling to tell me you're on your way over?"

"I wish I were. Hillary, can I take a rain check till Monday afternoon? My boss wants . . . actually he is demanding I go with him to Marietta to talk to a builder who is considering giving us the sole representation of his new development. It's such a coup, I can't say no. I should be back by three, no later. You can use the time resting up and getting ready for me. You almost killed me last night. You know that, don't you?" He forced a lilt to his voice that surprised even him.

There was more small talk as Kent prowled through the downstairs, opening and closing drawers, leaving no stone un-turned. When he finally ended the call to Hillary, he turned his phone off, jammed it into his hip pocket, and raced up the stairs, where he went from room to room. He blinked at the change in furnishings in the master bedroom. Silver must like a king-size bed. More power to him. He would have opted for a sleeping bag, so he wouldn't have to sleep next to Rosalie. To each his own.

The day after Rosalie had booted him out, she'd been in the guest room when he'd arrived at the house. He crossed the hall to see his old bed. He ignored it as he opened drawers and closets. He pawed through everything. He finally found the five lottery tickets in a box of sanitary nap-kins under the vanity in the guest bath-room. He stared at them before he walked back down the long hall to a room at the end. It was Rosalie's office. There was a separate phone line, computer, fax machine, and copy machine. He made two copies of the tickets. He was careful to turn off the machine.

Back in the bathroom, he replaced the tickets just the way he'd found them. Why was she keeping them if she hadn't won? What was it she'd said? Oh, yes, "my proof that I didn't win." She won all right. He was certain of it. He just didn't know where the damn winning ticket was.

Maybe he was spinning his wheels at Rosalie's house. Maybe she had put it in a safe-deposit box. No, that wasn't his wife's style. Rosalie liked things where she could either see them or where they were within easy reach. She'd hide it, that's for sure. Just the way she'd hidden the five tickets.

Kent knew the ticket was somewhere on the second floor. He'd bet his life on it. What he needed to do was think like Rosalie. She'd pick someplace obvious. Someplace a normal person wouldn't think to look for the simple reason it was too obvious, like under the mattress or under the carpet.

He was galvanized as he set out to go through the house again.

Ninety minutes later, all he had to show for his efforts was a sweaty body and a messy house. He looked around at the chaos he'd created. There was no way in hell he was going to tidy up the mess he'd made. Let Rosalie think burglars had broken in. He needed to take something to make it look like an anonymous burglary. What?

Kent's gaze fell on her jewelry box. Once she'd told him she kept her good pieces, which weren't many, among the costume jewelry in case anyone ever did break in. How could he have forgotten the false bottom where she kept cash? He lifted out the tray of jewelry to see a thick wad of bills. He rifled through them — over four thousand dollars. He didn't think twice about taking the jewelry and the money. Suddenly, he slapped at his forehead. Of course, Rosalie probably kept the ticket in her purse, which she kept with her at all times. How stupid could he be? The purse was obvious. Like Heather, Rosalie was predictable.

Angry with himself that he had wasted so much time, he sat down on Rosie's favorite rocking chair. It wasn't a total loss, he had four thousand dollars and a pile of jewelry that he could take to Atlanta and pawn. Within seconds he was sound asleep.

★ ★ ★

"Oh, this is beautiful, Jack," Rosie said, getting out of the car. "So this is your parents' house."

"It was. My dad gave it to me when I got married. I love this place, always have. It was wonderful growing up here with the river in the backyard. I think everyone says that who has ever lived on or near a river."

Rosie's heart thumped in her chest. *Married.* She backed up a step and then another. Kent was right, she was stupid. "You're married?" Damn, her words sounded so anguished like she'd just found out she'd been betrayed.

"I was. My wife died. It was a long, painful death. Martha, that was my wife, wanted to die here in this house by the river. I think she loved this place more than I ever did or could. You're the first person I've brought out here since she died. For some reason I thought you would like it. You remind me a lot of Martha. I guess that's why I like you. You would have liked her, Rosie. She was kind, always smiling, and she had the most wonderful sense of humor. We both wanted kids, but it didn't happen. I had all these plans for a houseful of kids and a couple of dogs and a cat or two. See that big old oak on the

265

front lawn? I always wanted a swing there for the kids. Eventually, I put one up, and it's still there. The day before Martha died she wanted me to carry her out to the swing and push her. She kept saying, 'higher, higher!' I was petrified she would fall off because she was so weak, but she didn't. She said it was like reaching for heaven. I think I bawled for two solid hours after I carried her back to bed. She was so exhausted she couldn't lift her head."

"Oh, Jack, I'm so sorry. I didn't know. What did she die of?"

"Ovarian cancer."

Rosie shook her head sadly. "How did you get through it all?"

"With the help of my dad and my uncle. The fitness centers required my time twenty-four/seven. I didn't think I could survive, but I did. I think the hardest time was the day I scattered her ashes on the river the way she wanted. I saved some. I suppose it sounds ghoulish, but I buried what I kept under the oak. There's a round patch of moss covering it now. It's the only spot of.moss under the whole tree. I took that to mean it was okay with Martha that I did that. I needed a place, you know. Someplace where I could sit and talk and relive old memories.

"I thought we'd picnic there, but if you'd rather not, I understand. I'm not real smart when it comes to women and how they think and feel. We have a lot of equally old trees in the back. It's just that this one is special. It's well over three hundred years old and shades the entire yard, as you can see."

Rosie didn't know what she felt or what she should do. Overwhelming sadness swept through her for Jack's loss. "It's the perfect spot for a picnic. I'm flattered that I remind you of your wife. She must have been a wonderful person."

"She was. Come on, let me show you the house. Pop and I kept it up. It would be sacrilegious not to. I haven't been here for a long time, but there is a caretaker. The guy that owns the Buick dealership in town owns the house on the left. You really can't see it through the shrubbery. They maintain their property also. They have two little cottages in the back. We just have extra lawn and a dock. Some rich tycoon from up North owns the one on the right. To my knowledge he's never come here. My caretaker said the house is falling to ruins. I guess it was some kind of historical write-off for him. The last house on the road will eventually be owned by the town.

It's in litigation. Some distant relatives of old Mrs. Lackland are contesting the will.

"Did I tell you I also know how to cook?"

Rosie burst out laughing. "Sort of. You said you cooked all the stuff for the picnic, so I just assumed you could cook. Thanks for clarifying that for me, Jack."

Jack reached for Rosie's hand. She clasped his willingly. It felt good. "C'mon, I'm giving you the tour. Now, this is the front door! Solid mahogany. A master craftsman did the glass inserts at the top. We could have a category-four hurricane, and this door will still be standing. I don't know about the rest of the house, but I do know about this door and all the others. I had hurricane shutters installed about ten years ago to protect the stained-glass windows.

"It smells kind of musty in here right now, but once the doors and windows are opened, the smell goes away. The floors are the original floors. They're called heart of pine. You clean them with beeswax. Jeez, I'm sorry, Rosie, you have the same floors in your own house, so I'm not telling you anything new. I envy you that second-floor verandah on your house. When Martha was confined to bed at the end, I moved her down here to the music room so she could be wheeled, bed and all, out to the verandah. We had tons of summer flowers and ferns out here. It looked just like a garden. Someday I am going to move back here. Let Buddy loose so he can wander around."

Rosie unhooked the leash, told the big dog he could go. He did, sniffing everything as he went along.

"It's beautiful," Rosie said. "I can understand why you would want to return here. I love walking along the river. I get some of my best weeds on the riverbanks. One good thing about weeds, they grow fast. I'd like to check yours out before I leave."

Jack threw his head back and laughed. "Be my guest. By the way, your room is at the top of the stairs, second door on the right. It has its own bathroom. I'll sleep down here. I like sleeping on the verandah if the weather is good. Do you hear something?"

Rosie frowned. "Music."

"That must mean someone is staying at the Daniels place. Oh, well, they won't bother us. For sure we won't be bothering them. I don't know about you, but I'm starving. Let's eat."

"I thought you were never going to suggest it. I didn't eat any breakfast. I guess we're having brunch, eh?"

"I have some salmon in the freezer. I'm going to thaw it out, and we can grill it tonight for dinner. Yeah, we're having brunch." Jack reached for her hand again to draw her forward. Together they walked out to the verandah, down the steps, and on out to the front yard, where they'd left the picnic basket.

"I have to warn you, Rosie, I cannot guarantee the ants. As many times as I picnicked under this tree, there were never any ants." His voice turned fretful when he said, "A picnic is not a real picnic unless you have ants."

"If it's all the same to you, Jack, I'll take an antless picnic anytime."

Rosie watched as Jack spread a huge blue-and-white-checkered tablecloth on the ground. She noticed that he was careful not to cover the rich mound of emerald green moss directly under the old swing. She wondered if, later on, he'd allow her to swing on the swing. On the other hand, maybe the swing, like the moss, was taboo.

"Oooh, that all looks soooo good, Jack. I love fried chicken. You took the skin off, right?"

"Yep, and I fried it in canola oil. You shouldn't be eating it, but once in a while you have to break the rules. One piece won't hurt you."

Jack watched as Rosie fixed a plate of food for Buddy, who was waiting patiently. He liked what he was seeing. He knew he hadn't been wrong about this woman. He looked upward in the still air. His eyes lit up when he saw the leaves of the old oak start to rustle. The swing seemed to be moving of its own volition. He looked around to see if anything else was moving in the breeze. The funny thing was, there was no breeze. He smiled. Martha was letting him know she approved.

Later, their picnic debris cleaned up, Rosie held out her wineglass. "I can't remember the last time I was this contented, this lazy. I don't know how I'm going to run later."

"It's the wine. We could take a nap right here on this fine tablecloth where there are no ants. We can't run now for two reasons, one, it's too hot, and two, we just ate."

"Hmmm," Rosie said, setting her empty glass aside. A minute later she was asleep, Buddy at her side. The dog looked at him with unblinking intensity, almost daring him to move closer. He didn't. He leaned back and rolled over on his side. He, too, was asleep within seconds.

Overhead, the branches in the angel oak continued to rustle as the swing moved back and forth, going higher and higher until it reached the tip of the highest branch.

It was late afternoon, the golden sun starting its downward spiral, when Rosie rolled over. Her legs stretched out just as her face touched something warm and scratchy. She opened one eye and then the other. She squeezed both eyes shut, her first thought was she was dreaming.

He wasn't moving. Should she move? She felt his warm breath on her cheek. No, she wasn't dreaming.

Then his lips moved, and he was saying something. What the hell was he saying? She felt so befuddled, she lay frozen. "Your call," the voice drawled.

Your call. Rosie's befuddled brain told her that meant Jack was waiting to see what she did. Vickie would say, seize the moment. God alone knew what Luna Mae would say. The voice whispering against her cheek was so sexy, so intimate, Rosie felt light-headed. *Your call.*

Rosie wanted to kiss this man more than she ever wanted anything in her life. Her thoughts were jumbled, frantic. Kissing, the kind of kissing that would happen here on the blue-and-white-checkered table-cloth, would be intense and lead to other things. She simply wasn't prepared to shed her clothing, to let a man, any man, see her naked body. Not yet. Then again, maybe it was the *swooshing* sound she could hear overhead or maybe it was the movement of the swing, reminding her of Jack's late wife. Whatever it was, it was taking its toll on her.

All the anguish and frustration she felt came out in her whispered reply. "This isn't the time or the place, Jack. Cut me some slack. When I'm ready for . . . for this, I want it to be for all the right reasons." But unable to resist her attraction to this wonderful man, she leaned a little closer and kissed him lightly on the lips. Her mouth felt seared, as if it had touched a flame. She quickly turned, rolled over, and was on her feet a moment later, her hand outstretched to help Jack to his feet. His eyes looked as glazed as she knew her own were. "Just so you know, Jack, I have never been so flattered in my life and . . . and I like you a lot. Probably more than I should. There will be another time, another place, and then look out, Jack Silver, I'll blow your socks off."

She heard that sexy, intimate whisper again. "Is that a promise or a declaration, Rosie?"

Rosie's hand reached out to stroke Jack's cheek. "It's a promise."

Buddy wiggled between them, his massive body pushing first at Rosie's legs, then at Jack's. He wanted to wedge between them. Satisfied when they moved apart, he barked his approval.

"I see this dog as a possible problem," Jack laughed. "It might be time for me to get a dog of my own, a female to keep him occupied."

"Good idea." Rosie looked upward. The angel oak was still, the swing at rest.

"It's four-thirty, Rosie. Are you up for a short run?" Jack asked, pushing the moment into the background. "I thought we'd do a two-and-a-half-mile run each way, then take the canoe down the river. You need to get the feel of it."

"I've never been in a canoe before. Or any kind of boat for that matter." Her voice was cold, distant, when she said, "Kent said I'd tip the boat because of my weight."

"Kent's an asshole, Rosie. You will not tip the boat. Now, let's run off that fried chicken we had for lunch. I slept like a log. Best nap I've had in . . . years. I'm raring to go."

"You know what, you're right. We slept for four straight hours. I can't remember when I slept straight through for four hours."

"Imagine how much sleep we'd get if we were in a bed," Jack quipped.

Rosie's face turned brick red. "Oh, yeah."

"Okay, let's go. Side by side, Buddy in the middle. I want you to pick up those legs and *GO*, Rosie."

Conditioned now, Rosie sprinted off, Jack and Buddy at her side. She was keeping up with Jack, and she knew he was giving it all he had. She had no idea what speed she was running at but she was *moving*, and she wasn't sweating half as much as Jack.

"Show-off!" Jack gasped at the turn-around point.

"You taught me too well, Jack," Rosie gasped in return. "I'll meet you back at the house!" She picked up her feet and sprinted ahead, her arms and legs pumping furiously.

"Like hell!" Jack gasped again. Rosie laughed again, so far ahead of him she felt pleased. If there was one thing she knew in her heart and in her gut, it was that Jack was *not* letting her win.

She kept running, Buddy way ahead of her. She wanted to look behind her, but that was a luxury she couldn't afford. She reached the house and was sitting on the old stone wall two full minutes before Jack arrived.

"Beatcha," Rosie drawled. She held out her arms. Jack fell into them and hugged her hard. It felt so wonderful, so warm and comforting. And even though they were both sticky and sweaty, she felt comfortable touching him.

Jack sprawled out next to her. "You sure did. You've been holding back on me. How many miles are you running these days?"

"I just started a ten-mile run."

"Ten miles! Every morning!"

Rosie grinned. "Yep!"

"Lady, I am impressed!"

Rosie beamed her pleasure.

"How are you on a real bike?"

"Wobbly. I am going to have to find a place to ride. I was never very good on a bike, even as a kid."

"The track at the high school is a good place to ride. I'll see about getting you permission to use it. We need to drink a couple of glasses of water before we set out in the canoe."

"You're a slave driver, Jack Silver!" Rosie

said, leading him toward the house and the kitchen. Off in the distance she could hear loud music. Puffs of gray smoke swirled above the shrubbery that separated the two river properties. Someone was cooking over a charcoal grill. Rosie felt hungry.

"I want you to win the triathlon in November," Jack said. "You'll get your picture in the paper and all that jazz. Winning one of those events is more powerful than any aphrodisiac. I want you to win for yourself, Rosie, not for me, not for anyone else, just you."

"Jack, you have too much faith in me. Three months is not a long time to train. I have a business to run. There's the divorce and all kinds of emotional issues I have to deal with. I'm willing to give it my best shot, but I don't want you to be disappointed if I don't win. I might come in last. All those guys and women who have been going to the gym for years are so far ahead of me, I don't know if I can catch up."

"You can do it, Rosie. Even if you came in last, I'd still be proud of you." Jack handed her a huge glass of ice water with a circle of lemon perched on the side. She gulped at it.

You can do it. He believed in her. She believed in herself, too, but it was an awesome task he was setting for her. *You can do it.* She smiled and nodded.

Both runners finished the water before they headed for opposite bathrooms, then it was down to the boathouse and the canoe Jack had tied to one of the pilings.

Ten minutes into the river ride, Rosie's face darkened with pain and frustration. "This is torture! I can't do this!"

"Yes, you can. You have strength you haven't even tapped into. Paddle and shut up. Count. We have fifty minutes to go! Do it!"

Rosie clenched her teeth, her eyes sparking with anger. "Damn it, didn't you hear me? I can't do this."

"You can do it! Seems to me that's your favorite expression."

"My arms feel like they're being pulled out of their sockets. Have you no mercy?" Rosie screamed.

"No! Either you paddle, or we sit here! Move!"

The ensuing dialogue was colorful to the point that Jack had to turn his head so Rosie wouldn't see him laughing. "C'mon, dip that paddle, put some muscle in it! You want to get back to the house, you have to help. Don't think this is a joyride down the river. You're a *wuss*, Rosie! Your husband works out for an hour a day on the rowing machine! You gonna let him beat you?"

Rosie bit down on her tongue, her eyes spewing something that made Jack sit up and take notice. *Damn. Maybe I went too far.*

"Kiss my ass, Jack Silver. I'll get back even if I have to swim. I quit!"

Jack laughed. "Yeah, right along with the alligators. You know this river is full of them. Now, paddle and shut up!"

Rosie raised her middle finger. Jack laughed and laughed.

Forty minutes later, Rosie slammed the paddle into the middle of the canoe. "My blisters have blisters. Paddle this damn thing yourself."

"Then I guess we're going to sit here. Ten more minutes, Rosie. You can do it. I didn't think you were a quitter."

"Jack, please, I can barely move my arms. My hands are full of blisters. Look!"

He hated to look, but he did. He remembered the first time he'd paddled a canoe and the same thing had happened to him. He shook his head. "Pick up the paddle, Rosie, and let's get home. Otherwise, we sit here. Whatever you do, don't put your hands in the water."

"Why?" she snarled.

Jack pointed to the bank of the river, where four monster gators were sunning themselves. Rosie's eyes widened as she picked up the paddle and dipped it in the water. "Before," she gasped, "when I said I hate your guts, I was wrong. I hate your guts and everything else about you! Do you hear me, Jack?"

"I hear you! Paddle!"

Rosie paddled.

Jack scanned the edge of the river and the tall grass before he decided it was safe to pull the canoe to the dock. He hopped out and tied the canoe to a piling. He reached down for Rosie's arm to pull her up.

"I will get out of this damn ship on my own. I do not need your help."

"Canoe."

"What?"

"It's not a ship. It's not even a boat. It's a canoe. If you don't let me help you, you're going to fall in the water."

"Then maybe I'll drown, and I'll be out of my misery." Plop. She was in the water, the brackish, smelly water settling over her head. She came up gasping. "Don't just stand there, help me!"

His eyes sharp, Jack watched for any sign of a gator. "Why should I? You declined my original offer. Did I or did I not say you were going to fall in the water?"

"Okay, you said it. If I was on the ground, I'd be groveling. Now, will you please help me out of this water? Please."

Jack held out a muscular arm and pulled Rosie to the dock. She smiled and thanked him graciously before she turned around, her foot lashing out. A second later, Jack was in the water. Rosie did her best to run to the house, where she galloped up the steps to her room and the shower, Buddy barking and howling right behind her.

Rosie stepped under the steaming spray, fully clothed. It was a repeat of the first morning she'd gone running with Jack. How, she wondered, as spray billowed out and around her, could one person be in so much pain and still stand up and survive? How?

It was torture to raise her arms to take off her shirt and bra, but somehow she managed. She kicked off her sneakers, then her Capri pants. Her cotton underwear cleaved like glue. She should have gotten the thongs. They would have peeled right off, or she could have ripped the skinny string in the back.

Rosie stepped out of the shower and reached for a huge pink bath sheet that she wrapped around her body. A smaller towel she wrapped around her head. She headed for the bed, pulled down a lemon yellow comforter, and climbed in. She was asleep a moment later.

Buddy whined softly before he hopped on the bed and settled himself in the crook of Rosie's bent legs. He faced the doorway, his big head on his paws. Buddy jerked to attention an hour later when the door opened quietly. The big dog waited to see what Jack would do. The moment he stepped over the threshold, Buddy bared his teeth, his ears going flat against his head.

Jack backed up a step and closed the door quietly. Rather than wake her for dinner, Jack went to fire up the grill and broil the salmon steaks. Maybe Rosie would like salmon for breakfast tomorrow morning. In the meanwhile, she was in good hands.

It was more than he could say for himself.

12

Kent Bliss leaned back and watched Heather at the grill. He was so damn tired he couldn't see straight. He was hungry, though. He struggled to keep his eyes open. Why, he didn't know. All Heather had done was glower at him from the minute they'd set out for the river house. He told himself all he had to do was get through the weekend, then it was bye-bye Heather. Not a minute too soon to suit him. She'd filled what he called a short-term void.

If there was one thing he'd learned during that short-term void, it was that Heather was a whiner, and she was vindictive. It would be just like her to follow and spy on him. Maybe what he needed to do was make his getaway slowly. If he was lucky, she'd get fed up with him and end it herself. Either way, he was going to have to return the Buick and the cell phone. The loan now was something different. He hadn't signed anything, and the money had been in cash. *So prove it and sue me.*

He was rather flush at the moment with

the money he'd snatched from Rosalie's jewelry box, and he still had a healthy chunk from the ten thousand Heather had given him. Plus, he had some commission checks coming due. All in all, he was okay for the moment. He needed a plan, though. But more important, he needed to find a way to get hold of Rosalie's purse.

Kent reared up in the chair when a wave of smoke circled overhead and settled on the terrace. He was about to snap at Heather, telling her she was burning something, when he realized the smoke was coming from behind his chair. "I thought you said no one was on River Road but us." The accusation was so cold, Heather flinched.

Heather looked up at the swirling smoke the strong breeze was carrying in their direction. "I don't own those properties, Kent. That means I have no control over who comes and goes. I haven't seen anyone there for over a year. The last two houses on the row are empty. I guess the Silvers are in residence. I saw the canoe leaving the dock a couple of hours ago. That particular house is the only one with a boathouse and a dock. You know Jack. He owns the gym. He's got a powerful cabin cruiser in the boathouse. I saw him take it out last year. Since his wife died, my dad told me he never comes here. My dad and his dad are good friends," Heather said breathlessly.

"Jack Silver owns that *mansion?*" Kent asked incredulously.

"Yes. The Silvers are incredibly wealthy. That's according to my dad. They don't act like they're rich, do they? Real down-home people. Their company is on the stock exchange, too. You sound surprised, Kent. I had the impression you and Jack were friends. Jack's really a nice guy once you get to know him. His father and uncle are just as nice. It was a shame his wife died. I really liked her because she was an incredible person. In fact, she's the one who showed me how to put makeup on, how to choose the right perfume, and how to dress and walk like a lady. She took a real interest in me because I was a real tomboy when I was a kid. That lady could cook and bake like you wouldn't believe. They had help, but she liked doing everything herself.

"When Martha got really sick, I came out to see her a few times, but Jack said she wasn't seeing visitors. I went to the service, though, when they scattered her ashes on the river. I cried for days."

"That's more than I wanted to know,

Heather," Kent snapped. "Does he come alone?"

"There were two people in the canoe. I really didn't pay attention. Do you want me to invite them over for a drink?"

"No, Heather, I do not want you to invite them over for a drink. When are we going to eat, for God's sake?"

"When your steak is done, that's when. If you don't change your attitude real quick, you are going to be *wearing your dinner*."

Kent waved away Heather's comment. Just his damn luck that Jack Silver owned the house next door. A house that was a mansion compared to the one he was visiting. As far as he knew, Hillary didn't have anything half as grand as either one of these houses. Her own mansion was beautiful, but she shared it with a husband. Hmmm. Maybe he could dangle both Hillary and Heather on a string. He was now thinking about classifying both women as sexual predators. He wasn't sure what that made him. Nor did he care.

He was almost certain the woman in the canoe with Jack Silver was Rosalie. He needed to get Heather drunk enough so she would fall asleep. Then he could mosey over to the bushes and do a little spying. "I'm three glasses ahead of you, sweetie. C'mon, you said you could keep up with me," he teased lightly. He watched as Heather polished off the wine in her glass and poured another. Her back to Kent, she didn't see him toss his wine over the railing of the terrace. When she turned around, he held out his glass. She dutifully filled it. He pretended to drink.

By the time the steaks were done, the salad tossed, and the baked potatoes taken out of their foil, Heather was unsteady on her feet. So unsteady, Kent had to help her to the chair.

Kent gobbled his food while Heather picked at hers. He kept filling her glass, tossing his over the railing when she wasn't looking. "This is delicious, sweetie. You do know how to grill a filet mignon. The salad is scrumptious. Did you see me take two helpings? I just love potatoes on the grill. You sure do know the way to a man's heart. Since you did all the cooking, I'm going to clean up. You sit right over there, stretch out, and I'll open this bottle of wine. Good year," he said, looking at the label.

Heather kicked off her high-heeled sandals and tottered over to the chaise lounge next to Kent's.

Kent filled two glasses and held out one. "Let's drink to *us*."

"Us? Oh, that's so nice, Kent. Yes, to us." Heather brought the glass to her lips, spilling half of it. Kent was Johnny on the spot to refill it.

"Bottoms up, baby." Kent moved behind her chair, the wine going over the railing. "I have an idea. That dinner was just too, too delicious. Let's take a little catnap so we can . . . do *other things* later."

"Ooohh, that sounds . . . wonder—"

She was out. Kent waited a few minutes before he entered the house and exited by the front door. He picked his way carefully out to the road. There was no kind of outside lighting whatsoever. That was good. The moon was gone, hiding behind a thick cloud cover. Heather had told him earlier, in a gleeful voice, that it was supposed to rain over the weekend. Rain meant they would stay in bed. Heather didn't know what the word *sleep* meant.

It was so dark, he could barely make out where he was going. Twice he tripped on the thick gravel that seemed to be scattered in small mountains on the unpaved road. He saw the car then. The silhouette of the house showed him there were no lights on in front of the house. That would make it all right to open the car door even though the light would go on. What he hoped to find, he didn't know. Some sign that his wife had been in the car, the house, and in the canoe. He heaved a sigh of relief when he opened the car door. He almost fainted when he saw a woman's purse in the backseat. Rosalie had a habit of tossing her purse in the backseat when she got in a car. Most times she forgot it and her keys. He'd lost track of the number of times she'd locked her keys and purse in the car.

At that moment, he would have parted with his right arm for a flashlight. He smacked at his forehead. Superduper man of the hour Jack Silver would have a flashlight in the glove compartment. He opened it. Sure enough, his hand found a small flashlight. And a gun. He debated for a full minute. Should he take the gun or not? Better not. But it was nice to know where he could get one if the need ever arose. He wondered if Jack had a license to carry a gun.

Kent went through Rosalie's purse, item by item. He checked her billfold four times but didn't find the lottery ticket. He did take the $297 that was in it. He tackled the zippered compartments and found another fifty dollars but no lottery ticket. It was a bust. Where in the damn hell had she hidden the ticket? He was so disgusted, he tossed the straw purse on the ground and stomped on it. He felt pleased when he heard the crunch of his wife's sunglasses. Picking the purse up, he carefully replaced it on the backseat.

Kent was angrier than he'd ever been in his life. For spite, he opened the glove compartment and took Jack Silver's gun. He shoved it in the waistband of his khaki shorts. When he heard a dog bark in the front part of the house, he eased himself out of the car and headed back to the Daniels house, a murderous look on his face.

What he needed to do, even though he was exhausted, was to get Heather into the car and head back to town. He'd drop her off, go back to his own place, and sleep. He didn't want to be anywhere near the Silver house when Jack found out his gun was missing.

Rosie woke, her body screaming in protest. She reached out to pull the covers over her, but her arms wouldn't move. She felt cold and wet. How was that possible? Then she remembered. "Oh God," she groaned.

The bedroom was totally dark. She had to move to the other side of the bed so she could turn on the lamp. Tears burned her eyes as she inched her way to the edge. She had to struggle to lift her arms, but she managed after several tries. She gasped when she looked down at her blistered hands.

It would be a miracle if she managed to get out of bed and into the shower. Could she do it? She had to do it. She pep talked herself as she wiggled and squirmed into a sitting position. Buddy whined at her feet. "I think I can do it, Buddy," Rosie whispered. "No, no, that's all wrong. I *know* I can do it. I *have* to do it."

Rosie felt like she'd climbed the Himalayas when she made it to the shower and turned it on. As the hot water sluiced over her body, Rosie reveled in it, holding up her face to let it beat at her. It felt better than a massage, better than a multiple orgasm. Not that she'd ever had a multiple orgasm, but she did have an active imagination.

The sun was starting to come up when she finally managed to dress herself. She needed to go out to the car and get some aspirin out of her purse. Maybe coffee would help. She looked down at her feet. She'd pulled on some socks, but her sneakers were soaking wet. That was okay, she'd brought an extra pair, and they were on the floor in the back of the car.

Rosie was by the front door when she sensed a presence.

"*Hello!* Aren't you going to say good morning to your host? I see you're ready for our run. I've been waiting. What took you so long, Rosie?"

Rosie whirled around, a look of horror on her face. No sane person was this cheerful so early in the morning. If she'd had a stick in her hand, she would have jammed it down Jack's throat. "You better not have said what I just think you said," she snarled.

"No pain, no gain. Those are the rules. Then we're going canoeing. You said you could do it. Are you telling me you're going to chicken out? I thought more of you, Rosie." Jack's voice no longer sounded cheerful. Rosie felt instant depression.

"Not only do I hate your guts, I'm going to kill you when you fall asleep. As you can see, I have no shoes."

"You were going out to the car to get them. Probably some aspirin, too."

"Why do you always know everything? It's true, I am going for my sneakers and some aspirin, but I am not going running or canoeing. Chew on that, you miserable cretin."

"I'll give you ten minutes," Jack said.

Rosie stared at him. He looked so good this morning in his denim shorts and yellow tee shirt. His sneakers were so beat-up she didn't know how they stayed on his feet. Her shoulders slumped as she walked through the doorway, tears rolling down her cheeks. She wondered if they'd put her in one of those fancy, copper Springfield caskets when they carted her dead body back to town.

Somehow Rosie managed to get her sneakers on her feet and two aspirin down her throat. She wanted to shout with glee when she also managed to tie the laces. When she looked up, she saw Jack watching her. She wished she knew what he was thinking. She did her best to square her shoulders.

Jack wondered if he was doing the right thing. His heart and mind said yes. And yet, she looked so miserable. But she looked wonderful to him, with her wet hair plastered against her head and curling about her ears. She was wearing a lime green outfit that looked to be roomy and comfortable.

"Let's do some stretches to work out the kinks, Rosie." She nodded, but didn't say a word. Ten minutes later, he said, "Okay, let's go! Take the lead. We'll do it single file today in case you need a cushion when you collapse. Meaning, of course, that I will cushion your fall." He waited for the sharp, blistering retort he knew was coming. When it didn't come, he was disappointed. She eyed him stonily before she set off. Jack stayed a good distance behind, Buddy in the middle.

Jack bellowed to be heard. "I want to see those arms move. Pump, pump. Lift those legs. C'mon, you're running like an old lady with hemorrhoids."

Tears continued to roll down Rosie's cheeks. "A pointy stick up your butt is too good for you, Jack Silver," she muttered. She did as she was told, though, and felt better for it. Why was he always right? Some of the soreness was actually abating.

"All right, let's move here!" Jack bellowed. *"Show me what you got!* No pain, no gain! *Do it. Rosie!"*

Rosie gritted her teeth. "I'll show you what I have, you son of a bitch!" She picked up her feet and took off. Sweat poured off her body as she ran at full throttle, leaving Jack in her dust. She was far enough ahead to slow suddenly. Then, dancing on one foot, then the other, she slid her sweats halfway down over her rump and mooned the trainer. Buddy barked shrilly, enjoying the strange show. Rosie took a few seconds to look over her shoulder to see Jack at a dead stop. She didn't want to think about the startled expression on his face. "You said, *show me what you got.* Now you know," she bellowed before she took a deep breath and raced off.

The harder and the faster she ran, the better she felt. This time when she made it back to the house she had to wait for nine minutes before Jack joined her. For spite she was smoking a cigarette she'd taken from her purse. Jack knocked it out of her hand.

"Damn you, get me another one. You *said* whatever it takes. It takes a cigarette right now. *Do it. Jack!*"

She was right, time to eat his own words. He had no other choice.

Jack watched as Rosie blew one perfect smoke ring after another. He knew his pupil was angry. At him. He felt like a chastened schoolboy. "How do you feel now, Rosie? Did you work out some of the soreness?"

"I hurt, Jack. All over. Yes, some of the soreness eased up. Listen, I think someone was in the car last night." She tossed the half-smoked cigarette she no longer wanted on the ground, then used the heel of her sneaker to grind it into the soft dirt. "Even though my purse was on the backseat, my sunglasses are smashed. My first thought was someone stepped on my bag. I was just about to check my wallet. Do you have thieves out here?"

Jack was already opening the door of his car. She watched as he popped the glove compartment panel. "My gun's gone!"

"Gun! What gun?" Rosie bleated as she raced for her purse to rifle through it. "Someone took all my money! Damn. I thought you said it was safe way out here. You're going to call the police, aren't you?" The cell phone was already in Jack's hand.

Fifteen minutes later the local police were filing their report. Rosie showed them her purse and gave them the amount of money that was missing. The officer looked at both of them, frowning. Rosie knew he was thinking, *what kind of idiots leave a purse and a gun in an unlocked car.* He was right, they were both idiots.

Both she and Jack signed the report, received their copies, and watched the police cruiser reverse and drive away.

Jack scratched his head. "I don't get it. No one ever comes down this road. Most people don't even know this street is here.

I deliberately let the vegetation grow out of bounds for just this reason. Mr. Daniels and I agreed to keep River Road as private as possible. The other two owners couldn't care one way or the other what happens on River Road."

"Why don't you go over to the Daniels house and ask them if they saw or heard anything last night?" Rosie suggested. "Someone is there because we heard the music playing yesterday afternoon. While you do that, I can make breakfast."

"Does that mean you aren't angry with me anymore?"

"No, that's not what it means. What it means is I am starved since I missed dinner last night. I'm not angry with you. I was venting, and you were handy. And, don't even think about telling me what I can and cannot have to eat this morning." To make her point, Rosie stomped her way past him. Buddy avoided him as if he smelled.

Jack sighed. He turned, looked up at the big angel oak, whose branches were still. He threw his hands in the air before he, too, stomped off. His destination, the Daniels house.

There was no car in the driveway. For all he knew, some vagrant or perhaps some kids had spent the day on the terrace or one of the back decks, having themselves a good old time with no one the wiser. He certainly hadn't bothered to check, which didn't exactly make him a wonderful neighbor. He walked around, checking all the doors of the Daniels house, but they were locked. The barbecue grill showed signs of recent use. It was even faintly warm. The deck was neat and tidy. He pulled out his cell phone and dialed information to get the number for Sinclair Daniels's home phone number.

"Sinclair, this is Jack Silver. I'm out at the house on River Road. Last night someone broke into my car, stole some money and my gun. I was wondering if anyone was staying at your house because I heard music playing. There's no one here this morning. I checked your place, and it appears to be okay."

"That's terrible, Jack. I gave the house to my daughter sometime ago. It's possible she was out there. Give me your number. I'll check with her and get right back to you. Appreciate you taking the time to check the house for us. Sorry about the gun. That's serious business."

Jack was walking up the steps to his own house minutes later when the phone in his hand rang. He flipped the cover up, and said, "Hello."

"Jack, I spoke to my daughter. She was at the house with a friend, but they left right after dinner. She said the bugs were out in force. She also said she cleaned everything up and locked all the doors. I told her what happened, and she said she hadn't seen or heard anything but did know you were at the house because the smoke from your grill made its way to her deck. She said you can call her if you want." He rattled off a number that Jack immediately forgot.

"Okay. Thanks, Sinclair."

Jack walked into the kitchen, his steps hesitant. Rosie smiled at him. "Just in time. I made omelets and some toast. Fresh-squeezed juice and lots of coffee."

Jack sighed with relief. "Guess we won't be having the second salmon steak I grilled last night. I'm starved. And this looks wonderful. I didn't know you could cook, Rosie."

"I like to cook when I have time. Unfortunately, my cooking tended to be all the wrong kinds of food. Everything I made had to have gravy so I could sop it up with bread that had butter on it. I cooked a lot with cheese, wine, and butter. The more calories, the more fattening the dish was, the better I liked it. I felt so good when I ate. I made cakes, pies, then added ice cream or whipped cream. I didn't just eat one helping or one slice. Oh, no, I had to have two or three helpings and at the very least, two slices of cake or pie. When I would order pizza, I ate the whole thing myself. With every topping they offered. I used to love to eat. These days I hardly think about food. I guess that's a good thing. Sometimes, I crave sweets or a load of mashed potatoes and gravy."

"Me too. Sometimes I even indulge," Jack confessed.

Rosie reacted with surprise. "You!"

"I used to be a fat kid. You know the kind the other kids made fun of. Then my dad laid down the law when I got to high school. My dad scheduled a workout at the gym for me three days a week. He wouldn't let me take the bus to school which, by the way, was five miles away. I had to ride my bike. He consulted a nutritionist on my behalf, and she made up a month's worth of menus. One day a month I was allowed to eat whatever I wanted. After the first couple of months, I didn't even want to do that. I was able to stick to the diet because it was good food, it tasted great, and after a while it wasn't that hard to give up the junk. Even way back then when no one was health-conscious the way they are today, I knew I had to take the weight off. And, girls never looked at fat boys. My dad was right even though I fought him tooth and nail in the beginning. I'm glad he kept at me, twenty-four/seven. It was a new way of life. It stayed with me. How about you?"

Did she really want to confess about her life to this man sitting across from her? What would he think of her? She grimaced, why not. "I wasn't fat exactly, but I was pudgy. Vickie was so thin, so petite. As much as I loved her, I was jealous of her. She could eat anything and not put on an ounce. To this day she can still eat anything and not gain weight.

"It was hard being the chubby one in my group of girlfriends. They were all active, cheerleaders, involved in the marching band, track and field. I ate and studied. College was pretty much the same. No, that's not true. In college I ate more and studied because I was the one no one asked out to the frat parties. I wasn't invited to join a sorority. Vickie was invited to join all of them. She didn't accept any of them because they didn't want me. I made it through okay. I had a few dates. Nothing memorable. I hung out with the nerds."

Jack listened and thought about his wife Martha. She'd been all the things Rosie hadn't been. She'd been a cheerleader and had been invited to join every sorority on campus. She'd been homecoming queen and one of the most popular girls on campus. He had never been able to understand what she saw in him. She said he had kind eyes and a kinder heart. Plus, she'd said, "You're cute."

Rosie finished the omelet. "Nothing changed after college. I was a prime candidate for someone like Kent Bliss although he didn't come along until ten years later. Vickie and Luna Mae tried to warn me, but I wouldn't listen. That's my story."

She put her napkin down next to her plate. "Since I cooked, you get to clean up."

Jack wanted to say something, something profound, but he wasn't sure he could find the words. Even though it might sound stupid, he took a stab at it anyway. "Yeah, but look at you now. You have your ducks in a row, and you're moving forward. I just want you to understand something, Rosie. Being skinny won't make you happy. Happiness comes from within. I'm sure you heard that before. It's true. Whatever you do in life, do it for the right reason, and you'll be happy." Damn, it didn't sound stupid at all. He looked Rosie in the eye and grinned. She grinned back.

"Oh, let's forget about the dishes and finish our coffee out on the porch. There's something I want to tell you."

Rosie flinched. *Here it comes,* she thought. *It's probably something terrible. Damn, why am I such a pessimist?*

Out on the porch, Jack lowered the back of his chaise until he was stretched out completely. "I can't prove this but I think your . . . I think your husband was next door yesterday. I'm almost certain he was over there with Heather Daniels. Remember, we saw them together at the cafe a while back? Think about it, Rosie. Somebody stomped on your purse. Who would do that? Your regulation burglar doesn't take time to stomp on a purse. That was a spiteful thing." He went on to tell her about his conversation with Sinclair Daniels. "He called Heather, and she told her dad that they left right after dinner. I can call her and ask her if it was Kent with her."

Rosie focused on a trellis at the far end of the porch that held confederate jasmine, whose scent was wafting her way. How strange that her heart wasn't lurching, that she wasn't breathless with what Jack was telling her. She closed her eyes for a moment trying to picture Kent going through her purse, looking for what? The lottery ticket, what else? Then when he didn't find it, he stomped on her purse in a fit of anger. Yes, she could picture Kent doing that. The gun, though, that was different.

"No, don't call her." Rosie told him what she thought happened and why.

"He thinks you won that big Wonderball! Is the man obsessed? Why does he think that?"

"Because I did win," Rosie blurted.

Jack gaped at her. "You won all that money! Jeez."

"That's all you can say, 'jeez!' I didn't know what to do. I still don't know what to do. That's why I didn't come forward to claim it. Now that Kent, and I'm sure it was Kent, stole your gun and my money, things are going to change quickly. Even if you called Miss Daniels, and she said Kent was with her, we can't prove he's the thief. There were no witnesses. Kent is very sly."

"Rosie, I'm so sorry. I don't know what to say. I hope you have that ticket someplace safe."

"You don't have to say anything, Jack. I'm not giving half of that money to Kent.

That's all there is to it. It's safe." At least she hoped it was safe.

"Rosie, do you have any idea of all the good you could do with that money? You need a good lawyer. One of those chew-nails-spit-rust lawyers. How long do you have to claim the prize money?"

"A year from the date of the drawing. I probably shouldn't have told you. You won't tell anyone, will you?" Rosie asked anxiously.

"Hell no! I'm flattered that you trusted me enough to tell me. A little while ago you wanted to kill me."

"I apologized. Sometimes I get carried away."

"I forgive you," Jack said softly, gazing deeply into her eyes. Then he looked down at his watch and his manner changed abruptly. "In thirty minutes we have to go canoeing!"

Rosie's eyes popped wide. She held up her blistered hands for Jack's inspection. He shrugged and shook his head. "I have just the thing for those hands."

Rosie started to cry. Her tears didn't faze Jack at all.

Buddy leaped onto Rosie's lap and licked her tears away.

13

Kent Bliss shoved the gun he'd taken from Jack Silver's car under the love seat in his room. His eyes were wild and full of panic. Where to hide the damn thing? Keep it in his car? Under his pillow? In a locked drawer in his office? Brilliant thinking there. The girls in the office could open any locked drawer, which they did all the time, with a nail file. What in the hell was he thinking when he took the firearm? Guns had serial numbers. It could be traced. He could wipe it clean and dump it somewhere. Hell, he didn't even know how to shoot a gun. And he hated and yet loved the way it felt in his hands. All cold and silky, kind of like the way a woman felt sometimes.

He was overtired. He needed to sleep, but it was still light out. Not that it mattered. He closed the ugly orange-and-brown drapes before he stripped down and slipped between the sheets. The gun went under his pillow. He hoped the safety was on. He was asleep within seconds.

Kent woke a little after two in the

morning and was instantly wide-awake. He looked over at the small travel clock he kept on the nightstand and quickly calculated how long he'd slept. Twelve hours since he'd hit the bed a few minutes past four in the afternoon.

He'd never used the little kitchen area, but this morning he made coffee, and, while it dripped, he showered, shaved, and dressed in jeans and a beige tee shirt. He gulped at the terrible coffee, smoked, and when the room grew cloudy with smoke, picked up the gun and dumped it in his shaving kit. He left the room and headed for his car. Time to take another crack at Rosalie's house. This time he would check Luna Mae's room and the attic as well. The damn ticket was somewhere in the house. All he had to do was find it.

He was almost certain Rosalie didn't have a safe-deposit box. She'd never had one when they were married. There wasn't a safe-deposit key on her key ring either and none in her jewelry box. The winning ticket was somewhere in Rosalie's house. He'd stake his life on it.

Kent felt like a vampire as he drove out of the parking lot. He didn't turn his lights on until he was out on the main road. He looked over at the passenger seat. His shaving kit and his breaking-and-entering tools nestled together. He felt jittery as he wondered what the penalty was for carrying a stolen gun.

This time, Kent parked around the opposite corner from where he'd parked the first time. No reason to give some nocturnal housebound neighbor an eyeful.

The clock over the stove in Rosalie's kitchen read 3:27 when he disarmed the alarm system and rearmed it. He gingerly laid the shaving kit holding the gun on the counter. He took a full minute to realize he actually missed this house and the freedom that had come with living here. He used up another minute thinking about his present lifestyle. There was no comparison. He wasn't meant to scramble for money. He realized now what a good thing he'd had.

He wanted the lifestyle back and, by God, he would do whatever he had to do to get it. His eye fell on the shaving kit. *Whatever it took.*

It was 4:55 when Kent, his face murderous, plopped down in Rosalie's rocking chair in the guest room. His feet tapped the floor as he rocked. He was missing it. It was here. Why couldn't he find it? He'd checked his wife's shoes, the pockets of her clothes, everywhere he could think of. The elusive piece of paper was not to be found. He hadn't tackled the attic yet. He needed to get to it before it got full light out.

Kent jumped off the chair, the flowered cushion sliding onto the floor. He didn't bother to give the cushion a second look or pick it up.

At the top of the attic steps, he turned on the light. He looked down at the dusty floor. There was no sign of footprints. No one had been in the attic for a very long time.

He was beyond furious as he made his way back down the steps.

Once more, he eyed Luna Mae's room. He'd found nothing of interest except the housekeeper's bankbook, according to which her account had sixty-seven thousand dollars in it, and two hundred and forty dollars in cash in the bottom of one of the drawers. The cash was now in his pocket, along with an old Rolex watch that had belonged to her friend Skip. He was scrounging up a really nice little nest egg.

Kent made one last round of the entire house. He went from room to room, standing in the doorway, eyeing each and every little thing to see if he'd missed a hiding spot. And only when he reached Rosie's guestroom did a smile break over his face.

Rosie sat on the front steps leading up to the verandah as she waited for Jack to secure the canoe and lock up the boathouse. She ached from head to toe. It was a good ache, not an angry one like she'd had the first day. She couldn't wait to get home so she could relax in her Jacuzzi with a nice glass of wine. She'd earned it, and she deserved it.

In her wildest dreams she never thought she'd spend a weekend like this one. She'd half hoped it would be a romantic weekend, one whose memory she could cherish. Jack had acted like he was willing. The problem was her. She still didn't have the self-confidence to believe a man could seriously be interested in her. *Talk about shooting yourself in the foot.* She grimaced at her lack of self-confidence.

From her position on the steps she could see the huge tree in the front yard with the swing. Even from this distance, she could see the round emerald patch of moss where a little bit of Martha rested. She took a moment to wonder why she wasn't jealous.

Holding on to her hips because they ached so much, Rosie walked down the steps and over to the tree and the swing. She was careful not to walk on the lush mound of moss. She wanted to sit on the swing so bad, to kick her feet and sail high into the branches of the tree. She reached out tentatively to touch the ropes holding the swing, but she drew her hand back as though she'd touched something red-hot. The swing belonged to Martha and Jack. Not her. Something pricked at her eyelids. She rubbed them with her knuckles. When the branches started to sway, Rosie looked up. "He must have loved you very much. He's a kind, caring man. I can see how and why you loved him," she whispered.

Rosie backed up when she saw the swing start to move. At first it just moved back and forth a little with the breeze in the tree, but then it started to sway faster and faster. Rosie stumbled in her haste to get away. "I'm sorry, I didn't mean . . . I only wanted . . . You don't have to worry about . . . please don't be upset. I won't . . ."

"You ready, Rosie?" Jack called from the verandah.

Rosie nodded. "Look!" she said, pointing to the swing that was sailing as high as it could go. She was startled when Jack let loose with a loud laugh. "What? Why are you laughing? The air isn't even stirring."

"That's Martha telling us it's okay. Us.

She likes you. That swing only moves when she approves of something. I was holed up here with my dad and uncle during the last hurricane. Seventy-mile-an-hour winds. That damn swing didn't move. Neither did the branches of the tree. I know it's hard to believe, and I would have thought I was dreaming or imagining it, but Dad and my uncle saw it, too. Ask them."

"But . . ."

"It's Martha's tree, Rosie. She's very protective of it, and her space underneath it. Martha will let you know when it's time for you to get on that swing. I tried it once, and she booted me right off. My dad saw that, too. Don't even try to figure it out, Rosie."

"Okay, I won't," she said, eyeing the tree warily before she turned back to Jack. "Are you ready?"

"I packed up the car, and I'm good to go. How about you and Buddy?"

"He's been sitting in the car waiting for the last fifteen minutes. He's ready to go home, too."

"Then let's go."

Weary to the bone, but contented, Rosie leaned back and listened to Jack chatter about the November triathlon, her training, the gym, and anything else he felt like talking about. She was glad she didn't have to contribute to the conversation. Even so, she felt connected to the trainer. Somehow, this holiday weekend, they'd forged a bond she couldn't explain. She felt attracted to him, her thoughts and desires going off in all sorts of directions, but the timing wasn't right. And then there was Kent and the missing gun. Along with all her other emotions, a feeling of dread settled between her shoulder blades.

An hour later, Jack swung into her driveway and parked by the garage. "Home sweet home," he said, laughing.

"No place like it. Your house on the river is beautiful though. I can see why you love it so much. It's too bad you can't spend more time there. I don't know if you realize it or not, but you turn into a different person when you're there."

Jack looked at Rosie in awe, "You picked up on that? Martha used to say that to me." He linked his arm with hers and walked to the house, stopping twice while they waited for Buddy to do what he had to do. He growled, though, when he raced up the back steps to the door. His body slammed the door as Rosie stuck the key in the lock, her own nerves twanging at the dog's apparent anxiety.

Buddy barreled through the open doorway as his mistress ran to the keypad to turn off the alarm. Her feet crunched on the broken glass and china, ground coffee and rice littering the floor. "My God, what happened?" she said, looking around at the mess.

"I think it's safe to say your house was broken into, Rosie. Stay here while I check the other rooms."

"But the alarm was on. You saw me turn it off. The windows are locked and armed."

"Then it must be someone who knows your code. Stay here, Rosie."

"Like hell! This is my house. No one but Vickie, Luna Mae, and I have the code. It had to be Kent. He's looking for the ticket."

Jack stopped in his tracks. He turned around to look at Rosie. "And now he has a gun."

Rosie ran her hands through her short-cropped brown hair before she jammed them into the pockets of her olive green slacks. "If you're trying to scare me, you're succeeding, Jack. The house is empty. Otherwise, Buddy would be going ballistic. Well, let's see if he found the ticket."

Rosie's heart fluttered in her chest when she walked into the guest room. She struggled to take a deep breath when she saw the floral cushion on the floor. She ran over to it and picked it up. The small white ticket sailed downward.

Rosie let out her breath in a loud *swoosh* of sound as she bent down to pick up the ticket.

Jack could only gape, his jaw dropping. "*That* was your safe place! Under the cushion!"

"Hey, it worked, didn't it?" Rosie quipped. "The ticket stuck to the bottom of the cushion when the cushion fell to the floor." She unbuttoned the button at the top of her shirt, which matched her slacks, folded the ticket, and stuck it down her bra.

"Women!" Jack said, disgust ringing in his voice. "Why didn't you take it to a safe-deposit box, Rosie?"

"I don't have one. I thought if I had the ticket in a hiding place, Kent would have a better chance of finding it. He has a shrewd, devious mind. I know he did this. I can't explain about the alarm, but I know it was him. I just know it, Jack."

"Okay, I'll go with that because I think you're right. I also think you better check around to see if anything else is missing."

"Well, he took my jewelry box and the money I had in it. I think I had about four thousand dollars. You know, for emergencies. I hate waiting in line at the bank. I hate waiting in line, period."

"Did you ever hear of the word *safe?* You could have one installed in half an hour. Hell, I can install one for you. Anything else?"

Rosie looked around at the mess in her bedroom. The mattress and bedding littered the floor, the box spring was tilted askew. The contents of her dresser drawers were scattered everywhere. The bathroom fared no better. Body powder was everywhere, coating everything with a white glaze.

Her clothes in the closet were on the floor, the pockets of everything inside out. Her shoes had been tossed in all directions. She felt sick, violated by what had been done to her home. What bothered her more than anything, though, was the look of disgust she was seeing on Jack's face.

She reacted.

"Don't look at me like that, Jack. This is my home. My castle, so to speak. I should be able to do things the way I want. I took the time, the effort, and paid for a top-of-the-line alarm system. I shouldn't even have had to do that, but I did. Most people keep a certain amount of cash handy. Maybe I had a little more than most, but that's my right, too. What good is having jewelry locked up in a safe-deposit box? I'm calling the police and the alarm company to find out how this happened. We probably shouldn't touch anything until the police make their report and dust for fingerprints. The only ones they're going to find are mine, Luna Mae's, and Kent's. I can tell you that right now."

Jack walked over to where Rosie was standing. He cupped her chin in his hand. "Look at me, Rosie. I'm not judging you. I would never do that. If you think I'm angry, I am. I'm angry that I agree with you that your husband did this, and I'm angry that we both think he stole my gun. I am not angry with you."

Rosie's eyes filled with tears, blurring his sturdy figure. She felt his lips on hers as tears splashed between them. It was the sweetest, sexiest, most mind-boggling kiss she'd ever experienced. She swayed with dizziness, wanting it to go on forever.

It was Jack who drew away first, a look of stunned wonderment on his face. "Uh-huh," was all he could think of to say.

Rosie was a little more verbal. "I liked

that. Want to do it again?"

"I do, but we aren't going to. We are going to call the police and the alarm company. Then we are going to clean up this mess. After which, what do you say to the two of us taking a nice shower together? I wash your back, and you wash mine."

"That sounds wickedly delicious." She turned around so Jack wouldn't see her worried face. Taking a shower meant he would see her naked body. And feel it. Did she care? She had cared earlier in the weekend. Now she decided she didn't give a tinker's damn if he saw her naked body or not. If he couldn't handle it, it was his problem. She did take a moment to wonder what his wife had looked like. Was she thin and petite? Was she beautiful? Did she have a wonderful smile? Well, there was only one way to find out.

"Jack, what did your wife look like?"

"Would you like to see a picture of her, Rosie?"

"I would, Jack."

Jack pulled his billfold out of his hip pocket and withdrew a picture of Martha. His thumb traced her likeness for a second before he handed it over.

"She's beautiful, Jack." Rosie's voice rang with sincerity.

"And she was just as beautiful inside as she was outside. Like you, she was a pretty woman. I'm thinking you thought she was a little woman, maybe a size six or something like that. Am I right?"

"Yes," Rosie said honestly.

"No. When I first met her she was a little bit of a thing, but Martha had a weight problem. She worked at it, though. She was never able to drop below a size fourteen. She used to call herself a plump pigeon because she was short and round. Look at me, Rosie. It's what's inside that counts. Some people, no matter how hard they try, no matter how hard they work at it, are never going to be little and skinny. As long as you exercise and eat right, that's all you have to worry about. I told you I was a fat kid. I learned to be tolerant."

Rosie's eyes misted. She watched as he slipped the picture back into his wallet. She turned around, picked up the phone, and called the police.

Two hours later, Rosie walked the two police officers to the door. When the door closed behind them, she looked at Jack. "They're going to talk to Kent. He will be livid. If you don't mind, I think you should call Heather and ask her point-blank if Kent was with her at the river house. I'd like for you to do that before the police get to him. That way, he won't be able to coerce her into lying for him."

"Did the alarm company guy say anything?"

"He's on the phone with the monitoring station now," Rosie said.

"Okay, you deal with him, and I'll call Heather."

Rosie nodded as she walked down the steps and into the kitchen where the alarm pad was located. The technician was just hanging up the phone. She looked at him expectantly.

"There's no malfunction. You said you were away for the weekend. Someone entered your house, turned off the alarm, then rearmed it. They did it twice over the weekend. The last time they did it was yesterday, a little after three-thirty in the morning. That's all I can tell you, Ms. Gardener. I checked the locks on your doors. There's nothing wrong there. Someone must have a key. Sign here."

Rosie scrawled her name at the bottom of the slip, folded her copy, then shoved it into a kitchen drawer that held hundreds of other receipts.

Rosie crunched her way over to the table where she sat down. She eyed the broken teapots and wanted to scream in anger. Kent would do something like this.

Vickie and Luna Mae had keys to the house, and both of them knew how to arm and disarm the alarm system. It had to be Kent. There was no other explanation.

That damn lottery ticket was making her life a living hell. She needed to do something about it, and she needed to do it soon. Real soon since Kent now had a gun.

Rosie heard Jack before she saw him, Buddy at his side. "Heather said it was Kent with her at the house. She wanted to know why I wanted to know. I told her the truth. I don't know if that was wise or not, Rosie. It's too late now, though. When she finally figured out why I was asking, she was quick to point out that Kent was with her the whole time and never out of her sight. When I pressed her for more details, she said she'd fallen asleep, then Kent woke her up saying he felt sick and wanted to go back to town. I guess her father is on her case over this, too. I'm sure she's talking to your husband right now."

"Poor Heather. I say that, and I don't even know the young woman. That will be the end of their relationship. Kent will view it all as a betrayal on her part."

"Does Kent know anything about guns, Rosie?"

"I don't think so. However, there are a lot of things I don't know about Kent. For all I know, he could be a crack shot. If it's considered fashionable to own a firearm and be a good shot, then, yes, he knows how to use one. Whatever is 'in' at the moment is what he's most interested in. He is no longer on my radar screen, Jack."

"Let's get this all cleaned up. I'm staying here tonight. Either in your bed or on the couch. Your choice." Jack grinned.

"Then I opt for the bed," Rosie said boldly.

"Attagirl. Come on, let's get to work."

Shortly before six, Jack and Rosie looked at each other before they dusted their hands dramatically. Now it was relaxation time. Rosie's heart thumped in her chest. Her eyes were bold, her cheeks slightly flushed. "You said something about taking a shower together. Or would you rather go in the Jacuzzi with a nice glass of wine?"

Jack leered at her. "Right now I'd settle for someone running the garden hose over me. If my opinion counts, let's take a shower and hit those pretty sheets I just saw you put on the bed. What's your vote?"

Rosie had never done a wicked, unplanned, spontaneous, serendipitous thing in her life. She pursed her lips. "I have a garden hose. It's been a while since I scampered through the tall grass buck naked."

"Uh-huh," Jack said. He was breathing hard, Rosie noticed. She quirked an eyebrow in his direction. Buddy stared at them both before he threw back his head and howled.

"Exactly where is this hose of yours?" Jack drawled.

"Why don't I show you," Rosie drawled in return as she stuck her hand down her bra to pull out the Wonderball ticket. She stuck it back under the cushion on the rocking chair before she crooked her index finger. "Follow me," she whispered. She kicked off her sneakers and heard them thump on the hardwood floor. She heard two more thumps as Jack's sailed across the room.

She ran then, like a gazelle, out to the hall and the stairway, where she galloped down, Buddy behind her, Jack bringing up the rear.

Rosie reached the hose first and turned the nozzle. Water shot everywhere before she aimed it at Jack. He wrestled it from her, water shooting upward to catch him full in the face. It was just enough time for her to scamper to the other end of the porch and grapple for a second coiled hose. She turned it on full blast as she whipped it around.

"I think this is called frolicking," Jack gasped.

Rosie started to giggle. "Frolicking is good. How about tomfoolery?"

"Tomfoolery is real good."

"If it's so damn good, why aren't we doing it?" Rosie said, spitting out a mouthful of water.

Jack dropped the hose in his hand. It danced across the lawn till it came to a stop, the spray shooting upward. Rosie dropped hers at the same time. It snapped into place, finally coming to rest next to Jack's hose.

"Our own waterfall," Rosie purred, water dripping down her body. She struggled to pull off her olive green shirt. "I could use some help here."

Jack took it to be the invitation it was.

"You are *sooo* slow," Rosie said, whirling the sodden shirt over her head. Her bra was suddenly in her hands. She twirled it around before she whipped it behind her.

"Uh-huh," Jack said.

"You need to play catch-up here!" Rosie trilled.

"I can do that! Yes sirree, I can do that."

Buddy ran between them, barking and howling. If it was a game, he wanted to play, but both players were ignoring him.

"Oooh," Rosie said, her eyes growing big.

"I'm all caught up," Jack growled.

"Up, up, up!" Rosie chortled as she finally got the olive green slacks and her soaking-wet panties down to her ankles.

He reached for her and she let him, as their wet, slick bodies melted together.

Disgusted with this turn of events, Buddy dragged the wet clothes out of the way before he lay down, his big head on his paws.

Dinner was going to be late tonight.

Kent Bliss stepped from the shower and wrapped one of the Days Inn towels around his middle. He spread a second towel on the scratchy love seat with its mysterious stains. His dinner, a meatball sub and a bag of greasy french fries along with two cups of coffee, glared up at him from the coffee table. He unwrapped the sandwich, and chomped down, his thoughts on what had transpired back at Rosie's house. He'd looked everywhere and still he couldn't find that goddamn ticket.

He'd been so angry, he'd wrecked her kitchen and broken her prized teapot collection. He knew as sure as he knew he needed to keep breathing to stay alive that the winning ticket was somewhere in Rosie's house. Fresh anger ripped through him all over again.

Never content to do one thing when he could do two at the same time, he flipped open the cell phone to retrieve his messages. There were four from Heather, each more agitated than the one before, and three from Hillary demanding to know when she was going to see him again. It was the last call from Heather that made the fine hairs on the back of his neck stand at attention. The police wanted to talk to him.

The meatball sub and the french fries went back into the paper bag. He scalded his tongue on the hot coffee but barely noticed.

"Son of a bitch!" he shouted, as his fist pummeled the love seat he was sitting on. The last call had come in from Heather at three minutes past six. It was now eighteen minutes past ten. He didn't want to call her but knew he had to. Just as soon as he could get his breathing under control. It took him a full ten minutes before he felt comfortable enough to dial Heather

Daniels's number. He tried to make his voice sound unconcerned and cheerful. "Hi, darlin', what's up?" Not bothering to wait for a response, he gushed on, "What did you do today? Anything exciting? You know, I hate paperwork, but I finally got caught up. Maloy might even be so happy with me he'll shower me with bonuses. So, tell me what you did all day without me at your side."

"Kent, the police were here. Twice. Daddy's got a wild hair up his butt, and he's on my case. Jack Silver's gun was stolen from his car while it was parked on River Road, not far from my house."

"What's that got to do with me? Hell, I barely know Jack. Just to talk to him at the gym sometimes. I think I can count on one hand the number of times I've spoken to him. You know him better than I do. What's he doing with a gun anyway?"

"I don't know, Kent. He had a friend with him, and money was stolen out of her purse. I didn't find out until a few minutes ago, when Daddy called me back for the tenth time, that the friend Jack was with is your wife. I guess that's why the police want to talk to you."

Kent struggled to whip some outrage into his voice. "Well, thanks for getting me involved in your mess, Heather. I hope to hell you aren't implying or even thinking I had something to do with stealing the man's gun. Jesus, I don't even know how to shoot a gun. Guns kill people. Now why did you go and get me involved in this? I was with you the whole time till I got sick. I hope you told them that."

"I did, Kent. I told them everything. Police are just naturally suspicious. You were there, and your wife was right next door. She's probably having an affair with Jack like you're having an affair with me. They probably find that strange, then Jack's gun is suddenly missing. Surely you can see the way their minds work."

"No, I can't see it, Heather," Kent snarled. "This is going to be all over town by morning."

"I'm sorry, honey. Daddy said I wasn't to dare lie to the police or him. I don't know who I'm more afraid of, the police or Daddy. And, honey, I had to tell them about the ten thousand dollars I loaned you. I didn't tell Daddy, though."

Kent started to sweat. "For God's sake, Heather, one thing has nothing to do with the other. You should have kept your mouth shut. I can't believe you were so stupid you told them about the money."

Heather started to whine. Kent clenched his teeth at the sound. "It wasn't like I volunteered the information," she said. "They asked me questions. Pointed questions. They asked me about your marriage, why it broke up, where you work, everything. They asked me about your financial situation. I had to tell them about your cell phone and the Buick. Daddy said you should never lie to the police. I didn't lie. Anything to do with a gun is serious business."

Kent broke the connection and turned off the cell phone. His insides started to quiver. With fear. He stripped off the skimpy towel and headed back to the shower.

There was nothing worse than the stink of fear, especially when it was your own.

14

The knock sounded on the door at twelve minutes past eleven. While Kent was expecting it, he still felt jittery. He didn't bother to ask the person on the other side of the door to identify himself. Instead, he threw open the door, allowing his eyes to grow wide and his eyebrows to shoot upward. "Yes?" He made a pretense of trying to look over the two officers' shoulders. All he could see were the lights in the motel's parking lot.

"Kent Bliss?"

"I'm Kent Bliss. What can I do for you at this hour of the night?"

"May we come in?"

"Show me some ID first." The officers obliged. Kent pretended to scrutinize the credentials. He nodded and held the door open so they could step into the efficiency. He motioned for them to sit down at the two chairs next to the round table. Both officers remained standing.

"What's this all about? It's rather late for a visit from the police. Am I supposed to have done something?" Kent was amazed at how brisk and professional his voice sounded. The air-conditioning vent spewed cold air that made the hair on the back of his neck dance. He stepped slightly aside as he was bare-chested, wearing only a pair of sweatpants.

One of the officers consulted his notes. "Were you out on River Road at the Daniels house over the holiday weekend?"

"Yes, I was. Unfortunately, I got sick and we had to come home early. Why?"

"Do you know Jack Silver, Mr. Bliss?"

"Well, sure. I have a membership to his gym. We aren't personal friends or anything like that, but we speak when we see each other. He runs a first-class facility. Why are you asking me these questions?"

Instead of answering Kent's question, the second officer asked another question. "Did you know Jack Silver was out at his house, which is next door to the Daniels house?"

"No. How could I know that? I didn't even know the house next to Miss Daniels's house was his until she told me right before we left. The only reason she even mentioned it was because smoke billowed over toward the Daniels's deck, where we were sitting. That's when

Heather said Jack must be there. Did something happen to him or his house?"

"His gun was stolen from his car."

Jack allowed surprise to show on his face. "What does that have to do with me? Oh, I get it! You think I stole it, is that it? Well, I didn't. I was with Heather Daniels the whole time. She can verify my whereabouts if you ask her. I didn't even know Jack owned a gun. Hell, I don't know *anyone* who owns a gun."

Both officers scribbled something in their notebooks. The first officer looked up, and asked, "Did you know your wife was at the Silver house with Mr. Silver?"

"No. How could I know that? What I mean is, I know it *now* because I spoke to Heather, Miss Daniels, a while ago, and she told me. Again, what does that have to do with me? Rosalie has her life, and I have mine. We're getting a divorce. Thousands of people get divorced every day."

"Is your divorce a bitter one?" the second officer asked.

Kent pretended to think. He opted for a semblance of the truth. "I guess on my part it was a little bitter back in the beginning. I didn't see it coming. I forgot our anniversary. Rosalie booted me out that same night when I got home. I tried to talk her out of it, but her mind was made up. Yeah, you could say I'm a little bitter. How would you like to live in this Halloween nightmare?" he said, waving his arms about to indicate the orange-and-brown decor.

"All right, Mr. Bliss, it's late. Stop by the station tomorrow and sign the report."

Kent nodded and opened the door for both officers. He waited until he heard their footsteps fade away before he double-locked the door and slid the flimsy chain into the groove. Then, he literally ran to the bathroom and threw up. Drenched in his own sweat, he turned on the shower again. While he waited for the water to warm up, he brushed his teeth with shaking hands.

If Heather Daniels had been standing next to him, he would have strangled her.

While he stood under the shower, Kent's mind raced. *Am I a suspect? Will the cops put a tail on me? Taking the gun was the stupidest thing I've ever done. Now I have to find a way to ditch it* and *the stuff I took from Rosalie's house. Jesus, what if they come back with a search warrant?*

Even though he knew he wasn't going to be able to sleep, Kent crawled into bed and stared at the dark ceiling, his eyes wide-open. *This is all Rosalie's fault.*

"I think it's time to go in," Rosie whispered in Jack's ear. "I don't want to give up this moment, but I'm getting cold. I have never been naked this long in my life. I like it," she blurted.

Jack burst out laughing. "Me too. We've been out here for *hours*. We made love twice. In an hour," he said, his voice ringing with awe. "I love it that we can talk about everything and anything and never miss a beat. It's like we're meant to be together. I just feel so peaceful, so content, so happy. And I know I feel that way because of you, Rosie."

Rosie playfully chucked his chin with her clenched fist. "Are you sure?" she teased. "I think maybe the food and wine have something to do with that contentment."

"You feel so good next to me."

For a brief moment Rosie was embarrassed. How could she have forgotten that she was stark naked? Just minutes ago she was feeling comfortable and happy. "I want to lose twenty more pounds," she said defensively.

Jack propped himself on his elbow. "I hope you aren't doing it for me. I love your body, Rosie. I love everything about you. I just want you to be healthy and strong."

"I don't want to lose the weight for you, Jack. I want to lose it for me. *For me.* I have to do this for myself. I made goals for myself, and I haven't reached them yet, but I will!"

It was midnight when the two naked figures wearily climbed the steps to the second floor. Both were shivering but laughing. The sound was an intimate one. They headed for the shower to warm up.

Buddy waited in the doorway. The moment the shower door opened, he beelined for the big bed, hopped up, and tugged at the coverlet until he had enough room to settle between the two pillows. His favorite spot.

Jack chuckled. "Do you think this means the only time we can have sex is under a garden hose? I see your dog has staked out his position."

"Yep, I think that's exactly what it means." Rosie giggled.

No amount of coaxing or cajoling could convince the big dog to move. He showed his teeth when Jack made a move to pick him up. "I don't think I ever slept with a dog before," he grumbled as he climbed into the big bed.

"He's warm and comforting," Rosie said

as she, too, climbed into the bed. "He usually goes to the bottom of the bed after I fall asleep."

"Fat lot of good that's going to do me now," Jack said, pretending to grumble. Rosie giggled again.

" 'Night, Jack. 'Night, Buddy."

Rosie smiled in the darkness when she heard Jack's light snore. She continued to smile as she thought about what had transpired. It was probably the most enjoyable, the most wonderful five hours she'd ever spent in her life. She continued to smile, wondering if she was falling in love with the trainer. More than likely, she decided.

She closed her eyes and was instantly asleep.

Jack Silver opened one eye, then the other, when he felt something warm and soft. Something that was moving, featherlike, across his abdomen. He closed his eyes, savoring the feeling. When he opened them again, he looked down at his stomach and saw a fat black tail swishing back and forth. Buddy. He grinned in the semidark room. He propped himself up on one elbow to stare down at Rosie, who was sound asleep. Little puffs of sound escaped her lips.

The memories of the night before slid over him. He remembered how good Rosie had felt in his arms. He remembered her delicious sense of humor, and he remembered how she'd given as good as she got. He continued to smile, wanting to reach out and brush her hair away from her forehead, but he knew he would be minus a hand if he even thought about touching the black dog's beloved mistress. A phone call later would have to do. Perhaps a note.

Jack wiggled to the edge of the bed, swung his legs over, and dressed. The dog looked at him but made no move to get up. He felt like a teenager when he blew Rosie a kiss. Either he was nuts, or he was still half-asleep, because he thought Buddy smacked his lips in return. As he walked down the steps he wondered if he was falling in love with Rosie Gardener. More than likely he was already in love and in denial at the same time.

Jack disarmed the alarm, waited two minutes, then rearmed it, giving himself twenty-five seconds to get out the back door. He waited on the porch until he heard the beeping noise that all was secure, the red light glowing brightly.

Rosie woke, uncertain what noise had penetrated her sleep. She rolled over, stretched, then realized she was naked beneath the covers. Last night's memories engulfed her. She craned her neck to see if Jack was still sleeping, but he was gone.

Rosie rolled back over and stared across the room at the light of the new day starting to filter through the window. She stretched like a jungle cat. How powerful she felt, how deeply satisfied. There was sex, and there was sex. And then there was sex with Jack Silver. She knew she'd been more than enough woman for him. She'd pleased him, excited him, taken him into the universe with her when they'd both exploded into one. For one wild moment she'd thought she had died until Jack gave voice to the same thought.

Perfect harmony.

Perfect everything.

She was far from an authority on sexual romps, but she knew it probably didn't get any better than last night. She felt like shouting her pleasure from the rooftops.

Rosie knew she should get up even though she'd made the conscious decision last night not to run this morning. She could run later, when the sun went down. She felt guilty, though, so she got out of bed and headed for the bathroom. This time she looked at herself in the mirror, trying to see what Jack had seen last night. She wasn't skinny, but she wasn't fat either.

Her hands clenched into tight fists, she beat on her chest. "I am woman!" she yelled at the top of her lungs. Buddy charged into the bathroom and skidded to a stop. Rosie started to laugh as she pulled on her robe and walked the big dog downstairs. She was about to open the door when she saw Luna Mae getting out of a taxi. She waved and ran out and down the steps to hug her housekeeper.

Rosie, her arm around the housekeeper, started to babble the moment Luna Mae finished paying the driver. She finally wound down, and said, "Check your room to see if anything is missing."

Luna Mae stopped on the front porch. "So, you went for it right there on the back porch?"

"Not *right* there. Over on the grass. Best sex I ever had. I still think I'm in orbit. How was your weekend?"

"Tip-top," Luna Mae said, avoiding her employer's intent gaze. "You look like you lost some more weight, Rosie."

"Probably," Rosie said happily. "I keep forgetting to eat. I'm starved now, though. How about if I make us some breakfast.

You've been flying all night and I've been
. . . doing other things. What would you
like?"

"Scrambled eggs and bacon. Toast with
soft butter. Coffee and a big glass of orange juice. I'll check my room while you're
doing that."

Rosie hummed under her breath as she
set about making breakfast. Sex made a
person ravenous. She hadn't known that.
Maybe because it burned off so many calories. She'd probably burned off *thousands*.
She was flipping the bacon for the second
time, the flame low, when she realized
Luna Mae was still in her room. She'd
been rather quiet, subdued actually. She
knew instinctively that something was
wrong.

Rosie knocked on the door, opening it at
the same time. Luna Mae was sitting on
the cedar chest at the foot of her bed,
crying. Rosie ran back to the kitchen,
turned off the stove, and raced back to the
housekeeper's room. "What's wrong, Luna
Mae? Oh, God, you aren't sick, are you?
What? I've never seen you cry. Dammit,
Luna Mae, what's wrong?"

"I'm leaving."

Rosie felt her heart flutter in her chest.
"W-when?" she asked.

Luna Mae swiped at her eyes, then blew her nose. "As soon as I take care of all my business. I hate leaving you, Rosie. You saved my life. I'd probably be dead now if it wasn't for you."

"Don't say that, Luna Mae. I'm sorry that I went off on you about that Curly person. I had no right to do that. I just want you to be happy, and if Curly makes you happy, then go for it. I don't know what I'm going to do without you, but I'll manage somehow. I don't want you worrying about me. Life's too short. All I want for you is happiness."

"You have Vickie, Buddy, and Mr. Silver now. You won't hardly miss me. I'll call you." Luna Mae sobbed.

Rosie wanted to stamp her feet and cry. "Yeah, but they aren't you. What do you want me to do? I want to do something to help you."

Luna Mae swiped at her eyes again. "Nothing. I don't want you to do anything. Just be happy for me. I want to walk away from here knowing you're okay with me leaving you."

"I'm okay with it, Luna Mae. You have to do what you have to do."

"Hey!" A female voice called from the kitchen. "Anyone home? It's me, Vickie!

Boy, I couldn't have timed it better. I love it when someone else makes me breakfast!"

Rosie heard her friend's suitcase drop on the kitchen floor.

"We're in here," Rosie called tearfully, her arm still around Luna Mae's shoulders. She quickly explained the situation to Vickie, and Vickie started to cry.

Luna Mae unwrapped Rosie's arms and stood up. "All right, that's enough crying. I'm not dying, just going away. I'll call and write. I thought you said you were making breakfast, Missy."

"I am. I am. Are any of your things missing?" Rosie asked, changing the subject.

"My cash. A few hundred dollars. And Skip's old Rolex, which had sentimental value. I think it was that *smarmy* husband of yours who went through all my belongings. Thank goodness I had my jewelry hidden in the tool drawer in the kitchen. I'm assuming it's still there. I'm going to change my clothes right now. I'll be ready for breakfast in ten minutes."

"Yes, ma'am," Rosie said. "I'm sorry that creep took Skip's Rolex. Maybe we can get it back."

Luna Mae rolled her eyes before she turned away, dismissing them.

In the kitchen, Rosie dropped to her knees to look in the tool drawer where she kept a pink hammer, matching screwdrivers, and other assorted women's tools. A pink velvet pouch was nestled under the pile of tools. She pulled it out and handed it to Vickie, who placed it next to Luna Mae's breakfast plate.

Rosie wiped her eyes on the sleeve of her robe. "She's really going. I didn't think she would. She's making a mistake, Vickie."

Vickie sat down on one of the kitchen chairs. "Don't do to her what you did to me, Rosie. Leave the door open. If things go bad, she needs a place to come back to. I'm sure, considering her age, she thinks this is her last chance at happiness. Listen, it might work. We could be wrong."

Rosie flipped the bacon one last time. "I know, I know. This is going to take some getting used to. She's proud, Vickie. If things go awry, she won't want us to know. My God, what if she ends up on the street again?"

Vickie fiddled with her paper napkin. "We'll stay on top of it, Rosie." She changed the subject. "Want to hear about my weekend?"

"Nope. Want to hear about mine?"

"You mean you have something exciting

to report?" Vickie leaned across the table, her eyes wide and sparkling.

"She had sex," Luna Mae said, coming into the kitchen. Rosie rolled her eyes. "And this house was broken into, probably by that husband of hers. She told me Jack Silver's gun was stolen from his car. I bet her husband did that, too!"

Vickie sat up straighter in her chair. "Wow! Those were the highlights. Now, give me the details, and don't leave anything out, Rosie. Not a thing."

Vickie looks so pretty today, Rosie thought. She didn't even look tired from her transatlantic trip. She wore a melon-colored summer suit. With the gold winking in her ears and around her throat, her summer tan looked like rich honey. She must have highlighted her hair either before she went to Paris or while she was there. The soft glistening curls around her face only enhanced her tan.

Rosie filled her in as she scrambled a dozen eggs and filled their plates. When she finally wound down, she looked shyly at her friend to see what she thought.

"Hot damn! Good going, Rosie! Happiness is oozing out of your pores. Boy, are these eggs good. I didn't eat much this weekend for the same reason you didn't, Rosie."

Rosie flushed a bright pink. Both women eyeballed Luna Mae. In unison they said, "Well?"

"You're thinking because there's snow on the roof that there's no fire in the chimney. Well, ladies, you are wrong." Luna Mae cackled.

Later, when they'd finished eating breakfast, the women sipped at their last cups of coffee. Vickie broke the silence. "Listen, Rosie, I was thinking on the flight over and on the flight back that I'm going to take over the business for you for the next couple of months so you can train full-time for your triathlon. Luna Mae has her seniors lined up to step in and help. They're due in tomorrow morning if I remember correctly. I can handle it, Rosie. I owe it to you for the three years I was gone and you did all the work. I want you to *win* that triathlon."

"Vickie, you're making it sound like I'm training for the Olympics. It's just a race, where you run, bicycle, then paddle a canoe. I can't let you do all the work."

"I won't be doing all the work. Luna Mae's people are going to be our new employees. I want you to go out there and be the best that you can be. I want to see you even more happy than you are right now. If you set your mind to it, Rosie, you can win that thing."

Rosie stared off into space, envisioning herself crossing some imaginary finish line. "Are you sure, Vickie?"

"I'm positive."

"Okay, I'll give it my best shot."

Vickie clapped her hands in glee. So did Luna Mae.

"I want to be the one to plan your victory party. Calvin is going to do his best to be here for Thanksgiving, so we can really do it up big. Luna Mae can come back for the holiday with Curly, and it will be a wonderful time for all of us. How does that sound to everyone?"

"Like a real plan," Rosie said.

"I agree. Now, scoot. I have to clean up this kitchen and do some laundry," Luna Mae said. "I'll call an agency and see about getting you a housekeeper."

"No! I don't want a housekeeper. I can manage by myself. Besides, no one could ever take your place, and I don't want anyone sleeping in your bed but you. No housekeeper, Luna Mae!"

"I'm not deaf. I heard you." Luna Mae rolled her eyes for their benefit.

Both young women could see the housekeeper was pleased with Rosie's declaration.

"Are you coming by the house today, Rosie?"

Rosie nodded. "I have to shower, do some paperwork, then I'll be over. I'll have plenty of time to do all the paperwork for the business, so don't give that another thought. Supplies are low. Orders have probably come in over the weekend. You'll have your hands full."

"I'm going to leave my suitcase here and pick it up later, okay?"

Rosie nodded.

"Hey, girlfriend, did I tell you that you look great?" Vickie said, then watched as Rosie blushed with happiness.

Rosie laughed as she headed up the steps.

It was high noon when Luna Mae tooted the horn on the van in front of the Simmons house. Vickie and Rosie watched in stunned amazement, their jaws dropping, as sixteen seniors climbed out of the vehicle, purses and knapsacks slung around their shoulders. Walkers, canes, and one wheelchair followed.

Luna Mae made a low, sweeping bow with her arm. "I bring you your new employees." She rattled off introductions. "The two in the front are the brains of the outfit," she whispered. "This," she said, "is Mitzi Glass, and this is Ben Black. They have the most spit and vinegar. Not that the others don't, they're just a little slow. Trust me, you'll want to give them a bonus when you see how they work."

"Ladies, gentlemen," Rosie said, extending her hand as she went down the line to greet each new employee, Vickie right behind her. Buddy, thinking it was a party, barked joyfully as he allowed himself to be petted and tickled behind the ears.

Mitzi Glass was a round ball of a woman with a hennaed topknot and bright blue eyes, which were sparkling behind granny glasses. She had rosy cheeks that weren't real and a set of dentures that positively glistened. She wore sneakers with holes cut in the side for her bunions and corns. A giant whistle hung around her plump neck.

Ben Black was tall and lean, with stooped shoulders and a dark brown toupee that was slightly askew. His eyes were denim blue behind trifocals that rested on his bony nose. No one was sure if his pearly whites were real or manufactured. He sucked on peppermints, his shirt pocket full of the wrapped candies. He doled them out to his friends, sometimes giving the ladies two. With hands as big as ham hocks, he offered them to Vickie and Rosie.

The whistle sounded. Rosie cringed, and Vickie backed up a step. "It has to be loud in case their hearing aids aren't turned up. Listen up, people," Mitzi barked. "This isn't a social. We're here to work. So, let's get to it!"

As the parade passed them, Luna Mae, her hands on her skinny hips, looked at both young women. "What do you think?" Not bothering to wait for a reply, she said, "I'm leaving you both in good hands. Oh, I forgot to tell you, you'll have to pick them up and take them home. They're up for overtime, too. See ya," she said, bouncing away. "Don't worry about me. I'll walk home. By the way, don't let their infirmities scare you. They're all sharp as tacks."

"Uh-huh," Rosie said, borrowing Jack's favorite comeback.

"I can see it working, Rosie," Vickie said, nodding. "I'm almost certain this is a good move. Age is just a number. They looked real alert. Sharp as tacks is good, isn't it, Rosie?"

"Uh-huh. Spunky. I like that. Okay, let's see what we can do," Rosie said, leading the way into the house.

Inside, Mitzi eyeballed Rosie, and told

her, "Luna Mae explained your business to us. We understand it. So, if you show us what you want us to do, I'll assign our people their jobs. We all have our specialties. We should probably put our lunches in the refrigerator if that's all right with you." Vickie nodded. "Ben, bring in our lunches."

"How we work . . ."

Mitzi cast a critical eye around the storage room. "Assembly-line style. Luna Mae explained all of that to us. Drying the weeds, spraying them to preserve them, spreading them out. We have to wear goggles. You need to relax, ladies, we do meticulous work. You won't be sorry you hired us. It doesn't look like you have much stock. Are you sure you have enough business to keep us busy? We agreed to this job because we need to earn money."

"You're right about our stock. Weeds are not as plentiful as one would think. At least the kind we use. My other two employees are in charge of product," Rosie said defensively.

"Then they're falling down on the job. Put us in charge, and this room will be filled to overflowing," Mitzi said firmly.

Rosie blinked. "Well, okay. Where . . . do you know a place . . . ?"

"Honey, I'm eighty years old. I know

where every weed in this state is. So do Fred and Estelle. If you have someone to drive them, they can be back here by the end of the day with so many one-of-a-kind weeds, they'll blow your mind. Do you have snake boots? We only have one pair between us."

"I do," Rosie said smartly. She looked at Vickie, her eyes full of questions.

"Okay, I'll drive," Vickie said.

"You should get a trailer hitch and one of those things you pull. That way we won't waste time, and we can have tons of weeds in various work stages," Mitzi called out.

"I'll get one," Rosie said hastily. "Just tell us what you need. You know, make a list."

Three hours later, while the seniors were eating lunch, Rosie made her way home, comfortable in the knowledge that Mitzi Glass had matters in hand. A germ of an idea started to form in her mind.

Rosie lowered her gaze to her watch. Almost six. The ten-mile run left her with sweat running down her cheeks and neck. She couldn't wait to take a shower. Buddy started to bark just as Vickie rolled into her driveway. She ran over to Rosie, laughing.

Overhead, a roll of thunder sounded. "Rosie! You are never going to believe this! We have enough product to last us through spring even if the buying public goes nuts! That guy Fred, the one who had his own snake boots, took me to places I didn't know existed. Three hours, Rosie! That's all it took, and we're loaded! They are *un-bee-leave-able!* They *love* working. And they work as a *team.* Mitzi cracks a silken whip. It's just perfect. The whole time they were working they talked about what they're going to do with their money. Hiring those seniors is the best thing for all of us. I just love it.

"They were all living in one of those re-tirement places. You know the kind. Some-times your kids visit, more often than not, they don't. They kind of banded together and moved out to this rental property, where they look after one another. All most of them have is their social security. Fred and Ben have pensions in addition to their social security, so those two are the heaviest contributors. The ladies cook and clean. John does the marketing. Everyone has a job. They work in tandem. And, Rosie, they have *ideas.* Helen thinks you should go global with a special catalog. They also think we should have an after-

Christmas sale catalog. And . . . they have hundreds of friends in the same position they're in."

"That's wonderful! Too bad they aren't interested in doing the bookkeeping," Rosie grumbled as she massaged her leg muscles.

"Ah, there is one person who used to be a bookkeeper at a tire company. She's a whiz on the computer. Why don't we try her out and see how it works? It would free you up for sure so you can concentrate on your fitness program. But best of all, you'll have more time to spend with Jack."

Rosie stared at her lifelong friend, a smile stretching across her face. "Okay. As long as you're comfortable with all this. Do whatever you want."

Vickie nodded. "Now, Rosie Gardener, I want to hear everything about your weekend. And I mean *everything*. You look happier than I've ever seen you. Are you falling in love with Jack?"

Rosie shrugged, then squealed with happiness. "In your wildest dreams, in my wildest dreams, I never thought . . . experienced such . . . oh, God, I don't know the word."

"You don't need words. Your face says it all."

Rosie sobered almost instantly. "Vickie, do you believe in the afterlife, or in things paranormal?"

"Spirits and spooks, that kind of thing? Yes and no. I have an open mind. Why are you asking?"

Rosie explained about Martha, the tree, the swing, and the moss. "While I was out at the river house I believed implicitly. Away from there, I'm not so sure. I think I felt her presence. I think she approved of me. Maybe I just want to think she approves because I care about Jack. It's a magical, for want of a better word, kind of place. Maybe I fell under a spell or something."

"What does Jack say?" Vickie asked curiously.

"He sees *signs* in everything in regard to the tree and swing, but he's okay with it. It's so weird, Vic. I wanted to get on that swing so bad. I was almost desperate about it. Jack said he tried sitting on it once, but Martha booted him off. It's *her* swing, *her* tree, *her* mound of moss, which, by the way, is as green and smooth as an emerald."

"I don't know what to say. What's the house like, Rosie?" Vickie asked as she tried to change the subject.

"It's beautiful. It has lovely French doors in every room. Curtains billow inward with the breeze from the river. The floors are magnificent, and it's full of antiques. Everything is old, worn, and so very comfortable. The kitchen is modern with a brick floor. Some of the nicest features are the deep window seats and the wide windowsills. If I lived there, I'd have herbs and flowers on all the sills. The verandah has bamboo blinds and a green fiber carpet on the floor with white wicker furniture. It's old world yet new world. The shrubbery is ancient, pruned, and lush. There are flower gardens everywhere. Each bloom more beautiful than the next. It's like a rainbow. The crepe myrtles were mind-boggling, all deep purple and deep crimson. Jack has a private dock and a boathouse. I loved it. It would be a great place to live and raise kids. Jack grew up there, you know."

"No, I didn't know. I hope everything works out the way you want it to, Rosie. Now, tell me about Kent, the gun, and the break-in."

Rosie's good mood changed instantly.

"Kent is no longer on my speed dial. I'm beginning to feel afraid of him, Vickie."

15

Kent's briefcase on the floor next to his desk drew his gaze like a magnet. He couldn't seem to keep his eyes off it. He'd wrapped the gun in two towels from the Days Inn and stuffed another towel into his briefcase so it wouldn't slide around. He had to find a place to stash it or get rid of it altogether. He'd toyed with the idea of wiping it clean and hiding it in Rosalie's garage in the middle of the night. Then he thought about driving back to River Road and tossing it in either the bushes or the river. His third thought was to take it apart and get rid of the pieces one by one. At the moment he was leaning more toward his second option — tossing it in the river. Just as soon as he felt safe enough to do it.

On top of that particular worry, he had an appointment with his sleazeball lawyer, and it probably wasn't going to be good news. Something about listing his assets and bills. He snorted at the thought. Obviously, there was no news on the Wonderball end of things, or he would have already heard something.

Kent tore his gaze away from his brief-case to stare at the stack of pink message slips lying on his desk. There had to be at least thirty, 90 percent of them from Heather and Hillary he noticed as he flipped through them. Not bothering to read the messages, he tossed them in the drawer and booted up his computer. He had to act normal. Whatever the hell normal was. While he waited for the computer to come to life, he buzzed the front-office receptionist. "Hold *all* my calls until I tell you otherwise. Just say I'm across town at a closing or something," he barked into the phone. He cursed under his breath.

A picture of an antebellum mansion ap-peared on his screen. Kent narrowed his eyes. He knew the house but couldn't place it. He'd seen it recently, but where? Was it for sale? If so, he had three Northern buyers who might be interested. He scrolled down to see who had the listing. Century 21. Four million dollars. A drop in the bucket to the Yankees who had buckets of money and wanted to claim a piece of history. If he sold it, he'd have to split the commission with the Century 21 gal. Half of something was better than nothing. Lillian Ormandy was the agent. He knew her. A loudmouth, obnoxious Chicagoan who took no prisoners. She was even greedier than he was. And she was long in the tooth, not to mention a good hundred pounds overweight.

As he continued to read the description of the property, his eyes popped. Of course, the last house on River Road, the property two houses down from Heather Daniels's house. The one Heather said was vacant or belonged to some estate. He'd had to drive all the way to the end of the narrow, private road because Jack Silver's car prevented him from turning around. He clearly remembered staring at the dilapidated building, wondering if it would ever go up for sale, and, if it did, who would be dumb enough to buy it.

His ticket to safety. All he had to do was call Lillian Ormandy, make arrangements to pick up the key to the lock box, drive out to River Road on the pretext of examining the house, and dump the gun in the river. It was the perfect solution to a nasty problem.

Kent spent the next forty-five minutes calling his three clients in upstate New York. Bob and Sara Schwager expressed interest when he told them there was a quilting room and a loom and a fully equipped workshop and a library with tons of books. The Logans said they could drive down in two weeks to take a look and requested a video. The Dennys said 4 million was a little steep and would have to call their business manager and get back to him. They, too, requested a video.

Kent's next call was to Lillian Ormandy. She told him he could pick up the key after lunch and had no problem if he wanted to video the property.

It was all almost too good to be true. He'd covered his butt as far as having a reason to go to River Road. The police could find no fault with his trip if they were watching him. For the first time in days, he felt good.

Kent was on his way to the kitchen for coffee when he heard his name called. He whirled around to see an angry Heather glaring at him. He sucked in his breath and led her outside but in view of his office window, where his briefcase sat.

"I want an explanation, Kent," Heather shouted.

Kent squared his shoulders. "That's my line. Don't ever screech at me again. It's not ladylike, and it certainly is not becoming. Do not, I repeat, do not, ever come to this office again and pull a stunt like you just pulled. I won't tolerate it. Now, if anyone has a right to be angry, it's me. What the hell are you trying to do to me? For starters, you never tell police anything. That whiny, schoolgirl confession of yours to the police has just put me on the hot seat. You need to grow up."

"But Daddy . . ."

"Screw your daddy. This is between you and me. Your father has nothing to do with me. If you were a real woman instead of a schoolgirl pretending to be a woman, you'd have the guts to handle your own affairs. *Our* affairs. You know what, we need to take a break from each other. I'm too angry right now to deal with this. We're both going to say things we'll regret; and then for sure it will be over. When this is resolved, I'll call you."

"But . . ."

"There are no buts, Heather. You screwed up. That's not something I take lightly. Where is your loyalty? I'll tell you where it is. It's with your father. Go there and cry to him. See if he makes you feel better."

"You're dumping me, aren't you? If you are, I want my money back, and the car has to be returned. If you don't listen to me, I'll go to the police and . . . and . . . make up something terrible." Heather stamped her feet in anger, her beautiful face turning ugly.

"Stop acting like a petulant child. I hate temper tantrums, and do not ever threaten me again. Do whatever the hell you want to do, but leave me alone." Kent shook his head from side to side. Finally, he threw his hands in the air and stalked back into the office. He didn't look back.

Heather sobbed as she walked back to her car.

Rosie shoved the papers she was working on to the side of the kitchen table so Luna Mae could set her plate down. Rosie looked at the mound of tuna salad, the little pile of crackers, and the apple. She grimaced. Food like this was a way of life now.

"Is Jack coming over for lunch, Rosie? I made extra." Luna Mae pointed to the bowl of tuna salad she'd just covered with plastic wrap.

"I don't think so. He just said he was stopping by for a minute. Go ahead, put it away." She took a bite of the salad and, good as it was, it tasted like sawdust. All Rosie could see or think about was the two big suitcases standing next to the kitchen door.

"Okay. I'm going to get dressed now. A taxi is picking me up in half an hour."

Rosie shoved her plate across the table. "I wanted to take you to the airport. I wanted to say good-bye the right way." Her eyes filled with tears. "You are so damn stubborn sometimes, Luna Mae."

"Now you know you'd cry and blubber and carry on, then I'd start to feel bad. This is the best way. You're starting to waste away to nothing, Rosie. I spent a lot of time making that salad for you. There's enough to last you for three days. Eat!" she ordered, a catch in her voice, as she left the kitchen.

"Yes, ma'am," Rosie said as she reached for the plate. Her eyes were wet. She wiped them with the napkin she was holding in her hand. She'd promised herself she wasn't going to cry, but it was a fool's promise, and she'd known that when she made it. She tried again to eat, but the food kept sticking in her throat.

Rosie was pouring herself a second cup of coffee when the door to Luna Mae's room opened. All she could do was gawk. Who was this person walking toward her?

"What do you think, Missy?" Luna Mae

asked, twirling around. "Curly's picking me up at the airport, and I want to blow his socks off."

"You . . . you're going to do that for sure," Rosie gasped as she eyed the trim, tailored Armani suit. Ostrich skin shoes and purse completed the outfit. "You look . . . breathtaking." Luna Mae had spent a fortune to blow Curly's socks off. She hoped the man appreciated it. "I . . . I like the way you made a coronet of your braids. You look elegant and beautiful. Oh, God, I am going to miss you so much! Promise to call me. Every day, Luna Mae. Promise! I want to hear you say the words."

"I promise," Luna Mae said solemnly. "You promised not to cry, Missy."

"I'm not crying," Rosie said, sobbing.

Buddy barked as he sidled up next to Luna Mae. He wiggled, his tail swishing furiously. Luna Mae bent down and whispered, "You take care of her, you hear me. If you don't, I'm coming back to swat you." Buddy threw back his head and howled.

Rosie held out her arms. Luna Mae stepped into them, all eighty-nine pounds of her. "Don't mess me up," she said, a sob catching in her throat.

"God forbid I should mess you up. Go

on, go. Hurry up! I can see the taxi."

Luna Mae looked over her shoulder, her eyes full of tears. She could see Rosie biting down on her knuckles. She waved. Rosie waved back.

Rosie closed the door and ran into Luna Mae's tidy room. She threw herself down on the bed and sobbed, her whole body shaking with the misery engulfing her.

Rosie rolled over when she felt the mattress sag. "Oh, Jack! Luna Mae just left to go live with Curly in Indianapolis. I promised myself I wasn't going to cry, and what do I do? I cry. I can't believe she actually left. I don't know what I'm going to do without her. The selfish part of me wanted her to stay, the generous part of me just wants her to be happy. Do you think she'll come back, Jack?"

"You left the door open for her to come back. It will be up to her, Rosie. Listen, I wish I could stay and comfort you, but I have to head for the airport myself. I'll be back Sunday night. I'll call you every night. I know you're hurting right now, but this is all about Luna Mae, not you. She deserves to be happy."

"I know that, and that's what I want for her. I just don't think it's going to happen. Where are you going, Jack?"

"Chicago, Minnesota, and Montana. I have to check on our gyms there. I hate leaving you like this. I'm going to worry about you, Rosie. Are you going to be all right?"

Rosie reached for a tissue. "I'll be fine once I get used to the idea that Luna Mae is really gone. You better hurry, so you don't miss your plane. I don't think anyone ever actually said they were worried about me. It's a nice feeling. I have Buddy." She was babbling and couldn't seem to stop.

"Here's the key to the boathouse. The silver key is the key to the house. Remember everything I taught you about canoeing. An hour. If the river is choppy, don't go out. Be sure to check the weather report. Are you planning to go out there today?"

"In about an hour."

"Make sure you tell someone when you do go out. That's a rule, Rosie. One you never break."

"I understand."

Jack leaned over and cupped her face in both hands. He kissed her lightly on the lips. "Are you going to think about me while I'm gone?" he whispered.

"Every waking moment," Rosie said honestly. She smiled tremulously. Jack kissed her again, more deeply this time. When he broke away, his eyes looked glassy. "I have to go."

"I know."

"I don't want to go."

"I know."

"I'll be back," Jack said, stepping away from the bed.

"I know."

"I'll call you tonight, okay?"

"Tonight is good." Rosie's head bobbed up and down.

Buddy, jittery with these strange goings-on, lunged at Jack to make him move faster. The minute he was through the door, the big dog used his rump to close the door. He then ran across the room and leaped on the bed. He lathered Rosie's face with wet kisses. She laughed.

"You aren't Jack, but you'll do." She hugged the dog, tussling with him before she got up to go into the bathroom to wash her face.

Sadness, then happiness. All within minutes. She stopped to ponder the thought. Back in June she wouldn't have been able to handle Luna Mae's departure. Back in June she never would have thought her world would continue without Kent in it. Back in June she never would have thought she could fall in love with someone like Jack Silver.

Maybe that's why it was called life.

Kent Bliss drove down River Road, trying to avoid the deep ruts in the narrow road. As he bounced along, he cursed under his breath. The damn road was a real kidney crusher. He pulled into the driveway as he skirted a young sapling growing in the middle, up through a deep crack in the concrete. Just to be on the safe side, Kent got out and opened the garage door, which creaked and groaned as the rusty hinges gave way. For some reason he expected to see all kinds of junk, but the garage was bare. There wasn't anything hanging on the walls either. Strange.

He drove the Buick inside, got out, and closed the door, the firm's video camera in hand.

Kent eyed the terrain. All he could see was a tangled mass of vines and overgrown shrubs. He hated the outdoors. The closest he ever got to real grass was when he played golf. He looked around again. It looked like a jungle to him. He was a concrete-and-glass kind of guy.

A cloud of gnats swarmed in front of him. He ran out to the road, knocking over the FOR SALE sign. He stopped to right it, then ran through the opening in the iron fence. The rusty iron gate hung drunkenly on one hinge. Four million for this white elephant. "I don't think so!" he muttered as he picked his way up the rotted wooden steps that led to an equally rotted verandah. The difference between this house and Heather's was like night and day. There was no way this property would go for four million. Not a chance.

The floorboards on the verandah were rotted through. He had to step carefully. If he fell through and hurt himself, he could be out here forever. Zigzagging this way and that, he managed to get to the door. He had some trouble with the lock box but finally got it open. He sneezed and kept on sneezing as, dust flying everywhere, he opened the warped and discolored plantation shutters. It would cost a fortune to refurbish this nightmare. His gut told him none of his clients would gamble on this one. Still, he had come here for a reason. He turned the video camera on and walked through the house.

An hour later, Kent dropped the video camera by the front door to make sure he didn't forget it and walked back to the kitchen, which was the last room in the old plantation house. What he could see of the back verandah told him it was in as bad shape as the front. There, though, the spindles from the railing were missing. They would also be impossible to replace.

Nevertheless, the view of the river was spectacular. The problem was, how to get to it. He had visions of snakes and alligators chewing at his feet and legs. A person could die out here, and no one would be the wiser. Maybe that's why Heather didn't like coming alone. Jack Silver was a different matter entirely. He closed his eyes and envisioned the trainer wrestling an alligator. He knew in his gut that Jack would be the winner. He'd probably skin the damn gator and have a pair of shoes made for Rosie.

Kent looked down at his Bally shoes, knowing they'd be ruined the minute he started to tromp through the underbrush. The closer he got to the river, the more sodden the ground would be. He'd be up to his ankles in mud and water moccasins within seconds.

Screw that.

Kent opened the back door and the squeaky screen door, its screening curled into a roll at the bottom, and stepped carefully out onto the verandah. All he could see were overgrown vines and trees.

Maybe he needed to cross the verandah to get a better view of the river and the neighbor's house on the left. He wasn't sure, but he had the impression it wasn't nearly as overgrown as this property. Then there was Jack Silver's property. Worst-case scenario, he could stash the gun somewhere over there. Let Silver try to explain that to the authorities if it was ever found.

Kent jerked to watchfulness when he saw movement out of the corner of his eye. Movement on the river. He squinted for a better look. *Well, what do you know,* he thought gleefully. *My wife in a canoe. All alone.* He cupped his hand behind his ear to pick up any sound, either Jack calling out encouragement or the dog barking. He heard nothing.

He backed into the house, knowing he needed to rethink his plan.

Kent picked up the video camera before he locked the lock box and carefully picked his way across the rotted floor and down the equally rotted steps, where he made his way through the gate and back out to the road. He laid the camera down and walked up the road to the Silver house. Rosie's car sat in the driveway. He crept up behind it, half-expecting the dog to lunge at him.

When nothing happened he grew bolder and made his way across the front yard. As he approached the huge oak with the mound of moss underneath, a fierce, galelike wind whipped up, pushing him backward. He stumbled, going down on one knee. *What the hell is going on?* He looked up at the cloudless blue sky. None of the branches on the other trees were moving. *Am I caught in some kind of dry vortex?* He struggled to move, but couldn't do so on his own, the terrible wind driving him farther and farther from the tree. He could see the swing attached to one of the thick limbs swinging wildly.

Finally, the galelike wind wound down. Kent looked around wildly to see where he was. He was in the driveway behind Rosalie's car, hardly knowing how he'd gotten there. He felt dazed, disoriented. He eyed the expanse of lawn again with suspicion. The only way to the front verandah or the back of the property was to walk across the lawn. He felt bruised and battered as he struggled to his feet. That's when he noticed that one of his expensive Bally shoes was missing.

How in hell did Rosalie get to the back of the house and out to the river? His head down, Kent gritted his teeth and charged across the lawn. This time when the wind whipped up, it grabbed him and tossed him all the way back to the driveway, where he landed with a painful thump. He looked at his feet. His other shoe was missing.

Fear, unlike anything he'd ever felt, shot through him. The swing was still moving crazily, higher than a swing should be able to go. He ran back to the vacant house, his heart pounding as he grabbed the video camera and headed for the garage.

Sitting in his car, the door locked, he calmed down. Silver's house must be haunted. What other explanation could there be?

And he still had the damn gun.

Kent hugged his arms to his chest as he sweated with fear. He lost time as he cowered in fear.

Finally, he was able to start the car and drive up the narrow road. He had to get out of there before Rosalie returned and spotted him. For one crazy moment he thought about lying in wait somewhere and shooting her.

Where in the hell are my shoes? If Rosalie finds them, she'll know they're mine. "Shit!" he fumed. *Is anything ever going to go my way?*

Rosie limped her way up the path from the river. She turned to look back, knowing she'd secured the canoe and locked the boathouse. Lately, it seemed she double-checked everything. She longed for a cold drink and a tube of liniment. She had a key and knew she could go into Jack's house if she wanted to, but she didn't feel right about it. She did stop long enough to sit down on the bottom step to rest.

It's so beautiful out here, so quiet and peaceful. And safe.

Rosie reached for the railing to pull herself to her feet. Time to head home and do her five-mile bicycle ride. She groaned. She'd do it, though. She made her way from the back of the house to the front and was about to cross the lawn when she heard the rustling sound in the big oak. She found herself smiling. "Hi, Martha! I was rowing. I hope you don't mind. I didn't go in the house, though. It looks like it's going to rain." *Am I nuts? If anyone saw me talking to a tree and a swing, they'd lock me up and throw away the key.*

The swing started to move, slowly. Rosie closed her eyes, imagining Martha sitting on it, moving her legs back and forth. "I never had a swing as a child. I had a metal gym, but it wasn't the same as a *real* swing like yours." One of the lower branches waved, then dipped, as though someone was sitting on it.

"I gotta go now, Martha. The next time I come out, tomorrow if the weather is nice, I'll sit and talk." The branch waved again, this time dipping lower. Rosie walked over. "Do you want me to climb on the branch? I could, you know, it's just low enough." Rosie watched as the branch moved even lower. She laughed as she scrambled onto the branch, her grip secure. She laughed again as the branch gently lifted upward until she was nestled in green leaves. "Oh, this is wonderful! I can see everything. Oh, oh, what's that? Oh my God, that's Kent! I have to get down, Martha."

The branch dipped and swayed as it gently bent down to the ground. Rosie jumped off and ran toward the road. She was just in time to see the taillights of a silver-colored car turn onto the main road. Was he spying on her? Of course he was. She thought about Jack's gun. She'd also forgotten to tell Vickie she was coming out here to River Road. *Stupid, stupid, stupid!*

Rosie was almost to her car when she heard the wind whip up again and whistle through the monster oak. Mystified, she looked around, thinking she was supposed to hear or see something. She saw them then, side by side, right next to the door of her car. A pair of Bally shoes. Kent's shoes. She should know, she'd paid for them. She hated touching them, but she picked them up, one at a time, and pitched them across the road into the underbrush. Then she had second thoughts, crossed the road, and rummaged in the brush for the shoes. She held them between her thumbs and index fingers before she tossed them onto the floor in the back of the car.

Rosie looked over her shoulder for one last look at the angel oak. There was no wind, the leaves and branches still. The old-fashioned swing was at rest. Rosie nodded, waved, then gave a tap to the horn. She looked through the window to see the same branch she'd sat on dip and sway. She laughed, a sound of merriment. "See ya, Martha! Thanks!" she called through the open window.

16

Back from her early ten-mile run, Rosie showered and dressed. She forced herself to eat her unappetizing breakfast as she scrutinized her day planner. She had an appointment with her lawyer, Kent, and his lawyer today. She also had a dental appointment, and Buddy was scheduled for his rabies shot. She was undecided if she should go out to River Road later in the afternoon or not. Certainly she wasn't going to go alone. Perhaps if Vickie could spare the time, she could coax her into going with her.

She wondered now if she should have told Jack what had happened yesterday when she'd talked to him last night. For some reason she hated talking to Jack about Kent. They'd talked for over an hour about everything and anything. Talking about Kent would have ruined her mood and the conversation. She smiled when she remembered how sexy she'd felt while she was talking to Jack, how warm her body had felt. She missed him. He said all he did was think about her. Did that mean they were in love?

Twice she'd started to tell him about her experience with the tree, but at the last second switched the conversation to something else. That, too, would have ruined the mood.

She'd been restless after the phone call and unable to sleep, so she'd gotten up and sat on the rocker with the warm night breeze that swept through the window cloaking her in a delicious ambiance she was at a loss to explain.

She'd thought a lot about Martha and finally decided it was a special, private experience and not to be shared with anyone. At least until there was some kind of a sign that maybe she should share. Maybe she just wasn't supposed to share it with Jack. Telling Vickie would probably be okay. A woman thing? Her overactive imagination? She simply didn't know. What she did know was she wasn't spooked in any way. That had to mean something.

Rosie started to tingle when she thought about taking Vickie out to River Road and having her take a look at the tree. Vickie had a good head on her shoulders. Maybe her friend would see or feel something she was missing. Then again, Vickie might think she was a total nutcase.

Rosie checked her watch. Time to head

for the meeting with Tim Donovan. She looked down at Buddy, who was sitting with his leash in his mouth. "Sorry, baby, but it's way too hot to leave you in the car. I won't be long, then we can go to the school and do our bike ride. My dental appointment is just a checkup. You'll get a good run, and all the kids will play with you." The dog tilted his head as though he knew that was exactly what she was going to say to him. He dropped his head between his paws, his leash at his side. Rosie offered up a rawhide chew that he totally ignored, as though to say, you can't bribe me.

In the foyer, Rosie looked at her reflection in the mirror. She was wearing one of her new outfits, a cranberry silk dress. She'd chosen it because it had a pretty gold-braided belt, and at last she had a waistline. She winked at herself. She knew she looked good, and she felt even better. She was a smart, pretty woman with only eighteen more pounds to lose.

One time after a particularly bitter quarrel with Kent, Luna Mae had said something to her she never forgot. She'd said, never fight with a boyfriend or a husband if you don't look good. Looking good gives you confidence. She'd also said, stand tall and don't slouch and do not ever let someone tower over you while they are talking to you. Luna Mae said that allowing something like that was gross intimidation. Something Kent excelled in. Well, not today or any other day. This wasn't the old Rosie Bliss. This was the new improved Rosie Gardener.

Rosie was almost to the door when she backtracked to the kitchen for a plastic grocery bag. She stuffed it in her purse before she set the alarm, then exited the house. In the car, she picked up Kent's Bally shoes and tossed them into the grocery bag.

She was going to get such pleasure out of returning the shoes to Kent in front of both lawyers.

The ten-minute private conversation with her attorney was not all that she wanted it to be. Rosie listened intently, her eyes sparking with anger. "No, no, and no. I'll deal with the lottery ticket in my own way. I'm not settling with Kent, I'm not paying him alimony, and I'm not giving him half of my private pension plan. No, no, no!"

The lawyer stepped back to get a better look at his client. This was definitely not the same woman who had first appeared in his office. This woman was a fire-eating *dragoness*. He was pleased with the thought until he wondered if there was such a thing as a *dragoness*. He liked the change in his client.

"I hear you, Rosie. Okay, let's go to the conference room."

Her head high, her eyes still blazing, Rosie followed the attorney to the conference room and sat down across the table from her husband. Kent was the first to look away. He did raise his eyes long enough to glance suspiciously at the grocery bag Rosie dropped on the conference room table.

Rosie listened while the two lawyers went at it with their legalese. To Rosie's ears it sounded just a little too civil for her. For all she knew the two attorneys were friends, although from the looks of Kent's slick-looking attorney, she wouldn't bet her pearls on it. They'd probably go to lunch together when the meeting was over. On her dime.

Rosie stood up. "That's enough! I'm sick of this. I'm not paying four hundred dollars an hour to beat around the bush." She placed the palms of her hands on the table and fixed her gaze on Kent. "Listen to me, Kent. You are not getting half of my private pension. I am not settling with you. Do you understand me? You broke into my house twice. I have a witness who saw you," she lied with a straight face. "You stole Jack Silver's gun out of his car, and you stole money and jewelry from me and

Luna Mae at the house and from my purse out on River Road. Just so you know, Kent, I have a private detective watching you twenty-four/seven," she lied again.

"In addition, don't you think it's time for you to give up on that Wonderball nonsense? I am going to file a harassment suit against you. Now, is there any part of what I just said that you don't understand?"

All Kent heard were the words *private detective* and *twenty-four/seven.* He stared at his wife as he tried to control his rage and the fear that was threatening to choke the life from him.

"Here!" Rosie said, sliding the grocery bag across the table. "Your shoes are in there! The shoes you left behind yesterday when you were out on River Road. I saw you, you son of a bitch! You were trespassing on Jack Silver's property."

Rosie turned her wrath on the two lawyers. "Here," she said, withdrawing a stuffed manila folder from her straw carryall bag. "Every receipt, every penny I gave this man is accounted for. He contributed nothing to our marriage. All he did was take and take and take. Add it up, and it will blow your minds. I-want-every-damn-cent back! Otherwise, I will go to Kent's employer, Jason Maloy, and ask him to garnish his wages. I will do that, and don't think I won't. The man is an alley cat. He feeds off women because he isn't man enough to take care of himself. He has no pride, no integrity, and, on top of that, he's *STUPID.*

"When I leave here, I am going to the police station to get a restraining order against you, Kent. Then I am going to tell the police how you broke into my house not once but twice. They're going to look at you real close, Kent. They probably have a tail on you, too. You now have a gun in your possession that you stole. In my eyes, that makes you a dangerous person because you're a hothead, and that frightens me. Your stupidity is exceeded only by your greed. I must have been out of my mind to have married you. Oh, one last thing." Rosie leaned farther across the table. "I'm going to make you look like the arrogant fool you are in that November triathlon because I'm going to beat you. You'll eat my dust."

I hope I did that right, Luna Mae. I stood up. I towered over him just like you said. I did my best to look good. I feel good. She worked her facial muscles into something that resembled a smile and said "Good day, gentlemen! I can see myself out."

The two lawyers looked at one another. Then, as one, they looked at Kent.

Flustered and frightened out of his wits, Kent stood up. He had trouble meeting the lawyers' eyes. "All right. Just file the damn divorce papers, and I won't contest it. However, I want to reserve my right or whatever it is you have to do in case Rosalie ever comes forth with that Wonderball ticket. I'm going to want my half."

Both lawyers watched as Kent reached for the grocery bag and exited the office.

The lawyers sat down when the door closed, legal pads in front of them, their respective Mont Blanc pens at the ready.

In the parking lot, Rosie pressed the remote to open the car door. Out of the corner of her eye she saw Kent approaching her. She held her arms out in front of her. "That's far enough, Kent! Just so you know, the private detective I hired is around here somewhere, and he's probably taking pictures," she fibbed. "Keep it in mind from this moment on. Every move you make is documented."

"You're crazy! I always knew you had a screw loose, but this just proves it," Kent snarled. "You better not go to Maloy with your garbage. Don't worry about getting a restraining order. I have no desire to get within spitting distance of you. To me you're still the tub of lard I married.

"In addition, *Rosalie*," Kent sneered, "I had a legitimate reason for being out there on River Road. The house at the end of the road is up for sale, and I went there to take a video for two different clients. I can show it to you and your lawyer if you want. I was walking up and down the road shooting different angles. Yeah, I stepped foot on Jack Silver's property, and some goddamn freaky wind whipped up and blew me all the way across the yard and also blew off my shoes. I know it sounds crazy, but that's what happened. I was not spying on you. Why would I? You don't mean anything to me. You never did."

Once those words would have burned her to her soul. *Freaky wind? A wind so strong it blew off Kent's shoes? Martha?* She forced a laugh she didn't feel. She'd think about that later. "You're looking a little ragged, Kent, not your usual snappy self. You need a haircut, your clothes are wrinkled. Dry cleaning is expensive, isn't it? What, no manicure? They're expensive, too. Is that a zit on your face? By golly, it is. I couldn't believe it when Vickie, Annie, and Danny said they saw you going through the drive-through windows of some of Savannah's finest greasy fast-food restaurants.

"Luna Mae told me you're residing at the Days Inn. My, oh my. How *can* you stay there? You were always so fastidious. Just thinking about all the people who slept in that bed doing God knows what? Roaches. All kinds of people doing all kinds of things in those beds. Probably doing things *you* wouldn't even *think* of doing. It just gives me the creeps thinking about it. You have a nice day, you bastard."

Kent shouted something, but Rosie couldn't hear once she closed and locked the door. She gave the horn a zippy three-note tap and sped off.

Kent sat in his hot car until the air-conditioning finally cooled it down. It shouldn't be so hot in early September. He turned the key and drove away, aimlessly driving up one street and down another. Where should he go? What should he do? He kept his eyes on the rearview mirror, hoping to spot the detective Rosalie said she'd hired. Of all the damn, dumb, stupid breaks. He was sorry now that he never watched cop shows and all those legal programs where detectives gave away their secrets. He could use the trick called "how to spot someone following you."

Maybe he should just go back to work and forget about everything except showing houses and making money.

His wife's words rang in his ears. It had all been so humiliating. He knew he was slipping, and he hated it. He'd always strived to match his appearance to his Porsche. He had to dress and look like a person good enough to own and drive a Porsche. People expected it, and he had been more than glad to comply. You could dress any way you wanted if you drove a leased Buick, just like you could wear overalls and drive a Toyota. Those vehicles simply weren't dress-up cars that shouted, "Hey, look at me!"

Kent steered the Buick into the parking lot of a strip mall and headed for the liquor store. He had his hand on a bottle of scotch when he realized he didn't really like scotch. He only drank it because it was a man's drink and fashionable at the same time. He moved his hand and picked up a quart of gin, an inferior brand given the price. At the register he bought two packs of cigarettes, paid the bill, and walked away. He was going back to the Days Inn to get soused. But before he did that, he had some heavy-duty thinking and planning to do.

In his room, Kent covered the small sofa with the skimpy towels. The ice bucket was full, and his bed had been made, so that meant none of the housekeeping staff would be knocking on his door. He opened the bottle of gin and poured it over the ice in his glass. He stared at the glass in his hand. Maybe he should have gone to the gym and worked off his anger instead of coming here to drink.

Dammit to hell, where does Rosalie get off talking to me the way she did? Like she's really going to win the triathlon in November. He snorted. *God, how I hate her.*

Kent downed his drink and poured another. And another, then still another. When he couldn't hold his eyes open any longer, he kicked off his shoes and crawled between the sheets.

Life is such a bitch, was his last thought before he passed out.

It was two o'clock when Rosie returned from the vet's with Buddy. She watched, smiling, when he went to his bed and lay down. Poor baby, he hated the vet and all the poking and prodding he'd done. He hadn't liked the two shots he'd gotten either.

Rosie was now free and could do one of two things. She could either go to the high school with her bike and do her five miles or she could go by the Simmons mansion to see how the seniors were working out. She opted for the seniors. She could bike tomorrow and really start her training with a hard-and-fast routine. She had no pressing engagements to interfere with her program.

Fifteen minutes later, Vickie's voice rang out loud and clear. "The boss is here!"

Rosie blushed as her new employees looked up, smiled, and waved.

"What are you doing here, Rosie? You're supposed to be training. That's what this," she said, waving her arms, "is all about."

"Tomorrow I start in earnest. I had an appointment with the lawyers. Kent was there. It wasn't nice. I wasn't nice. I had to go to the dentist, then take Buddy to the vet. I also had to go to the grocery store and the drugstore. Jack doesn't want me canoeing on the river unless someone is there with me. I thought about asking you if you'd go with me. Not in the canoe, but just so you can keep your eye on things." Rosie lowered her voice. "There's also another reason why I want you to go with me out to River Road if you have the time." She quickly explained about her experience with the tree and swing. Vickie's eyebrows shot upward, her eyes wide. "Can you leave them, or do they need you to be here?"

"Are you kidding! They are so on target it's almost scary. Come over here, I want to show you something. What do you think?" Vickie asked, pointing to a box made of thin wooden lath and filled with gold-and-silver pinecones. A bright red velvet ribbon finished the pretty box.

"It's gorgeous. Did you buy it?"

"No. Lettie made it. She went out in the yard when she finished her lunch and picked the pinecones. Sally sprayed them, and Mitzi made the bow. Ben made the box in under five minutes. No nails. He used super wood glue. The pinecones dried in seconds. Mitzi has some kind of gadget that actually makes bows. You'd be surprised at the stuff she lugs around in that satchel of hers. A person could set up housekeeping with what she carries around. What do you think of $49.95?"

Rosie looked surprised. "For that!"

"Yeah. It costs about thirty-nine cents to make. This yard is littered with pinecones. So is your yard and so is mine and practically every yard in Savannah. I took a picture of the box when it was finished, and Fred already added it to the Web site. That was a while ago. We got six orders that just came through. But I can top even that, Rosie." Excitement rang in her voice when she said, "Willie, the man in the wheel-chair, is a whiz with Web sites. His nephew showed him how to do it, and that's what he's been doing for the past year as a hobby. We now have animation on our site, and it's terrific! He geared it all to Christmas, with Santa, elves, and a sleigh loaded with our products. I'm telling you, Rosie, it's a work of art. The best part of all this is, all these ladies and gentlemen love what they're doing. Forget working part-time. They want full-time, and they are in no hurry to go home at six o'clock. They are worth every penny we're paying them plus more."

"This is just so awesome." Rosie laughed. "Does that mean you can go with me to River Road?" Her voice dropped to a low whisper. "Is there a reason why all of our new employees wear so much jewelry? Do they buy it by the pound?"

Vickie broke into hysterical laughter as she led Rosie out of earshot of their new employees. "It's magnetic jewelry. For their aches and pains. That's why they're so spry and upbeat. They have a magnet for every-thing. We had to do some organizing when we first got started because all our metal tools kept gravitating toward them. It's under control now, though. Who knew?" she quipped.

"That's great. I should get some for my knees," Rosie said, laughing. "Hey, if it works, more power to them. So, can you go with me or not?"

"Yep, I can go with you. Just let me tell Mitzi I'm leaving. I'll meet you in the car."

Shaking her head from side to side, Rosie walked outside to follow the path that led to the backyard. She looked up at the tall pines and down at the ground, where hundreds and hundreds of pinecones of all sizes lay. The magic of throwaway stuff.

Unbelievable.

Rosie parked the car, and both women got out to look around. "Oh, this is so beautiful, Rosie. I'm not being nosy, but how does a physical fitness trainer own something like this? Just maintaining it must cost a fortune. Do trainers make that kind of money?"

Rosie shrugged. "He runs the gym here in town and oversees the others. He travels a lot to make sure they're up to speed. I never got into financials with him. It's none of my business. We were just trainer and pupil until a few days ago. He did say he grew up here, so that has to mean the house was in the family. He lived here all his married life. Oh, I remember. Jack said that his father deeded it to him when he and Martha got married."

"What's it like inside?" Vickie asked, as she stretched her neck to look around at the landscaping.

"Really nice. Worn, homey, and comfortable. Kind of like Jack when you get to know him. It's the kind of house that screams out for a bunch of kids, a couple of dogs and cats. Maybe even a bird that sings in the morning. You can't see it from here, but there's a real nice boathouse with a cabin cruiser and, of course, Jack's canoe.

"Kent's new girlfriend, at least I think she's new, owns the house on the left. The last two on the street are empty. The very last one is for sale. Kent said he was out here doing a video for two customers. Since he said he could prove it, I guess I have to believe him. We have to cross the front lawn — that's where the tree and swing are — to get to the back. Come on, follow me. Whatever you do, don't step on the green moss under the tree. That's Martha."

Vickie rolled her eyes. "Gotcha."

A foot away from the tree, Rosie stopped short, Vickie bumping into her. "Hi Martha! I brought a friend out today. I hope it's okay. I heard what you did to Kent. I approve and want to thank you for that, too."

Rosie reached for Vickie's hand, her gaze going to the lowest branch. She smiled from ear to ear when it dipped and swayed. She could feel Vickie's nails biting into the palm of her hand. "This is Vickie Winters. We've been friends since we were little kids. Say hello," she whispered in Vickie's ear.

"Hello, Martha. I'm Vickie," she said self-consciously. She'd never talked to a tree before. *How silly can one person be?*

Both women watched as the branches, big and small, whipped upward and then gracefully slipped downward. They continued to watch as a single, lone leaf sailed downward to land in Vickie's outstretched hand. Her eyes full of awe, Vickie nodded. The tree rustled once again, then remained still.

"She likes you," Rosie whispered. Then she told Vickie what Kent had shared with her in the lawyer's parking lot. Vickie shivered in the bright sunlight. "It's okay.

Come on, I want to show you the river."

Rosie and Vickie crossed the wide expanse of lawn under the giant angel oak. Rosie pointed to the emerald patch of moss and smiled. Vickie shivered again.

"See ya later, Martha," Rosie called over her shoulder.

Neither woman spoke until they were on the dock. "Well?" Rosie said.

"Well what? Good God, Rosie, I don't know. It was . . . eerie and yet it was . . . was . . . uplifting somehow. Only one leaf fell." She opened up her closed fist. "It feels warm. Maybe that's from the heat of my hand. Maybe it was just a wind of some kind. You know, sometimes it rains and blows up in front of the house or across the street, and it's calm and dry in the back. That kind of thing. No, huh? Okay, I concede that Martha's spirit hangs out in the tree. It doesn't scare me, but it does make me jittery. You know me. How did that happen?"

"I don't know, Vickie. I can give you Jack's explanation. They were very much in love, but Martha died of ovarian cancer right here in the house. She used to swing on the swing, going as high as a swing can go. Jack would push her. The day before she died, she wanted to go out on the swing, and Jack carried her out. He gave her a little push and she kept going higher and higher of her own volition. He said she went all the way to the top and when she came down, she had leaves in her hand. He has them pressed into a book. I haven't seen them. He just told me that the other day.

"Anyway, Martha wanted to be cremated, her ashes scattered on the river. He did that, but he kept a little and buried them under the tree. He did it for himself, so he would have a place to go where she was. You know, to talk, to grieve. Then the moss grew over the spot. He accepts the moss as a sign that Martha is okay and looking out for him. However, she won't let him on the swing. He said that the one time he tried to get on it, she booted him off. I think it's okay to believe all this if it makes you feel better and enables you to go on without the most important person in your life." Rosie looked out over the river.

"I'm a believer now. I can only go by what I feel and see. I'm sure there could be another explanation, but whatever it is, it eludes me. I might have been a little more skeptical, but when Kent told me what happened, that turned the tide for me.

Okay, enough of this. I have to take the canoe out. I want you to sit on the dock and wait for me. Whatever you do, Vickie, don't set foot on the riverbank. There are all kinds of alligators around here. If one ever takes off after you, run. Zigzag while you're running. Gators can only go in a straight line. I didn't know that until Jack told me."

Vickie grimaced. "You're just full of information this afternoon, aren't you? Don't worry about me and gators. Are you sure you're going to be okay out there on the river by yourself?"

"Yes, I'm sure. Just sit there and daydream about Calvin till I get back. I always need help tying up the canoe. I can get it out okay, though. Don't put your feet in the water either."

"Yes, Mother," Vickie drawled. She watched as Rosie worked the canoe. She thought she was going to bust with pride for her friend when she saw the hard muscles in her arms ripple. She gave an airy wave as Rosie expertly maneuvered the canoe out to open water.

Vickie sat on the deck and hugged her knees. Every so often she turned her head to look at the top of the angel oak, which could be seen over the rooftop of Jack's house. She wished she knew more about the spirit world. Was it possible for a spirit to inhabit a tree and make overtures to *live* people? Obviously Rosie and Jack both thought so. If what Kent Bliss told Rosie was true, he was also probably a believer. Who was she to say it wasn't possible?

Vickie turned around again to stare at the treetop and saw it start to move. Her gaze ricocheted around at the other trees and shrubbery. Not a leaf stirred anywhere that she could see. The air was hot and still, stagnant really, and yet the treetop was gyrating back and forth. Vickie continued to watch, fascinated, her eyes wide.

"Okay!" she shouted. "I believe you're there, Martha. Nice to meet you!" The tree branches instantly grew still, then they moved upward till all Vickie could see was the underbelly of the leaves. She laughed then. Rosie was right, there was a comforting feel to what she was experiencing.

Vickie turned her attention back to the river. She could see Rosie in the distance. She waved.

Rosie was finally going to be the person she was meant to be.

17

Rosie was dreaming, she was almost sure of it. Why else was she being nice to Kent Bliss?

". . . Isn't it kind of late for you to be crying, Kent? You said you hated me. If you hate me and can't stand to look at me because I'm fat and smell, what is it you want from me? I'm fresh out of absolution."

"It was a mistake, Rosalie. I'm sorry. It wasn't you, it was me. Can't you see your way clear to giving me another chance? I won't screw up this time. I promise to work on all my shortcomings."

"Didn't you hear me, Kent? It's too late? I've moved on. I'm in love with someone else now. There's no room in my life for someone like you. You actually did me the biggest favor of my life. For that I will always be grateful. Now I know what it's like to love someone and have that person return my feelings. If you hadn't done what you did the day of our anniversary, and if I hadn't kicked you out, I would never have met Jack. To show my gratitude, I'm going to share my Wonderball winnings with you.

I won't give you half, Kent, but I will give you some. Are you agreeable?"

"What does 'some' mean, Rosalie?"

"I don't know yet. I have to talk to my lawyer and tax man. It will be enough to allow you to lead the lifestyle you want and crave. There will be strings and stipulations. You will have to agree to my terms."

"So you did win, and you lied to me," Kent said, outrage ringing in his voice.

"Yes. However, if I decide I can't trust you, the deal is off. There's no way you can prove I did or did not win. I don't need that kind of money, Kent. I prefer to work for what I get. I'll simply give the ticket away, then you'll get nothing."

"You're insane."

"I *was* insane when I met and married you. Now that I have my wits about me and think like a rational person, I know what my limits are. So, get out of my dream and bother someone else."

"You can't get away with this any more than you can win that triathlon in November."

"Wanna bet?"

"Yeah, I'll bet I can beat you, and if I do, you have to give me the Wonderball ticket. What's it going to be, Rosalie?" Kent pressed, an evil glint in his eye. "Remember, I have Jack Silver's gun. So, what's your answer?"

. . . Rosie bolted out of bed screaming the one word, *"NO!"* at the top of her lungs. Buddy backed up and started to howl, his tail sliding down between his legs.

Rosie dropped to her knees and motioned for the dog to come closer. "Shhh, it was just a bad dream. A real bad dream."

Buddy bellied up to Rosie and started to lick her face.

Rosie closed her eyes, willing her heart to resume its natural beat. She really had to do something about the Wonderball ticket. She took a deep breath and exhaled slowly as she tried to make sense of the dream.

For weeks now she'd been thinking about turning the ticket in and simply giving Kent half. Then she'd vacillate and think about giving half to the seniors. Every time she brought it up to Jack, he just looked at her and refused to comment. She really wished she knew what he thought. It wasn't that she wanted all the money for herself; she didn't. She was honest with herself — she didn't want to share it with Kent. She'd set a deadline of December 1 to decide what to do.

Was the dream she'd just had an omen of some kind? Dreams were supposed to be about a person's subconscious worries. Well, she was worried all right, that was for sure. But would she wager the Wonderball ticket on the triathlon race as Kent suggested in her dream. *Only if I'm a fool,* she thought.

Rosie looked up at the little bedside clock with the digital dates on it. She had a full month of training to go till the triathlon. The last seven weeks had passed in a blur. In another few days, Halloween would be here. How she'd loved that holiday when she was a kid. Vickie had loved it, too.

Her mind racing, Rosie led Buddy down the steps and let him out. While she waited, she made coffee. The moment Buddy barreled into the house they raced through the rooms and up the steps. Today, Rosie won for the first time. Buddy barked his approval.

"I'm just a lean, mean, fighting machine, Buddy. And, I'm forty-seven pounds lighter. And, I feel damn good." She tweaked Buddy's ears as she stripped down to take a shower. These days she did look in the mirror. She preened this way and that way, admiring her flat stomach, her firm hard breasts. Her arms were as hard and muscled as her legs. All the cellulite was gone. The best part of it all was she no longer lived to eat. She ate to live, oftentimes forgetting. Since Labor Day, she'd only cheated twice on the special diet, then felt so guilty, she'd worked out extra hours to burn off the calories.

Mentally, she wasn't the same person she'd been back in June and the months prior to her anniversary. She knew now that if something went awry between her and Jack, she wouldn't turn to food. She'd suck it up, pull up her socks, and get on with the business of living. One day at a time.

Her low self-esteem had evaporated on the wind once she'd stood up, admitted her shortcomings, and made a pact with herself never to go backward. She was poised these days, according to Vickie, and could hold her own anywhere. She had self-confidence, and she now owned a kick-ass wardrobe that screamed to be noticed.

She'd done it on her own, too. Well, almost on her own. Jack had steered her in the right direction, and Vickie had made it easy for her to train by taking over the reins of the business. She'd done the work, and she had the bumps, the bruises, and the calluses to prove it. "Yippee!" she shouted to the reflection in the mirror.

"Time to run, Buddy. We can't rest on our glory just yet."

She was running fifteen miles a day, biking for another five, then paddling up and down the river. Five days a week.

Could she win the triathlon? She thought so, but she wasn't sure. Most of the people who had entered worked out at the gym. According to Jack, she was one of only four or five who did their training outdoors. The others ran on treadmills, rode the stationary bike, and rowed on the rowing machine. The odds, he'd said, were in her favor since she was doing her training the *right* way. Then he'd said something that made her double over laughing. "Those guys aren't going to know what hit them when you take off." He'd beamed with pride at her accomplishments.

How she loved him. She'd skimmed all the sappy romance books, all the slick magazines, and what she'd read couldn't hold a candle to what she had with Jack. Jack was real. He was warm, honest, caring, compassionate, and said he loved her so much he ached with the feeling. Real words, honest words that he acted on.

The only bone of contention, if it was a bone of contention, between them was the Wonderball ticket. When she brought it up, a veil would drop over Jack's face. He absolutely refused to discuss it. It was the only negative between them.

As she ran, her mind raced. Due to the triathlon, they were having Thanksgiving dinner out at the River Road house since the foot race was the last event in the triathlon. Jack's father and uncle were doing the cooking and everyone who participated in the event was invited. Even the seniors and Vickie. She'd just sent Luna Mae a special invitation. Each night since she'd mailed it, she prayed that her housekeeper would return. They all had so much to be thankful for. She'd included the faceless Curly in the invitation. She crossed her fingers that Luna Mae would come to cheer her on.

"I'm going to win, Buddy! I really am!"

Vickie Winters gaped at the man getting out of the car in the driveway of the old Simmons mansion. Kent Bliss was the last person she expected to see on this dreary, rainy day. Her first thought was that he looked awful. Her second thought was that he was trying to do something about it. He looked thinner, and yet more muscular, like he'd been working out. What *did* he want? She waited expectantly as he knocked on the door and one of the seniors let him in. When he walked over to where she was standing, she said, "Rosie isn't here."

"I didn't think she would be. I came here to talk to you, Vickie."

Vickie crossed her arms over her chest. Body language that said, stay away from me and make it quick.

"I'd like it if you would arrange a meeting between me and Rosalie. You can be there if you like. I need to talk to her."

"About what?"

"Several things. Personal things. Look, I'm not looking for trouble. All I want to do is talk to her." He advanced a step and held out a card. "This is my cell phone number. Have her call me if she's agreeable."

"What if she doesn't want to see or talk to you? You're such a louse, Kent. Why are you doing this? Didn't you do enough to her in those three years? Why do you have to shove yourself at her like this? She's doing just fine these days without you."

"The question remains, will you ask Rosalie?"

"That's another thing, Kent. Why do you call Rosie Rosalie? No one else does. Not that I really care. I will tell her, but don't expect me to endorse the idea."

"All right, that's fair. The reason I call my soon-to-be-ex-wife Rosalie is because when I was growing up, our neighbors had a vicious pit bull named Rosie. It bit me when I was five years old. I had to have sixty-seven stitches. I almost lost my arm."

Vickie watched as Kent walked back to his car, her thoughts chaotic. Rosie was so happy these days. It sounded corny to say she was fulfilled, but that's exactly what she was. Talking to Kent might throw her into a tizzy, but Vickie had no right to ignore Kent's request. It would have to be Rosie's decision. If she didn't want to talk to him, she wouldn't talk. It was that simple. Still, Vickie stewed and fretted all afternoon until she walked over to Rosie's house after she dropped the seniors off.

Rosie was standing at the kitchen sink rubbing cocoa butter into the palms of her hands. She turned when she noticed Vickie standing in the doorway. "You scared me, Vic! What are you doing here? Want some coffee? I just made it."

"Nah, I'm *coffeed* out. The seniors drink it by the gallon, and they drink it black.

Must be all that magnetic energy or something. Listen, Rosie, Kent stopped by and asked me if I would ask you to call him. Here's his card with his cell phone number on it. He told me something today I never knew. I asked him why he always called you Rosalie, and he said when he was five years old, a neighbor's vicious pit bull named Rosie bit him. He had to have sixty-seven stitches and almost lost his arm. Did you know that?"

"No." Rosie continued to rub the cocoa butter into the palms of her hands. "Did he say what he wanted to talk about?"

"No, just that it was personal. You don't have to talk to him if you don't want to."

"I know that. I can handle talking to Kent these days. Listen, Vic, I had this dream early this morning. Maybe I had it because I've been thinking so much about that damn Wonderball ticket. When I'm running, biking, or paddling, I think about it. I've just about made up my mind to turn it in and give him his half. I just want to get rid of it. I don't care about the money, I never did. I've tried to talk to Jack about it, but he won't say one word. I'm taking that to mean he disapproves of the whole ugly drama that's sprung up around the ticket.

"This is what I've been thinking. I turn it in, give you and Luna Mae a really nice nest egg so that you never have to worry about your kids' futures. I'd keep a good amount to secure my own kids' futures in case I ever have kids. Then, I'd give the rest away to all kinds of charities. You know, the seniors, women's shelters, animals, children. Then there's Bobby. I promised to pay for his education, and I will honor that promise.

"I just can't see myself handing over that much money to Kent. He'll go public, I'll get all this unwanted notoriety that he will thrive on. I'm trying to find a way to share it with him without actually giving it to him. I know that doesn't make sense. Something like a trust that would give him so much a year to live comfortably on."

"For God's sake, why would you do that, Rosie?"

"Because I was a gutless wonder back then. Because I enabled him to continue to be who he is. I bought and paid for a husband, Vickie, then I chopped him off at the knees when I finally had enough. Was that fair? At the time, I thought so. I wanted him to feel the pain I was feeling. You know what, Vickie, it wasn't pain I was feeling, it was humiliation. Gut-level humiliation. Each of us has to take responsibility for our actions. If we don't, we never learn. I don't want to lose what I've struggled for so hard these past five months.

"You aren't saying anything, Vickie."

"He broke into your house, stole four thousand dollars and your jewelry, not to mention Luna Mae's money. And he stole Jack's gun. He has a gun, Rosie. Are you forgetting all that?"

"No, I'm not forgetting it. Unfortunately, we can't prove any of it. Now, if this were a perfect world, I would ask him to go away, relocate with enough money to live out his life. Since it isn't a perfect world, that is not going to happen, and I have to think of something else. The fact that Kent wants to talk to me has to mean he's about at the end of his rope. I think he might be looking to strike some kind of deal. Stop and think about it, Vickie. I'm in the catbird seat right now. I'm the one in control. He knows that, and he knows I know it. Great bargaining position from where I'm standing. I'll call him later. Let him sweat for a while."

"I don't trust him," Vickie grumbled. She looked around. "These flowers and plants are dying. Luna Mae would have a fit if she could see how you're neglecting her plants."

Rosie looked around at the yellowing leaves of the plants. "Was that just to have something to say, or did you mean it?"

"Both," Vickie snapped. "Do you have anything to eat?"

"Nothing you would like. Want to go out for some pizza and a beer? Once in a while it's okay to break the rules."

Vickie threw back her head and laughed. "Oh yeah!"

"Then let's do it! Maybe two beers!"

"Attagirl," Vickie said happily. "What about Jack?"

"He won't be over till he closes the gym. Around nine or nine-thirty. That gives us three whole hours for eating, drinking, and girl talk. Let's walk, though. I don't like having even one beer and driving."

"Fine with me." Vickie locked her arm with Rosie's. Together, they left the house and literally skipped down the street, young girls again with no worries.

Kent felt like an errant schoolboy when he stood before Jason Maloy. "It's slow, Jason. You know no one is looking for a house before Christmas. If you can't see your way clear to giving me the time off, then I'll have to resign. This triathlon is very important to me. You know what my life has been like these past five months. I need to get back on track. Five weeks, that's all I'm asking, Jason. Oh, yes, one other thing. Would you be interested in sponsoring me? It's for a good cause, and it's good publicity. I think I can win it, Jason."

Maloy pretended to think. It was true, it would be good publicity. Business was slow this time of year, so Bliss was right about that, too. Still, he hated doing favors for his jackass employee. He stroked his chin like he couldn't make up his mind. "What exactly will this cost me in terms of dollars, Bliss?"

"The thousand dollars to the purse, which goes to charity. Every sponsor has to donate a thousand dollars. A pair of running shoes for me, and an outfit. We all have to wear the same thing for the races. I don't know the cost yet, and it has to be purchased through the gym. Plus two hundred bucks a week for me until the race. You can deduct it from my next commission check.

"Jack Silver is throwing a Thanksgiving dinner at his house out on River Road after the triathlon. Everyone who participates is invited, and the press will be there. Like I said, good publicity for the agency."

"How confident are you of winning, Bliss?"

"I've been training for some time now, and I think I have a better than average shot of coming in first. To date, according to the posting at the gym, there are 225 entries. The newspaper is saying this is the biggest turnout since the gym's first race."

Maloy had read the same newspaper article, so he knew Kent wasn't putting him on. "Okay, Bliss, it's a deal." Maloy turned around so he wouldn't have to shake hands with his salesman. The bottom line was the guy made his skin crawl.

No one was more surprised than Kent when his cell phone rang at five-thirty. He said hello and waited. Rosalie's voice came over the wire, cool and aloof. "If you want to talk to me, come by the house at seven o'clock." The moment Kent got his wits about him and said, "Okay," the connection was broken.

Rosalie Gardener Bliss had an attitude.

Kent spent the next twenty minutes practicing looking humble in the agency lavatory's mirror. He filled the rest of his time diddling around and doing a crossword puzzle until it was time to leave. He allowed himself an extra ten minutes for the short trip to the house in which he'd once lived.

His heart was thundering in his chest when he climbed out of the car. He'd shaved for the second time that day at four-thirty because he had a date later with Hillary. He was dressed in casual slacks with a white shirt whose sleeves were rolled up just enough to show off his Rolex and his lingering tan.

He'd turned himself around by eating decent food and getting nine solid hours of sleep a night. The strenuous exercise regimen he'd put himself on gave him the glow of fitness and good health. He was still juggling Heather and Hillary, but he was in control, and that pleased him also.

When he saw her coming down the front steps he couldn't believe his eyes. His first reaction was that he'd pulled into the wrong driveway. He actually looked over his shoulder at both houses next door. The creature walking toward him was *ravishing.*

All Kent could do was stare at his wife, his mouth hanging open. He finally found his tongue and said with all honesty, "Rosalie, I didn't recognize you. You look *great.*"

"Is that another way of saying I'm not fat and I no longer smell?"

Kent had the good sense to look embarrassed. He also had enough sense to clamp his mouth shut.

This is one of those defining moments in life that will never be forgotten, Rosie thought as she walked over to where Kent was standing.

She'd taken pains with her appearance tonight because she was going out to dinner with Jack at a new restaurant in town. She wore lined, white linen slacks and an electric blue sleeveless silk top. A slender silky chain with a gold medallion on the end and a gold belt were her only accessories. High-heeled sandals made her appear taller than she was. Jack said she looked tall and willowy. That had been the single most wonderful compliment she'd ever received in her life. She'd almost swooned when he'd carried it a step further and said she looked sexy.

"So, what do you want to talk to me about, *Mr.* Bliss?" Rosie drawled.

"I'll get right to the point, Rosalie. Look, I know you have the winning Wonderball ticket. I know it in my head, in my gut, and in my heart. You don't want to share it with me, and if I was standing in your shoes, I wouldn't want to share it with me either. The past is past, Rosalie, we can't change it. What I want to do is make a deal with you. I heard the guys talking at the gym, Jack Silver to be specific. He thinks you're going to win the race next month. Aside from me, the rest of the guys and gals are a bunch of slugs. They'll be lucky if they finish the footrace. If I win, we split the ticket. If you win, it's all yours. We can draw up an official agreement."

"You're assuming I have the winning ticket, Kent. What if I don't have it?"

"I know you have it. You know what else, that kid Bobby knows you have it. His parents know you have it. I've talked to all three of them. They're taking the position you're going back on your word. The father wants to file a suit against you. I talked him out of it. You don't need that kind of bad publicity. Hell, it could ruin that nice little business you have. All that money, and you're trying to deny some poor kid who pumped gas all summer the education you promised him. Jack Silver isn't going to think very much of you when he finds that out, now is he? This town won't think very much of you either if the kid's parents file a lawsuit.

"I went one step further, Rosalie. I got in touch with the Wonderball's legal department, and if a lawsuit is filed, that's when they can run the numbers off that particular machine and it will show that all five of your tickets were bought within seconds of each other. Somehow, you managed to throw in a bogus one. The machine will also show the time at which you bought the tickets. See what I'm talking about here?"

Rosie felt her insides start to crumble. She could see what he was talking about all right. One of Luna Mae's ditties popped into her mind. She'd always cautioned her when it came to Kent. Never let him see you sweat, baby. It was right up there with always look your best and wear your good underwear when you fight, and never let a man tower over you in an argument.

"Let's say I agree with you, just for the sake of argument. I'm not admitting I have the winning ticket, so make sure you understand that. What do you say to this, Kent? Let's say you win, which you probably will because you're a guy and in good shape. Would you agree to donating 75 percent of your half to charities and good causes? If I win, I can do whatever I want with the money, and you get nothing."

"It's something to think about," Kent said carefully as he tried to keep the elation out of his voice. He needed a calculator.

"I'll tell you what," Rosie purred, "I'll call my lawyer in the morning and have him call your lawyer to set up a meeting for the four of us. Mind you, I am not admitting I have the winning ticket, so let's be clear on that. Are we clear on it, Kent?"

"Crystal."

Rosie looked down at her watch. "We're adjourned."

"Rosalie, wait a minute." Kent shuffled his feet, then blurted out, "Can I kiss you?"

Rosie didn't know if she should laugh or cry. For three long years she'd yearned and hungered to hear those words. Now, when she finally heard them, they were just words. She fixed her gaze on the man she'd lived with for three years. "Do you know what the word *kiss* stands for, Kent?" When there was no reply, she said, "*K*eep *I*t *S*imple *S*tupid."

Rosie carried the vision of her husband's stunned, baffled look with her as she turned and, without another word, walked up the steps and into the house. The moment the door closed behind her, she leaned against it and closed her eyes. *What in the name of God did I just do?*

18

What a beautiful restaurant, Rosie thought as she followed the hostess to a table with a magnificent view of the river and the boats sailing lazily to their docks for the evening. The decor was nautical and yet whimsical, with fishermen's nets, captain's wheels, and pictures of children catching fish. Supposedly the food, especially the catch of the day, was mouthwatering. Captain Tom's was the third in a chain of what the owner hoped would be seven restaurants spread across the South.

"Best view in the house," Jack said as he sat down across from her. "I do like a table with a real tablecloth and real napkins. How about you? You look preoccupied. Is something wrong, Rosie?"

She wanted to tell him. She probably should tell him. She was never good at keeping secrets. Instead, she smiled, and said, "No, why do you ask?"

Jack shrugged. "I'm pretty good at picking up on moods. Guess it goes with the territory. You look . . . stressed. Did I ever tell you what my mother used to do when she got bent out of shape? She swore that it worked."

Rosie leaned across the table and reached for Jack's hand. She smiled again, her entire face lighting up. She loved it when Jack shared things from his past with her. "Tell me."

"My mother would go to the open-air market and buy a watermelon. She lugged it home, cut it up, and took out all the seeds, one by one. She said it was a mindless thing to do, and by the time she was finished, whatever stress she was feeling would be gone. My father finally got the hang of it and had watermelons delivered to the house. Sometimes, it would take two watermelons to relieve her stress. Like the time I fell out of the oak tree in the backyard and sent the clothes she'd just hung out to dry into the mud. The clothesline broke my fall. I bawled my head off because Mom was more interested in the laundry than me. At least that's what I thought at the time. That was what my dad called a *twofer*. Then, Mom would make me and dad eat the watermelon. To this day, I hate watermelon, and so does my dad. We'll buy a couple on the way home, and I'll show you how to do it."

Rosie leaned back and laughed till her sides hurt. "Okay," she managed to say. She was going to add this to the Memory Book that she was keeping on Jack. Someday, when they were old, she'd show it to him, and they'd hug and smile at one another. Memories, at least some of them, were wonderful.

"Do you want to talk about *it*, Rosie?"

It. Rosie fixed her gaze on a picture of a sailboat with children hoisting the sail behind Jack's chair. "No. Not now. I'm fine, really. Let's talk about the triathlon. The local papers are giving you a lot of press. Vickie is sponsoring me through Nature's Decorations. I bet this is going to be your best year yet." She was talking way too fast, proof that something was bothering her. Obviously, she needed a watermelon.

"Looks that way. I'm betting on you."

Rosie's heart fluttered in her chest. "What if I don't win, Jack?"

"Then you don't win. The winning isn't important. It's how you play the game, Rosie. This is all about good health, fitness, building self-confidence, giving to others, and doing the best you can do. I don't give two hoots if you come in last. You're doing it, and you're doing it for all the right reasons."

But am I doing it for all the right reasons? Rosie's insides started to shake. She nodded because she didn't trust herself to speak.

"Have you heard from Luna Mae, Rosie?"

Rosie worked her tongue from side to side. "No, and I'm worried. It's not like Luna Mae either. I'm just hoping nothing is wrong. She usually calls once a week, and I haven't heard from her in three weeks. I've been calling every day, and I wrote, too, but so far she hasn't responded. I keep telling myself she went off on a trip with Curly What's-his-name, and she'll get in touch when she returns."

"I'm sure that's exactly what happened. Let's give her another week, and if you don't hear anything, I'll fly out to India-napolis and check on her."

Rosie's eyes filled. This man sitting across from her had to be the dearest, sweetest, kindest man she'd ever met. She offered up a tremulous smile.

"So, what looks good to you?" Jack asked as he opened the menu.

"The smashed potatoes with garlic and chives," Rosie replied, laughing. "Do you think if I have that, and the pecan-crusted salmon they will even each other out? Plus a salad of course. I'm also going to have those bananas that are coated in crushed pecans and then set on fire in rum and butter."

"We'll have to walk home, Rosie, to work it off," Jack laughed.

Rosie sipped at her wine. It was good. She took a second sip before she said, "I don't care. Once in a while you have to break the rules. Otherwise, there's no point to having rules."

"I couldn't agree with you more. Listen, Rosie, I . . . I want to . . . talk to you about something."

Rosie could feel her heart start to sink in her chest. *Please, God,* she prayed, *don't let him say something I can't handle. Please, God.* She struggled to work a smile onto her face. The smile was to encourage Jack to keep talking. It felt like her heart was sinking further when it appeared Jack had trouble meeting her eyes.

"Rosie, you know how I feel about you, don't you?"

Until a minute ago, she thought she knew. Nodding seemed to be her safest bet. Her mind raced. *How can I run out of here and still keep my dignity if he says something I can't handle? Where's the damn exit?*

"I never thought I could . . . feel . . .

want . . . I bought this," Jack said, fishing in his pants pocket. He withdrew a small jeweler's box. "I guess this is kind of stupid on my part because you aren't free. I saw it and bought it. It's a . . . what it is . . . is a ring that I want to give you when you're free. Doyawannaseeit?"

Rosie swayed dizzily in the chair. She reached out to grasp the ends of the table. "Uh-huh."

Jack slid the small box across the table. Rosie reached for the box and, with shaking hands, opened it. Nestled in a small bed of black velvet was the most exquisite marquise-cut diamond ring she'd ever seen in her life. She wasn't going to have to use the exit after all. Her eyes started to burn from what she was seeing and feeling. She wanted to say something, but she couldn't make her tongue work. Her mouth felt like it was full of peanut butter. This had to be the most wonderful moment of her life.

"Do . . . do you like it? When the time is right, will you . . . will you wear it?"

"Oh, yes, yes, yes. It's beautiful, Jack," she whispered.

Jack beamed. "Why are we whispering?" Jack whispered.

Rosie continued to whisper. "Because

. . . because it's a hushed moment. The kind you want to remember forever and ever." She fought with herself not to take the ring out of the box and put it on. It was the same feeling she'd had about Martha's swing. The time wasn't right. It was that simple. She slid the box back across the table and watched, her heart in her eyes when Jack pocketed the box.

"We aren't crazy, are we?" Jack asked.

"Boy, I hope not. The minute I'm free, the very second the judge says the word, I want you to put that ring on my finger. Promise."

"I promise," Jack said solemnly. "Will you marry me?"

This time Rosie had no trouble making her tongue and voice work. "Oh, yes. A thousand times, yes. I want that more than anything." She wished she had the nerve to hop up on the table and shout to the other diners that the wonderful man sitting across from her had just proposed marriage. She knew her eyes were wet, but she didn't care.

"Me too," Jack said hoarsely. "Then it's settled. When exactly will your divorce be final?"

"February 14. Valentine's Day."

"Then we're getting married on February 15," Jack declared.

Rosie felt a warm flush flood her entire body. In her life she'd never been as happy as she was at that moment. "O-kayyy."

Jack reached across the table to take both of Rosie's hands in his own. "If you're half as happy as I am right this minute, then we are on the first step to heaven."

Rosie squeezed his hands. Poor thing, he looked so flustered. She laughed again, and he smiled.

"I want lots of kids!" Jack blurted.

Rosie's eyes twinkled. "Do you now?"

"Uh-huh."

"How many is lots?"

"A houseful of little Rosies and little Jacks. Some dogs, a couple of cats, maybe a bird that sings in the morning. It's my dream for us, Rosie. I want us to live out on the river. Can you see yourself living out there?"

Could she? She wanted that as much as Jack did. "Oh, yes. What about . . ."

"Martha? It's all right, Rosie. I'll put away all the pictures and pack up her things. Anything less would be unfair to you."

"Oh, no! I don't want you to do that until you're really ready to do it. I would like you to keep that painting you have of her on the swing. I'm not jealous of her, Jack. If anything, I feel . . . I don't know what the word is, maybe, kinship or something with her. Another time, another place, had we met, I think she and I might have been friends. If her spirit lives on there, it's okay with me. It will be like she's watching over us and our family."

"God Almighty, how did I get so lucky as to meet you?" Jack said, looking awestruck.

"I don't have the answer to that, but what I do know is that the day you rang my doorbell was the best day of my life. Even though I hated your guts when you left."

The waiter arrived with their food, saving Jack from a retort.

Dinner passed in a blur for Rosie. Later, she couldn't even remember how the food tasted. All she could think of was the ring in the little black box and Jack's proposal.

Rosie started to get jittery all over again as Jack paid the bill. She should have told him about Kent.

Jack frowned as he cupped her elbow in the palm of his hand to usher her through the crowded restaurant. Something was bothering the love of his life. Something she wasn't ready to talk about with him.

"Let's go get that watermelon."

Rosie sighed. If only a watermelon could solve her problems. If only.

Jack pretended to huff and puff as he carried the fifteen-pound watermelon into Rosie's kitchen, where Buddy pounced on them both. They stopped long enough to tussle with the big dog before Jack picked up one of Luna Mae's wicked-looking carving knives. Rosie blanched when she saw that it was the same one she'd gone after Kent with.

"We need aprons," Rosie said.

"Yesss, we do!" Jack said as he plopped the huge melon into the stainless-steel sink. He waited while Rosie put hers on and tied another one around his waist. They were both bright yellow with orange sunflowers. "Very chic!" he said, as he whacked the melon with the knife.

Rosie took a deep breath. "Would you look at *all* those seeds! How . . . how long is this going to take?"

Jack grinned as he perched himself on the counter. "As long as it takes. My father and I eventually decided it all depends on how stressed you are. Maybe we should have bought *two*." A wicked grin played around the corners of his mouth.

"I think one will do. I need a smaller

knife." Jack handed over a paring knife with an easy-grip handle. Rosie dug into the watermelon with a vengeance. Jack watched, offering up advice when it came to the two thick rows of black seeds.

"Just scoop that right to the end, then run the knife . . ."

"Shut up, Jack! Whose stress reliever is this anyway, yours or mine? I hate wasting food with all the starving people in the world. Are you sure these seeds won't clog up the garbage disposal?"

"I have no idea. My mother didn't have a disposal when I was little. She just scooped out the seeds and put them in the trash. You do know you're supposed to cut up a lemon and run it through the disposal to take away the odors, don't you?"

Rosie flicked one of the thick black seeds at him. He caught it with an expertise that surprised her.

"So, is it working?" Jack winked. "Are you experiencing less stress?"

Rosie eyed the luscious melon and the rows of black seeds in front of her. There had to be at least a million of them. *That* was stress. She flicked another seed at him. Her gaze went to the two bowls full of the seedless melon. Maybe the seniors over at Vickie's would like it for lunch tomorrow.

"Rosie, did I tell you I hate watermelon?"

Rosie clenched her teeth. "At least ten times," she muttered. Suddenly a devil perched itself on her shoulder. Instead of digging her knife into the melon, she dropped it and reached down to scoop a handful of the pink fruit into her hand. She looked at Jack, then pitched it, hitting him smack in the nose. He howled his outrage as his hand dipped into one of the bowls. Rosie took the hit high on her cheekbone.

All hell broke loose, with Buddy running for cover as chunks of watermelon sailed in all directions. From his position at the side of the refrigerator Buddy could see his mistress take aim and pepper the man who was growling until he yelled for mercy.

"Who's going to clean this up?" Jack demanded. He answered himself by saying, "Since I don't live here, I guess it's you! Would you look at that ceiling!" A chunk of rind clunked him on his ear. "Okay, that's it! Now you're in for it."

"It? Is that what you said, it? No, no, this was your idea! I used to like watermelon. I am probably never, ever, going to eat watermelon again." Rosie danced away from Jack's outstretched arm. She saw him sway, windmill his arms, and then he was flat on his back and sliding across the slippery floor. In her wild dance to get away, Rosie, too, went down on one knee. She was reaching for one of the legs of the chair to get back on her feet when she felt herself slide backward. She struggled to roll over until she realized what was happening, at which point she rolled back over on top of Jack. Then she did what she'd always wanted a man to do to her, she took the initiative. Her mouth found his and she kissed him hard. When she came up for air, all she could see were Jack's glazed eyes.

A heartbeat later he was on his feet, and she was in his arms as he carried her up the stairs to her bedroom.

They shed their clothes quickly. And then they were on the bed, both of them burning with the desire to please each other. His hands were hot, searching, hers just as fiery and demanding. "Now," she gasped. "Now!"

Rosie woke with a start. For a moment she felt disoriented until she saw Jack standing in the doorway. He blew her a kiss that she returned. Buddy hopped onto the bed and proceeded to nuzzle her neck. She smiled as she tickled him behind the ears.

Jack returned to poke his head in the doorway. "Rosie, I don't want you running this morning. Do the treadmill. The rain is coming down in torrents, and the wind is whipping up. I think this is the tail end of the tropical disturbance they were talking about on the news. Promise me."

"I promise," Rosie said huskily.

"With all this rain, you can use your spare time to clean your kitchen. I'll call you." He ducked just in time to avoid getting clunked by the small travel clock on the bedside stand.

Jack laughed all the way to his car. He couldn't remember ever feeling happier.

Life took on a whole new meaning as the days and weeks passed. Rosie worked out with a vengeance from sunup to sundown, oftentimes forgetting to eat as she dropped off to sleep, only to wake up and start all over again.

She was returning home now from her latest physical, having been told she was in the best physical shape of her life. She was down to her desired weight, topping the scale at a mere 122 pounds. Dr. Benton said he was going to put a little side wager on her to win the race. Rosie felt her chest puff out with pride at his words.

Rosie fit the key into the lock, turned off the alarm, and headed for the coffeepot. She'd had to fast before getting her blood work done, and she was not only thirsty but starving as well. She'd just pressed the button for the coffee to start to drip when the phone rang. "Hello! . . . Luna Mae! Oh, my God, is it really you, Luna Mae? Where have you been? I've been calling and writing, and Jack even went to Indianapolis to find you. I'm pissed, Luna Mae! Say something! Are you all right?"

Rosie listened as Luna Mae explained that she'd gone to California with Curly to meet his brothers and sisters, who numbered eleven in the family tree. "They love me," she chortled.

"Why wouldn't they love you? You're a wonderful person when you aren't being thoughtless and uncaring. Do you have any idea how worried we've been? I know how old you are, and that you can take care of yourself." Rosie burst into tears. In between sobs, she blubbered, "You're supposed to be here to see me run and Jack has an engagement ring for me and he asked me to marry him. I wanted to call you and tell you, but you were . . . off meeting the family tree. . . . Of course I'm jealous. I love you like a mother, Luna

Mae. . . . Oh, you got the invitation and all the piled-up mail. What does that mean? . . . You are! You're really coming home! With Curly. You want to get married here in the house. Curly is retiring, and you and he are going to take care of me and Jack? Are you just saying that to shut me up or is it true? . . . True! Oh, God, Luna Mae, it is going to be so good to see you. Are you happy? . . . You're delirious? That's good. . . . You're going to cheer me on at the race? . . . Kent who?" Rosie laughed.

Ten minutes later when Rosie hung up, she sat down and cried with happiness. "She's coming back, Buddy. She's going to take care of us again. Not that we didn't do okay by ourselves, but it just wasn't the same without her." Buddy sat at attention, listening to his mistress. At one point, he raced across the kitchen to the door of Luna Mae's room, where he barked and pawed the door.

"Yes, Luna Mae is coming back. Guess you'll soon be getting all those treats she used to give you. This is wonderful, absolutely wonderful."

While Rosie sipped at her coffee, she dialed Vickie's and Jack's numbers to relay the good news. Neither one of them picked up their cell phones. She left a happy, cheerful message on both cells.

Before Rosie changed into her running clothes, she peeled and ate a hard-boiled egg, a fat-free yogurt, a banana, and a protein bar. Buddy chomped on a cheddar cheese stick.

Rosie Gardener's world was right side up.

Finally.

No one was more surprised than Jack Silver when he parked in the gym lot to see Kent Bliss waiting patiently for him to open the door. They made small talk as they walked side by side to the back entrance.

"Early day, Kent?"

"On a gray, miserable, rainy day like this no one wants to look at houses. Might as well work out. How's it going? Anyone new signing up for the race?"

"Don Connors signed up yesterday morning, but I haven't posted his name yet. There are a few others that need to be posted also. Time just seems to be getting away from me these days. It's going to be an impressive race this year. Just about everyone in town has entered. Good causes and all that. I doubt very much if more than a handful will cross the final finish line."

"You could be wrong, Jack. Most of the guys at the gym are pretty competitive. The women have their own reasons for wanting to beat us guys. I think it's going to be one lively race."

Why in the hell is this guy being so chatty? Jack wondered. The past few weeks he's seemed like a different person. Jack knew for a fact that Kent wasn't messing around because Heather Daniels constantly quizzed him about Kent's whereabouts. Hillary called on a daily basis checking on him, too. When Jack told Kent about the calls, he didn't seem interested. That alone was more puzzling than the change in his manner. However, it didn't change the fact that as far as Jack was concerned, Kent still had his gun. If Kent was up to something devious, Jack sure as hell hadn't been able to figure it out.

Jack switched on the lights to the main part of the gym. He parted company with Kent and headed for the kitchen, where he made the day's first pot of coffee.

Ten minutes later, the early birds, as he called them, were lined up at the door for their workout before heading for the office. This was the part of the day that he liked best, talking to the guys who were so gung ho to get their day off to a good start. He liked the easy camaraderie. Over the past month, even Kent Bliss had somehow become part of the team. He actually talked and joked with the guys. And, he'd stopped hanging around to watch the women's aerobics class. In fact, it seemed to Jack that Kent had sworn off women. On more than one occasion he'd wondered if Kent was going to make an attempt at winning Rosie back. Then and now, the thought sent a chill up his spine.

The other trainers straggled in and made small talk in the kitchen while they waited for the coffee to finish dripping into the pot. Jack stood on the side and listened as they kibitzed and grumbled. His ears perked up when he heard his best trainer, a young guy of twenty-six, start to extol Kent Bliss's accomplishments. "This guy is gonna take it hands down. I'll cover any and all bets right here, right now." He had no takers.

"What makes you so sure, Scotty?" Jack asked nonchalantly.

"The guy's a powerhouse. He's dedicated. In the beginning, he was just horsing around, like most of the guys. Then, all of a sudden, about a month ago, he hunkered down, and, I gotta tell you, he is obsessed with winning this thing. He's gonna do it, too."

A chill ran up Jack's arms.

"You know what they say, guys, the best man or woman, always wins. My money is on a woman this year."

"Would that be Rosie Gardener, boss?" the guys heckled good-naturedly.

Pride rang in Jack's voice when he said, "Yeah, it's Rosie Gardener."

19

Kent Bliss settled himself comfortably in a muddy-colored brown chair in his quarters, propped his feet on the coffee table, turned on CNN, and sipped at his Dunkin' Donuts coffee.

This was home whether he liked it or not. The truth was, he was getting used to the Halloween decor of the orange-and-brown suite. The past months had convinced him that he was never going to live high on the hog again. The realization had stunned him for all of thirty minutes or so. Then he'd hunkered down and tried to make sense of his life. Looking in the mirror, one of his favorite pastimes, convinced him that he needed to make life-altering changes. It was then that he forced himself to look deep into his mind, his heart, and his soul, and he realized he didn't like who he was. It was not a happy realization. He was fast approaching middle age. Definitely time to take stock of one's life and get on with living a good, decent life. He wondered if it was possible to make such a dramatic turnaround at this point in time. His thoughts took him to a place he really didn't want to go. Rosie. Rosie was his motivating force no matter how he tried to convince himself otherwise. If Rosie could turn her life around and make life worth living again, so could he. It was time for him to give up the playboy image, time to get back on track and contribute something along the way. Rosie again.

He couldn't keep going at full throttle, chasing other men's wives, cheating and lying just to make himself feel good. He had to close that chapter in his book and get serious.

Rosie did it.

He could do it, too.

He also realized there was no way to make amends for all the misery he'd caused the people in his life, especially Rosie. What that meant was, he would have to move on. The idea was not unappealing for some reason.

He was mesmerized by his wife these days. She'd changed and become a stronger person and, if she could do it, so could he. That knowledge and his subsequent decision had left him breathless. And, with that decision, he'd concentrated on the race as if it were the only thing that mattered in his life. Maybe seeing it through to the end would somehow validate him.

As Kent watched the international news, his mind wandered to the two H's, as he thought of Heather and Hillary. Before he left town, he'd have to settle up with both of them. Somehow, some way. It was important to him that when he left Savannah, he left with a clean slate. That meant giving Jack Silver back his gun. Making amends to Rosie, apologizing. As if an apology could ever make up for the way he'd treated her.

Kent settled deeper into the worn, comfortable recesses of the chair. It boggled his mind that he had no desire to go out and cat around. He felt good after training all day, ridding his body of all the toxins his trainer said were locked in his muscles. He was content, and looking forward to a nice hot shower, clean clothes, a good order-in Italian dinner, then eight hours of uninterrupted sleep.

He was no longer obsessed with the Wonderball ticket. His gut still told him Rosie had it. If she wanted to share, she would. If she chose not to, he would have to accept her decision. The truth, hard as it was to accept, was that he had no right to it. The other truth that was hard to accept was that he had no best friend. No guy he could call up to go have a beer with, no guy to slap on the back, no guy to go to a ball game with. His own doing, of course. Maybe the only way he was going to get a best friend was to get a dog the way Rosie had.

All his plans, all the wheels were in motion. The day after the race, he was moving on. A sad ending to a less-than-fruitful life. But still time to make a new one. There was no one to say good-bye to except maybe Rosie, who would probably kick his ass all the way to the highway. Then again, that wasn't Rosie's style. They'd probably shake hands, and that would be that.

One more week to go. One more week of intense training. One more week until it was time to say good-bye. He looked around. He was going to miss this crummy place. He really was.

Kent's thoughts took him in another direction as he tried to remember the last time he'd had sex. Even sex wasn't important these days. He wished he could remember the precise minute when his life had taken a 180-degree turn. Maybe someday when he had nothing better to do, he'd figure it out. Then again, maybe he wouldn't. Right now, it simply wasn't important.

His thoughts were interrupted when a knock sounded on his door. His Italian dinner. He smacked his hands together in glee as he stood up to open the door to accept the white bag with the green-and-red logo. He tipped 15 percent and closed the door.

Life was looking pretty darn good, he thought, as he spread out his dinner on the small round table in front of his chair. He switched television channels and watched a rerun of *Seinfeld*.

Rosie limped the last quarter mile of her morning run. Her right leg ached, and she didn't know why. Buddy came to a full stop and barked. Usually, at this point in the run, his mistress increased her speed and shouted to him to *GO!* He barked again as he waited for the signal that didn't materialize. He did a wild, dizzy circle, hoping to spur his mistress on, but it didn't work.

"I think I pulled a muscle back there somewhere. Probably when I came down on that rock that wasn't supposed to be there," Rosie groaned. "I'm doing the best

I can, Buddy." The big dog barked again as he fell in behind her. His snout nudged her on. Rosie started to laugh and couldn't stop. "It's not going to work," she gasped. "This is as fast as I can go. *Go!*"

Buddy looked at her as if to say, are you out of your mind? He moved ahead, sat down, and waited. When Rosie caught up to him, he moved again and sat down. It was a pattern he repeated all the way to the house, where he let loose with a bark that raised the hairs on the back of Rosie's neck. Someone was getting out of a taxi in front of her house. She gaped at the sight.

"Luna Mae!"

"It's me, baby. This is Curly. What's wrong?"

Rosie collapsed against the skinny woman, tears blurring her vision as she watched a butterball of a man crouch down to tussle with Buddy. He looked like Santa Claus. "What took you so damn long, Luna Mae?"

"We missed our flight yesterday. If I recall correctly, I did *not* give you my ETA. What I said was, you'll see me when you see me. Now, what's wrong?"

"I think I pulled a muscle. This can't happen, Luna Mae. The race is the day after tomorrow. You always have the an-

443

swer for everything. Think! What can I do?"

"Curly!" It was a declaration, an order, a command. The Santa Claus look-alike with the potbelly looked at both women over the top of his wire-rim glasses. "What can I do for you, darlin'? I'm mighty pleased to make your acquaintance, Miss Rosie. Luna Mae does nothing but talk about you." He extended a chubby hand with a magnificent diamond pinkie ring. Rosie shook it.

"Rosie pulled a muscle, sweetie. You got any of that liniment you used to smear on Skip and the others when they pulled muscles? If so, haul it out and let's go to work. My girl is racing the day after tomorrow, and we need her fit and rarin' to go."

To Rosie, she said, "Curly is better than any doctor. He's got cures for everything. He'll have you right as rain in no time. Trust me, baby."

Rosie hobbled up the steps and inserted the key in the lock. Curly stayed behind to carry up a mountain of designer luggage. "This is a *twofer*. I just know it," Rosie muttered as she headed for the kitchen where nine watermelons graced the counter.

Luna Mae eyed the fruit, and asked, "Are

you on a watermelon diet or something?"

Rosie explained Jack's theory about the watermelons as Luna Mae doubled over laughing. "Stop laughing, Luna Mae. It works. You'll see. He looks like Santa," she said, changing the subject.

"And he's rich. He loves every inch of me. He cooks for me. He makes the bed. I do the dishes. He also gives the best back rubs. Did I say he's rich? He bought Cisco when it was two dollars a share. Thousands and thousands of shares. He has other stuff, too. That ring on his finger, five carats. He kisses me all day long. He sings to me sometimes, and he reads to me in bed when we aren't doing *other things*. He just pretended to be poor so people wouldn't take advantage of his good nature. So, do you like him?"

"How could I not? He sounds like the perfect man for you. I can see how happy you are. That's all I want for you, Luna Mae. God, I missed you." Rosie threw her arms around Luna Mae's shoulders and hugged her until she screamed for mercy.

"I missed you, too, baby. As happy as I was, I still missed you. Curly knew that, and it was his idea to come back. We'll still go off to the races from time to time, but this or wherever you end up living is going to be home for us. We're going to be your loyal, devoted, family retainers. We both want to dandle your children on our knees. We'll make good grandparents, Rosie. I promise."

Rosie started to cry. Luna Mae crooned to her the way she had in the past. Eventually, she calmed down when Curly dug into one of the designer bags for what Luna Mae called his medical kit. Before she knew what was happening, Curly's short stubby fingers, which were like tensile steel, probed her leg, digging and rubbing until she thought she would scream. Then, miraculously, an hour into the massage, all the pain disappeared. Curly continued to rub and massage, then instructed her to go into the Jacuzzi and let the jets beat on the sensitive area. "We'll do this again in a few hours, into the night, and tomorrow, too. By race time, I guarantee you will be one hundred percent."

Rosie wanted to hug him to death. She told him so.

The little round man with the sparkling blue eyes laughed, and said, "Luna Mae now, she doesn't take kindly to other ladies hugging me. Get along with you. One hour in the Jacuzzi, then back down here for some more liniment."

"Yes, *sirrr*," Rosie said, saluting smartly as she made her way through the kitchen to the stairs that would take her to the Jacuzzi.

While Rosie soaked and pulsated, Luna Mae and Curly chattered like two magpies as they unpacked, stowed their luggage, then eyed the watermelons on the counter.

"I don't think I'd touch those melons, lovey. They serve a purpose for Miss Rosie, and you don't want to do anything to upset her. She's strung real tight. I could tell that the minute I started working on her leg. She kept eyeing those melons. Now, what's for breakfast, lunch, or brunch?"

"Good question," Luna Mae cackled. "What are you making, and it better not be watermelon?"

Curly kissed the tip of Luna Mae's nose. "What would you like, darlin'? How does an omelet sound? This refrigerator is rather bare. I can see we have to take a trip to the market."

"Just whip up some magic, honey. I'll make the coffee. Rosie does love her coffee, almost as much as you do. She looks wonderful, doesn't she? Aside from her injury, she looks happier than I've ever seen her."

"She's everything you said she was,

darlin'. I like this dog. Very protective. I like that, too. Set the table. Excuse me, please set the table."

"For you, sweetie, anything," Luna Mae said.

An hour later, the threesome sat down to brunch, Buddy's plate under the table.

"This is awesome," Rosie said as she forked the omelet into her mouth. "You have to make this for Jack. He loves omelets."

"It's the basil and cilantro," Curly said proudly. "I used to cook on the circuit. I'm really looking forward to meeting your young man."

"He'll be here soon. Downplay my . . . whatever it is that's wrong with my leg. He might want to pull me from the race. He can do that, you know."

"Only if you allow it," Curly said.

"Oh. All right. That makes me feel better. I'm entering that race if I have to crawl. Kent's racing, too, Luna Mae."

Luna Mae's brow furrowed. She made an unladylike sound. "A turtle and a greyhound. There is no comparison." The old housekeeper's voice rang with loyalty. Curly patted Rosie's shoulder. It felt comforting.

"I'm going to go over to Vickie's and check on the seniors. You said they're doing well. Are you still happy with the way things are working out, baby?"

Rosie reached for the sharp carving knife on the table. She gave a hard whack to one of the melons Curly had placed within her reach. First, though, he'd spread a layer of brown grocery bags to sop up the juice.

"This is mindless," Rosie said defensively, as Curly and Luna Mae stared at the speed with which she ripped at the seeds. "I don't know what it is about doing this, but it does work. See, I'm less jittery about my leg." To make her point, she wiggled her foot and leg. "Tell the seniors I'll send over this watermelon when I'm finished."

Luna Mae looked as dubious as Curly as they continued to watch the succulent fruit find its way into a large earthenware bowl. "I never really liked watermelon," Luna Mae said to have something to say.

"I hate it!" Rosie said vehemently. "Are you sure my leg is going to be okay, Curly?"

"I can almost guarantee it. We won't be long. You just sit here and wait for us to get back, and we'll do another treatment."

Rosie whacked at the melon again. A spurt of juice spiraled upward and plopped on the floor. Buddy looked at it with disdain. "He hates watermelon, too," Rosie said. "I'm calm. See, I'm really calm," Rosie repeated.

"I can see that," Luna Mae said tongue-in-cheek as she backed out of the doorway. "We won't be long."

"Take as long as you want. I have eight more melons to go. If I get that far," she muttered. "I'm usually in a stupor when I finish two."

Outside, Curly looked at his beloved and whispered, "You didn't tell me she had a watermelon fetish."

Luna Mae tweaked Curly's cheek. "That's because I didn't know, sweet cheeks. Are you sure her leg is going to be all right to run?"

"Yes, darlin', it is going to be fine. We'll put a pressure bandage on it just to be sure. Stop worrying."

Luna Mae dabbed at her eyes. "I don't want anything to go wrong. Rosie is happier than she's ever been. I worry about her. She's like the daughter I never had, so I have a right to worry."

"All right, then worry. Come along, dumplin', show me the way to Rosie's weed business. Weeds!" he said, throwing his hands in the air. Luna Mae chuckled as she linked her arm through his as they walked around the corner to the old Simmons mansion.

The seniors heard the footsteps cross the porch and looked up from their work. Mitzi quickly ran to the door to bolt it. "No more watermelon!" her cohorts shouted.

Vickie reached the door a second before Mitzi. "It's Luna Mae, and she doesn't have any watermelon!" Her voice rang with relief as she threw open the door to hug the housekeeper. "Thank God you are empty-handed."

Luna Mae didn't have to ask what she meant as she introduced Curly to Vickie and the seniors.

An hour later, Luna Mae held up her hands. "Girl, I cannot tell you how impressed I am. I never saw such a tight-knit operation."

"We owe it all to the seniors. They love what they're doing. We even put an ad in AARP magazine. The orders almost killed us, but we managed. They might be doing an article on us next year. There is one small problem, though. If any more watermelon shows up here, they're quitting! I just dumped the last three batches down the disposal."

"Well, Rosie has nine lined up on the counter as we speak. She hurt her leg this morning, and she's stressed out. Don't be alarmed, she's fine, and Curly said she will be able to participate in the race."

Alarm washed across Vickie's face. "Are you sure, Luna Mae? Rosie has worked so hard, trained just about every day for the past three months. She *needs* to be in that race. Do you think I should go over there and talk to her?"

"No, Vickie. She might take your visit as a sign that things aren't as good as Curly said they are. We need to downplay it. She's got the watermelons."

"It is kind of funny, if you think about it," Vickie laughed.

"It was hard not to laugh," Luna Mae giggled. "Hey, if it works, there's nothing wrong with it."

"Darlin', you are so right," Curly chirped. "Nice operation you have here, Vickie."

"Thanks, Curly. It wasn't in such good shape before the seniors came. Like I said, they love what they're doing. We wouldn't be where we are now if it weren't for them. We've had queries about franchises. I haven't mentioned it to Rosie because she has enough on her plate at the moment. I plan to talk to her after the race."

Vickie hugged the housekeeper again as she walked to the door with them. "Tell

Rosie I'll stop by after I close up. I usually do that anyway, so she won't think I'm worried about her. You do know Kent's going to be racing, right?"

Luna Mae's face darkened. "She told me. I'm not worried. Our girl looks fit, and I know she can do it. She just has to stay focused. That's the right term, isn't it?" the housekeeper fretted.

"*Focused* is the right word, dumplin'. Now, you said something about showing me this fair city. We both need the exercise. It was mighty nice meeting you, Vickie." He waved at the seniors, who waved back.

Two hours later, Luna Mae and Curly walked into the kitchen, both their jaws dropping at the sight of bowls and bowls of watermelon lined up everywhere. "I'm done for the day!" Rosie said dramatically. "I did four! Do you believe that? Four! Can you take it over to the Simmons mansion for me?"

"Watch this!" Luna Mae said as she carried one of the earthenware bowls over to the sink, where she dumped it in the disposal and turned on the switch. To Rosie's horror, she did the same thing with all the other bowls. "The seniors said they were going to quit if you made them eat any more watermelon."

"They said they loved it!"

"You're their boss. What did you expect them to say?"

Rosie started to cry. "Damn, I can't do anything right. Jack said this worked for his mother. It isn't working for me. I wanted it to work. I needed it to work."

"What you need, Rosie, is to sit there and tell me what's wrong while Curly works on your leg. Take it from the top, baby, and tell me every single thing from the moment I left. I'll make us some coffee, and it will be like old times."

Rosie talked and talked, then she talked some more. When she finally wound down, she looked at Luna Mae with tears streaming down her cheeks. "What if I don't win, Luna Mae? What if Kent beats me?"

"If that's your mind-set, Rosie, you're doing this for all the wrong reasons. This is all about you. It's not about Kent or Jack, me or Vickie, it's about you. Have you looked in the mirror lately, baby? You're beautiful. You're beautiful because you're happy, and you're in love. Do you think winning a race is going to change that? It isn't. So what if Kent or someone else wins the race. So what? It's all about giving it your best. Your best, Rosie. There can only be one winner. That doesn't mean the rest are losers. They aren't. You're only a loser if you think like a loser."

"That's what Jack said," Rosie hiccuped. "I need to win, Luna Mae. For me. Not for Jack, or in spite of Kent or anyone else. For me. I understand everything you just said, truly I do. This is my own personal battle, and I need to win it. Did they really say they would quit if I sent more watermelon over?"

Luna Mae looked at Curly. "She sounds like a winner to me. What's she sound like to you, sweet cheeks? Yes, they now hate watermelon. How does your leg feel?"

"Wonderful!"

"All right, young lady, get upstairs and into that Jacuzzi. One hour. We'll clean up the kitchen and toss these melons."

"Oh, thank you, thank you. Don't tell Jack, though."

"Baby, we wouldn't think of it. Scoot!"

20

Rosie stared at the dark ceiling. Why in the world had she thought she'd be able to slip into bed and actually sleep? With the race just hours away, she was wired so tight she felt like she was going to explode. She rolled over, swung her legs over the side of the bed, and walked to the rocker. There was no moonlight, no stars to be seen through the sheer curtains. On the late-night news the weatherman had predicted a light drizzle that was to start around midnight. She'd shivered when he'd droned on, saying the temperature was going to be unseasonably cool at fifty degrees for the next four days. In his short monologue, he'd used the term, *freaky weather* three times. "Perfect Thanksgiving weather," he'd chortled when the cameraman moved the southeast map to show viewers where it was already snowing in New England. *Freaky* was definitely the right term to use.

Seven more hours!

She was just too damn jittery. That was her bottom line.

What if she failed?

What if she disappointed . . . *herself?*

Worse yet, what if she made a fool of herself?

What if? What if? What if?

Rosie stood up and reached across the back of the chair for her robe. She might as well go downstairs and have some coffee and orange juice. Buddy got up, stretched, then padded over to her chair. He watched as his mistress lifted up the cushion to look down at the Wonderball ticket. In the end, after her house had been ransacked, she'd replaced the ticket under the cushion. It had turned out to be the safest hiding place in the house. Monday morning she was driving to Atlanta to turn in the ticket. In her mind, she likened Monday morning to the first day of her new life. As she crept down the steps, she couldn't help but wonder if she was being premature in her thinking.

Rosie pushed the swinging door that led from the dining room to the kitchen. She was stunned to see both Luna Mae and Curly sitting at the table eating breakfast. "Are you up early, or haven't you gone to bed yet?" she asked as she made her way to the coffeepot.

"Both," Luna Mae said cheerfully. "I turned the heat up." Her voice turned anxious when she said, "Will the rain and the cool weather affect you, baby?"

Rosie was wondering the same thing. She'd trained in the rain but not the cold. She forced a light tone to her voice. "I don't think so. A while back, we had two solid weeks of rain. I ruined nine pairs of running shoes. We'll all be running, biking, and canoeing under the same conditions. None of us will have an edge. Don't worry about me. My leg is good as new and feels fine. I can't thank you enough, Curly."

The rotund little man smiled. "I heard you on the treadmill at around eleven last night. Did you experience any stiffening or cramping?"

"Nope, and I ran at 5.0. I wish you two would stop looking so worried. I'm going out there, and I'm going to do my best. That's it. I'll live with whatever happens."

"Good girl! Where is Jack? I thought he'd be over last night."

"He had to go to Baltimore yesterday morning on business. He got in late last night. He'll be here around eight to pick me up. I told him not to bother because he has so many details to tend to, but he insisted. The Rotarians are all acting as volunteers, and he has to get that organized plus a hundred other details. This race has really turned out to be a huge event for Savannah. I never really paid attention in years past, did you, Luna Mae?"

"I'm sorry to say, I never paid attention either," Luna Mae said.

Rosie guzzled her orange juice and went back to her coffee. Buddy barked at the door to be let in. Rosie blinked at how wet he was. She stepped outside to see how hard it was raining. Hard. Really hard. And, it was damn cold. She shivered inside her warm robe.

In the laundry room, Rosie plucked two thick, thirsty towels from the laundry basket and proceeded to dry the big black dog. When she was finished, she reached for a third towel and laid it down by the vent in the kitchen. Buddy literally purred his pleasure.

"I think I'll take a shower now. By the way, I'm going to turn the Wonderball ticket in on Monday. Start making a list of what we can do with the money."

"What about . . ."

"Don't go there right now, Luna Mae. Monday will be time enough."

In the bathroom with the door closed and locked, heat spewing from the heating vents, Rosie clutched at her stomach. Nerves. Don't give in to it, Jack would say.

Mind over matter. *This isn't the Olympics, Rosie. It's a damn race. Chill out.* Easier said than done. She stripped off her robe and sleep shirt and stepped into the steaming water. It felt so good. A balm to her weary body. The cramps were easing up, too. *Jack is right, it's just a damn race. Why am I making this a life-and-death event? It's me. Some flaw in me. I worked so hard. I didn't weaken. I stayed the course, and on those rare occasions when I cheated, I made up for it. I did the best I could. I gave a hundred percent. I don't have any more in me to give.*

Why can't I accept what everyone is saying? Is it because I'm stupid like Kent said I was? Once words are spoken aloud, they can't be taken back. I bought into all that stuff he said, and I came to believe it. It's ingrained in me now, and I can't let it go. It doesn't matter if I get down to skin and bones, it doesn't matter if I have an earthy smell or not. What mattered then, and even now, is that someone thinks of me in those terms. Why haven't I been able to rise above all that? Why?

Rosie felt tears rush from her eyes as her slumped shoulders squared imperceptibly. "I don't want to fail," she blubbered.

A niggling voice in her head attacked her. *C'mon, c'mon, what happens if you fail?*

What's the worst possible scenario? Spit it out. Say the words out loud. No one can hear them in the shower. Let's hear it!

"All right, damn you. If I fail, I'll be all those things Kent said I was. I won't get a second chance. This is it for me. I get one shot at proving him wrong."

You don't have to prove anything to anyone but yourself. You're smart enough to know that. Why are you even thinking like this? Kent Bliss is not some god you have to appease or prove anything to. He's just a sorry excuse for a man. A man you had the misfortune to marry.

"I bought and paid for him. I didn't get my money's worth," Rosie gasped.

Aha! So that's what this is all about. You feel cheated, and now you want to win so you can rub it in his face. Will that give you your money's worth?

"Damn straight it will."

I hate to be the one to rain on your parade, but no, it won't. What happens if you don't win? Does that mean you didn't get your money's worth? Are you then going to arrange another race, another something, to get your money's worth if you don't win?

"Yes! I mean no, of course not."

You realize, don't you, that if you fail to win, as long as you have these feelings and thoughts in your head, it will affect your future relationship with Jack?

"No, it won't. I won't let that happen."

Then why didn't you tell him about the deal you made with Kent?

"Because that's my baggage, and Jack doesn't need to be burdened with my past. Now shut up and leave me alone."

Oh, no. No, no, no. You're afraid. Admit it. You thought because, as you put it, you bought and paid for Kent, that it was all right. You didn't buy Jack. Jack can walk away anytime, and you have no hold on him. C'mon, Rosie, back in the beginning, you thought Kent would come crawling back because of your comforting lifestyle and your money. And, of course, that fancy sports car. There was a very small window of time where you actually got up on your hind legs and said enough is enough. You took charge. You really did. You made him pay the only way you knew how. You chopped him off at the knees. In the end, you got your pound of flesh. Now, you're looking for another pound. It doesn't work that way.

"Well, if I'm as bad as you say I am, maybe I need a shrink to set me straight," Rosie snapped to the foggy mirror as she belted the robe she had slipped into.

Let the past go. It's gone. All you have is today because yesterday is gone and tomorrow isn't here yet. Let it go. You allowed it all to happen. Now you have to move on, and winning a race isn't going to make it one bit better. Ask yourself who you are, Rosie Gardener. You see yourself as a victim. A victim is someone who is helpless against a situation. You are not helpless.

Rosie picked up the wet towel she'd dried herself with and threw it at the foggy mirror before she marched out to her bedroom.

Soul-searching was not for the faint of heart.

Ten minutes later as Rosie finished tying her sneakers the phone rang, the ring exceptionally loud in the early morning. Who would be calling her at four o'clock in the morning? Kent? Vickie? Well, there was only one way to find out.

"Jack! What's wrong? Why are you calling me so early?" She listened, her brow furrowing. "Okay, I got it. I don't have a problem with the switch up, and, yes, I understand that you're under the gun. I can make my way out to River Road with Luna Mae and Vickie. I understand glitches happen, and there's no controlling the weather."

Rosie continued to listen to the man she loved. He sounded harried and stressed. "I have a couple of watermelons in the kitchen you can have," she quipped.

"It's going to take more than a couple of watermelons to calm me down. I was so sure everyone would want to postpone the race, but there wasn't one dissenter in the bunch, so we're on. The weatherman is predicting heavy rain for early in the afternoon, so we all agreed to get the canoe race out of the way first while the river is still calm. Less chance of the canoes filling with rainwater. You didn't sleep, did you?" Jack asked, changing the subject.

"I tried, but, no, I didn't sleep. How is everyone getting to the river?"

"Joe Mallory brought six school buses over to the gym. We've been working on this all night long. At this point, everything is ready to go, and of course there are some of the contestants who will make it to the river on their own. You're sure you're okay, Rosie?"

"Never better," Rosie lied.

"Then I guess I'll see you out at the river. Good luck, Rosie."

"Thanks, Jack. I love you."

Rosie smiled when she heard Jack groan. "I love you, too. More than you can ever know. Remember now, pace yourself. Don't worry about what anyone else is doing. Concentrate, focus, and do your best."

"I will, Jack. See ya at the finish line. I'm

not saying what number I'll be crossing it, but I *will* cross it."

"I know you will. Good luck, Rosie."

Rosie replaced the phone. A glitch. A glitch was a glitch was a glitch. So what if the canoe race came first. So what? All things considered, that might be best in the long run. She would be fresh, her torso strong. The five-mile bike ride, then the ten-mile run would take a toll on her. *Better this way,* she told herself. She hoped she was right.

Back in the kitchen she said, "Change of plans. That was Jack on the phone. We're doing the canoe race first, then the bike race, and the run last. Most of the contestants are going in the school buses out to the river. I told Jack we could get there on our own."

"Why the change, baby?" Luna Mae queried.

"Jack said hard rain is predicted for early afternoon. The river will be rough, and the canoes might fill with rainwater. Jack thought everyone would want to cancel, but that didn't happen."

Curly stroked his snow-white hair. "You look worried, Rosie."

"It's out of sequence. I know how my body responds to the training. I trained by running, then biking, then canoeing. This is backwards for me so, yes, I'm a little concerned. I hate being thrown a curve."

"Won't everyone else be in the same boat? No pun intended," Luna Mae said.

Rosie poured a second cup of coffee and knew she shouldn't drink it, but she did anyway. "Jack told me only a few other contestants trained on the river. The others used the rowing machines at the gym, assuming that they'd be able to make the transition from rowing a boat to paddling a canoe. The UPS guy did the river on weekends. He's like a Goliath. Jack said he was really good. Then there's Kent. Jack said he was just as good as the UPS guy. It's only a mile up and a mile back. It was supposed to be three miles, but that changed this morning, too. I can do it."

Curly was still stroking his white hair, twirling it between his fingers just the way Luna Mae did. "Luna Mae told me it doesn't matter if you win the canoe race or the bike race. The winner is the first person to cross the finish line after the run. Is that correct?"

"Yep. You would think that three races would mean three winners, but that is not the case. Whoever crosses the finish line is first. It's all about stamina."

Buddy suddenly reared up and barked,

then he stretched out again when the door opened and Vickie blew into the kitchen, her umbrella sailing out of her hands.

"I knew you guys wouldn't be sleeping, and I couldn't sleep either, so here I am." She headed straight for the coffeepot. "I'm starved," she said. Her words had the desired effect. Curly got up and headed for the stove.

"It's cold out there. And it's raining like hell. They might cancel."

"No. Jack just called." Rosie repeated for Vickie's benefit what the trainer had told her.

"That changes things. I have to call Mitzi and tell her about the switch. I'm picking the seniors up at eight. Guess I better leave at seven-thirty if I have to drive out to the river."

"Be sure to tell them to dress warmly. They're all staying for the dinner, aren't they?"

Vickie laughed. "The whole town will be there for that dinner. Last night's paper carried the menu. It said the elder Mr. Silver has been cooking for two days. I guess it's going to be quite a spread. Our local television station will be on hand, and of course the newspapers. This is big stuff." She grinned, then winked at Rosie.

"I hope someone has the good sense to make a video so I can send it to Calvin. He had to cancel being here for Thanksgiving at the last minute."

Vickie sidled closer to Rosie. "You have to shift into neutral, Rosie. You're way too tense. C'mon, relax." Her voice dropped even lower as she whispered in her friend's ear. "Today is no different than yesterday or the day before yesterday. You were ready and confident then. Today is no different, so don't go blowing it now."

Rosie grinned. "Okay, coach, I hear you."

"Good."

The foursome watched the hands on the kitchen clock as they chatted. At seven o'clock, Vickie stood up and carried her plate to the sink. "I gotta run. I'll see you down by the river. We'll be cheering you on, Rosie." She hugged her friend and whispered in her ear, "I want you to go out there and kick some ass. You can do it. Just stay focused. I have ten bucks riding on you."

Rosie waved as the kitchen door opened, a cold blast of air whirling into the room. She heaved a mighty sigh.

"We should probably leave around seven-thirty ourselves. There might be a lot of traffic. Is that okay with you?"

"Of course. Curly and I are going to get dressed now. Since you don't have anything to do, why don't you take care of the dishes?"

"Okay," Rosie said agreeably. Her mind raced, her thoughts full of the three phases of the race as she filled the sink with soapy water. It wasn't until she'd finished washing the dishes that she realized she could have loaded everything into the dishwater. *I must be nervous.*

Rosie waved to what she called her fan club as she made her way down to the dock, where all the canoes were waiting. Rain fell in a slow, cold drizzle. Overhead, thick gray clouds scudded across the sky. She felt chilled to the bone, even though she was wearing lightweight dark blue sweats. But she knew the moment she picked up the paddle she would start to sweat, and her body would heat up.

She was in awe at what she was seeing, swarms of people, shivering and doing their best to chat with the person standing next to them. Rosie felt her stomach start to knot up as she accepted her sandwich board sign, which she slipped over her neck. She was number 9. She felt self-conscious as she worked her way through the throngs of people. She'd never been this visible; in fact, she couldn't ever remember being in such a crowd of people. Some smiled, some waved. The UPS guy was doing windmills with his arms. He looked formidable. Almost as formidable as the choppy river she was eyeing uneasily. The river could be a dangerous place.

Rosie looked around for Jack but couldn't see him. Maybe it was just as well.

"Hi, Rosie."

"Kent!"

"What do you think of the switcheroo?" His voice sounded curious and in no way threatening.

"Maybe it's not a bad thing. The river isn't looking too good. We're going to be fighting it every inch of the way. What do you think?"

Kent peered off into the distance. Rosie thought he looked a million miles away. She ran in place to keep warm. Kent did the same thing.

"I don't think it's a bad thing either. If it rains any harder, the canoes will fill. Jack has some speedboats on the side. He put a lot of work into this."

"Yes, he did." Rosie looked around. "Who's the best of the best?"

"You. Me. The little guy from Home Depot."

Rosie stopped running in place to stare at her soon-to-be-ex-husband. "What about the UPS guy? Jack said he was a real threat."

Kent laughed. It was a nice sound, Rosie thought. "He's going to get motion sickness the minute he starts paddling. I was out here one day when he was canoeing, and he puked over the side. That's just my opinion for whatever it's worth. The Home Depot guy is the one to watch. I heard someone say he used to be a Navy SEAL. He has muscles and stamina you and I only dream of. Don't let that scare you, though. He was treated and operated on for tennis elbow a while back."

Rosie digested the information. "Aren't the women any good?"

Kent shook his head. "No torso strength. None of them are a threat. They're signaling us to line up. Rosie, good luck." He stretched out his hand. Rosie reached for it and crunched it. She thought she saw approval in Kent's eyes.

"Same to you."

It looks like a regatta, Rosie thought as she climbed into her canoe. It would have been nice if the sun were out and colored flags whipped in the breeze like at a real regatta, where all the ladies wore straw hats and were dressed in linen. She took a minute to look around. She saw the seniors holding signs that said GO ROSIE and YOU'RE NUMBER ONE! Everyone was dressed in rain and winter gear, with wool hats and gloves. The men and women standing on the riverbank and dock wore high rubber boots, most of them Wellingtons in bright colors. Vickie's were purple, and Luna Mae's daffodil yellow. They gave her a thumbs-up. Buddy, on his leash, barked shrilly. She still couldn't find Jack.

Rosie looked down the row of canoes. Kent was number fourteen and easy to see. The UPS guy was number four and on her left, the Home Depot guy was somewhere after Kent, number nineteen, she thought. Her gaze swiveled to the mayor, who was getting ready to fire off the starter's pistol. She gripped the paddle, squirmed on the hard seat until she had a feel for it. She sucked in her breath and was suddenly calm when she exhaled. "Just let me do my best," she whispered to herself.

The pistol fired, high in the air. A burst of orange light fizzled in the rain as 257 paddles hit the water simultaneously.

Concentrate. Focus. Don't look back or side-ways. One, two, in, out. One, two, in, out.

472

Rosie moved the paddle through the water. *Yin, yang, frick, frack. One, two, in, out.* She was holding her own as she continued to fight the rain and the choppy water. So far no one was pulling ahead of her. Minutes wore into eternity, her shoulders and arms screaming in pain as she dipped the paddle first on one side and then the other. *Concentrate, focus. One, two, in, out.*

I can do this. I know I can do this. I spent days, weeks, months doing this. I goddamn will do this. I will.

Rosie repeated her mantra to herself over and over as she moved forward. She was soaking-wet, the paddle slippery in her hands even with the gripper gloves she wore. No pain, no gain. She thought about the first time she'd paddled the river, with Jack showing her no mercy. *One, two, in, out, Frick, frack, yin, yang. I can do this. I will do this. I will.*

She saw it then, a canoe edging ahead of the straggly line. In the dismal, gray morning, she couldn't see the number on the contestant's back. *Kent? The UPS guy? Or the guy from Home Depot?* She hunkered down, breathing deeply as she dipped the paddle into the choppy water. *Stay focused. Stay focused.* And then she was alongside him. The UPS guy. Not Kent. Not the guy from Home Depot. The water was getting more choppy, the canoe bouncing along almost as though it had a will of its own. *One, two, in, out. You can do this, Rosie. You know you can. C'mon, c'mon, put some muscle in it. Breathe! Breathe!*

She passed him, and, out of the corner of her eye, she could make out the strain showing on the guy's face. He was giving it all he had, but still she'd passed him. She'd actually passed him. *Focus, concentrate. One, two, in, out. Now breathe!*

Fifteen minutes later she saw the bright yellow buoy bobbing in the water just feet away. It was the most beautiful thing she'd ever seen. She was going to lose precious seconds when she reached it and had to reverse her seat. Precious seconds could mean losing the race. She could do it. By, God, she *would* do it. She'd practiced the move a thousand different times until she could do it blindfolded. All she had to do was pretend this was another training session.

Just the few seconds it took to change her seat was such a relief to her tortured arms she wanted to cry. Crying was for babies Jack said. That was right up there with the damn watermelon seeds. Crying had always been a release. *Focus, concentrate.*

She'd made the transition and was

heading back up the river, fighting against the current. Her whole body cried out in pain as she whipped the paddle from side to side.

There was movement on the side of her. *Stay focused. Don't look. You can do this. No pain, no gain. Breathe! Breathe!* Whoever it was wasn't inching ahead of her, but he was staying with her.

The rain was coming down harder now, plastering the hair to her face and neck. She was almost blind from the water pouring down her face. No one was in front of her. Not yet. And then she saw the canoe nose ahead of her. *Oh, no. No, no, no.* She whipped her paddle deep, her arms screaming out a protest that she ignored. They were neck and neck, and she mumbled and muttered, refusing to give even an inch.

Rosie could feel the rainwater in the bottom of the canoe. It was ice-cold as it splashed around her bare ankles. If she had water in the bottom, so did the person abreast of her. Who was it?

A voice rang in her ears. Kent!

"You're doing good, Rosie!" *Oh my God, a kind word from Kent. Will wonders never cease.*

Of course she was "doing good," she was

now ahead of him. The good Lord must be watching out for her. Where were the guy from Home Depot and the UPS guy? Like it really mattered.

The next fifteen minutes were the longest of Rosie's life as she pulled farther and farther ahead of Kent. She prayed, then she cursed, then she apologized for cursing. Would she make it? When she heard the seniors shouting her name and saw the mate to the yellow buoy ahead, she wanted to cry all over again. *One, two, in, out. Stay focused. You're almost there. Almost isn't good enough. Harder, faster! Move, move! You can do this.*

The nose of the canoe moving alongside her was like a dragon breathing down her neck. She reached down to that inner core of strength Jack told her all athletes had and summoned it, demanding it rise to the surface. She crossed the finish line with the opposing canoe a hair behind her. She turned then. The guy from Home Depot. Kent was behind him.

"I did it! My God! I did it!" Now all she had to do was get out of the canoe and stand up. She didn't need to worry. There were so many helping hands she was literally carried up to the top of the riverbank, where her bicycle waited for her. As she walked, Curly and Luna Mae massaged her wet arms and neck.

"You okay, baby?"

"Yeah. Yeah. I'm okay. I did it, Luna Mae. Me! I really did it! Kent came in third. I gotta go."

"Not till you put these dry shoes and socks on. It will just take seconds. Starting out dry will make all the difference," Curly said. It was Curly's words of, "Trust me," that convinced Rosie to take the few seconds needed to put on dry shoes because she knew he was right. She'd catch up to Kent and the Home Depot guy. She still couldn't see Jack anywhere.

She was off, her arms and shoulders numb with pain, her friends' shouts of encouragement ringing in her ears. What she needed now were her legs more than her arms. The best thing she could have done was to put on the dry socks and sneakers. She had to remember to give Curly a big hug.

Rosie bent low over the handlebars as she sailed down the wet, slick road. She knew there were a gaggle of people behind her, but it was the two in front that held her interest. Men, Jack told her, had powerful, muscled legs, and that gave them the edge. "Well, we'll just see about that," Rosie muttered to herself.

The bike route was one long five-mile run with no hills or inclines of any kind, and that helped her speed.

The rain sluiced down as she sped along. She could see the oil slicks on the road and knew how dangerous they could be. The bikes could slip and slide and go down, and that would be the end of the race for that contestant. "Pace yourself," Jack had said. "You know what you're capable of, you've been training longer than anyone else. Just pace yourself and go for it."

At the three-mile marker she passed Kent and didn't look at him. At the four-mile marker, her legs cramping up, she was right on the Home Depot guy's rear fender. He lost a second when he whirled around to see who was behind him. She ate up his second and cruised ahead of him, her legs moving like pistons.

Off in the distance she could see a crowd of people at the yellow tape stretched across the finish line. She bent even lower over the handlebars and forced her tired legs to pedal even faster. The rain was falling so hard she could barely see ahead of her, but she sensed when the cyclist from Home Depot was once again abreast of her. Rosie sucked in her breath and forged ahead, her legs moving at the speed of light. She pulled ahead, her body protesting every second. She tossed her head to get the rain out of her face, hoping it would enable her to see better. It didn't help.

Behind her she heard Kent shout. "Go, Rosie, go! Don't let that guy beat you. Go! You can do it!"

Stunned at what she was hearing, Rosie gave one last violent push and crossed the finish line, the yellow tape catching her in the throat. The Home Depot guy came in second and Kent took third place. She literally fell off the bike into Luna Mae's arms. All she wanted was to lie down and go to sleep. She said so.

"Sorry, baby, you have ten more miles to go. Come on now, dry shoes and socks and a dry shirt. I know it's going to get soaked in a minute but Curly says you have to start off dry. It helped you the last time. There's no time for modesty. Hold up your arms." The swell of people around her allowed Rosie to undress and dress within seconds. She felt a little better as she gulped a glass of orange juice.

"Have you seen Jack?" Rosie managed to gasp.

"Every now and then. I don't think he wants to distract you. How bad is it, baby?"

Rosie looked at Luna Mae. "I want to cry. Don't worry, I won't. Kent encouraged me to beat that guy from Home Depot. I wish you could have heard him."

"No thanks. They're starting off. Just so you know, I heard someone say a few minutes ago that the race is now down to twenty-three people. Two-thirds of the contestants wiped out in the canoe race. Guess they couldn't make the seat change successfully. The UPS guy you were worrying about fell into the river. They're picking up mangled bikes behind you. Good luck, baby. We'll see you for dinner when the race is over. I've got a bag of clean, dry clothes for you."

Vickie appeared out of nowhere to hug Rosie. "You are something else, my friend. I am so proud of you I could just bust!"

"Vic, I am so tired. I don't know if I can finish this. I hurt."

Vickie's head bobbed up and down. "I know, Rosie. All you can do is give it your best shot. Go on now. Those guys out there are a bunch of slugs. You're a *woman.* You can do it!"

"I hope you're right." Rosie stepped out from under the golf umbrella Vickie was holding and started off.

Pain was something she couldn't think

about as she ordered her feet and legs to obey her. Up ahead she saw faint splashes of color through the rain. She had no idea how many people were still in the race. Kent and the Home Depot guy for sure. She thought she saw the owner of the bakery pass by while she was changing, but it was just a fleeting glance. Whoever it was didn't matter anyway. The fact that there were people ahead of her was all that mattered.

Pace yourself. The first thing Jack had taught her. What he hadn't taught her was how to survive and win during a rainstorm, and it was now a full-blown rainstorm. The sky was almost black. Even the streetlights had come on. It wasn't that she'd never run or trained in the rain — she had — but the rain had been nothing more than a light drizzle with wet pavement. The rain on the ground beneath her feet was over the soles of her sneakers. Deep puddles were everywhere. Her sodden clothes plus her soaking-wet sneakers added to the weight she had to carry while she struggled.

Rosie did her best to pump her arms, but they felt like lead weights. She would have killed for a steaming-hot shower. Head down, she trudged on.

You call this running! I-don't-think-so. Jack is going to be so disappointed in you, said a niggling voice inside her head.

Rosie struggled with the rain slapping at her front and back. "This damn race should have been called off. Do not even presume to tell me what I am or am not doing," Rosie gasped. Her reward was a mouthful of rain. She spit it out and increased her tempo. "For your information, conscience, I guess that's who you are, I have blisters on my feet. Bad blisters. I'm probably raw down to the bone."

Tsk, tsk. You're whining. A sorry excuse for a runner. You're a slug like the rest of the contestants who dropped by the wayside. Slug!

Rosie picked up her legs and surged forward. Her muscles screamed in protest. She knew the heels of her feet were bleeding. She ignored the pain. This was all about endurance and stamina plus a bunch of other stuff she couldn't even remember. She wasn't sure she could remember her own name. What she did know for a fact was that Kent Bliss was ahead of her.

She couldn't pace herself for the simple reason there was nothing left to pace. She had to run full tilt or just give up.

Rosie saw the huddled form on the side of the road just in time to leap over it. She came down hard on her heels, her sneakers grinding against her tortured skin. Her feet felt like they were on fire. In the brief second as she leaped over the form she saw that it was the pharmacist from the drugstore, who signaled that she was all right and waved her on. One down. Who and how many were left? Where were the damn markers? Someone should be on the side of the road shouting encouragement and handing out drinks. She mumbled something that encouraged the niggling voice to vent again.

Your grandmother could run faster than you! What happened to all that talk about being the best of the best? You said you were going to win. It doesn't look like you're winning to me. Loser, loser, your name is Rosie. Rosie the loser!

"Shut up!"

You can't tell me to shut up. I'm you. That's like telling yourself to shut up. Will you move already. Go! I want to win this race. Don't you understand English?

Rosie started to cry. She'd never been in so much pain in her entire life. If she didn't quit now, she was going to die. Right there in some damn, dirty rain puddle.

Like hell!

"I thought I told you to shut up!"

She felt a body slam against her. She almost went down but managed to swerve just in time. Who? What?

"Kent!"

"Sorry, I slipped. I'm running barefoot. My blisters have blisters. How are you doing?" he managed to gasp.

"Where is everyone? I saw the pharmacist back there?"

"It's just you and me, Rosie. Home Depot got some bad cramps and fell. Some guy from the gym, the big redhead, the one with all the freckles, just up and quit. He grabbed his thigh, then sat down. He looked like he was in real pain."

"Count me into that category. I can't do it, Kent. I don't have one ounce of energy left. Looks like you're going to be the winner," Rosie said hoarsely.

"Oh, no! You're finishing this race if you have to crawl over that finish line. We shouldn't be talking, it takes too much energy."

"How much farther is it, do you know?"

"Only God in his infinite wisdom knows. No clue. Kick your shoes off."

Without stopping, Rosie kicked off her shoes. The exquisite relief left her giddy. She was going at a snail's pace, but she didn't care. At least she was moving, Kent at her side.

That's it, now you're getting it. You're pulling ahead. Keep it up and you just might beat him. Just so you know, he looks like he doesn't care, and that, my dear, does not compute.

"Get out of my head. I don't care if I beat him or not. I don't even care if he cares or not. All I want to do is finish or die right here. I can't do this. I really can't do this."

You WILL do this. See what happens when you slack. He's ahead of you again. Are you going to let that happen? No, you are not. Move your ass! Go!

Rosie didn't look at her husband as she plowed past him.

"There's a marker! The red one. Do you see it, Rosie? Three-quarters of a mile to go!" Kent shouted to be heard over the driving rain as he plunged ahead of her.

How could he possibly expect her to see something on his side of the road with the rain pouring over her in buckets? Three-quarters of a mile was the same thing as saying she had to run all the way to Alaska.

He was ahead of her again, she could see his bright yellow shirt. Rosie brought her hands up to swipe at the rain whipping against her face. She stumbled and went down hard. But whatever she hit was soft and unmoving. "Kent!"

485

"It's okay. Keep going. My knee went out. Go on, send someone back for me." His face twisted in pain as he struggled to talk.

"Are you crazy? I can't move, much less get up on my feet."

"Yes, you can move. You have to move!" Kent pushed her and she rolled over onto her back, the rain beating at her like a drum. "Get up!" he thundered.

"I can't."

"Then crawl. You are going to cross that finish line if I have to push you. Move, Rosie! If you won't do it for yourself, do it for me."

"Kent, my legs won't move. They won't move! I can't feel anything. I'm too numb."

"They'll move if you make them move. I'll crawl with you. It's no contest, Rosie. I blew my knee out. The only way I can go on is to inch my way on my side. I'll skin myself raw if I try to do that. Go on, you deserve to win."

"Wait a minute here! Are you saying you want me to win? You must be up to something. I don't trust you any farther than I can see you. If I win, you don't get a thing," Rosie gasped.

"I don't want it, Rosie. Look, it's a long

story. We can discuss it some other time. Will you just go on and win this damn race so you can send someone back for me. I'm in a lot of pain here in case you haven't noticed."

Rosie forced herself to sit up. She really did have to continue. Kent needed help fast. "If you cross the line, you win, right? It doesn't matter about the two other races and no time limit was set on the run, right?"

"Yeah. Doesn't matter if you crawl or swim, all you have to do is cross it."

"Okay, I'll crawl, and you *roll.*" They looked at each other and burst out laughing.

"Go for it, Rosie!" Kent said, tears of laughter and pain, rolling down his face along with the rain.

It took her fifteen minutes to reach the finish line. Rosie limped across it and fell to the ground. The roar of the rain-clad crowd sounded like thunder to her ears. Within seconds Luna Mae, Curly, and Jack were pulling her up and hugging her. "Someone has to help Kent. He blew out his knee about three-quarters of a mile back," Rosie whispered.

Jack ran to the ambulance that was standing by while Luna Mae and Curly whisked Rosie away from the crowd and into Jack's house. "Am I going to die, Luna Mae?"

"Kent's on his way to the hospital right now, Rosie. No, you are not going to die. I will not allow it!"

Rosie started to cry as Luna Mae peeled off her clothes and helped her into a steaming shower.

"It's okay, baby. It's all over and you won. You won, baby!"

"I was ready to quit. I wanted to quit. I got to the point where I didn't care. Kent is the one who made me go on. Kent, of all people. Without his encouragement, I never would have finished. No one got seriously hurt out there, did they?" she blubbered.

"No. They fished the UPS guy out of the water, and he's downstairs now with everyone else. You must be starving."

"Where's Jack?"

"Outside the door waiting to see and talk to you. Rosie, he was behind you every step of the way, you just couldn't see him. He told us he wanted to stop you a hundred different times. When he saw you kick off your sneakers Curly had to restrain him. That man loves you heart and soul, baby."

Rosie smiled through her tears. "I

know," she said softly. "You know how I know, Luna Mae? I know because that's how much I love him."

"Okay, let's get you outta those clothes so I can rub you down with Curly's liniment. I brought a nice fleece-lined sweat suit. You'll look good in it for the pictures. I'll bandage up your feet, but you'll have to wear socks, no shoes for you for a while."

Luna Mae was taping the bandage on Rosie's left foot when the door burst open, and Jack shouted, "Ready or not, I'm coming in!"

"What took you so long?" Rosie said, holding out her arms. "Damn, you smell good! And you look even better. Just so you know, I'm not entering your race next year."

"Why not?" Jack said, squeezing her so hard she yelped for mercy.

"Because . . . because . . . I'll be pregnant by then."

"Are you . . . ?"

"No, not yet, but I plan to do everything in my power to make that happen. It takes two people, though. You up for it?" she teased. Neither one of them noticed when Luna Mae left the room. Before she had time to close the door, Buddy raced through the room and leaped onto the bed.

He lathered his mistress's face with wet kisses as he snuggled and wiggled to worm himself between Rosie and Jack.

"Oh, well! There's always later. Your adoring public awaits, Miss Olympus. You have no idea how much pleasure it's going to give me to award you the Olympus Trophy," Jack said, beaming. "Listen, I'm not sure if you know this or not, but I *own* the Olympus gyms."

"And you have no idea how much pleasure it's going to give me to accept it, Mr. Silver. You *own* them! Oh, well, I love you anyway."

The rest of the day passed in a blur for Rosie. Her television, radio, and print interviews over, she settled herself in Jack's La-Z-Boy recliner. Vickie brought her a plate of food, which she devoured. Jack brought the second plate and her second glass of wine, and a third plate for Buddy.

Rosie basked in contentment as the other contestants stopped by her chair to congratulate her and to say good-bye. By eight o'clock, the house was empty of visitors. Only the kitchen crew remained.

"Jack, I wonder if you can do me a favor."

"He's doing fine, Rosie. I already called. He's out of Recovery, and they have him on

490

a morphine drip. I hired a private duty nurse for him for the next couple of days. I told the charge nurse to tell him you called."

"Thanks, Jack. Can I go to bed now?" Rosie asked sleepily.

Jack bent down and scooped Rosie into his arms and carried her upstairs. She was sound asleep before he hit the top step. He placed her gently in the bed and tucked the covers up around her shoulders. "Okay, Buddy, you can take over now," he whispered. The big dog looked from Jack to Rosie and leaped up on the bed. He lowered himself gently, then placed his head on Rosie's stomach. Jack petted the dog's head and whispered again, "If you need me, I'll be downstairs." He swore later that Buddy nodded.

In the kitchen, he finally took his Thanksgiving dinner out of the warming oven and carried it into the living room, where he sat down on his favorite chair. How in the hell could he have forgotten to eat? He took a slug of the beer in his hand before he tackled what looked to him like the best Thanksgiving dinner of his life.

Outside, the temperature dropped steadily as the rain continued to batter the house. Like he cared. His immediate world was perfect.

The fire crackled in the fireplace, casting the room in a delicious, warm orange cocoon. Jack looked over at the mute television screen. He should probably turn it off. It seemed like a tremendous effort. He reached for the lever that would lower his chair to the recline position and leaned back. Perfect.

A moment later, he bounced upright. He walked to the front door and opened it to stare across the yard at the big oak in the center. Unmindful of the rain, he ran across the yard to the swing. He wondered what would happen if he sat down on it. He needed to talk to Martha. One last time. He didn't know how he knew, but he knew that after tonight, Martha would be locked away in his heart. He had to tell her why. He sat down and waited to see if she would boot him off like the last time. He sat perfectly still, then smiled when the swing started to move on its own until he was almost to the top of the tree. He reached out and plucked a leaf. When the swing was still again, he started to talk.

A long while later, Jack stepped off the swing and walked over to the emerald patch of moss beneath the old tree. He dropped to his knees and ran the palms of his hand over the moss. A sense of peace and contentment washed over him. And then a strong gust of wind propelled him forward. He laughed, the sound echoing up through the dense foliage of the tree. "I'm getting on with it. I am."

Jack sprinted for the house. At the door, he turned and waved. The biggest branch, the one that held the swing, dipped, then righted itself.

In the house, Jack walked over to the bookshelf and withdrew his memory book. He slipped the leaf next to the ones Martha had reached for so long ago. There was a sense of finality when he closed the book and returned it to the shelf.

Jack took the steps two at a time. He stood in the open doorway to observe Rosie. She was still sleeping peacefully, Buddy's head still on her stomach. He smiled.

His little family.

Epilogue

Rosie was stunned to see all the Christmas decorations when she walked into Savannah Memorial Hospital. She blinked at the dazzling Christmas tree twinkling in the middle of the lobby.

She was tired, but it was a nice kind of tired. She'd driven to Atlanta, leaving the house at five in the morning and returning as soon as she finished her business. It was after eight now, almost the end of visiting hours.

Rosie looked around for a directory that would lead her to Kent's room. She wasn't sure if she felt guilty or not as she walked down the blue-zoned corridor that would take her to the orthopedic unit. Coming here was a private personal matter, and she really didn't owe anyone an explanation. Not even Jack.

Rosie stopped at the desk to ask which room Kent was in; 411 she was told.

The hospital bustled with early-evening activity, meds were being dispensed, visitors were preparing to leave, and hospital volunteers were busily pushing their juice and snack carts down the halls. Doctors' pages sounded over the loudspeaker, one after the other, jarring Rosie's thoughts. She hoped the pages weren't life-or-death calls.

She was brought up short by the number on the closed door — 411. She knocked softly and was told to enter. She did so, but cautiously.

"Rosie!"

Rosie turned, half-expecting to hear a trumpet blast heralding her arrival. She grinned. "That's my name. I just stopped by to see how you are."

"As good as can be expected." He patted the soft cast on his knee and pointed to the aluminum crutches leaning against the nightstand. "I get out of here in five days. Therapy is just about all day long and wipes me out. I know it's a little late but congratulations. When I woke up after surgery, all I could think of was that Thanksgiving dinner I missed. Believe it or not, I'm glad you won."

For some reason, Rosie believed him. She sat down on the only chair in the room. "What are you going to do now, Kent?"

"As soon as the doctor gives me the go-ahead, I'm moving on. I'm thinking of ten days at the most. Listen, Rosie, I'm glad you came by because I need to do some *fessing up* here. When I leave, I don't want any loose ends. I took Jack's gun. I think I was a little crazy back then. I'm also the one who broke into your house, and I stole your jewelry box and the money inside, and an antique Rolex from Luna Mae. The gun is in my locker at the gym. Your stuff is in the trunk of my car. I can say I'm sorry a hundred different ways, but it won't make a difference to you, I'm sure. Something happened to me when I took that gun. I started to see where I was going, what I had become, and I didn't like it.

"I started to train, and my life changed. I was so exhausted at the end of the day, it was all I could do to eat and go to bed. I can't explain it any better than that. Look, Rosie, I was a son of a bitch, and I apologize. You should never have married me. You were way too good for me. I'll be out of your life completely in a few months. I'll send you a Christmas card every year if you want one."

"Where . . . where are you going, Kent?"

"I'm thinking Montana. Big Sky country. Don't ask me what I'm going to do there because I don't know. Something. It won't be real estate, that's for sure. I can see myself working on a ranch."

Rosie burst out laughing and couldn't stop. Kent had the good sense to look embarrassed. Rosie continued to laugh. "I can see you as a ranch owner but not a ranch hand."

"Well, that isn't going to happen. I guess it is kind of funny. So, you look like you recovered from the race ordeal. It's a good thing I was knocked out from the operation, or I would have climbed the walls. Every bone in my body, every single muscle screamed in agony. You got the trophy, huh?"

Rosie reached into her purse and pulled out the trophy. "You would have won, Kent. It belongs to you. Consider it a going-away present."

"Nah, I can't take that. You won it fair and square. You were dead tired and about to quit yet you picked yourself up and ran ahead to get the ambulance for me. That tells me all I need to know about you, Rosie. I hope you and Jack have a good life."

"I hope you do, too, Kent. The past is gone. Hopefully, we both learned from it. I know I did. You know, right up until I stumbled across that finish line I had myself convinced that I was in that race for myself. I lied to myself. I did it to show you up. I was so bitter, so angry at you. I wanted to make you pay for what I allowed you to do to me. I'm okay with myself now. The trophy is yours. Be gracious in your acceptance, Kent."

"Okay. I'm glad you stopped by. I hate to ask you this, but do you think you could float me a loan until I get settled? I'll sign a note and pay you back."

"How come you don't watch television?" Rosie queried, ignoring his question as she tried to figure out if he'd seen her accept the check for the Wonderball lottery.

"I just haven't felt like it. Why, did something big happen in the world today?"

"Yeah, something pretty big happened." Rosie opened her purse again. She handed over a white envelope.

"What's this? Please don't tell me it's a subpoena."

"Nah. Just a little something to make your life easier. Oh, I almost forgot, here!" she said, tossing him a key ring.

"This is the Porsche key. Is it the spare?"

"Nope. The real thing. The dealer couldn't get me a fair market price, so I took it back. I paid it off, and it's yours.

You can go in style to Montana."

"Jesus, Rosie, I don't know what to say. Thanks."

"Thanks is good. See ya, Kent. Don't forget to send me a Christmas card." When Rosie reached the door, she turned around and waved airily, then blew him a kiss. She was about to step into the elevator when she heard Kent's whoop of pleasure. She laughed all the way out to her own car.

Nurses and doctors ran down the corridor only to see Kent hopping around on one foot waving a check for all of them to see. "Sixty-eight million dollars! Do you believe that?" The staff watched while their giddy patient did a one-legged dance, all the while kissing the check in his hand.

"Rosie," he whispered, when the door closed behind the staff, "I'm even going to send you a Christmas *present*."

Seeing Jack's car in her driveway, Rosie got out of her car and ran up the steps. Jack met her on the front porch. He picked her up and swung her around until she was dizzy. Buddy barked as he nipped at Jack's ankles, a signal that he wanted affection from his mistress. "Everything is ready, so we can leave anytime you want," he whispered, as Rosie bent down to hug the big black dog.

"Hey, I'm ready right now. River house, here I come!"

"You looked good on television this morning. How does it feel to have all that money?" Jack grinned.

"Not one bit different from before. I stopped by the hospital to give Kent his share. I gave him the keys to the Porsche, too. He's going to send us a Christmas card every year," Rosie giggled. "By the way, the gun he took is in his locker at the gym. You might want to stop and take it out before we head over to the river house. I don't know if this will mean anything to you, Jack, but Kent said he turned around his life, and he said it happened after he took the gun. Meaning, of course, that he had sunk so low there was no place to go but up. In the end it was a good thing, I guess. He's not our problem anymore. From here on in, it's just me, you, and Buddy."

"Sounds like a road song," Jack said, hugging her.

"I was hoping for something a little more substantial. Like an earth-shattering kiss that sends rockets off in my head. Or makes me weak in the elbows. Blowing my branch would dip. It did. She turned to run into the house and ran straight into Jack's arms.

"How did it feel?" he whispered.

"Like I could reach all the way to heaven. It was wonderful! Look!"

Jack looked down at the leaves, then up at the big tree. He smiled and waved. Rosie waved, too.

"I love you so much it hurts," Jack said.

"Me too," Rosie said.

Buddy barked.

"It's unanimous." Jack grinned.

"You bet it is. We're a family, and families have to stick together."

The big tree suddenly took on a life of its own as the branches rose and dipped, then up again and down. The wind seemed to be saying, welcome, welcome home!

socks off is good, too."

"If you'd shut up for a minute, I would be more than happy to oblige you."

It all happened, just the way she wanted it to happen. "Oooh," she murmured a minute later, "that curled my toes."

Jack laughed as he held the car door open for her. "What now?"

"Now, I have two weddings to plan before I start on my own. I promised Luna Mae and Vickie that we would throw each of them a wedding at the river house. Just us and immediate friends, you know, your dad, your uncle, all of Luna Mae and Curly's NASCAR buddies, all of Vickie's friends and her fiancé's fellow lawyers."

"Doesn't sound very little to me. The old house is going to rock, that's for sure."

Rosie's voice turned suddenly shy. "Jack, tell me the truth, are you as happy as I am?"

"Happier. I didn't think it was possible, but I am."

"Is this where one of us says, all's well that ends well?"

"This isn't the end, it's just the beginning," Jack said, nuzzling her neck.

The ride to the river house was made in record time. While Jack carried in her bags and all of Buddy's gear, Rosie walked across the lawn to the old tree. "Hi, Martha, it's me," she said softly. "I'm moving in. I wanted to tell you myself." Rosie looked up at the branch that held the swing, holding her breath. When it didn't dip in greeting, her stomach started to churn. She swallowed hard. "I will love him just the way you did. I'll do my best never to say a cross word, and I'll never let us go to bed angry with each other. And one thing's for damn sure, your pictures will always remain exactly where they are in the house. I just want you to know that." Still the branch didn't move, but the swing jiggled in the cool evening air. At first she thought she was seeing things until it whirled completely around. "You want me to sit on it? Are you sure?" The branch dipped. Rosie grinned from ear to ear as she sat down on the swing. When it started to move, she squealed with delight. Higher, higher, and still higher. From somewhere far off, she could hear gentle laughter.

Rosie held on to the ropes as the swing returned to a still position. In her hand were a bunch of leaves. A lone tear rolled out of the corner of her eye as she slid off the swing. "If it's okay with you, I'll be back," Rosie whispered. She held her breath as she waited to see if the big